Lord of
the Wings

Lord of
the Wings

A Meg Langslow Mystery

Donna Andrews

Minotaur Books

A Thomas Dunne Book
New York

A THOMAS DUNNE BOOK FOR MINOTAUR BOOKS.
An imprint of St. Martin's Publishing Group.

www.thomasdunnebooks.com
www.minotaurbooks.com

The Library of Congress Cataloging-in-Publication Data is available upon request.

ISBN 978-1-250-04958-2 (hardcover)
ISBN 978-1-4668-5056-9 (e-book)

Minotaur books may be purchased for educational, business, or promotional use. For information on bulk purchases, please contact the Macmillan Corporate and Premium Sales Department at 1-800-221-7945, extension 5442, or write to specialmarkets@macmillan.com.

First Edition: August 2015

10 9 8 7 6 5 4 3 2 1

Acknowledgments

Thanks, as always, to everyone at St. Martin's/Minotaur, including (but not limited to) Hector DeJean, Melissa Hastings, Paul Hochman, Andrew Martin, Sarah Melnyk, Talia Sherer, Emma Stein, Mary Willems, and my editor, Pete Wolverton. And thanks again to David Rotstein and the art department for the dramatic Halloween cover. I'm raven about it!

More thanks to my agent, Ellen Geiger, and the staff at the Frances Goldin Literary Agency for handling the boring (to me) practical stuff so I can focus on writing.

Many thanks to the friends—writers and readers alike— who brainstorm and critique with me, give me good ideas, or help keep me sane while I'm writing: Stuart, Elke, Aidan, and Liam Andrews, Renee Brown, Erin Bush, Chris Cowan, Meriah Crawford, Ellen Crosby, Kathy Deligianis, Suzanne Frisbee, John Gilstrap, Barb Goffman, C. Ellett Logan, David Niemi, Alan Orloff, Shelley Shearer, Art Taylor, Robin Templeton, and Dina Willner. Thanks for all kinds of moral support and practical help to my blog sisters and brothers at the Femmes Fatales: Dana Cameron, Charlaine Harris, Dean James, Toni L. P. Kelner, Catriona McPherson, Kris Neri, Hank Phillipi Ryan, Mary Saums, Marcia Talley, and Elaine Viets. And thanks to all the TeaBuds for years of friendship.

The Creatures of the Night exhibit in the Caerphilly Zoo was modeled closely after the Kingdoms of the Night exhibit in Omaha's fabulous Henry Doorly Zoo. I owe the late Sally Fellows and all of the organizers of the Mayhem in the

Midlands mystery convention a debt of gratitude for luring me to Omaha in the first place, and am particularly grateful to Lori Hayes, who is always eager to take me to the zoo and never complains when I want to take just another few dozen pictures of the peacocks or the meerkats.

And above all, thanks to the readers who continue to read Meg's adventures.

Lord of
the Wings

Chapter 1

"Someone's broken into the Haunted House!"

My cell phone almost vibrated from the excitement in my brother's voice.

"Calm down, Rob," I said. I wanted to add, "And what are you doing awake before eight a.m.?" but I suspected he would take it as a slur on his character. I punched the speaker button, set my phone on the kitchen table, and went back to painting a goatee on my son Josh's chin.

"But, Meg, the Haunted House—"

"Was anything taken?" I asked. "Or broken?"

"Not that we can tell," Rob said. "But Dr. Smoot is upset."

"That's his normal state of mind these days," I said. Then I winced, hoping the proprietor of the Haunted House wasn't close enough to Rob's phone to hear me.

"If you can call anything about Smoot normal." Okay, even Rob wouldn't have said that in front of the man. "But definitely more upset than usual. The closer we get to Halloween, the more hyper he gets."

Josh lifted up his piratical eye patch, twisted to look at his reflection in the shiny chrome side of the toaster, and frowned.

"I want to be more hairier," he said.

"Just hairier," I corrected. "I'm working on it. Did you report it to the police?" I added to Rob.

"Not yet," Rob said. "Dr. Smoot says Chief Burke never takes him seriously."

Dr. Smoot was probably right. Of course, it didn't help that while he was still serving as Caerphilly County's medical examiner, Dr. Smoot had taken to dressing as a vampire, complete with a long black cape and fake fangs, and collecting vampire-related paraphernalia. Chief Burke had been vastly relieved when Dr. Smoot had resigned his post to pursue this strange new hobby full time, complete with travels to such vampire meccas as Transylvania and New Orleans. The chief probably wasn't thrilled to have Dr. Smoot not only back in town but also running the Haunted House that played a central role in the town's ongoing Halloween Festival.

"Never mind their past history," I said. "If there's any real evidence of a burglary, Chief Burke will want to investigate. In fact, he'll be pretty ticked off if he finds out you didn't call him right away."

"Dr. Smoot says since nothing was actually taken, he thought it was okay to call the Goblin Patrol instead."

"Rob," I began.

"Sorry," Rob said. "The Visitor Relations and Police Liaison Patrol. I still think Goblin Patrol's catchier. I'll call the chief. But Dr. Smoot's upset—he really wants to talk to you."

"I'm putting the boys into their costumes for school," I said. "And then Michael and I are going along as chaperones for today's school field trip to the zoo. And—"

"Great," Rob said. "The Haunted House is right on your way. You could just drop in for a few minutes—"

"After the field trip," I said. "Or if more than enough parents come to wrangle the kids, I might be able to break away once we've delivered our carload to the zoo. Call the police, and tell Dr. Smoot I'll be there as soon as I can."

"Roger," Rob said.

"Uncle Rob," Josh said. "I'm a pirate today."

"A pirate?" Rob echoed. "I thought you were a cowboy."

"A cowboy? Yuck. That was yesterday."

"Today he's a pirate," I said. "I've been trying to explain

to the boys that when their teacher said they could wear costumes every day this week, it didn't mean a different costume every day."

"But it's more fun this way," Josh protested.

"Absolutely!" Rob said. "Goblin Patrol, over and out."

"Rob," I began, but he'd already hung up. "Josh, can you punch the button to turn off my phone? My hands are full."

He obliged, then turned back to me and lifted his chin as if silently demanding that I add another layer of painted beard.

"Mommy—look!" I turned to see Jamie, Josh's twin. "See my new costume! Isn't it cool?"

"Very cool!" I stopped myself before asking, "But what is it?" and studied his outfit for clues. Like most first graders, he had only rudimentary costume-making skills, so at first glance, his new outfit looked exactly like Monday's dog costume, Tuesday's raccoon, and Wednesday's penguin. They all used as a base the same set of faded beige footed pajamas. Today he'd stuck tufts of fur rather than feathers to the flannel, so I deduced that he was a mammal rather than a bird. The catlike whiskers stuck on his cheeks with Scotch tape didn't help much, but then I noticed that the rope he'd tied around his waist, leaving one end trailing six or seven feet behind him, now bore a tuft of fur at the tip.

"So you're going as a lion today?" I guessed.

Jamie beamed.

"Look, Josh," he said. "Rowrrrr!"

Josh was studying himself again in the toaster.

"I guess it's okay," he said. "But I want a really cool costume for the real Halloween on Saturday."

"Josh," I said. "That's only two days away. I'm not sure we have time to make another costume. Can't you just go as a pirate or a cowboy or a space alien or a wizard? We can make some improvements to whichever one you choose."

"I want to be a robot," Josh said.

It could be worse, I decided. I could easily make him a robot suit with some cardboard boxes and tin foil.

"But not one of those lame robot costumes like Victor's mother made him out of cardboard boxes and tin foil," Josh said. "A *real* robot costume. It should be metal. And the eyes should light up when I get mad. And you should be able to open up my chest to see my motor."

"I'll think about it," I said. "No promises," I added. "You know I'm pretty busy with the Halloween Festival."

"But I really want to be a robot!"

"No whining!" I exclaimed.

Josh recognized the wisdom of shutting up, and shifted tactics. He sighed and donned a look of patient, wistful longing—rather like Oliver Twist holding up the empty gruel bowl.

Maybe Michael could enlist some help in making a robot costume. An extra-credit project for a couple of his drama department students with prop and costume shop experience. I could ask him.

And come to think of it, maybe Michael could drive the boys to school, pick up the other two kids we were supposed to transport, and take them to the zoo. Then I could drop by to soothe Dr. Smoot and still meet them there in time for the tour.

"Where's your daddy?" I asked the boys.

"In the backyard, chasing the llamas," Jamie said.

"Why is he chasing the llamas?" I asked. "Are they loose?"

Jamie shook his head.

"Then why—"

"Who's ready for waffles?" my cousin Rose Noire called out, as she sailed in, already dressed in her costume for the day, as Glinda, the Good Witch.

"Yay!" Jamie exclaimed.

"Blueberry waffles?" Josh asked.

"*Organic* blueberry waffles," Rose Noire said. "With artisanal maple syrup."

The boys sat down and looked expectant. On mornings like this, I was profoundly grateful that Rose Noire still showed no signs of moving out of the third floor spare bedroom she'd occupied since before the boys were born.

I strolled outside to see why Michael was chasing the llamas.

Actually, he wasn't so much chasing them as being followed by them. He was jogging briskly around the perimeter of their pasture and the llamas, ever curious about human eccentricities, were loping along behind him.

I leaned over the fence and watched until he drew near, then climbed over the top rail and fell into step beside him.

"What's up?" I asked.

"An actor's body is his instrument," he puffed.

"That's nice," I said. "What does that have to do with your taking up jogging?" Then enlightenment struck. "You tried on your wizard costume last night, didn't you?" I asked.

Michael frowned and nodded.

"Too tight?"

"Not *too* tight," he said. "But a little tighter than it used to be. Tighter than it *should* be."

Not surprising, since it had been a few years since Michael had donned the costume he'd once worn to play the evil wizard Mephisto on *Porfiria, Queen of the Jungle,* a long-canceled cult TV fantasy show. In fact, although die-hard fans kept inviting him to Porfiria fan conventions, he hadn't gone since before the twins were born, and they were six now.

"I could let your costume out a little," I suggested.

"No," he said, and picked up his pace a little. "I need to get down to my proper weight. An actor's body is his instrument."

"Okay," I said. "Carry on tuning your instrument. I'll figure out something healthy and low calorie for dinner."

"Thanks," he said. "And keep all that damned Halloween candy away from me."

"Roger," I said. "By the way, can you take the boys to school and pick up the other two kids we're taking to the field trip? I can meet you at the zoo—I have an errand I should run on my way."

"Goblin Patrol business?"

"Something like that." As I explained about Dr. Smoot, I considered whether I should stop fighting this Goblin Patrol thing. It was certainly catchier than Visitor Relations and Police Liaison Patrol. "If I hurry," I concluded, "I can deal with Smoot and still make the zoo tour."

"I don't envy you," he said. "And yes, I can take the boys."

We'd done nearly a complete circuit of the pasture now, so I decided I'd jogged enough.

"I'm going to peel off now and get ready for my busy day," I said.

"Not as busy as it would have been if Randall Shiffley hadn't hired Lydia," Michael called over his shoulder.

I made a noncommittal noise and headed back to the kitchen.

Yes, if Randall hadn't hired Lydia Van Meter to the newly created post of Special Assistant to the Mayor, I would probably have been running the whole of Caerphilly's ten-day Halloween Festival instead of merely heading up the Goblin Patrol. I definitely preferred my more limited role.

But that didn't mean I had to like Lydia.

Just thinking about her soured my mood. And it wasn't because she was doing a terrible job at organizing the Halloween Festival. Considering that it was her first major project, she was doing okay. Not perfectly—certainly not the way I'd have done it—but things were lurching along, and she was learning. She'd probably have an easier time with the much bigger Christmas in Caerphilly event that would start right after Thanksgiving, because we'd been doing that for several years now, and Randall and I had done a pretty good job of setting up procedures and training the townspeople in them. By summer, when it was time for the Un-Fair, the statewide agricultural exposition Caerphilly hosted every year, she should be in fine shape—again, thanks to all the ground work Randall and I had done on past Un-Fairs.

Since, in the long run, she was going to make my life easier, it was probably ungracious of me to dislike her. Maybe I was the only one who minded her constant griping about how hard she was working and how impossible the job was. I couldn't count the times I'd had to bite my tongue to keep from saying, "You think you've got it bad—I used to do all that and more, as a volunteer." And was it just my imagination, or was she developing an annoying tendency to ask me how I would handle something and then do exactly the opposite?

"Chill," I muttered. After all, Lydia was making it possible for me to spend more time with Michael and the boys, doing things like today's field trip to the Caerphilly Zoo.

And accompanying the boys to the zoo was definitely important, and not just because I wanted to see their reaction to the brand new Creatures of the Night exhibit. As the zoo's proud owner, my grandfather was planning on conducting the tour himself, and I knew better than to expect common sense from him. What if he gave in to some first grader's pleas to be allowed to pet the arctic wolves? Or began explaining the curious mating habits of the greater short-nosed fruit bat, as he had a few weeks ago when giving a preview tour to the Baptist Ladies' Altar Guild?

I ran upstairs to throw on the last few bits of my costume—a modified version of the red satin and black leather swordswoman's outfit I wore whenever I exhibited my blacksmithing work at a Renaissance festival. I added the festive black-and-orange armband that marked me as a member of the Goblin Patrol and headed for town.

The first few miles of my journey lay through farmlands—pastures dotted with grazing cows or sheep, fields filled with late crops or post-harvest stubble, and orchards picked clean of all but the latest fruits. Closer to town, I began to see Halloween and harvest decorations on the gates and fences. I particularly admired the farmer who'd used a collection of scarecrows to simulate a zombie attack on his cow pasture. The contrast between the bloodstained shambling figures clawing at the outside of the fence and the Guernsey cows calmly chewing their cuds inside never failed to amuse me.

I was nearing town when my phone rang. Lydia. I considered letting it go to voice mail. Then I sighed, and pulled over to answer it. She was probably calling about something she considered important. Her definition of important rarely coincided with mine, but I'd already figured out that the best way to keep her calm and off my back was to talk to her. She seemed to resent having to leave a voice mail.

"Thank goodness I caught you!" she exclaimed as soon as I answered. "Can you drop by to see me as soon as possible? Something important's come up. Festival business! Thanks!"

"I'm already on my way to take care of festival business," I began. But before I could make the case for discussing whatever had come up over the phone instead of face to face, I realized she'd hung up.

"Damn the woman," I muttered as I punched the button to call her back. But her phone line was already busy.

So I muttered a few words I didn't usually let myself say (for fear the boys would pick them up) and pulled out onto the road again. Dr. Smoot's burglar would have to wait while I tackled whatever crisis Lydia had to offer.

Chapter 2

Even Lydia couldn't spoil my enjoyment of the Halloween scenery. Closer to town the farmlands gave way to houses whose yards almost universally contained some kind of decoration. Strings of orange pumpkin- or skeleton-shaped lights festooned at least half of the fences. Most of the steps bore jack-o'-lanterns. Some yards contained miniature graveyards, with or without skeletons or vampires digging their way out of the earth, and I lost count of the number of witches that appeared to have slammed into trees.

In the outskirts of town I passed by the left turn onto the Clay County road that would have taken me to Dr. Smoot's Haunted House and then on to the zoo. Instead I continued on toward the town square.

The official town decorations, though attractive, were somewhat more sedate, reflecting a harvest theme rather than a Halloween one. The streetlights had been enclosed in plastic covers to make them look like pumpkins—just pumpkins, not jack-o'-lanterns. Graceful black, brown, and orange garlands hung between the lampposts, and all the trash cans and benches and other public fixtures were festooned with gourds and sheaves of dried grass and flowers. "It's the Caerphilly Garden Club," Randall Shiffley had said in a slightly apologetic tone when he showed me the design. "They always like to err on the side of good taste, and I don't think most of them really like Halloween all that much."

They probably didn't—but they were clearly in the minority. Most of the shops and houses contained enough jack-o'-lanterns, faux skeletons, black cat window decals, bat garlands, and rubber rats to make up for any excess of good taste on the part of the Garden Club.

It was early enough that I had no trouble finding a parking spot near the courthouse. As I climbed the long marble steps up to the front portico, I could see that the two small groups of protesters were already on duty. I turned to study them for a moment. To the right were a small group of people who objected to our Halloween Festival on the grounds that it was a godless pagan holiday that a respectable town shouldn't be celebrating. To the left was a group of about the same number of devout pagans who were protesting our commercialization of what was for them an important religious holiday and our use of decorations that perpetuated society's negative stereotype of witches.

Neither group had started picketing yet, only milling around as if waiting for something. The arrival of the first tourists, perhaps.

If I'd been in charge, I'd have long ago sent a couple of local ministers out to placate the Halloween haters and tasked Rose Noire with figuring out what we could do to calm down the pagans.

Then I saw them all perk up as two figures approached. It was Muriel, owner of the local diner, and one of her waitresses, both carrying trays laden with doughnuts and carry-out cups of coffee. Muriel began serving the pagans while the waitress continued on toward the Halloween haters.

"You were right," said a voice from over my shoulder.

I looked up to see Randall standing at the top of the steps, gazing down at the protesters. His buckskin costume already looked wrinkled, and his Davy Crockett-style coonskin hat was askew.

"I usually am right," I said, as I made my way up the rest of the steps. "What in particular am I right about today?"

"We never should have tried to chase them off," he said,

nodding at the protesters. "Should have killed them with kindness from the start."

I refrained from saying that it was Lydia who tried to order the protesters away, and demanded that the police step in when her efforts failed. Fortunately Chief Burke had a cool head and a strong respect for the First Amendment.

"I see you're taking my idea about the refreshments," I said.

"Yup." Randall smiled with satisfaction. "Coffee and doughnuts every morning from Muriel, and tea and cookies every afternoon from one of the churches. If the forecast calls for rain, we put up those little canvas shelters for them, and they know they're always welcome to use the courthouse bathroom."

"You're spoiling them," I said.

"And we're down to about a third of the number we had last week this time," he said. "Clearly it's no fun protesting people who seem perfectly happy to have you stay around. What brings you downtown? I'd have thought you'd be out at the zoo with the first graders today."

"I will be," I said. "As soon as I talk to Lydia and find out what's so important that she had to drag me all the way downtown."

Randall winced, and I felt slightly guilty for venting at him.

"Sorry," he said. "She means well, and she's learning."

Not learning fast enough to suit me, but I refrained from saying so aloud. I just nodded, went inside the courthouse, and took the elevator up to the third floor where Lydia had her office, a few doors down from Randall's office.

As usual, Lydia was on the phone. Not just on the phone, but switching back and forth between the two lines on her desk phone while texting something on her cell phone with her right hand and clicking something on her computer keyboard with the left. She nodded and smiled when she saw me, and held up two fingers, like the peace sign. Her intent, of course, was to say that she'd be with me in two minutes. I knew better by now.

I sat down in one of her desk chairs and resigned myself to wait. If I were a snarkier person, I'd have brought along a thick book—*War and Peace,* perhaps—and made a show of settling down to read it while she talked. Instead, I pulled out my notebook-that-tells-me-when-to-breathe, as I call my giant to-do list, and made productive use of my time.

Other people rarely understood how comforting I found it to spend time with my notebook. Knowing that everything on my plate was captured between its covers cleared my brain to concentrate on whatever I was doing. Since the boys' arrival, life had grown even more complicated than before, and I'd traded in my original spiral notebooks for a small three-ring binder, but apart from that my system was the same. My notebook gave me peace of mind, and all it asked in return was that I tend it for a few minutes here and there. I marked a few tasks as done and added a few new ones.

"Yeah, yeah," Lydia was saying. "I'll take care of it."

I glanced up to see that she was scribbling something on a yellow sticky note.

She stuck the sticky on the left side of her computer monitor, where it was largely indistinguishable from the hundred other yellow sticky notes that clung to the monitor, gradually encroaching on the viewing space. Her calendar and the wall it hung on were similarly encrusted. As I watched, one lonely yellow square gave up hope of ever being read and let itself fall to the floor.

By contrast, her desk contained only a few sticky notes, hidden here and there among the books, folders, paper stacks, and yellow legal pads that covered every inch of horizontal space and in some places had begun to slide off onto the floor.

Every time I walked into her office, my fingers itched to start organizing it all.

Not for the first time I wondered where Randall had found her, and how in the world she had convinced him that she was good at organizing.

"Chill," I murmured under my breath. Lydia's organizing skills might be overrated, the festival might not be running the way I'd like to have seen it run, but it was limping along adequately without me doing anything other than organizing and running the volunteer security force. I reminded myself to be grateful for that.

"Sorry." She hung up and turned to me with a perky little smile that didn't really reach her eyes. "There's just so much going on."

"Understandable," I said. "What did you need to see me about?"

"Oh!" She began scanning the sticky notes on the left side of her monitor and plucked one off. "Here it is. Dr. Smoot called. He seems to think someone broke into the museum very early this morning. Could you check to see if it's something the police should handle or if he's just being hyper again?"

"You could have told me about it over the phone," I said. "As it happens, one of my volunteers already told me about the break-in, and I was on my way over there when you called. If you'd told me that was why you were calling, I'd be there by now, dealing with it."

"Oh, sorry," she said. "But it's only a little detour, after all."

"Only ten miles." My smile probably didn't reach my eyes, either. In fact, it was probably more of a grimace. But since Lydia had already half turned away to dial another number on her phone, she probably didn't notice.

I closed my eyes and counted to ten. Then I stood up and left her office, ignoring her cheerful good-bye wave.

Luckily Randall wasn't still at the top of the courthouse steps, so I was spared the temptation to tell him what I thought of his assistant.

The protesters had finished their morning coffee break and were marching up and down their assigned sides of the sidewalk. The anti-Halloween crew carried signs with slogans like "Halloween Is the Devil's Nite." The pagans' signs all had a picture of a spectacularly ugly cartoon witch riding a broomstick. The witch was in a circle with a line through it, reminiscent of a no-smoking sign. During the first few days they hadn't had any slogans on them, giving some of the tourists the erroneous impression that they were against witches, or possibly declaring the town a no-fly zone for broomstick riders. So they'd added slogans like No STEREO-TYPING and CAERPHILLY UNFAIR TO WITCHES.

The protesters were all remarkably well behaved, especially considering the fact that each group probably considered the other its archenemy.

Behind them, in the town square, the farmers and crafts-people and other merchants were starting to set up for the farmer's market. I could see merchants and volunteers performing a few last minute tasks, finishing up the job of switching things over from the Night Side, our evening mode, into the family-friendly Day Side.

In the daytime, we insisted that none of the festival attractions display any excessively graphic or scary decorations, and we discouraged overly gory or provocative costumes. We had no control over what the owners did on private property, of course, but most of them voluntarily complied with the daytime guidelines. Then, an hour after sunset, dozens of volunteers throughout the festival rushed to transform everything. Smiling pumpkin heads turned into evilly grinning ones. Fluffy black cats gave way to snarling wolves. Instead of "Ghostbusters" and "Monster Mash" on the loudspeakers we played "Night on Bald Mountain" and Bach's "Toccata and Fugue in D Minor" and, as the night wore on, truly sinister-sounding mood music. Welcome to the Night Side.

Most of the volunteers found it easier to switch things back before going home, so there was less to do in the morning, but as long as the switch was complete before the tourists streamed in we were okay with it. Members of the Goblin Patrol checked every morning to make sure the switch was complete by 8:00 A.M. That was probably why Rob had been out at Caerphilly Haunted House so early, since the Haunted House and its environs were a hot spot for inappropriate decorations.

My route out of town passed by Caerphilly Elementary and I could see that the children were lined up on the curb in groups of four, being given their marching orders by Mrs. Velma Shiffley, their teacher. I spotted Michael easily. At six four he towered over all the children—and for that matter, all the adults. He looked very impressive in today's costume—a Union general's uniform that he'd originally acquired for participating in the town's Civil War celebrations. Probably more suitable for a school outing than the over-tight evil wizard costume.

On impulse, I made a U-turn and pulled into the school parking lot. Lydia be damned. Dr. Smoot could wait. I was going to the zoo with my boys.

Chapter 3

"Mommy! You came after all!" Jamie was overjoyed to see me, and had to be restrained from running up to my car when I turned into the parking lot. Josh acknowledged my arrival with a casual wave.

I parked my car and joined Michael at the Twinmobile, where Jamie and Josh and their two best friends, Mason and Noah, had resumed squabbling mildly over who got to sit in the third row. I wondered, for a moment, if Mrs. Shiffley's decision to put these four together was wise. On the one hand, Michael and I had long ago realized that when the foursome got together they produced at least eight times as much noise and mischief as they did singly. But on the other hand, at least the odds were they'd comply pretty well with Mrs. Shiffley's orders to stay together as a group. And we'd have plenty of help. There were almost as many chaperones as children, probably because the Creatures of the Night exhibit was usually crowded beyond belief during the zoo's normal visiting hours.

Once we'd settled Josh and Mason in the third row, promising Jamie and Noah that prized position on the way back, we headed out. I distracted the boys by pointing out all the Halloween decorations we passed and challenging them to pick their favorite. At first, the army of skeletons outside the Caerphilly Hospital was running neck-and-neck with the Caerphilly Garden Center's display of three animated witches stirring a kettle that emitted dry ice fumes. But once we sighted the Haunted House it blew all its competition out of the water.

"Awesome!" Josh and Noah whispered in unison, while Jamie and Mason just stared.

"It is pretty cool, isn't it?" Michael said.

The Haunted House had started life as the Smoot family house. Like our house, it was a sprawling three-story Victorian. But in the last ten years we had transformed ours from a seedy wreck into a showplace, under Mother's guidance and with much expensive help from the Shiffley Construction Company. After inheriting it from his aunt last year, Dr. Smoot had taken his house in the other direction. The white siding and woodwork were now gray and black. The ornate gingerbread trim was still intact, but painted in gray and black it gave the impression that the house was trimmed with sooty geometric spiderwebs. Many of the windows had faux cracks painted on the glass, and flickering candles in a few of them seemed to be the only light. Right now the irregular slate front walk still looked ever-so-slightly too new, and I was suspicious that the weeds springing up between the stones were planted, since it was a little too soon for even the most enterprising weeds to grow quite so tall. But time would no doubt mellow all that. I'm not sure I would have replaced a perfectly nice white picket fence with an eight-foot black wrought-iron fence, but it looked elegant. Although I hoped the skull-shaped lights on the posts were Halloween decorations, not permanent features.

"Look!" Noah said. "Is that a vampire?"

"No," I said. "That's just Dr. Smoot, who owns the Haunted House."

"Awesome," Josh said. "Does he live there?"

"Yes," I said. "On the third floor."

"I bet he has fangs," Mason said.

I decided to ignore that remark. Where did they learn

about such things? At least, since it was Halloween, I wouldn't
have to answer questions about why Dr. Smoot was dressed
like a vampire. Their parents could explain that later, when
the kids noticed he did it year round instead of just at
Halloween, like most people. Halloween was the one time
when Dr. Smoot looked more or less normal. Normal for
Caerphilly, at least, where almost everyone would be dressed
in costume for the entire ten days of the festival.

Before the children could ask any more questions, fresh
sights pushed Dr. Smoot out of their minds. First the Halloween Fun Fair, a temporary amusement park complete with
rides, games of skill and chance, and food concessions—a
sort of Halloween-themed midway that filled the nine and a
half acres of Dr. Smoot's property not enclosed by the fence
around his house. It would be silent until noon today, but it
still captivated the children. And beyond the Fun Fair was
the field in which Randall had erected the Maize Maze—a
giant ten-acre cornstalk maze. He'd originally hoped to
plant the world's largest cornstalk maze, but upon learning
that the current record-holding maze was over forty acres,
he'd decided to start small and work up to world domina-
tion in the all-important maze race.

Then, shortly after we passed the maze, the children's excitement reached a fever pitch when the zoo gates loomed
into sight in the distance. Or maybe it wasn't the zoo gates
that excited them but the figure standing in front of them—
a tall figure in a homespun gray cloak. His hood was pulled
over his face, but as we drew closer you could imagine you
caught a flash of the piercing eyes beneath. He carried a staff
as tall as he was, with a carved raven at the top, and around
his shoulders swirled half a dozen ravens.

"Cool," "awesome," and "wow," were the small boys' ver-
dicts.

The birds banked and soared around the figure, occasionally landing on his arms or his shoulders. And as I

watched, one soared over its head and unleashed a spatter of droppings on his hood. The figure didn't seem to notice, but then perhaps that was the reason he was wearing the hood pulled up to cover his head so completely.

"Is that Gandalf?" Mason whispered.

"No," Jamie said. "It's Great-grandfather. He owns the zoo."

But even Josh and Jamie were slightly cowed by Grandfather's imposing figure in his unfamiliar garb. Our four charges scrambled out of the van and went to stand at a respectful distance from Grandfather. He waited while all the vans and cars emptied out and the children and chaperones gathered around him. The sooty black ravens all settled on his arms and shoulders and stared at the children as if studying them.

From time to time, the ravens would utter harsh cries and, occasionally, recognizable words.

"Nevermore!" exclaimed one who was sitting on Grandfather's shoulder.

"Nevermore!" agreed one who was trying to perch on his head.

"Doom! Doom!" croaked another.

"Room service," chimed in a fourth. Grandfather, who rather enjoyed the first three ravens, scowled at the fourth and shook his staff at it.

When the circle of children and chaperones was complete, Grandfather glanced up slightly, and seeing no wings directly overhead, he pushed the hood back, dislodging two of the ravens.

"Greetings, mortal children," he intoned. "Are you ready to visit the Creatures of the Night?"

Enthusiastic cheers greeted this. Mrs. Shiffley stepped forward.

"Before we get started, I want everybody to remember that we're guests here," she began.

Some of the children fidgeted, while others put on the sort of ostentatiously obedient and attentive faces that marked them in my eyes as potential troublemakers in need of watching.

"I think all of you know Dr. Montgomery Blake, the very famous zoologist and environmentalist who owns the Caerphilly Zoo," Mrs. Shiffley went on. "I want you to be quiet and listen to him. Anyone who misbehaves will be sent back here to wait in the parking lot while the rest of the class finishes the tour."

A hushed and anxious silence followed her words. Then Grandfather stepped forward.

"Don't worry," he said. "We won't be sending anyone back to the parking lot."

A few cheers greeted this statement. Mrs. Shiffley frowned.

"We'll feed anyone who misbehaves to the hyenas!"

Loud cheers, especially from the children who seemed most likely to become hyena bait if Grandfather were serious.

"Let me tell you about our new exhibit, the Creatures of the Night," Grandfather said. "A lot of animals in the zoo are hard for visitors to see, because they're nocturnal. That means they sleep during the day and are awake all night. And that's no fun is it—when you come to see the animals and they're asleep in their burrows?"

Much head-shaking by the children.

"So we built a new exhibit that's underground," Grandfather explained. "There are no windows, so the animals can't see the sunshine. We have really big lights that make it as bright as day when they're turned on, but when the lights are off, it's nice and dark, the way nocturnal animals like it. And once we got the animals settled down there, we started turning the lights on a little earlier each day. And then turning them off a little earlier each night. We gradually adjusted the lights so that now they go on at sunset and off at sunrise.

So during the night, when all of you have to be home and asleep, the bright lights are on and all the animals are asleep. But in the daytime, like now, the lights are low, and the animals think it's night and they come out to eat and play. So now you can see them."

More cheers.

"Now we have to be careful as we go through the Creatures of the Night," Grandfather said, with a slight but definitely menacing frown. "For most of the exhibit, we'll be traveling in a kind of tunnel. Most of the animals are behind one-way glass, so we can see them but they can't really see us. But to bother them as little as possible, we keep the lights in the human tunnel very low. You'll need to watch your step. And try not to make loud noises, because that might scare the animals. There are a couple of places where we won't be behind glass. In the Louisiana Swamp exhibit, for example, we'll have only a railing between us and the beavers and bullfrogs and alligators."

This statement seemed to alarm some of the children— at least, until Josh leaned over to one little girl who looked on the verge of tears.

"Don't worry," he said. "Alligators don't eat people. Only crocodiles do that."

"Very good, Josh," Grandfather said. "The other exhibit where you won't have glass between you and the animals is the Bat Cave—but I'll explain that when we get closer."

As he was speaking, a large bloodstained mummy came out of a nearby building and shambled over to stand at Grandfather's side. Its face was covered, but since it was slightly taller than Grandfather and much wider, I deduced that under its bloody bandages the mummy was Dr. Clarence Rutledge, the local veterinarian who looked after the zoo animals. The mummy bent over and whispered something in Grandfather's ear. Whatever the secret was, it turned Grandfather's usual stern expression into a scary scowl.

"Blast," he said. "I should go and deal with that. Meg, could you come and help me with something? Clarence, you take over the tour for a couple of minutes. Take them over to the Kingdom of the Night—but take them the long way round."

"Past the hyenas?" Clarence asked.

"No, through the aviary," Grandfather said. "That's about as far as you can get from the lions' habitat."

With that, Grandfather strode off. For someone in his nineties he had a remarkably fast and steady stride. Clarence began gathering the class and shooing them in the opposite direction from what Grandfather had taken.

"I'll keep you posted," I said to Michael, in an undertone, and then I set off to follow Grandfather.

"Why are you taking the children as far as possible from the lions' habitat," I asked when I caught up with him. "The lions aren't loose, are they?"

"Of course not." He came to a stop at the railing designed to keep people from falling into the moat around the lions' habitat. "But they do seem to have eaten a tourist."

Chapter 4

"Eaten a tourist?" Was he serious? "You're remarkably calm about the tourist's fate."

"I take a Darwinian view of it," Grandfather said. "We do what we can to keep the tourists out and the lions in. But if some fool tourist figures out a way to circumvent all our precautions—well, there you have it."

Grandfather was pointing to an area just outside the rugged faux-rock entrance to the indoor part of the habitat. Something was lying there. I shaded my eyes and squinted to get a better look. It appeared to be a severed hand, surrounded by a few ragged shreds of cloth.

We stood there staring at the hand for a few minutes. I found myself worrying about the repercussions for the zoo and the festival, and then mentally shook myself. I should be thinking about the poor misguided tourist. What on Earth had possessed him—or possibly her—to brave the lions' den?

"Where are the lions?" I asked.

He pointed to the highest part of the habitat, where a female lion was sitting on a rock, surveying her surroundings. On the ledge just below her a male lion was licking his paw and grooming his face with it.

"The keepers are trying to lure them inside so we can recover the hand and look to see if there are any other stray body parts," Grandfather said. "But they're not hungry yet, so it's slow going. And we'll be saving their scat for analysis. I suppose we should call Chief Burke now."

"Not just yet," I said. "Do you have your binoculars with you?"

He threw open his cloak to reveal that beneath it he was wearing his usual cargo pants and a faded khaki safari vest. He patted half a dozen of the vest's pockets and eventually pulled out the small but powerful binoculars he was in the habit of carrying.

I took the binoculars and focused on the hand.

"It's wonderful how well you can see things with these," I said.

"Let me have it when you're finished," Grandfather said. "Do you see any other body parts?"

"I don't see any body parts at all," I said. "That's a fake plastic hand."

"Are you sure?"

"Either it's a fake hand, or your lions' victim has 'Made in China' tattooed on the inside of his wrist," I said. "Rob's been annoying us all week with one just like it."

"You think Rob did this?" Grandfather frowned thunderously at the thought.

"He's not the only one with access to an Oriental Trading Company catalog," I said. "There must be hundreds of those things crawling around town. Sometimes literally—you can get mechanized ones with a remote control device."

Grandfather took the binoculars from me and made his own lengthy inspection of the hand.

"You're right," he said. "I'm relieved to know no one's going to blame my poor lions for simply following their natural appetites. But it's all part and parcel of the problem we've been having. I've been meaning to speak to you, since you're in charge of the Gargoyle Patrol."

"Goblin Patrol," I said. "Or more properly the Visitor Relations and Police Liaison Patrol—but never mind that. What problem?"

"We've had a sudden upsurge in trespassers last night and

this morning," he said. "People hiding in the Creatures of the Night exhibit and having to be kicked out at closing. People trying to climb over the walls after closing . . ."

"You think it has something to do with the festival."

"We don't normally get a lot of attempted stowaways," he said. "Especially not ones dressed up like vampires and zombies. So far all they seem to have done is strew empty beer bottles and soda cans around and take selfies in the Bat Cave—of course, that's probably because so far we've always caught them pretty quickly. But getting something like a dozen of them in the last twenty-four hours is strange and alarming."

"Have you told Chief Burke?"

"I have." Grandfather nodded sharply. "He says he'll do what he can, but the festival's got him stretched pretty thin. So I've put out a call for help to the Brigade."

Blake's Brigade was what we all called the loosely organized but fanatically devoted group of bird and animal lovers who regularly volunteered to help Grandfather with his animal welfare and environmental projects.

"That's good," I said. "Because my patrols are stretched pretty thin, too. And Randall says we're expecting the attendance to increase almost geometrically from now until Saturday."

"I figured we could add the Brigade people to your Goblin Patrol," Grandfather said. "Use them to keep an eye on the zoo. And on that haunted house of Smoot's. If you ask me, that's drawing in an unruly element."

"Certainly a weird element," I said. "I'll be glad to see just about any of the Brigade who show up." And come to think of it, the few I wouldn't be glad to see were probably in jail rather than the Brigade these days.

"No sense hanging around here," Grandfather said. "The keepers can take care of retrieving the fake hand. Let's get back to the tour."

Since Clarence had taken the children to the Creatures of the Night by a roundabout route to ensure that they couldn't possibly catch a glimpse of anything unfortunate at the lions' habitat, we caught up with them before they'd gotten too far in their tour. We found them standing in front of the Naked Mole Rat exhibit, a wall twelve feet high and twenty feet wide that was entirely covered with a six-inch-deep glass-fronted, dirt-filled habitat.

"It's like an ant farm," one of the first graders said. "Only bigger."

"And with rats instead of ants," another said.

"Naked rats!" Noah exclaimed, and at least half the children tittered. I sighed. Was it normal for first graders to display this mixture of embarrassment and fascination with words like "naked"? Surely I'd been older before I'd had any idea that some words held such power to shock the grown-ups.

"The naked mole rat is so called because of its almost complete absence of fur." Grandfather seemed oblivious to the children's glee at hearing the forbidden word uttered again. "Just as we humans have sometimes been called 'naked apes' because we have so little hair compared with other primates."

As I could have predicted, the children exploded into laughter and had to be shushed by Mrs. Shiffley and the nearby chaperones. Grandfather continued on inexorably, explaining how the naked mole rats regulated their temperature, how their social structure was similar to that of bees and ants, and how their colonies built tunnel systems several miles in cumulative length.

Perhaps Grandfather was wiser than I gave him credit for. By the time he began explaining how the naked mole rat could live up to thirty years and held the record for the longest life of any rodent species, the children had heard the word "naked" so often that they'd largely stopped snickering and were listening about as attentively as you'd expect for first graders.

"Let's move on!" Grandfather exclaimed, emphasizing his words by rapping his walking stick on the floor. He strode forward as if leading an expedition through the jungle or the veldt. Most of the class hurried to keep up with him, and Mrs. Shiffley brought up the rear, gently encouraging any laggers to keep up with their classmates.

We inspected fossas and cacomistles, aardvarks, spring-haas, and bush babies—the bush babies, who looked like animated teddy bears with enormous eyes, were a particular favorite. But the more bloodthirsty children—my own two among them—were growing restless to see more dangerous animals.

I suspected that Grandfather shared their eagerness.

"Let's move on to the Louisiana Swamp," he called.

"Are there crocodiles in the swamp?" Mason wanted to know.

"Of course not," Grandfather said. "There are no crocodiles in Louisiana!"

Many of the children, particularly the small boys, who had perked up when they heard Mason's question, slumped with disappointment.

"The only place in the United States where crocodiles live is in South Florida," Grandfather said. "In Louisiana, they have alligators."

Hope returned to the faces of the small children.

"And you have lots of alligators in your swamp, don't you, Great-grandpa?" Josh asked.

"We have eleven of them," Grandfather said.

Murmurs of satisfaction greeted this announcement.

"Do alligators really not eat people?" Noah asked.

Grandfather appeared to be pondering that question—perhaps weighing the dangers of alarming the timid children with the satisfaction of thrilling the rest.

"Well," he said. "They don't do it nearly as often as crocodiles do. Alligators are more timid, and when they see a human, they just want to run away from us. But if you annoy them or scare them, they'll attack. Or if they're really hungry. And unfortunately, alligators who see a lot of humans become less scared of them—and our alligators see a lot of humans. We try to feed them regularly, but don't stick your hands over the railing. You never know when one might feel like a snack."

Most of the children seemed quite eager to visit the swamp. But as Grandfather led the children out of the African habitat, I heard Mason's voice.

"But we don't get to see crocodiles." His tone wasn't quite a whine—more like a plaintive sigh.

"Not in the Louisiana Swamp habitat," Grandfather said. "I keep the crocodiles in the Australian Bush habitat. Five of them. We'll get to that before too long."

"Yay!" Mason exclaimed.

Visitors entered the swamp habitat through a replica of a bayou trapper's cabin, complete with rough board walls and several objects that I assumed were antique traps. It had two doors leading out into the faux swamp and several windows that let cautious visitors inspect the attraction before venturing out into it. The children hurried through the cabin without a second glance, swarming out of both doors onto the wooden boardwalk that wound through the dimly lit swamp. Michael and I paused in the cabin and found a window where we could watch what the children were up to without being caught in the middle of the noisy, jostling herd.

Although when he wanted to, Grandfather could do a great job of calming the herd.

"Let's be as quiet as we can so the alligators will surface to check us out," he said.

A hush fell over the swamp, so you could actually hear the

bullfrogs booming and small rustles and splashes as unseen creatures slipped through the underbrush or hopped into a pool. The pale trunks of cypress trees emerged from the murky depths and disappeared into the shadows overhead. Great swathes of Spanish moss trailed down into the water and shivered occasionally in what would be, in a real swamp, a passing breeze. Here, I knew, it was only a sophisticated ventilation system, designed to give the impression of random breezes, but it was still delightful.

"I like it," Michael murmured. "We should come back sometime when it's less crowded."

"Grandfather would be happy to give us a private tour, before or after hours," I replied. "Once the Halloween rush is over."

I heard a splashing noise, accompanied by gasps and a few squeals from the children.

"That," Grandfather said. "Is a thirteen-foot male alligator. His name is Vincent Price."

Clearly the children had never heard of the Merchant of Menace, but a few of the parents tittered. The children merely gazed down at Vincent with fascination.

The alligator habitat was between our window and the stretch of boardwalk where Grandfather had taken the class, so from our vantage point, we could see the alligator's eyes just above the surface and the children crowding closely around Grandfather to peer down at it. I worried briefly about how strong the fence between the children and the water was, and then reminded myself that Grandfather would have made sure it was strong enough to withstand anything the human crowds could do to it. Though I suspected his reasons had more to do with protecting the animals from the human visitors than vice versa.

The children oohed and aahed as he explained some of the alligators' most important features—including, since

Grandfather was a staunch environmentalist, the important service they performed to the environment by eating vast quantities of nutria.

"What's that?" one of the children asked.

"An alien invasive species," Grandfather said. And then, seeing that none of the children understood this, he added, "Think of a giant wet rat that eats everything in sight. They're destroying the environment in many parts of the south. The alligators help us get rid of them."

He and the children contemplated the alligator with renewed approval. The alligator seemed to be studying them back.

"Dr. Blake," one of the children piped up. "I thought you said alligators didn't eat people."

"Not usually," Grandfather said.

"Then what is that?" The child pointed to something in the water.

"It's a human foot!" one of the mothers screamed.

Chapter 5

The mother who had spotted the human foot continued to scream, and a few others shrieked with her, accompanied by exclamations of "gross!" and "cool!" from some of the boys.

Michael and I were about to dash out of the cabin by the nearest of the two exit doors to take care of our sons, when the other door opened and a figure furtively slipped in—a slender young man, dressed entirely in black, with a hooded cape swirling about his shoulders. He raced into the cabin and headed for the corridor by which we'd entered.

"Stop!" I shouted, and both Michael and I took off after him. He started and turned when he heard us, and that slowed him down long enough for us to tackle him. The three of us landed in a heap, with the intruder on the bottom. I suspected we'd all have bruises by the morning, but since I was five ten, Michael six inches taller, and neither of us undernourished, our undersized captive definitely got the worst of it.

Michael and I untangled ourselves, without letting the intruder up. I left Michael to keep him immobile while I raced to check on the twins.

But before I could dash out of the shack, they came pounding in.

"Mommy! We found a foot!" Josh said.

"I saw it first!" Jamie said.

More children were pouring in after them.

"It's not a real foot," Noah was saying.

"It's still awesome," Mason said.

"Stay out, all of you," I said. "I think we've caught the person responsible for this."

"Is he missing a foot?" Josh asked.

"I didn't do anything," the intruder wheezed from beneath Michael.

Grandfather pushed through the crowd.

"What's this?" he boomed.

"We caught him trying to slip out of the swamp," Michael said.

"I was just looking at the alligators," the intruder whined.

"The zoo is closed for a special tour," Grandfather said. "Only first graders and their parents allowed, and you're definitely not either. Michael, make sure this young gentleman stays just where he is. Meg, call 911 and report that we've secured an intruder."

"Roger," I said.

"Children!" Grandfather said. "You're going to get a special treat. Since the swamp is now a crime scene, we're not going to disturb it any more than we already have."

"It's only a fake foot," Mason grumbled.

"So I'm going to take you to the next exhibit—the crocodiles!—through the hallways that are normally open only to official zookeepers! You are about to learn the zookeepers' deepest, darkest secrets!"

The children cheered at this.

"Follow me!" Grandfather said. "Chaperones, make sure no one wanders off or touches anything."

The tour members began filing out, keeping their distance from the black-cloaked intruder, whom Michael was still restraining. As I dialed 911 I noticed that the children, intent on the promise of crocodiles, tended to ignore him, while the parents, particularly the mothers, glared at him so fiercely that I suspected he was lucky to have Michael between him and them.

I was waving bye to Josh and Jamie—not that they noticed,

since they were intent on being the first to enter the secret, zookeepers-only part of the Creatures of the Night—when Debbie Ann, the emergency dispatcher answered.

"Meg, what's wrong now?" she asked. Clearly, in the course of my Goblin Patrol duties, I'd been calling her rather often.

"Intruder at the zoo," I said. "Grandfather was taking the first graders on a special tour before opening time, and we caught a guy who's been trying to terrify the children by throwing fake body parts into carnivore habitats."

"No," the young man said. "That's not why I did it."

"Patrol car on its way," Debbie Ann said. "Is the intruder secured?"

I glanced over to see that Clarence the Mummy had arrived and was kneeling down to bind the intruder's wrists with a roll of leopard-print duct tape.

"Reasonably secure," I said. "And about to get even more so."

"Stay on the line in case anything happens," Debbie Ann said.

"You want to do his ankles?" Clarence tossed me another roll of duct tape—this one in a faux snakeskin pattern.

"Let's just keep an eye on him until the police get here," I suggested.

The young man groaned at the word "police." I squatted down by his head.

"What's your name?" I asked.

He clamped his mouth more firmly shut, as if afraid his name would escape by accident.

"You didn't actually say how he was secured," Michael suggested. "I think if we threw him in the alligator lagoon he'd be even more secure."

"Yeah, dead's pretty secure," Clarence added, clearly entering into the spirit of the occasion.

"You wouldn't dare," the young man said.

"Try me." I put on my fiercest expression. "I'm pretty sure

you just traumatized both of my sons for life. I'll be lucky if I can ever get them near the water again. So don't tell me what I wouldn't dare."

Actually, I was afraid the boys would never tire of scanning the alligator lagoon for rubber body parts, but I kept my expression thunderous. Michael scowled. Clarence's mouth was twitching, but he was behind the intruder's head.

"Justin," he said.

I frowned some more.

"Justin Klapcroft. And I wasn't trying to traumatize anyone, honest. It was just one of my tasks. If I finish the first set of tasks by midnight I advance to the next round."

"Next round?" I echoed. "So this is all a game?"

"It's an adventure!" It's not really possible to draw yourself up to your full height when you're lying on the floor of a fake Cajun swamp shack with your hands duct-taped behind your back, but Justin made a decent effort.

Just then Deputy Vern Shiffley loomed up in the doorway. He was carrying his service weapon, though the barrel was pointing up.

"All secure here?" Vern leaned down and tested Clarence's taping job. Then he nodded approvingly and holstered his gun.

"Vern's here," I said on my phone. "Want to talk to him or shall I hang up?"

"He'll call me if he needs me," Debbie Ann said. "Tell him I'll start looking for information on Mr. Klapcroft."

"Will do." I ended the call and pocketed my phone.

"So what did the creep do?" Vern asked. "Debbie Ann seemed to think he'd fed someone to the alligators."

"No!" Justin yelped. "It was fake! Honestly!"

I introduced Justin and explained about the fake foot, and its discovery by the school group.

"You see?" Justin said. "I didn't do anything awful. It was just a joke. And then these people tied me up."

"You're lucky Meg and Michael were here," Vern said. "'Cause if they hadn't been, my cousin Velma would probably have fed *you* to the alligators. Scaring a bunch of little kids like that. What were you trying to prove, anyway?"

"I want my lawyer," Justin said.

"Fine," Vern said. "Be that way. You can call your lawyer when we get you back to the station."

"Back to the station! No! Everyone else will get ahead of me and—"

Then Justin realized that maybe talking wasn't in his best interest. He closed his mouth and clenched his jaw.

"I think it's some kind of scavenger hunt," I said. "He said something like 'If I finish the first set of tasks by midnight I advance to the next round.' But he hasn't given us any more details."

Vern studied Justin for a few moments. Then he squatted down beside him.

"You carrying any weapons?" he asked.

"No!" Justin squeaked.

"I need to make sure of that," Vern said. He patted Justin down. Then he put on a plastic glove and searched his pockets. He found a wallet in the back pocket of the young man's jeans, and a folded piece of paper in one of the front pockets.

"This looks interesting," he said.

Michael, Clarence, and I gathered around to look over his shoulder. The paper was about three by five inches, but irregularly shaped, as if it had been cut rather haphazardly out of a larger piece of paper. It contained a list of five items.

1. Go to the graveyard and do a tombstone rubbing.
2. Visit the Creatures of the Night while the zoo is closed.
3. Eat a live insect.
4. Scare someone with a fake body part.
5. Steal a pumpkin.

"Yeah, sounds to me like a scavenger hunt," Vern said. "Pretty weird one, but—"

"It's an adventure!" Justin exclaimed. "A quest! But go ahead. You mundanes will never understand."

"May I?" I had pulled out my phone and was holding it up.

"Be my guest," Vern said.

As I took a couple of pictures of the list, I noted that the first, third, and fifth items were crossed off, leaving only "visit the Creatures of the Night" and "scare someone with a fake body part" to go.

"Evidently he was trying to knock off tasks two and four with one blow," I said.

"They would be the hardest," Michael said. "No one would pay much attention to someone doing a tombstone rubbing, and these days it's hard to walk through town without tripping over pumpkins everywhere."

Just then we heard a thudding noise out in the corridor.

"Tarnation!" someone exclaimed.

"Chief's here," Vern said. "Maybe I better shine a flashlight down the hallway so he won't trip again."

But before he could act on this plan, the chief limped in.

"I hope all these blasted night creatures appreciate what we go through for their comfort," he growled. "Is this the perpetrator?"

He glared down at our prisoner, who flinched as if expecting to be struck. Sterner souls had cowered under the chief's gaze, but if Justin expected mistreatment, he clearly wasn't from around here.

"Name of Justin Klapcroft," Vern said. "He seems to be playing some kind of game that involves terrifying the toddlers."

Justin uttered a small whimper. Vern showed the chief the small slip of paper with the list of five tasks. The chief read them, then shifted his gaze over to Justin.

"You want to explain yourself."

Justin shook his head.

"He wants his attorney," Vern said.

"Have we called his attorney?"

"He hasn't given me a name to call," Vern said. "I told him he could call when he got down to the station."

"Might save a little time if we have his attorney meet us there," the chief said. "Mr. Klapcroft, would you like to call your attorney now?"

Justin just frowned.

"Son," the chief said. "Do you even know an attorney to call?"

Justin shook his head vigorously. The chief sighed and turned back to Vern.

"Have Debbie Ann call the Public Defender's office," he said. "She can ask them to send someone down to the station. And then take Mr. Klapcroft in and book him for trespassing."

"And maybe disorderly conduct?" Vern sounded hopeful and eager. Maybe a little bit too eager. "And what about child endangerment?"

"Trespassing will do for the time being."

Vern looked crestfallen, and the chief relented.

"But that doesn't mean you can't start thinking about other things we might end up charging him with if he proves uncooperative. And get Horace to process his wallet and that piece of paper. Meg, Michael—you want to show me this fake foot?"

Vern looked cheerful again, and we left him and Clarence to deal with the intruder while we accompanied the chief out into the swamp exhibit. We followed the board walkway till we reached the place where Grandfather and the children had been standing. Then we leaned against the rail and gazed down at the dark water below. Vincent had submerged again, and we couldn't spot him or any of the other alligators. The chief fished a small flashlight out of his pocket and moved its beam over the surface of the water until he located the fake foot.

"That thing probably wouldn't fool anyone if the lighting in here were better," he said. "But I imagine the little ones got quite a shock. Nasty thing to do, and we've had quite a rash of that kind of doings in town lately."

"Justin did say that there were others who would get ahead of him if you took him down to the station," Michael remarked.

"To judge by what my officers have seen, at least half a dozen others," the chief said. "And that's only the ones who fooled someone into thinking they'd found a real body part and calling us. Who knows how many more people just wrote it off as a tasteless prank?"

"Grandfather did call you about the fake hand in his lion habitat, didn't he?" I asked.

"He did indeed." The chief shook his head. "Evidently Mr. Klapcroft is not the only game player trying to kill two birds with one stone."

Vincent—or one of his cousins—surfaced again and stared up at us with unblinking eyes.

"Shoo, you ugly reptile," the chief said.

Vincent ignored him.

The chief pulled out his cell phone and punched a couple of buttons.

"How's it going?" he asked whoever he was talking to. "Good. Can you send someone in here with a net to fish out this fake foot? No, that's fine. It's not as if the gators are likely to eat the evidence."

He hung up and turned to me.

"As it happens," he said, "I had a few words with your brother earlier today on the subject of tasteless pranks. Given his some-what exuberant sense of humor, I considered him a prime suspect when word of the first couple of fake body part find-ings reached me. I suppose I shall have to apologize to him."

"I wouldn't go that far," I said. "He did equip all our guest bathrooms with those creepy soaps shaped like severed fingers. He's probably not responsible for all the tasteless pranks, but I doubt if he's completely innocent."

"Point taken," the chief said. "Though Rob did assure me that he had been far too busy with his Goblin Patrol work to celebrate the Halloween season with his usual enthusiasm. You know, I don't want to second-guess the county board, but I wonder if they really thought through the ramifications of this Halloween Festival thing. I know the annual Christmas in Caerphilly celebrations have been quite successful. They're helping to get the town back on its feet financially."

"But the Christmas festival attracts a very different kind of visitor," I said. "More family oriented."

"Traditional," Michael put in. "Sentimental."

"Precisely," the chief said. "With this Halloween thing, we're trying to appeal to two very different audiences."

"Not just different," Michael said. "Antagonistic."

"We should have come down on one side or the other," I said. "Either made it a completely wholesome, G-rated, family-friendly event or warned the parents to keep their kiddies away and gone full-bore with the zombies and vampires. The mad scramble twice a day to switch between the Day Side and the Night Side is insane."

"I see I'm preaching to the choir," the chief said.

"And not saying anything that wasn't said in the town council and county board meetings before they approved Randall's plans," Michael added.

"Well, it doesn't matter now what we think of the festival, or whether we approve of having it next year," the chief said. "We're stuck with it. We invited all these people here and we owe it to them to do our best to keep them safe while they're having whatever kind of good time they're looking for."

"Provided their idea of a good time doesn't break the law or interfere with the other tourists' good times," I said.

The chief nodded.

Just then, my friend Aida Butler, who was one of the chief's deputies, strode in. She was carrying a net with a telescoping handle, just like the one we used to skim leaves out of our pool.

"That was quick," the chief said. "Thank you."

"I didn't have to go far," Aida said. "They keep a couple of these handy. Apparently the tourists are always dropping things into the ponds."

We all watched as Aida extended the pole to about ten feet and then maneuvered the net under the floating foot. Several more sets of alligator eyes surfaced to observe the process, but the pond's legitimate inhabitants kept their distance.

Aida carefully pulled in the net and held the fake foot out for the chief to inspect. He was right—close up it wasn't nearly as scary, and in proper lighting we'd probably find it ludicrously unrealistic. But so far, to my relief, the chief was respecting the swamp creatures' need for their normal dim night conditions. He probably wouldn't have if it had been a real severed foot, so perhaps we should be grateful to Justin for choosing such an obvious fake.

As we were watching, the chief got a phone call. His end of it was monosyllabic and not very interesting, but once he hung up, he filled us in.

"Sammy found where our intruder gained entry," he said. "Used a pair of wire cutters to make a hole in the chain-link fence at the far end of that big open field where Dr. Blake keeps all the antelope and buffalo and other herd animals."

"Grandfather's going to need better security," I said. "And for that matter, so is Dr. Smoot."

The chief nodded.

"Did you find any fake body parts when you checked out the haunted house?" he asked Aida.

"I found plenty of them, not that I was looking," Aida said. "Dr. Smoot has a bunch of them lying around as part of the décor. But I was looking for evidence of an intruder, not fake feet and such."

"Do you suppose Dr. Smoot would even notice if a prankster left more fake body parts in his house?" Michael asked.

"And more important, why would the pranksters leave them there?" I asked. "It wouldn't fulfill the task, would it? The list doesn't just say 'leave a fake body part lying around somewhere.' It says 'scare someone with a fake body part.' Who would be scared by one more disembodied hand at the Haunted House?"

"Let's hope that whoever is running the game is less particular than you are," the chief said. "Because having additional fake body parts turn up at the Haunted House would be a lot less disruptive than some of the places where the pranksters have been leaving them. And who knows where it could escalate by Halloween night?"

"Then if some of the pranksters consider the Haunted House a soft target for today's tasks, maybe a lot of them will be turning up there—so wouldn't it be a good place to catch them?" I asked. "Assuming we could enlist Dr. Smoot's help. Ask him to note the locations where he's already decorated with fake body parts, so we'll know if anyone adds any."

"Good point," the chief said. "I suppose I should go and talk to him."

He didn't sound that keen on the prospect. I remembered how much Dr. Smoot annoyed him.

"You're busy with actual crimes," I said. "How about if I talk to him? I need to go over there anyway. Rob seems to think I might have more luck than he's had at calming Dr. Smoot down."

"Be nice if someone could," Aida muttered.

"I'd very much appreciate it," the chief said.

"In fact, maybe while I'm there, I can get Dr. Smoot to give me a complete tour, and I can document all the fake body parts that are supposed to be there," I said. "I can take pictures of everything, and then at least we'll know how many of them are there, and where, so if any more turn up, we'll have proof."

"That would be excellent," the chief said.

"Let's catch up with the tour party and see if we can arrange an alternate ride home for the boys," Michael said. "Then we can go straight to the Haunted House when we leave here."

"What about that hand in the lion's den?" the chief asked, turning to Aida. "Are they making any progress toward clearing the lions out so we can process it?"

"They're working on it," she said. "It's not as if they can just pick them up by the scruff of the neck like kittens."

Michael and I followed the boardwalk through the rest of the indoor swamp. Along our way we spotted beavers swimming in their habitat. We resisted the temptation to peer into the glass side of the beaver lodge. We didn't pause to listen to the chorus of bullfrogs, perhaps croaking their relief at being in a separate pond from the alligators who, in the wild, would have found them delightful tidbits. We raced through the swamp and into the next exhibit.

"Smells a little like Vicks VapoRub," Michael said.

"We're entering the Eucalyptus Forest," I said, as I took a deep breath. "Come on—we might be able to catch up with the children at the crocodile exhibit."

But apparently we'd dallied too long talking with the chief. The children had all moved on from the crocodile exhibit—even bloodthirsty little Mason. Though I thought I could hear shrill childish voices not too far away.

"They must have gone on to the Bat Cave," I said.

I led the way through the Eucalyptus Forest, which was not

only aromatic but pleasantly dry after the dank humid air of the swamp.

"Brace yourself," I said.

"Why?" Michael asked.

I didn't answer. I just opened the door and let the bats do that for me.

Chapter 6

The Bat Cave was Grandfather's pièce de résistance. He'd wanted to give visitors the closest thing possible to what they'd experience if they went to a real Bat Cave—without, of course, subjecting the bats to any danger or annoyance from the humans intruding into their realm.

So the Bat Cave was built as a single huge space, several stories tall, in which the bats could fly freely and roost wherever they wanted. We mere humans traversed the floor of the Bat Cave confined to a narrow, winding tunnel. The sides of the tunnel were made of netting, so fine it was almost invisible—and in two layers, with a few inches of space between them, to keep us from sticking our fingers through the mesh to touch the bats. The roof was solid, to protect us from the bats' droppings, but made of clear glass, so we could look up and see the bats overhead—at least we could this early in the day, before the guano had piled up too badly. And we could hear the bats—the rustling of their wings and the squeaking noises they made—and feel the slight movement in the air as they rushed past.

Unfortunately we could also smell them. The bat guano reeked of ammonia. Not for the first time, I questioned the wisdom of having visitors go from the Eucalyptus Forest directly into the Bat Cave. I loved the way the gentle but pervasive eucalyptus scent cleared my sinuses and sharpened my sense of smell, but to go directly from that to the stench of the bats was cruel and unusual punishment.

And even though I knew the ultrasounds bats emitted as

part of their echolocation was too high for human ears, I couldn't help wondering if they didn't have some kind of effect on us—perhaps subliminally. Every time I entered the Bat Cave, it felt as if the air was pressing in on my ears and throat. Maybe it was those ultrasonic bat cries.

Or maybe it was just my claustrophobia kicking in. Either way, I had little desire to linger in the Bat Cave. But I wasn't about to let the children know how I felt.

I started to take the deep yoga breaths that Rose Noire always recommended I use to calm myself, and after the first one I decided that in the Bat Cave, I'd have to work on being calm while breathing shallowly.

We couldn't see the children but we could hear their voices somewhere ahead of us. I hurried to catch up with them. And the fact that catching up with them took me closer to the exit was also nice.

"No, the bats don't bite," Grandfather was saying. "Only vampire bats bite, and we don't have any vampire bats in the Bat Cave."

"I want to see the vampire bats." Mason again.

"We'll see some," Grandfather said. "They have their own habitat, just before the exit. But for now, enjoy the Bat Cave."

Most of the children seemed to be enjoying it. The group was only slightly smaller than it had been when I'd last seen it in the swamp exhibit. Perhaps a few children had freaked at the sight—and smell—of the Bat Cave and had to be taken out to calm down. Or perhaps a few parents decided to whisk their darlings away before more fake body parts appeared. A couple of the children seemed to be clinging to their parents in a way that suggested they were not wholly charmed by their surroundings. But most of the class were pressing against the inside of the mesh, trying to get as close to the bats as possible and muttering things like "awesome" and "wicked" and even that old standby from my generation, "cool."

As Grandfather lectured the children on the bats, he was holding his cell phone in his hand, and glanced down at it from time to time. He eventually wrapped up his spiel and walked over to Michael and me, leaving the class group to enjoy the bats on their own.

"Lot of Brigade people on their way," he said. "And Caroline's coming to help organize them."

"Good." I liked Caroline, who in addition to running a local private wildlife sanctuary was one of Grandfather's usual allies when he embarked on an environmental crusade or an animal welfare mission. She was cheerful, organized, and one of the few people in the universe capable of bossing Grandfather around.

"And I guess it's time I took your brother up on that offer of his," Grandfather went on.

"What offer was that?" Not, I hoped, his notion of opening a zoo annex in the building where Mutant Wizards, Rob's computer gaming company, had its offices. However much the programmers might enjoy the presence of wolves and badgers, I didn't think the feeling would be mutual.

"He says some of his techs can install cameras all around the perimeter of the fence, and also in key points inside the zoo," Grandfather said. "And then set up a big control room so someone on my staff can watch it all."

"Sounds like a good idea," I said. "But how long is that going to take?"

"No idea," he said. "So until we can get it up and running, we'll set up patrols of Brigade members. First thing is to get through this blasted spook fest without any more of my animals being upset."

I'd have been insulted at the implication that Grandfather cared more about protecting his zoo animals than his grandchildren if I didn't know that he more or less lumped them—and the rest of his family—in with the animals. He'd recently remarked that Josh and Jamie were admirable young primates, more amusing than spider monkeys and arguably as clever as baby orangutans—rare praise indeed.

Michael and I arranged for our two amusing young primates to ride home with Mason's mother and left the children to enjoy the Bat Cave for as long as their attention spans and Grandfather's patience would allow.

Crowds were already starting to gather outside the zoo. I checked my watch: 10:10. Still nearly an hour before the zoo opened. I saw two of my Goblin Patrol members standing nearby. One was Osgood Shiffley, a cousin of Randall's, who ran Caerphilly's only gas station. One of these days I'd ask Osgood why he'd chosen a giant chicken costume for Halloween. Left over, perhaps, from a long ago career with some obscure fast food chain? The other, Ragnar Ragnarsen, was the closest Caerphilly came to having a real celebrity. He was a retired heavy metal drummer—retired because the last three bands he had played in had self-destructed in ways that were pretty spectacular even by heavy metal standards, leaving Ragnar the only one still alive who wasn't committed, incarcerated, or in semi-permanent rehab. Although he was the mildest-mannered soul imaginable, Ragnar was taller than Michael—at least six eight—and built like a sumo wrestler, so in his black-leather Viking costume—complete with real, waist-length flaxen braids and a war ax whose edge I hoped wasn't too sharp—he made a satisfactorily intimidating presence. Osgood looked almost frail beside him, but I happened to know that Osgood was tough as rawhide and, unlike Ragnar, pretty cynically savvy about human nature. They made a great team, which was why I'd assigned them to the zoo, which had been something of a trouble spot ever since the festival had started. And I couldn't help thinking how nice it was that volunteering for the festival was bringing together people who might otherwise have never met.

We went over to wish them a good morning and pass along a warning about the scavenger hunt.

"So keep your eyes open," I said, when I'd explained the situation.

"We will." Ragnar opened his eyes very wide as if to demonstrate that he understood. I never knew whether he was pulling my leg or not. He had only a faint Norwegian accent, and spoke good and sometimes curiously formal English, but sometimes he seemed to take everything anyone said quite literally. "These tourists are far more weird than I expected," he added.

I had to suppress a giggle to hear that coming from a man who had redecorated his entire forty-room mansion in what Mother referred to, with a sniff, as a combination of late Gothic and early Halloween.

"At least the problem of people trying to sneak in goes away when the zoo opens," Osgood said.

"Until eight o'clock tonight, when the zoo closes again," Ragnar said. "Because if I wanted to sneak in here, I would wait until after dark."

"True," Osgood said. "I guess we'll have to keep our eyes out for fake body parts and entomophagy all day."

"Entomophagy?" I echoed. Not a word I'd have expected to find in Osgood's vocabulary.

"That's what your grandfather calls it," Osgood said, with a wheezy laugh. "Sounds less disgusting than bug-eating. This Goblin Patrol gig is turning out to be a lot more exciting than I expected. And I can tell you, it's going to get worse before it gets better."

"Grandfather's calling out his Brigade members to help patrol," I said. "We should have the first of them by sometime this afternoon."

"That won't be easy for a bunch of city folks," Osgood said. "Especially after dark. And some of the terrain on the far side is pretty rugged."

"The Brigade members aren't all city slickers," I protested.

"Once the gates open and things quiet down here, I'll

make a few calls to some cousins," Osgood said. "Pretty near every one of them's got one of those portable hunting stands you can set up in a tree, and they're all getting right bored, waiting for the deer season to start. We can probably put most of the perimeter under observation by nightfall."

The vision of the zoo ringed by a posse of armed Shiffleys perched in the trees was probably more reassuring to Osgood than it was to me.

"And what will they do if they spot an intruder?" I asked. "It's not tourist season, either."

"Always open season on tourists," Osgood said with a straight face. "The Virginia Department of Game and Inland Fisheries considers them a nuisance species, just like rats, pigeons, and feral hogs."

"And nutria, I suppose," I said. "But seriously—"

"Don't worry," Osgood said. "We spot anyone trying to break in, we'll call 911, and then follow them till a deputy arrives."

"Sounds good to me, then," I said. "But clear it with the chief, will you?"

"Will do," Osgood said. "And don't worry. One look at Ragnar here and the intruders will probably run away."

Ragnar grinned at that, and hefted his war ax.

"I know I would," I said. "Thanks again for volunteering," I added to Ragnar.

"Thank you for taking me." The subject seemed to depress him. "I was hoping to play a greater role, but . . ."

He shrugged.

"Yeah, Ragnar tried to offer his house for some of the events," Osgood said. "Still don't understand why you folks turned him down."

"Well, I didn't turn him down," I said. "I didn't even know he'd offered it."

"It was Miss Lydia," Ragnar said. "I do not think she likes me."

"Join the club," I said. "I don't think she likes me, either."

"I know she doesn't like me," Osgood said. "I told her a few plain truths about some of the mistakes she's made running things. I wonder if Randall's figured out what a mistake he made hiring her."

"I'll mention your offer of the house to Randall," I said to Ragnar. "Probably too late for this year, but come November first, we'll start planning for next year."

Ragnar beamed, and he and Osgood went back to the gate.

"Assuming this goes off well enough that we even have a next year," Michael said in an undertone.

"We will still have to plan for next year," I said. "Even if the plan is to lock all the doors, hide in our basements, and post signs at the county line saying 'Keep out! No festival this year!'"

Just then a young woman in a *Xena the Warrior Princess* costume burst out of the woods and looked around wildly. She spotted us and started running again, heading toward Michael and me. Osgood and Ragnar also noticed her and headed back our way.

"This doesn't look good," Michael muttered.

The young woman wore a Goblin Patrol armband, and I recognized her as one of Randall and Osgood Shiffley's many cousins. I even dredged up her name out of my memory by the time she neared us.

"Ashley, what's wrong?" I called.

"Meg! Thank goodness you're here! Thor and I found a body in the woods!"

Chapter 7

"A body?" I echoed.

"I'll call the chief," Michael said, pulling out his cell phone.

"Are you sure it's a real body?" I asked.

"We thought at first it was another of those fake legs like the first graders found in the alligator pond," Ashley said. "But then I tried to pick it up and—"

She burst into tears. I put my arms around her and she started crying on my shoulder.

"I'll call her ma." Osgood pulled out his cell phone.

Ragnar strode over to a bench some ten feet away, picked it up as easily as I could have picked up a folding lawn chair, and set it down gently behind where Ashley was standing. I steered Ashley down onto the bench.

"Chief's on his way," Michael said.

"Ashley, when the chief gets here, do you think you could lead us to where you found the body?" Her grip on me tightened. "Not all the way—just close enough that we can see it."

She nodded slightly.

I just let her cry, and she was a lot calmer by the time the chief arrived. And once we set out to lead him to the body, her normally sunny disposition began reasserting itself and she readily answered the chief's questions. No one objected when Michael and I tagged along. Maybe the chief wanted me around in case the tears reappeared.

"One of the deputies asked Thor and me to guard the place where that guy cut a hole in the zoo fence," Ashley explained as we made our way through the woods just outside the fence. "Until Cousin Randall could get someone down here to fix it. And it was pretty boring just standing around there, so we were patrolling up and down the fence and then Thor spotted a foot sticking out of some bushes. We thought it was a fake foot."

It was only a few minutes' walk. We passed the hole in the fence, now being repaired by two men in Shiffley Construction Company hats. Thor was standing in a small clearing another twenty feet or so farther along the fence line. He was muffled in a large gray-green cloak but his mop of bright red hair made him easy to spot. He was carrying a bow and arrow. Was he supposed to be an elf or one of Robin Hood's merry men? He didn't look particularly merry at the moment—just glum, and then relieved once he spotted us.

"Hey, Meg," Thor said. "When I tell your grandmother about this she'll be put out that she didn't come." Actually, I suspected Grandmother Cordelia could do without encountering another dead body, but I didn't argue with him. I'd met Thor through my grandmother, for whom he worked during semester breaks and summer vacations, and she had recruited him to serve in the Goblin Patrol. I hoped this didn't discourage him from continuing.

Thor pointed at a foot clad in a scruffy black boot, protruding from under the overhanging limb of a hemlock tree. The chief inched slowly forward until he could reach the limb and lifted it up to peer at the rest of the body. Then he frowned.

"I don't recognize him." He didn't sound happy about it. I could understand why. If the chief didn't recognize him, he was almost certainly not from around here. And therefore probably a tourist. Someone who had come for the Halloween festival. Just damn.

"Meg?" the chief said. "Perhaps one of your out-of-town volunteers?"

I stepped forward and peered past the chief's upraised arm. I had a good view of the dead man, including the curiously neat bullet hole in the center of his forehead. He was in his twenties, or maybe his early thirties. Since he was lying down, it was hard to tell how tall he was, and equally hard to assess his weight since he was dressed entirely in baggy black garments—black pants, shirt, boots, and cloak. His face was thin and sharp-featured; his eyes, though wide open, were still small and beady; and his mouth hung open to reveal prominent buck teeth. If Michael were casting a production of *Cinderella,* he'd probably consider the poor man perfect for the role of the rat turned coachman. And was it thinking ill of the dead to realize that if I'd seen him approaching me in the street, I'd probably have checked to make sure my purse was zipped shut?

"No." I shook my head. "Don't know him."

"Well, I won't keep you from your work," the chief said.

So much more polite than "get lost." I nodded and stepped back. The chief let the branch fall back.

"Osgood, can you stay here and give me a hand?" the chief asked. "Meg, it would help if you could reassign some of your volunteers to help with crowd control here. And Horace and Dr. Langslow are on their way—can someone lead them back here?"

The rest of us nodded and began making our way out of the clearing with varying degrees of reluctance or eagerness. And then, as luck would have it, I spotted something. At least if the chief asked, I'd call it luck, but the truth was that being banished from the crime scene fired up my curiosity, and I was walking away at a snail's pace, furiously scanning the ground for clues.

Had I found one? A torn bit of paper lying on the ground near the edge of the clearing. I veered closer, and peered down to see what it was.

Only two lines, obviously torn from the bottom of a larger bit of paper. The first line read "t a small fire." The second: "5. Take a selfie with a black cat."

"Chief." I pointed down at the scrap. "Take a look at this."

He walked over and glanced down at the paper.

"It reminds me of that list we found in Justin Klapcroft's pocket," I said.

The chief peered at it more closely, both through and over his glasses, before nodding.

"Mr. Larson," he called. "Ms. Shiffley."

Thor and Ashley turned and stopped where they were. The chief pulled out his cell phone, took a picture of the scrap, and walked over to them.

"This belong to either of you?" He held up the phone so they could see the picture.

They both shook their heads. Michael, Ragnar, and Osgood also disavowed any knowledge of the scrap.

"It might not have anything to do with the murder," I said. "Could just be a coincidence that someone dropped it here near the body."

"I'm not a big believer in coincidences," the chief said. "Carry on."

We left him and Osgood standing in the clearing. Osgood was peering around as if hoping to top my find. The chief was talking on his phone.

"Horace," I heard him ask, "what's your ETA?"

As we strolled back from the crime scene I mentally rearranged my Goblin Patrol duty roster and called to reassign a few more volunteers to the zoo. Thank goodness Grandfather was calling out the Brigade.

By the time we reached the front gate, three more police cars were there, and the first two reassigned Goblin Patrol volunteers were climbing out of a late-model pickup.

After I briefed them, Michael and I stood for a few moments, watching.

"Maybe we didn't just catch a trespasser," I said. "Maybe we caught a murderer. Two guys, both dressed like stereotypical Goths, both participating in some kind of weird Halloween scavenger hunt, and one of them turns up dead."

"I wouldn't make too much of the similar clothes," Michael said. "Half the tourists are dressed like that. But yeah. Maybe Justin Klapcroft could have a lot more reason than we thought to clam up until he gets a lawyer."

"Here's Horace," I said. We waved as he got out of his patrol car, and then watched as Ragnar led him off into the woods toward the crime scene.

"Meanwhile, you and I have work to do," Michael said. "Time to talk to Dr. Smoot."

"Fun," I muttered.

"You never know," Michael said. "The burglary could be related to the murder. After all, how many crimes do we usually have in Caerphilly? You could discover yet another significant clue."

"I know what you're doing," I said. "And it's not making me feel any better. You might convince me that talking to Dr. Smoot will be useful; nothing you say will make me like it. Let's go."

Thanks to everything that had happened here at the zoo, on top of Lydia's interruption, we were going to get to the Haunted House a lot later than planned. I hoped Dr. Smoot had grown calmer in the meantime rather than more agitated.

The early crowds were also gathering around the Haunted House and the Fun Fair, nearly an hour before their scheduled opening time—though at least here there was more for them to watch. In the Fun Fair, the ride operators were starting to get ready—turning on their rides, testing them, doing a few small repairs or safety checks. Delectable odors were already starting to waft from the food tents and concession stands. The game managers were unshuttering their booths, setting up their games, and refreshing their prize displays.

"How did they all get here?" I muttered. Meaning the tourists, of course. The Haunted House was several miles from the edge of town, with the zoo a few miles farther. We'd arranged for a fleet of free shuttles to ferry tourists from the town square to the zoo and all points in between, a combination of buses and horse-drawn wagons. But the shuttles weren't supposed to start running until ten. Had all these people come on the first shuttle?

We pulled into the "official business only" parking spot near the front door of the Haunted House and braved the resentful or merely curious stares of the costumed tourists. Most of their costumes were toward the scary end of the spectrum—vampires, zombies, werewolves, and other even more menacing monsters far outnumbered brides, nuns, pirates, furry animals, and characters from *Star Wars* or *Star Trek*.

Luckily for Dr. Smoot's peace of mind, the Haunted House was separated from the road by the eight-foot fence. Along the sides and the back of the yard the wrought iron was replaced by the same chain-link fence that surrounded the Fun Fair. Dr. Smoot had done his best to maintain the spooky atmosphere by painting the chain-link black and weaving black string through it in patterns that made it look as if a sinister creeping vine was gradually overtaking the fence. He'd hung flowers and fruit from the strings—also painted black, of course—to increase the illusion of a vine. All along the fence costumed tourists were peering through and taking selfies of themselves with the house in the background.

Michael and I pushed our way through the crowds and let ourselves in the gate with the spare key that Dr. Smoot had given me when I'd taken over as head of the volunteer security force. The loiterers began inching closer.

"Stand back," I snapped out. "Goblin Patrol!"

I put my hand on my sword hilt, and Michael followed suit with his. They were only hilts, of course, since the festival rules discouraged wearing real weapons. But the tourists would have no way of knowing our weapons weren't real.

They made way, and we were able to shut the gate behind us without any trespassers sneaking in. Though I noted that neither the wrought iron nor the chain-link looked particularly difficult to climb. I'd have gone for the chain-link myself, because the wrought iron was topped with wicked six-inch spikes, but I suspected that, all things being equal, some of the costumed crew would have tackled the wrought iron section simply because they'd look more picturesque flinging themselves over it in their flowing capes.

As we made our way up the front walk to the porch, I found myself wondering what Dr. Smoot's family would think if they could see their family house now. But there were no other Smoots in town to protest—the aunt from whom Dr. Smoot had inherited the house a few years ago had been his last living relative.

Looking up at the huge black-and-gray hulk looming above us, I suddenly realized what bothered me so much about it. It wasn't just the fact that he had inherited a house very similar to ours, and then spent good money to make it look like an abandoned and haunted house. No, what bothered me was that I realized for the first time that his house wasn't just similar to ours. They were almost identical—or had been before Dr. Smoot began his present quest. Watching him convert his family house into the Caerphilly Haunted House was like watching everything we'd done to our house unravel.

And maybe I was also a little bothered by the fact that poor Smoot lived here alone. Our house was usually overflowing with various friends and family members who either lived with or were visiting us, and yet most of the time it didn't feel crowded, and sometimes, when I was the only one home, I would find myself wishing, temporarily, for a smaller, snugger place. Dr. Smoot was always alone. Didn't that get a little lonely? And possibly, given the house's current condition, a little creepy?

Of course, Dr. Smoot probably enjoyed the creepy part. Ah, well. To each his own.

Though I suspected the late Miss Venicia Smoot would not have been nearly so philosophical if she saw what her nephew was up to. Perhaps I should ask the Reverend Robyn Smith, rector of Trinity Episcopal, if there had been any strange rumblings in the cemetery behind the church—rumblings that might be Miss Venicia spinning in her grave.

The porch was empty except for a few jack-o'-lanterns. In fact, the last time I'd seen it, the whole house was pretty empty. Anyone else might have been dismayed to find he'd inherited a three-story house with less furniture in it than most people would have in an efficiency apartment. But apparently Dr. Smoot was just as happy to be rid of the relatively conventional antiques Miss Venecia had sold off during her lean years. An empty house was easier to decorate to his liking.

I rapped the gargoyle-shaped door knocker firmly. The door opened almost immediately to reveal the black-cloaked figure of Dr. Smoot.

Chapter 8

"Good evening," Dr. Smoot intoned, in his best B-movie vampire fashion.

Out beyond the fence, the tourists murmured restlessly and several camera flashes went off.

Then Dr. Smoot's eyes lit up as he recognized us.

"Meg! And Michael! Thank goodness you're here!" Actually, it sounded more like "thank goodneth," because Dr. Smoot was wearing a particularly prominent set of vampire fangs. Rumor was that the fangs were permanent—fang-shaped crowns created by a Goth-friendly dentist in New Orleans—but no one had had the nerve to ask, so everyone in town was obsessed with peering at Dr. Smoot's mouth to see if the rumors were true.

"Happy to help," Michael said. I could tell he was peering, too.

"Why were all those police cars hurrying out to the zoo?" Dr. Smoot asked. "More burglaries?"

Michael and I glanced at each other. Well, the chief hadn't told us to keep our mouths shut.

"Yes," I said. "And someone was found murdered in the bushes outside the zoo. A tourist, as far as we can tell."

"Oh, my!" I wouldn't have thought it possible for Dr. Smoot to turn any paler, but he did, and he sat down quickly on one of the spindly little black chairs that formed the only seating in his living room. "I'm lucky to be alive!"

"The chief may already have the killer in custody," Michael

said. "And they're pretty busy down at the zoo with all the forensics, so Meg and I came to brief you."

"And inspect your crime scene, of course," I added. "Did they take anything from the Haunted House? Or leave anything behind."

"Actually, it was the museum they broke into," Dr. Smoot said. "Have you seen it yet?"

If I were wearing fangs, I'd have said "appear" instead of "seem." And "intent on" instead of "interested in." It would be possible to reduce the lisping, with a little ingenuity. But I was having a hard time thinking of a sibilant-free synonym for "museum."

I focused back on the problem at hand. The thought of the museum seemed to have distracted Dr. Smoot from his anxiety. He was pointing to a sign printed in an ornate, almost unreadable medieval-style typeface. It took me a few seconds to puzzle out that it read CAERPHILLY MUSEUM OF ODDITIES AND ANTIQUITIES. At the bottom of the sign, an arrow pointed downward. Beside the sign, through an open doorway, I could see the first few steps of a circular stairway.

"A lot of people in Caerphilly have been saying that it's time we had a museum," Dr. Smoot said as he led the way down the steep steps. "The town and the county have so much interesting history! But since we're still recovering from the tough times, I can understand that there's not enough tax money to pay for it. So I decided to start it myself."

He arrived at the bottom of the stairs and stepped aside, gesturing grandly to indicate the sights that lay before us.

I stepped out into the room and fought the impulse to stoop. The room wasn't really that low, but the black ceiling, floor, and woodwork and the blood-red walls seemed to close in on us. Just the sort of environment in which Dr. Smoot would thrive, but I wasn't sure how the rest of the town would feel about having our history displayed in a setting that seemed more appropriate for, say, a museum of medieval torture implements.

"Over there is the wax museum." Dr. Smoot pointed to his left while reaching with the other hand to flip a light switch.

The lights came on, though since the lights were all flickering LED faux candles in medieval-style black metal wall sconces, we got only a slightly better view of the row of figures trailing off into the shadows.

But we could see the closest two, and they didn't look like any wax figures I'd ever seen. In fact—

"Of course I haven't got the budget for real wax figures yet," he explained. "But I got a great deal on a large consignment of secondhand store mannequins, so I can get that feature going while I put together the funding for the real thing."

"Very ingenious," Michael said. Dr. Smoot probably didn't know that "ingenious" was Michael's tactful word, the one he used when he couldn't think of anything else positive to say. I choked back "interesting," since everyone in town knew that was what Mother had taught my siblings and me to say under similar circumstances.

We strolled down the aisle between the two rows of figures. Dr. Smoot—or whoever he'd enlisted to help with the fake wax museum—had obviously worked very hard on the costumes, including hats or hoods with as many as possible so it wasn't really too disconcerting that Vlad the Impaler, Jack the Ripper, Frankenstein's monster, and the inhabitants of the Zombie Apocalypse tableau had precisely the same tall, slender figures and bland, Barbie-and-Ken faces. In fact, it had a certain wacky charm. But the charm wore thin when we arrived at the second half of the exhibit, depicting events from Caerphilly history, and saw friends and neighbors depicted with the same smooth, blank features. I particularly disliked the diorama depicting me and my father and the penguins he had briefly tried to keep in the basement of our house.

"That doesn't look a thing like me," I couldn't help muttering.

"Well, the face doesn't, no," Dr. Smoot said. "But I think we've got the hair and clothes perfect. And aren't the penguins realistic! I found a Web site that sells fiberglass penguins for stores to use as part of their holiday decorations."

The clothes weren't too bad, since I very well might have been wearing a pair of jeans and a Caerphilly College t-shirt that day. But the hair—no. Right dark-brown color, right length, but I couldn't imagine my hair ever looking that frizzy and disheveled, even if I'd failed to comb it on a day when the humidity was near a hundred percent. Did Dr. Smoot really think I modeled my hairstyle on the Bride of Frankenstein?

Michael didn't look all that thrilled with his image, either. Dr. Smoot had chosen to present Michael in a replica of his Mephisto the wizard costume from the TV show and leading a shaggy object that vaguely resembled a mutant llama. Or what a llama would look like if sculpted by someone who had never actually seen one. Clearly Dr. Smoot had yet to find a Web site where realistic llamas could be cheaply purchased.

I wasn't sure who many of the other mannequins were supposed to represent—local in-jokes that I wasn't in on, no doubt. But I suspected other people would find their likenesses as disturbing as I did mine. And maybe it was a good thing the mannequins were so obviously fake. Visiting a realistic wax museum might have given me a serious case of the creeps so soon after inspecting a dead body.

"I've got a couple of requests out to foundations and wealthy families for funds to beef up the wax museum," he said. "But so far I haven't heard back from any of them. Not even the Brimfields, and I had such hopes of them."

"Who are the Brimfields?" I asked.

"An old Caerphilly family," he said. "They used to run a

bank here, but they lost all their money when the stock market crashed."

"Then maybe they're not the best people to ask for money," Michael pointed out.

"Oh, but then they moved out to California in the 1930s and made millions in real estate," Dr. Smoot explained. "Josiah Brimfield, the current head of the family, pops up sometimes on the lower reaches of that *Forbes* list of the wealthiest people in the country. He can definitely afford it. He just doesn't seem interested."

Considering that Josiah's family had left Caerphilly some eighty years ago and probably remembered it as the scene of a less-than-joyous phase of their family history, I could understand his lack of interest.

"And he was downright rude when I asked if he'd be willing to donate or at least lend any family artifacts," Dr. Smoot went on. "In fact, he tried to bully me into taking some of the artifacts I have off display. The nerve!"

"Was this where you had the burglar?" Michael asked, gently distracting Dr. Smoot from his diatribe against the Brimfields.

"No," Dr. Smoot said. "He—or they—were at the other end. In fact, most of the suspicious circumstances have occurred down there."

I'd more or less gotten used to Dr. Smoot's faint lisp by now, but I noted, in case I should ever find occasion to dress up as a vampire, that no one wearing fangs should ever attempt to utter the phrase "suspicious circumstances."

Dr. Smoot led the way back out of the non-wax museum into the main exhibit area. Michael and I followed slowly, examining some of the exhibits along the way.

Along one wall was a familiar-looking trunk. On the wall above it was a framed front page from the *Caerphilly Clarion*, with the headline "Body Found in Antique Trunk at First

Annual Countywide Yard Sale." A small glass case held a small heap of black-and-white feathers, with a sign proclaiming that they were authentic feathers from the actual bantam Russian Orloff chickens stolen in the course of the "Grisly Midway Murder Case." In fact, I could spot half a dozen bizarre exhibits commemorating events I had played a part in. And odds were a black-clad murderer waving an assortment of fake body parts was in the museum's future.

I was relieved to see that as we progressed down the room we moved away from recent history. One stretch of wall contained a series of photographs of soldiers and sailors in uniforms ranging from the Civil War to the Gulf War. The signs beside the photographs revealed that most of these were from the archives of the *Caerphilly Clarion,* our local weekly newspaper.

A couple of mannequins had strayed over from the faux wax end to model gowns. One was a black silk mourning dress from the 1890s, complete with intricate jet beading and enormous leg o'mutton sleeves, purportedly worn by Sophronia Pruitt to William McKinley's presidential inauguration. The other was a drop-waisted flapper dress, covered with silver beads and matching fringe, in mint condition except for the bullet hole and bloodstain near the left shoulder.

"That's the dress Arabella Shiffley was wearing when the G-men shot her," Dr. Smoot explained.

"What had Arabella done to upset the Feds?" I asked. Randall had never mentioned this particular black sheep.

"They weren't aiming at her," Dr. Smoot said. "William Pratherton, her boyfriend, was the county's biggest bootlegger. They went down in a hail of bullets, just like Bonnie and Clyde."

"Here in Caerphilly?"

He nodded.

"Why isn't this better known?"

"Well, there probably weren't quite as many bullets as with

Bonnie and Clyde," he said, looking at the single bullet hole in the dress. "And they didn't actually die in the attack. They eventually got married and lived to a ripe old age. Billy Pratherton died in the sixties, and Arabella lived on to see the millennium."

I noted on the sign beside the dress that it was on loan from Arabella Pratherton Walmsley.

"So the owner is a descendant of the once-wicked Billy and Arabella?" I asked. "Nice that she appreciates her family's colorful history instead of being embarrassed by it."

"She was their great-granddaughter," Dr. Smoot said. "Poor young woman—she was killed only a couple of months after she brought me the dress."

"Killed?"

"Very sad," Dr. Smoot said. "Hit-and-run. Not here, of course—out in California." His tone implied that such dire consequences were only to be expected if one foolishly left the safety of the Old Dominion for the Wild West.

"So the Prathertons also left Caerphilly for California," Michael said.

"Oh, no!" Dr. Smoot shuddered. "They moved to Richmond. And the Walmsleys are an old Chesterfield County family. Early on they made their money in tobacco, but they switched over to banking and insurance long before tobacco became problematic. Big donors to the Virginia Museum of Fine Arts and the Library of Virginia."

"And you're hoping they'll add the Caerphilly Museum to their charities?"

"Alas, no." Dr. Smoot's face fell. "Not now. I'm afraid they rather blame me for their daughter's death. Apparently she came home from her visit here all fired up to track down her ancestry. That's what she was doing when she was killed. I'm not sure they'd ever be willing to donate to the museum. I'm more than half expecting them to yank away the dress any time now. I wrote them a letter of condolence when I first heard the news. They haven't responded, so we're rather in limbo. I'd like to clarify the dress's status. But one doesn't like to press at such a difficult time."

He gazed sadly at the dress for a few moments. Then he shook himself and put on a deliberately cheerful expression.

"On a happier note, here's another prize." He pointed to a painting that hung in a place of honor with its own little light shining down to illuminate it.

A prize? Clearly whatever value or interest the painting had was in its historical value rather than any artistic merit. It was a family portrait from the Colonial era, and although all the people in it looked awkward and misshapen, I was pretty sure this was as much the painter's fault as theirs. The father, stern, large-jawed, and jowly in a powdered wig and a fawn-colored coat, sat at the far left of the canvas, while the mother sat to the far right, leaning away from the rest of the family as if hoping to slip off the canvas when the painter wasn't looking. Between them were seven or eight children— all girls, with the possible exception of the infant who was about to slide headfirst off his mother's lap. Most were seated behind or playing in front of a table that formed the center point of the painting and all shared their father's unfortunate jawline. The oldest daughter stood behind her father, plucking the strings of a lute and looking soulful, which might have been charming if she hadn't had the profile of a pit bull. The other children were all holding flowers or wearing headdresses made of flowers, and they all looked stiff, lumpish, and uncomfortable. Well, who could blame them? I had a hard time getting the boys to stand still for my camera. I couldn't imagine what would happen if I asked them to pose for a painting.

"The Paltroons," Dr. Smoot said with pride. "A very distinguished old Virginia family."

I noticed he didn't call them a very distinguished old Caerphilly family, probably because at the time the painting would have been done, Caerphilly was occupied mainly by cows, sheep, and a few early ancestors of the Shiffleys.

"Colonel Habakkuk Paltroon was a great patriot," Dr. Smoot went on. "And fought in the Continental Army."

"Is that why he's missing a leg?" Michael asked.

"Missing a leg?" Dr. Smoot peered at the painting. He sounded agitated. "He wasn't missing a leg when he got here."

"I don't think he's actually missing a leg," I said. "I think his other leg is just hidden behind the tablecloth."

We all three studied Habakkuk's one visible leg for a few moments.

"You're right," Michael said finally. "It just looks as if he is because from the waist down he's facing the table, while from the waist up he's looking out at us, with no real indication that his waist is twisted. A very uncomfortable-looking position."

And anatomically improbable, but I stifled the urge to say so. Dr. Smoot was so proud of the painting.

"You had me worried for a minute," Dr. Smoot said. "I was afraid maybe his leg had flaked off. There are a couple of areas where the paint is starting to buckle slightly. I'm afraid it may not have liked being moved. I've notified Mrs. Paltroon."

"The Mrs. Paltroon who runs the local DAR?" I asked.

"That's her," he said. "A very formidable lady."

I'd have called her a snob and a pain in the neck, but yeah—formidable also applied. Mrs. Paltroon treated the Caerphilly DAR chapter like a personal fiefdom, and her presence probably accounted for its remarkably small size— only half a dozen or so local women seemed to be members, even though I suspected a lot more were eligible. Most of them were probably like Mother, who was an active member of the DAR in our hometown of Yorktown, but turned up her nose at the local chapter because of Mrs. Paltroon.

Not someone I'd want to upset, though. I could tell from

the anxious expression on Dr. Smoot's face that he wasn't keen on doing so, either.

"Well, we have a restoration expert coming in tomorrow to take a look," he said. "And do any necessary conservation."

Now that Dr. Smoot had pointed it out, I could see the slight irregularities in the surface of the paint. It looked as if Habakkuk's coat was in danger, and also the blank back wall of the room. If I had been the unknown artist, I would have painted something along that back wall. A window, a fireplace—anything to break up the rather large area of muddy tan wall that loomed behind the assembled Paltroons.

"Well, we'll see what the restoration expert says," Dr. Smoot said, visibly wrenching himself away from the painting and looking back at us. "Meanwhile, you haven't seen the *pièce de résistance.*"

He pointed to a glass case at the very back of the museum. It was a display of jewelry. Some of the pieces looked old— Victorian, Art Nouveau, or Art Deco. Others looked modern and implausibly sparkly—like a rhinestone tiara once used, according to its label, to crown winners of the now defunct Miss Caerphilly Contest. But Dr. Smoot was indicating the object in the center of the case—the most spectacularly ugly brooch I'd ever seen. It was shaped like a black cat arching its back. The body was entirely covered with sparkly black-ish stones, except for the green eyes and the colorless claws.

"Impressive," I said. Actually, I started to say "interesting," but stopped in time. Michael managed to repress any urge to call it "ingenious."

"The body is covered with black diamonds," Dr. Smoot said. "The eyes are emeralds, and the claws made of white diamonds. It used to belong to the Duchess of Windsor."

I looked back down at the brooch. Knowing it had once belonged to a famous fashion icon didn't change my opinion of it. Spectacularly ugly.

"What's it doing here?" I asked.

"The Griswalds have lent it to the museum for the time being," Dr. Smoot said. "Mr. Griswald bought it in 2013 from Sotheby's, and gave it to his wife as a twenty-fifth anniversary present."

I wondered if Mother would have pointed out that the proper gift for a twenty-fifth wedding anniversary was silver, not expensive but tacky jewelry.

"So you think this is what your intruders were after?" Michael asked.

"It's the most logical explanation," Dr. Smoot said. "It's the only really valuable piece there."

"The ruby ring's fake, then?" I pointed to a white gold ring with what to my inexpert eye looked like a ruby the size of a small cherry.

"Cubic zirconia," Dr. Smoot said. "And the rest of this is costume jewelry, of mainly historical or sentimental value."

"Still, I hope you're insured."

"The Griswalds insisted," he said.

"Any idea how the intruders got in?" Michael asked.

"Through the back door," Dr. Smoot replied.

He pointed toward a black curtain that covered the back wall. I lifted one side of the curtain and saw a small, rather utilitarian black door.

"This leads outside?" I asked.

"Yes," Dr. Smoot pulled the curtain aside so I could see better. "There's an outside stairway that leads to the surface. I'd really rather close it off entirely, or bolt it securely, but the fire marshal would have a fit. So I installed one of those one-way emergency-exit-only doors."

There was a window in the top part of the door—small, and reinforced with a metal mesh grille over the glass. Outside, I could dimly see a concrete stairwell—painted black of course—and steep black concrete steps leading upward and then disappearing into the shrubbery that overhung the stairwell.

"I keep the curtain over it down here," Dr. Smoot said. "And it's mostly hidden by a holly hedge outside."

"May I?" I gestured to the door, which in addition to a push bar carried a sign that warned EMERGENCY EXIT ONLY—ALARM WILL SOUND.

"Wait till I disarm the system." Dr. Smoot stepped over to the far wall and removed a picture of a group of World War II soldiers from its hook, revealing a keypad. He punched in a four-digit code and a disembodied female voice said "The security system is disarmed" in a tone that suggested she was disappointed with us for scorning her protection.

"Go ahead," Dr. Smoot said. "Of course, the police have already checked the stairwell out."

I opened the door and stepped out into the stairwell. I wasn't sure what I was looking for. Maybe just a minute or two out of the basement, breathing fresh air instead of the slightly musty atmosphere of the museum. I climbed to the top of the stairs and looked around.

The hedge that hid the stairwell continued all across the back of the house, and apparently also provided camouflage for an outdoor spigot and several hoses, a wheelbarrow, and various other assorted yard and garden accoutrements. A break in the hedge at the head of the stairway gave access to the yard. Beyond the chain-link outlining Dr. Smoot's backyard, I could see the now-silent Halloween Fun Fair and beyond that the gently rustling stalks of the giant Maize Maze.

At night, when the Fun Fair was in operation, it would be hard for anyone to notice if someone climbed over the fence to hide behind the hedge. For that matter, it would be even easier for someone leaving the Haunted House to slip sideways into the shrubbery instead of walking out to the road, and then make his way to the back of the house.

I heard a noise and glanced over at the fence. A few tourists dressed as vampires or ghouls were peering through the fence with their fingers twined in the chain-link. They reminded me a little too much of some of the zombie apocalypse movies I'd seen, in which the menacing hordes of zombies surrounded the few surviving humans and reached through the barriers with clawlike hands—

Then one of the tourists dispelled my dystopian vision by sticking his phone through the fence and taking a selfie of himself peering through the chain-link. Zombie hordes, maybe, but not the kind that were apt to eat any of our brains.

I shook off my creeped-out mood and went back down the steps to where Dr. Smoot was holding the basement door for me.

"Anything interesting?" he asked.

"Anyone who poked around here long enough would probably assume this was the best way to sneak into the house," I said as I slipped past him into the basement again.

"But they'd figure out that the door was locked." Dr. Smoot was pulling on the door to make sure it was completely closed. "So they come down here and try to prop open the door so they can sneak in later, and the alarm goes off, and I catch them and kick them out and resecure the door."

He walked over to the keypad and pressed in a code.

"The door is alarmed," said the disembodied female voice. The door might be alarmed, but she sounded profoundly indifferent.

"Mind if I go around and check out the rest of the Haunted House," I asked. "The chief and I think it would be a good idea to take a lot of pictures of how things are supposed to be, so we've got evidence, in case one of these intruders steals or damages anything. And you never know what could turn out to be evidence in the murder case."

"What an excellent idea!" Dr. Smoot smiled so broadly that we could get a clear view of both fangs. "Let me give you a tour!"

I soon realized that my project might have been easier if Dr. Smoot hadn't been quite so keen on documenting the

contents of the house. He wanted to show me every item in
the museum and tell me every single shred of information
he knew about it, while I snapped photos from every possible angle. The inauguration ball gown alone took up seventeen photos—Dr. Smoot wanted to be sure I appreciated all
the intricate tailoring, beading, and embroidery. We managed to cover Arabella Shiffley's skimpy flapper dress in a
mere ten or eleven, and then moved on to the military photographs. Dr. Smoot seemed to know every biographical detail
of every soldier or sailor who appeared in them—at least
the ones from Caerphilly. Fascinating to know that soldiers
from tiny little Caerphilly had served in nearly every war our
country had ever fought. But I wished we could postpone the
full tour to a day when I didn't have dozens of other things
to do.

Michael finally intervened.

"Oh, my goodness!" he exclaimed, looking ostentatiously
at his watch. "It's getting close to your opening time! I think
I hear one of the shuttles arriving! You must have a million
things to do!"

"Oh, dear." Dr. Smoot looked harried. "But this is important."

"I tell you what," Michael said. "You go and get the house
ready to open. Meg and I will race through the photography
part of the documentation, and then we can come back before you open tomorrow to record the provenance of all the
objects."

"An excellent idea! Thank you!"

Dr. Smoot raced away and Michael and I both let out sighs
of relief.

"You're a lifesaver," I said.

"Let's hurry up and finish this," Michael said. "Before he
decides that what we're doing is more important than whatever he's doing."

Without Dr. Smoot's involvement, we finished off the rest of the basement in five minutes. Another ten minutes took care of the less-cluttered first and second floors. He'd set up each of the rooms as a spooky tableau. In one room, flickering candelabra and arrangements of black flowers surrounded a coffin that slowly opened to reveal a grinning, fanged vampire. In another, he'd set up a trestle table covered with herbs and flasks and other alchemical accoutrements. Jars with labels like EYE OF NEWT and FILLET OF FENNY SNAKE suggested that this was intended to represent a sorcerer's potion lab, and I suspected he'd be throwing bits of dry ice in some of the flasks and test tubes from time to time to produce suitable fumes.

Still, the rooms weren't cluttered—he'd left plenty of room for people to crowd in to admire each tableau—so photographing them was quick. Since the third floor contained only Dr. Smoot's private quarters, we decided it fell outside the bounds of our project—though we did test to make sure he'd locked the door at the foot of the stairs that led to it.

The whole time we were working, I couldn't help thinking about that clearing outside the zoo fence, where Cousin Horace and the other police officers were probably taking pictures of their own. By now they'd probably already found my father, who had succeeded Dr. Smoot as the local medical examiner. Maybe the sad, rat-faced dead man was already on his way to the hospital, where Dad would perform the autopsy. And perhaps it was illogical, but I felt bad that I hadn't stayed long enough to learn his name.

"Mission accomplished," Michael said, rousing me out of my preoccupation.

"Some mission," I said. "I know we're mainly doing this to document how the Haunted House looks now, and maybe I should feel happy that we didn't find anything that looked like an important clue to the murder. But still—not sure we need to rush down to the station to deliver these photos to the chief."

"Probably not," Michael said. "And we have other things to do. Let's make tracks."

Chapter 9

We slipped out the front door just as Dr. Smoot was scurrying down the walk to fling open the front gates, and although I felt like a salmon swimming upstream, we eventually fought our way through the crowd of ghosts, pirates, zombies, and ghouls to our car.

"Of course, you do realize that now he expects us back to finish the tour tomorrow morning," I pointed out.

"I'm sure we can think of some emergency to postpone it," Michael said. "Better yet, when you get a chance to send your photos to the chief, send Smoot a copy, too, and tell him that it would be so much more helpful, since he's the expert, if he wrote up the descriptions."

"I like the way you think," I said.

Michael dropped me off at the school, where I reclaimed my car. He was due back at the college to teach his afternoon classes.

"A pity the college turned down Randall's proposal that they give the students today and tomorrow off so they could join the celebration," I remarked.

"They didn't actually turn it down," he said as he kissed me good-bye. "They just pretended not to have ever received it. Much more tactful that way."

With that he drove off to the delights of Drama 350 (Advanced Theater History), Drama 380 (Script Analysis), and Drama 730 (Graduate Vocal Technique). I hopped into my car, pulled out my notebook, and began adding items to my day's to-do list.

My phone rang. Looking at the length of my list, I wasn't sure whether to welcome a distraction from it or worry that the call would add to it.

It was Chief Burke.

"Meg? Are you still out at Dr. Smoot's?"

"No," I said. "I've finished up there and I'm back at Caerphilly Elementary, picking up my car. What's up?"

"If you can spare the time, would you mind dropping by my office? I could use your help."

Did he mean that literally, I wondered? Or was "I could use your help" a euphemism for "I want to chew you out for butting into my case." The way "helping the police with their inquiries" often seemed to mean "being interrogated as a really suspicious person but not technically under arrest . . . yet." Or—

"Meg?"

"On my way in a sec," I said. "I was just trying to calculate an ETA. Normally I'd have said I can be there in five minutes if you like, but given the crowds, I suppose I'd better double that estimate."

"Avoid the town square if you don't want to quadruple it," the chief said. "We're having a bit of a problem down there. Vern's arresting some people who are running around without costumes."

"I thought the town council vetoed Randall's suggestion that we require everyone to wear costumes," I said.

"By without costumes, I actually meant without any clothing whatsoever," the chief said. "Apart from some remarkably extensive tattoos. We do have statutes against public nudity."

"Roger," I said. "Okay, I'll take the long way round to avoid the copiously inked streakers and see you as soon as possible."

I did a quick calculation of the route least likely to take me past any crowd-pleasing attractions and set out. I was delighted when I managed to reach the police station in only nine minutes. And as I strolled into the station I realized that while I was still a little apprehensive that I'd done something to irk the chief, I was also elated that I might have a chance to find out what was happening with his murder investigation.

"He's waiting for you," said a voice from the Jabba the Hutt costume that occupied most of the space behind the front desk. "Go on back."

"Thanks," I said, while trying to recognize the voice. Clearly not one of the sworn officers, since the chief had vetoed Randall's suggestion that they be allowed—or even required—to wear costumes on duty during the festival. Probably one of the volunteer auxiliaries, or even a member of my Goblin Patrol, helping out while all the officers dealt with the arrest of the clothing-impaired tourists. I gave up trying to identify Jabba and just waved as I went past.

The chief was sitting in his office, frowning down at a piece of paper.

"What's up?" I asked.

"Our prisoner isn't talking much," he said. "In fact, I think he said more to you when you captured him than he's said the whole time we've had him."

"I'm sorry," I said.

"Don't be sorry," he said. "I'm not going to fault you for talking to someone you didn't know was a suspect in a murder we hadn't even found yet. And thank you again, both for spotting that little scrap of paper at the body dump site and for not just picking it up and handing it to me, the way some people would."

"Body dump site?" I echoed. "Does that mean he was killed elsewhere?"

"Not enough blood and . . . er, other tissue at the scene, according to Horace and your father," the chief said. "Someone killed him elsewhere, drove to the edge of the parking lot, and dragged the body into the woods a ways, presumably to delay its discovery. Or possibly because it was convenient on his way to breaking into the zoo."

"So you think it was Justin Klapcroft who killed him."

"Too early to tell." The chief sighed and rubbed his temples. He looked exhausted. "The evidence is against him. But if he did it, he's one heck of an actor. Tell me, does the name Arabella Walmsley mean anything to you?"

"Arabella Walmsley? Yes, of course," I said. "Though it wouldn't have an hour ago."

"An hour ago?" The chief sat up straighter and looked a lot less tired. "What happened an hour ago?"

"Michael and I went over to the Haunted House and took pictures of everything—remember?" I gave him an overview of our visit and the details on Arabella's connection to the museum through her namesake.

"Interesting," he murmured.

I waited a moment to see if he'd explain. And then I gave up waiting.

"Interesting how?" I asked.

"We didn't find any identification on our murder victim," he said. "No wallet, no phone—we've sent his fingerprints to AFIS to see if they have him on file, and I borrowed a digital photo technician from your brother to clean up our morgue shot of the victim so we'll have something to give the newspapers if we need to ask the public to help us identify him. But we did find this in his pocket."

He handed me a photocopy of an article from the *Caerphilly Clarion*. The headline read "Tragic Death of Richmond Resident with Caerphilly Roots." I scanned the article. The first paragraph reported the scant details of Arabella's death—she was the victim of a hit-and-run a few blocks from the hotel where she'd been staying in San Francisco. In typical *Clarion* fashion, the rest of the article focused on her connection to Caerphilly, with much the same information I'd heard from Dr. Smoot about Billy and Arabella Pratherton, and the present-day Arabella's generous donation to the museum. I'd be willing to bet that Dr. Smoot was the reporter's main source.

"So I wasn't lying when I told Dr. Smoot that there might be a connection between his burglary and the murder." I handed the article back to the chief.

"Although precisely what connection I haven't the slightest idea yet," the chief said. "For that matter, I'm still trying to figure out how the scavenger hunt fits in. So tell me again about your encounter with Mr. Klapcroft. I want to know everything he did and said."

I followed orders. When I'd finished, he nodded slightly and handed me two more papers—photocopies of the small folded paper that Vern had taken from Justin's pocket and the scrap I'd found near the body.

"What do you make of these? Mr. Klapcroft refuses to tell me anything about them. Even tried to deny that he owns one of them."

"And you reminded him that Vern took it out of his own pocket?"

"Claims he picked it up somewhere intending to recycle it."

"How civic minded of him."

"Hmph!" He looked down at his notebook. " 'Just one of my tasks,' " he read. " 'If I finish the first set of tasks by midnight, I advance to the next round.' And when you called it a game, he said it was an adventure."

"And a quest," I reminded him.

"It looks as if he was almost finished with his day's tasks. His cell phone contains a photo of him eating a small cricket—he's got that as his wallpaper or whatever you call what you see when you turn it on. He'd also completed the tombstone rubbing—we found it in a knapsack that he hid in the shrubbery behind the reptile house, near where he gained entry to the zoo. And we found one of those tiny apple-sized pumpkins at the bottom of his knapsack."

"So he was taking care of the last two tasks when we tackled him," I said.

"But he won't tell us anything else," the chief said. "He continues to assert his right to an attorney, and since he doesn't know any, I'm trying to scare up a court-appointed one for him. Which is not going to be easy. Two of the public defenders chose this week to take vacation, and the third's in Richmond representing a client who's in court down there."

"You'd think the PDs would have realized that this might be a busy time for them," I said.

"I think they realized it all too well and fled town."

"Don't you have a roster of local lawyers you can call on to do pro bono work?" I asked.

"Yes, and we're working through it, and as soon as we actually reach one who's in the same time zone as we are, we'll demand that he or she come down here to represent Mr. Klapcroft."

"Can't you get the paperwork you need to check out his cell phone?" I asked. "I'd be astonished if he hasn't called, e-mailed, or texted anyone about this scavenger hunt thing."

"I agree," he said. "Assuming we're ever allowed to get into it, the phone could give us a great deal more information. I've asked Judge Shiffley for a warrant. She's thinking about it. We'll probably get it eventually, but you know the judge. Big on protection of privacy. Likes to think through all the ramifications, and I suppose in her view, since we have the kid in custody, there's no big rush."

"Of course, that's assuming Justin's the killer," I said. "If he's not—"

"Precisely," the chief said. "There could still be a killer out there, and even if there isn't, these players are potential witnesses in a homicide, and I want to talk to them ASAP. Get the word out to your Goblin Patrol members about these lists. If I had unlimited personnel, I'd have officers watch-ing all the town cemeteries to watch for people doing grave rubbings, and more officers patrolling the perimeter of the zoo, to catch intruders. And have them keep their eyes open for people eating insects and stealing pumpkins, and if any more fake body parts turn up to frighten the tourists, I defi-nitely want to hear about it."

"Already on my list," I said. "And just so you know, Grand-father's sending out an urgent call to the members of Blake's Brigade. He's going to put them to work patrolling the zoo."

"Good," the chief said. "How many of them does he ex-pect?"

"With the Brigade, you don't always know till they show up," I said. "They're all volunteers. But his friend Caroline Willner has already said that she can come to help out, so if the turnout is light, she'll start twisting arms and drumming up participation."

"Excellent," the chief said. "Maybe you can have them con-centrate on the zoo, and leave your Goblin Patrol for the town proper."

"And the Haunted House," I suggested. "It's connected somehow."

"Blamed if I know how," the chief said. "None of the tasks seem to have anything to do with the Haunted House."

"None of today's tasks," I said. "But we only have part of that second list. What if it starts out with 'steal something from the Haunted House'?"

The chief nodded.

"You know," I mused. "If everyone playing the game is sup-posed to break into the zoo today, after the first few who get caught, it gets increasingly difficult. They'll be tripping over each other."

"Although that could be part of the game," the chief replied.

"It could," I said. "But it's also possible that different players have different tasks. We know Justin's task number five was to steal a pumpkin, but the murder victim was supposed to take a selfie with a bat. Was that an older list, or a different list? What if some other players' assignments for today included covering their entire bodies with temporary tattoos and walking around in the town square with no clothes on?"

The chief's eyes narrowed at this.

"We don't know that the people Vern's arresting are wearing temporary tattoos," he said.

"But we don't yet know that they aren't," I said.

The chief brooded on this for a few moments.

"That makes sense," he said at last. "It'd be a good way to organize this thing. Make up one list for each day it lasts. Say three days, for today, tomorrow, and Halloween itself, since most of the trouble started after midnight last night. And assign the players to three groups, so they're not all doing the same crazy things on the same day."

"But they all have to do the same crazy things to win," I said. "That sounds fair. So we not only have to watch out for people doing the crazy things we already know about from Justin's list and the scrap I spotted, we also have to watch out for people doing other, similar crazy things from the rest of the murder victim's list, plus who knows how many other lists we haven't yet seen."

"Blast!" the chief exclaimed. Since that was about as bad as his language ever got these days, I assumed that he was definitely not amused.

"I'll also tell my Goblin Patrol to be alert for people who appear to be consulting lists," I said. "And to try to get their hands on the lists if they see one."

"And I'm going to make a few calls for reinforcements," the chief said. "Several local jurisdictions have agreed to send a few extra officers to deal with the crowds. Though none of them can spare many—they all know they could have problems of their own this weekend."

"But let's hope we're the only one with a murder," I said. The chief winced and nodded at that.

It occurred to me that having Halloween fall on a Saturday was potentially a boon for the Halloween Festival, since it could significantly increase attendance. But for law enforcement, the increased crowds could mean an exponential increase in the amount of crime and trouble they had to deal with.

"And then I'll have to make another round of calls to all those lawyers," the chief muttered. "At least the ones who haven't already told me they've left town till the craziness is over."

"Could I make one more suggestion?" I asked.

The chief nodded.

"Let's call Rob about this."

Chief Burke looked pained.

"Meg," he began. "I know that technically your brother is an attorney, but, while I don't want to cast any aspersions—"

"Oh, I didn't mean you should call him about representing Justin," I said. "Because yeah, he is only technically an attorney and he'd be the first to admit that he's barely ever practiced. No, I meant about this game."

"You think he might know something about it?"

"Unlikely," I said. "Because I think even Rob would have the common sense to realize that this could be a very bad thing for the festival." At least I hoped he did. "He's very keen on the festival—he's even working as part of the Goblin Patrol. I think if he knew people were planning this, he'd have warned them, and if they went ahead, he'd have asked me what to do. But just because he might not know about it now doesn't mean he can't find out about it. After all, he owns a computer game company. Which means that over at the Mutant Wizards office he has dozens of people who do nothing but think about games."

"Their own games," the chief said. "Doesn't mean they know about this one."

"They might," I said. "It's called competitive intelligence. If someone invents a game, they all want to know about it, so they can invent one that's bigger and better and sells more copies."

"So maybe someone on his staff has heard of this game?"

"Right. And even if none of them has, they have years of experience finding out about competitors' games. Let's use that."

"They always say 'set a thief to catch a thief,'" the chief said. "So 'set a gamer to catch a gamer'?"

"What do we have to lose?"

"Okay," he said. "Worth trying. Especially since our department has only limited cybercrime resources. In fact, our cybercrime resources are Horace and Aida, and they're going to be pretty busy with other parts of the homicide investigation. But if Rob's people find out anything, they do not wade in like vigilantes. They come and tell me and let me figure out how to proceed."

"Absolutely," I said. By which I meant that I absolutely understood. Conveying these marching orders to the Mutant Wizards and getting them to follow them was going to be a challenge.

"Keep me posted." He picked up his phone, and I deduced that I was dismissed.

I pulled out my own cell phone as soon as I reached the parking lot.

"Junior Goblin Rob here," my brother answered. "What is your will, O mighty queen of the Goblin Tribe?"

"Rob, can you meet me over at the Mutant Wizards office ASAP?" I asked.

"What's wrong?" Who knew Rob could suddenly turn so businesslike?

"Nothing's wrong at your office," I said. "But I have a special Goblin Patrol assignment for you, and it involves Mutant Wizards. How soon can you be there? And is there any chance you can arrange to have an all-staff meeting so once I've cleared it with you I can tell everyone about it?"

"On my way. Goblin Rob, over and out!"

Chapter 10

I headed over to the Mutant Wizards office. Fortunately, it wasn't quite in the tourist-filled center of town. Rob had originally rented the top floor of a ramshackle two-story office building from the 1930s. Eventually he'd taken over the ground floor as well, and about the time his staff had completely outgrown that, the Pruitts, the family that had been running Caerphilly since shortly after the Civil War, went bankrupt and Rob had been able to buy the building that had housed their once-great financial empire.

I pulled up in front of what had at one time been a dignified if somewhat conventional six-story building. Clearly Rob and his employees liked decorating for Halloween. The trees and shrubs surrounding the building were draped with orange fairy lights as well as strings of skeleton lights. Most of the lawn was covered with what was undoubtedly the town's largest collection of fake tombstones. All of the windows bore decorations—silhouettes of black cats, pumpkins, witches, or skeletons. Two realistic-looking skeletons clung to the door frames on either side of the double front doors, which had been painted black for the occasion.

I pushed open one of the doors and a bloodcurdling scream rang out in the reception room.

"Welcome to our dungeon," the receptionist intoned. She was dressed in a long black Morticia Addams-style gown, and was somehow managing to work her computer keyboard in spite of six-inch blood-red nails.

The vast two-story reception area was completely redecorated in orange and black. The enormous crystal chandelier that had once hung from the ceiling had been replaced by an equally enormous light fixture made of black wrought iron and faux human bones, draped with spiderwebs and strings of red crystals. The double stairway that swept up each side of the room to the mezzanine level was also decorated with fake bones, and several lifelike skeletons posed on it, including one apparently about to take a header over the railing of the mezzanine and one sitting near the bottom of the right-hand stairs with his skull resting on one bony hand in a pose that echoed Rodin's "The Thinker."

A bit over the top, but not inappropriate for a computer game company, and I had to admit that I liked it all better than the rather pretentious and overwrought Pruitt décor it had replaced.

"Is Rob here yet?" I asked.

"Hi, Meg," the receptionist said. "He told me to convene an all-staff meeting as soon as you arrived. Shall I give the signal?"

I had figured Rob would want to hear what I had in mind before committing his staff to work on the project, but apparently he trusted me.

"Go for it," I said.

She reached down and pressed a button, and the room filled with fiendish laughter. Vincent Price's laughter, I suspected. The building erupted into activity. Doors slammed. People in costume began popping out of doors and swarming down the stairway. The elevators began dinging and disgorging more people.

I made my way against the tide up to the mezzanine level. I'd seen Rob hold all-staff meetings before, and he usually chose to address the troops from just about where the skeleton was attempting to end it all.

Sure enough, within a few minutes, just about the time the flood of witches, wizards, zombies, vampires, mummies, and other unearthly creatures slowed down to a trickle, Rob stepped out of the elevator and joined me.

"You want me to fill you in on what this is all about?" I asked.

"Nah." Rob waived his hand in a nonchalant way. "Let's just go for it. Attention, everyone!" he called out loudly.

The almost deafening clamor of conversation in the room rapidly faded into silence.

"Most of you know my sister, Meg," Rob said. "She's got something to tell us. Meg?"

They didn't stand much on formality here.

"Chief Burke and I want to ask your help on something that could affect the success of this year's Halloween Festival."

A murmur of interest rippled through the crowd and then died down.

"This morning, we apprehended an intruder at the Caerphilly Zoo," I began. "He apparently threw a fake foot into the alligator habitat just before a class of first graders was about to tour it."

Disapproving mutters.

"We think he was doing this as part of some kind of game—although he called it a quest or adventure. We found a piece of paper in his pocket that apparently listed the tasks he was supposed to complete today as part of this game. Let me read it to you."

I read out the task list, studying the faces below as I did— at least those whose faces were visible rather than obscured by some kind of mask, makeup, or headgear. Some of the Mutant Wizards looked puzzled. But a lot more looked interested.

"Chief Burke is worried about this game. He wants to find out who's behind it. Shut it down if possible."

I could tell from the faces that many of the Wizards were inclined to side with the gamers.

"Because shortly after we caught the guy who was terrifying the kids, we found the body of someone who the chief believes may also have been playing the game."

I could tell they were taken aback, but still not ready to side against the game's organizers.

"You know," Rob piped up. "The idea of a giant scavenger hunt sounds kind of cool."

Murmurs of agreement from the audience. Did Rob not get the point?

"But you know what's not cool? They come to our town—our turf. And they're running a game here. Without even including us. I don't like that!"

Noisy agreement from the troops.

"And then, to top it off, they kill a gamer!" Rob shouted. "A *gamer*! Let's get 'em!"

The bony chandelier shook from the resulting cheers.

"By which Rob means we need to collect competitive intelligence on this scavenger hunt," I put in. "We need to find out who's organizing this game. Who's playing it. And what other pranks they intend to pull."

"And then maybe we can prank them back, big time!" Rob added.

We'd see about that.

"I figure there's a slight chance one of you might have heard something about this game," I said. "Because I know all of you are passionate about studying anything that might possibly turn into an exciting new game. If anyone does have any information, please let Rob or me know. And if no one knows anything—is there any team in the world better able to find out!"

Cheers greeted this pronouncement, and Rob high-fived me, from which I deduced that he approved.

"Now remember," I said, when the crowd quieted again. "We're working to find evidence that Chief Burke might need to use. Someone was murdered here in Caerphilly, and it might have something to do with this game. So be careful."

"And don't do anything we know we shouldn't be doing," Rob said. "No vigilante, cowboy stuff. And no risking your own necks. Anything else, Meg?"

I shook my head.

"Everyone," Rob said. "Mission Scavenger Hunt is our number one priority from now until Halloween is over! A day's vacation to anyone who can prove he or she has found some useful intel. Let's roll!"

Most of the crowd stampeded out of the lobby and into the stairwells, while a few formed lines for the elevators. Most of them looked cheerful. I suspected the few who weren't were project leaders who hadn't quite lost sight of the deadlines they were paid to meet.

"And how badly is this going to disrupt your company's workload?" I asked Rob. "Don't you have a new game rolling out in a few weeks?"

"*Vampire Colonies II,*" he said. "And hey—want to see the final on the packaging? Your ironwork looks great."

He pointed to a poster hanging in the foyer. On it, a woman in a black-and-silver dress stood on a balcony, holding an elaborate candelabra that looked as if it had been constructed out of human finger bones painted black. Below her, in a moonlit courtyard, stood a man in a black cloak holding an ornate dagger with a sinister wavy blade, like an Indonesian kris, and a handle shaped like a bat with half-furled wings. The balcony was made out of oddly curly rails with gargoyles and bats entwined in them, while teeth, claws, and sinister slitted reptilian eyes erupted asymmetrically out of the railings. The whole effect was eerie, ominous, and almost monochromatic, the better to showcase the words *Vampire Colonies II* in dripping blood-red letters. I liked to think that my work helped achieve the creepy effect— because yes, the candelabra, the dagger, and the intricately wrought iron of the balcony were all my work. Below the poster stood a DVD case with a smaller version of the artwork on its cover, and the real items were in a glass case nearby.

"Looks great," I said. I confess, I breathed a small sigh of relief that if the posters and packaging were made, Rob and the art department were probably not going to come back to ask me for yet another variation. "Just a little creepier, Meg," were words I'd learned to dread over the past few months. Although I had to admit, Rob paid very well, and made sure my contribution was boldly highlighted in the game credits.

"But getting back to your schedule," I said.

"Don't worry. We're in good shape, and this should only take a couple of days. And who knows? Maybe we'll get a cool game out of it. The idea of a scavenger hunt in a town that's celebrating Halloween—the visuals would be awesome."

"Hey," said a programmer who happened to be passing. "What if it's like Groundhog Day Halloween. The town's stuck in Halloween unless someone can finish the quest and end the curse."

"I like it!" Rob said. "Keep thinking—but first let's find the other team so we can milk their brains for everything they know. Could be LARPers, you know. Live action role players," he added for my benefit. "They act out games in the real world."

"Definitely a possibility," the programmer said. "And there's no way they could plan something like this without leaving some tracks online. I'm going to go work some chat rooms where some of the LARPers hang out."

"Hey, count me in!" Rob said.

The two of them hurried off together.

As I was about to leave, I remembered something. I needed to alert the Goblin Patrol. A blast e-mail would probably be the easiest way to do it. But I hated typing more than a few words on my phone. It would be so much easier to do it from a full-sized keyboard. Where better to do that than in the

Mutant Wizards building, which probably contained more computers than every other building in town put together.

"Is there a computer I could use to send an e-mail?" I asked the receptionist.

She led me to a small cubicle near the back of the lobby where they had a computer set up for guests to use. I logged into the Web-based version of my e-mail and quickly composed my marching orders to the rank-and-file goblins. I outlined what we knew about the scavenger hunt and the murder and ordered them to be alert for people eating bugs, stealing pumpkins, carrying fake body parts, doing tombstone rubbings, or anything else weird.

And then I went back and deleted the word "weird." It was Halloween. Weird was the new normal. I changed it to "anything else you reasonably suspect could be part of a Halloween-themed scavenger hunt."

I added in a line asking everyone to reply or text me to confirm that they'd gotten the message, printed out a copy of my Goblin Patrol roster so I could check off the replies as I got them, and shut down the computer.

I left the Mutant Wizards building in a good mood. My phone was already dinging with acknowledgments from Goblin Patrol members. If the tourists were up to something out on the streets, the Goblin Patrol was on the case. And if there was any information on the scavenger hunt to be found on the Internet, the Mutant Wizards would find it.

I'd done everything I could do to help the chief's murder investigation. At least everything I could do without crossing that invisible line between helpful citizen and interfering busybody. And the festival wasn't going to slow down. Time for me to start making my rounds. And then my stomach growled, and I decided to start my rounds with a visit to the town square, where all the churches had set up their characteristic food tents.

And since it was only a few blocks to the town square, and

I already had free parking that was closer than anything else I was liable to find, I hefted my purse and my tote bag and set off down the street on foot.

I'd had mixed feelings about the festival itself from the beginning, but I loved the enthusiasm and ingenuity that the townspeople showed in their decorating. The town had opted for its generic fall/harvest decorating scheme to placate those who weren't sure they approved of Halloween, but the houses and small shops had gone in for Halloween by a ten-to-one margin. Hardly a house was without its pumpkin, and most people had gone in for groups of pumpkins, either ingeniously carved into jack-o'-lanterns or *au naturel*. And I had to remind myself that these were just the pumpkins left behind after the best had been gathered into the tent in the town square in preparation for Saturday morning's jack-o'-lantern judging. In one yard a huge mobile of paper bats fluttered from the limb of a towering oak tree. In another a bony hand slowly crept out of the ground in front of a fake tombstone and grabbed at the ankles of anyone walking toward the front door. One resident had woven orange and black ribbons between the pickets of her picket fence. Another had tethered a filmy ghost to her chimney so that the slightest breeze or puff of smoke would set it to dancing. I made a mental note not to bring the boys down this street after dark—the ghost was slightly spooky even in the daytime.

Before long I'd arrived at Caerphilly's tiny commercial area. The tourists were already out in force, and from their festive mood I suspected word of the murder hadn't yet started to spread. People were pouring into and out of the bakery with pumpkin bread and cookies shaped like cats and frosted with chocolate. They were standing in line halfway down the block from the coffee shop, which advertised pumpkin lattes and apple cider. They were admiring the *Nightmare Before Christmas* display in the front window of

Caerphilly Cleaners and the animated skeleton string quartet on the flat roof of the Caerphilly Supermarket.

My own enjoyment of the beautiful fall day faded as I found myself staring at the tourists, expecting every moment that one of them would reveal him- or herself as part of the scavenger hunt—or maybe even a killer. Was that a fake finger sticking out of that cup of hot chocolate? No, only a biscotto. Was that a spider on that pumpkin muffin? No, only a dribble of chocolate. I kept an eye out for people who might be consulting lists and then, after a few minutes, realized that if I were participating in the scavenger hunt, I'd put the list in my phone, so I could consult it without anyone realizing I was doing anything other than checking the time. Suddenly, every other tourist I saw seemed to be staring at a phone screen.

"What's wrong, Meg?" I glanced up to see the tall, lanky form of Randall Shiffley.

"These people came all this way to see the Halloween festival," I muttered. "You'd think they could take their noses out of their phones for five minutes to look at it."

"Oh, I expect half of them are using their phones to take pictures." He pointed at a woman who was using her phone to take a picture of three children beside the Headless Horseman scarecrow in front of the hair salon. "What's gotten into you?"

"It's been a crazy morning," I said.

"Yeah. The chief filled me in on the murder, and Lydia seems to be miffed that you haven't dropped by to brief her. She seems to think she's responsible for your finding the body because she sent you out to investigate something at the zoo."

"I didn't find the body, and she sent me to the burglary at the Haunted House, not the zoo, and I had no idea she wanted a briefing." I was careful to keep my tone light. "She just told me to take care of it. Which I'm doing. Want me to fill you in?"

"That'd be great," he said. "Mind if we do it over some lunch? I was just headed for the food tents."

"Great minds and dishwater run in the same channels, as Mother always says," I replied. "I'm going to start with Baptist chicken and mashed potatoes, and then finish up with some Episcopalian pumpkin pie."

"If you pick me up some Baptist bread pudding, I'll get your pie. I'm doing the Episcopalian ham and green beans."

"It's a deal," I said. "Meet you on the steps."

Chapter 11

Randall and I made our visits to the church food tents and a few minutes later we joined the crowd who were using the front steps of the courthouse as a picnic site. At my suggestion, we climbed all the way to the top of the steps where we could have a little privacy. In between bites, I filled him in on what I knew about the murder as well as the pranks at the zoo and the Haunted House.

My phone dinged several times during the telling. I noticed Randall frowning when I pulled it out to check it.

"Sorry," I said. "I sent out a briefing to the entire Goblin Patrol and asked them to acknowledge. After lunch, I plan to track down the holdouts to see why they haven't answered."

"That's great," he said. "I was worried it was Lydia bothering you for a report."

"She usually calls," I said. "And asks me to drop by her office so she can issue whatever orders she has in person."

Randall winced.

"I'll talk to her," he said. "She means well, but she still has a lot to learn. She still seems to be under the mistaken impression that in our quaint little town everything's only a few steps away."

"Thanks," I said. "I do have two voice mail messages from her, but I'm going to wait to answer until I finish my lunch."

"I can beat that," he said. "I have five."

I rolled my eyes.

"Oh, it's fine," he said. "Five's better than none. Last week I went for two days without getting a single message from her.

Quite a relief until I figured out she'd mixed up two digits of my cell phone number and left forty-seven messages with poor Branson Flugleman down at the feed store. He was a mite peeved."

I shook my head in commiseration, although I had to admit, I was secretly relieved that Randall was no longer singing Lydia's praises. Maybe he'd actually do something to get her to shape up. Or fire her. Either would be fine with me.

"Anyway—back to our crime wave," he said. "I heard that Dr. Blake has called out his brigade. Are you going to try to manage them along with our lot?"

"Caroline's coming up to take charge," I said.

"Good." He sounded pleased. "Tell her to make sure they know they're just here to patrol. I know some of them tend to get a little agitated when the welfare of the animals is at stake. We don't want anyone going all vigilante on us."

"Roger," I said. "Which reminds me—Osgood Shiffley came up with the idea of calling a bunch of your cousins and surrounding the zoo with armed Shiffleys perched in the trees on hunting platforms. I told him to clear it with you first. Has he?"

"I'll talk to him." Randall set his jaw and exhaled noisily, as if letting off steam. "The idea of watchers in the trees doesn't sound that crazy actually," he said. "As long as they're unarmed. Between Blake's Brigade and your scavenger hunt players and all the crazy teenagers who've seen *The Blair Witch Project* and want to go off and scare themselves in the woods, we've got too many mostly harmless but potentially unruly people who might be wandering around out there. No sense adding firearms to the mix. And frankly, I'm not sure if even our family has enough cousins to defend the entire perimeter of the zoo. If we did a little scouting around we could probably figure out the most probable points of entry and cover those."

"That sounds like a better idea than ringing the entire

zoo," I said. "By the way, on a not completely unrelated subject, what do you know about Arabella Shiffley?"

"Arabella?" Randall frowned slightly as if thinking, and then shook his head. "Sure you don't mean Amanda or Ashley? We've got a few of those, but I can't think that we have any Arabellas."

"She's dead now," I said. "And her married name would have been Pratherton."

"Oh, her." He grimaced slightly. "Family's not too proud of her. In fact, they disowned her. Struck her name out of the family Bible and everything."

"Because she married a bootlegger?"

"Shoot, no." He chuckled and shook his head. "We were bootleggers ourselves back then. No one would have minded if she married another bootlegger, as long as she picked an honest, plain-dealing one. But she had to pick Billy Pratherton. We couldn't sit still for that."

I found it amusing that he said "we," as if he were one of the Shiffleys who had disowned the wayward Arabella. Mother was the same, talking about things the Hollingsworth family had done in World War II, the Great War, or even the Civil War as if she'd been there to witness them.

"What was wrong with Billy?" I asked.

"The Shiffleys were honest moonshiners," Randall said. "We made a good, clean product. Potent as hell—you drank more than a sip and you might find yourself howling at the moon, and God help you when you woke up the next morning. But our moonshine wouldn't kill you or blind you."

"And Billy's did?"

"Yes." Randall scowled and nodded. "Even after they passed the Prohibition, the Feds couldn't stop people from making alcohol—too many industrial uses for it. So they tried to stop people from drinking industrial alcohol by adding in chemicals that would make you sick or even kill you. Kerosene, gasoline, benzene, iodine, nicotine, ether, formaldehyde, chloroform, camphor, acetone, and especially methyl alcohol. You name it. If it was poison, someone probably tried adding it to industrial alcohol between 1920 and 1933. And then the gangsters would steal the industrial alcohol. The smart ones would hire chemists to redistill it to get the poisons out. But that cost money. The stupid, careless ones like Billy just sold it the way it came."

Clearly Randall had spent some time studying this era of his family's history.

"Why would people buy from Billy, then?" I asked.

"They didn't always know that's who they were buying from," Randall said. "He had a lot of middlemen who actually sold the stuff. Billy kept his own hands clean. And not all his stuff was poisonous. He was always raiding our stills and warehouses, so some of his stuff was as good as ours—because it was ours."

"I can see why your family weren't thrilled about Arabella's marriage."

"Yeah, it was pretty much Hatfields and McCoys between us and Billy's mob," Randall said. "And they didn't get married right away—for a good ten years, she was just a gangster's moll. There's people in my grandfather's generation who not only wouldn't say her name, if someone else said it they'd spit on the ground. And then when Prohibition ended, Billy and Arabella decided to turn respectable. They got married, bought a big house with all those ill-gotten gains, and tried to bust their way in society."

"Tried?" I echoed.

"Turns out all the Caerphilly bigwigs were happy to buy booze from Billy during Prohibition, but they didn't want to share a dinner table with him after the Repeal. Billy and Arabella knocked their heads against that brick wall for a few years and then they moved away somewhere, and that's the last we ever heard of them."

"So I guess Dr. Smoot didn't go through your family to

find Arabella's descendants and get her dress for his museum."

"Her dress?"

"He's got a nifty little 1920s flapper dress that's supposed to be the one she was wearing when the Feds tried to do a Bonnie and Clyde on Arabella and Billy."

"News to me," Randall said. "And not just the dress but the shoot-out. Then again, the old people don't talk about Arabella much."

"Any of them dislike her enough to try to sabotage Dr. Smoot's exhibit about her?"

"Seems unlikely." He frowned as he said it as if this was a new and not particularly welcome idea. "But not impossible. I can look into it if you think it's important."

"It could be," I said. "The only thing the police found in the dead guy's pockets was an article from the *Clarion* about how Arabella's modern-day namesake was killed in a hit-and-run accident a few months ago."

"I'll look into it," he said.

"Well," I said. "Unless you have any more marching orders, I'd better go follow up on those nonresponsive goblins. After I've listened to Lydia's voice mails, of course."

I pushed the buttons to call my voice mail. And then I pushed my phone's speaker button. If Lydia's messages were particularly annoying or condescending, it might not be a bad thing for Randall to hear them.

"Hi, Meg," she said in her usual breezy tone. "Could you call the Griswalds about their cat? Thanks."

"Why is the Griswalds' cat my problem?" I asked. "Is Animal Control closed for the festival? And does she think I'm psychic and can guess the Griswalds' number?"

Randall just shook his head.

I pushed the button to listen to her second message.

"Meg, the Griswalds are driving me crazy!" She sounded less cheerful this time. "Can you *please* go over and calm them down? And if possible get their cat back from Dr. Smoot and take it back to them."

"Go over and calm them down," I repeated. "Again, why is this my problem and where are the Griswalds? Mrs. Griswald's technically a member of Trinity Episcopal— I've seen her name when I helped Robyn with some church paperwork—but she must not go often, because I don't recall meeting her and we're certainly not on visiting terms."

"Lydia seems to think we all know each other and spend all day sipping iced tea on each other's porches," Randall said. "And since when has Dr. Smoot taken up catnapping in addition to all his other peculiarities?"

Enlightenment struck.

"Oh, good grief," I muttered. I opened up the photo album in my phone and clicked through it till I found the shot I thought I'd remembered. "Aha! That's why I already heard the Griswalds' name today. Dr. Smoot hasn't stolen their cat. He borrowed a jeweled cat-shaped brooch from them to exhibit in his museum. Borrowed in what sounded like a completely businesslike and aboveboard way."

"I'm guessing they heard about the security problems at the Haunted House and have maybe changed their minds about the loan. I gather the thing is valuable."

I showed Randall my picture of the brooch.

"I repeat my question—is that eyesore actually valuable? Because if it were mine, I'd be over the moon if someone stole it."

"All the sparkly stones are real," I said. "No matter how ugly it is, it's worth a mint, so I can understand how the Griswalds might be a little worried about it. As soon as I find out where they are, I will happily go over and talk to them."

"They live in Westlake," Randall said. "I've got the address here in my phone. I've been over there a time or two for committee meetings."

Randall read me the address, and I entered it into my own phone for safekeeping.

"You take care of the Griswalds," he said. "I'll make your report on the Haunted House to Lydia. And then I'll go figure out if any of the old folks in my family are still worked up about Arabella."

"Or if they know anything that could explain her obituary being found in the pocket of a murder victim," I suggested.

"That too." He squared his shoulders and marched into the courthouse.

I hurried down the steps and back to the Mutant Wizards parking lot.

"Of course it would be Westlake," I murmured as I made my slow way through the crowds. Westlake was where Caerphilly's truly rich people lived. At least the ones who wanted to make sure you knew they were rich. Grandfather could probably have afforded a house there if he wanted one, but he considered that entire section of town a hideous example of rampant environmental unsustainability. Come to think of it, given how profitable Mutant Wizards had become, Rob could probably also afford a house there. But he made fun of Westlake as pretentious and seemed as content with his room on our third floor as Grandfather was with his pied-à-terre at Mother and Dad's farm.

Maybe if one of them had moved to Westlake I'd feel less like an intruder on the rare occasions when I had to go there. Most of the houses there were built in the faux Tudor style that was popular throughout much of the town, but in Westlake the houses looked more like medieval manors than quaint cottages, and a mere two acres was considered a tiny lot. Most of the houses were set back so far from the road that they could barely be seen, and a few were probably large enough to qualify for their own zip codes if they wanted them.

And clearly Westlake wasn't nearly as keen on Halloween as the rest of the town. I didn't spot a single fake tombstone or skeleton. Not a single witch had collided with any of the residents' numerous and well-tended trees. No fake bats anywhere. Where there were decorations, they were definitely of the low-key, tasteful fall/harvest school. Some of the front porches bore small, carefully arranged collections of gourds in muted earth tones—nothing so gaudy as a pumpkin. Some doors displayed wreaths of dried flowers or arrangements of two or three ears of Indian corn. Clearly Halloween was not nearly as much of an occasion here as it was in the livelier parts of town.

I wondered if this was how they decorated every year, or if their militant avoidance of Halloween trappings had anything to do with the Westlake neighborhood's bitter opposition to the festival plan. An opposition I suspected was largely due to the fact that a Shiffley was promoting the plan.

When I found the Griswalds' house, I stopped by the curb for a few moments to assess it. By Westlake standards it looked about average. It was set back fairly far from the street on top of a gentle hill. From the street it gave the impression of being one of the neighborhood's rare normal-sized houses—a sprawling ranch at the large end of normal, but nothing you might not see in a nice suburban neighborhood.

But once I turned into the driveway and made my way slowly up the hill, I revised my assessment. The higher I went, the more house I saw. It didn't just sprawl along the top of the hill, it also wandered all the way down the other side in a confusing mass of wings, terraces, gables, decks, covered walks, and outbuildings. Far from being modest, the Griswalds' home was toward the upper end of the range here in Westlake.

I was expecting a butler, or at least a uniformed maid, but a small, nondescript man in a brown suit met me at the door.

"It's not Halloween yet," he said, eyeing my swordwoman's costume with distaste.

"And Halloween can't be over soon enough for me," I said. "Lydia Van Meter asked me to come and see you. I'm Meg Langslow, head of the Visitor Relations and Police Liaison Patrol. Hence the costume." He didn't look like someone who'd be amused by the Goblin Patrol name. In fact, he looked like someone who disapproved of trick-or-treating but couldn't be bothered with the custom of turning out your front lights as a signal that you weren't giving out candy. Then again, only the most naïve trick-or-treaters would climb all the way up his driveway with no more encouragement than a single, tasteful sheaf of dried grass on the door.

"I see." He waited a few moments, then sighed and beckoned me in.

Without another word he led me across half an acre of foyer, our footsteps echoing on slate tiles that were bare except for a small and hideously expensive-looking oriental rug right in the center of the room. Above it hung a crystal chandelier that would have looked over-the-top in Versailles.

"My wife is in the great room," he said as he opened a set of double doors at the far side of the foyer and gestured for me to walk in.

The great room had size going for it, and very little else. The cathedral ceiling dwarfed the furniture, which was formal and uninviting. It was a prime example of what Mother called "decorating only for the camera and the magazine editors." Not that she didn't enjoy all the photography in her rags, as she called them—every month she read *Architectural Digest, Elle Decor, Elle Decoration* (its English cousin), *House Beautiful, Martha Stewart Living, Traditional Home, Veranda, World of Interiors,* and probably others whose names I was blotting out of my mind. But she didn't read them uncritically. And she saved the worst of her scorn for the houses that, as she put it, were just decorated to look good in a magazine feature rather than to be lived in. The Griswalds' living room struck me as a textbook example. I wished I could pull out my phone and take some photos, to see if she agreed with my assessment.

And on top of the rather chilly, minimalist décor, no fire burned in a fireplace that was almost as large as the one I remembered from the mansion in *Citizen Kane*. A pity, since the one thing the Griswalds weren't extravagant with was heat.

I had plenty of time to study my surroundings as we made our way across what seemed like several square miles of carpet so deep it was like walking through mud, to a distant pair of sofas upholstered in white brocade. But when we finally reached the sofas, Mrs. Griswald, who was sitting in a corner of one of them, came as a pleasant surprise.

"Meg Langslow! How nice of you to come!"

I recognized her as the sweet and bubbly woman who was a regular at Grace Episcopal Church's Sunday services, though she declined with seemingly genuine regret when invited to various social and volunteer activities. "I'm afraid Harry doesn't approve of my gadding about too much," she had said, more than once. If this was Harry, I now understood. And of course, I knew her as Becky, not as Mrs. Griswald—I couldn't remember ever hearing her last name.

"Ms. Langhorn has come about the cat," Mr. Griswald announced.

"Langslow, dear," Mrs. Griswald said. "And Harris, we don't really need to bother her about that now. She has such a lot to do for the festival. I'm sure the brooch will be fine."

The brooch, as opposed to the cat. I deduced that Mr. Griswald was the one who had called Lydia. And had I misremembered his name, or did she call him Harris to his face and Harry behind his back?

"Nonsense, Rebecca," Mr. Griswald said. "The brooch is worth four hundred and fifty thousand dollars. I think we need to find out whether the festival management is taking proper care of it."

"I can't speak for festival management," I said. "I'm only in charge of the volunteer security force. But as far as I know, the festival management isn't taking care of the brooch at all. It's not our job."

"What do you mean, not your job?" Mr. Griswald snapped.

"The festival made an arrangement with Dr. Smoot to use his land to house the Fun Fair, and he agreed to provide the Haunted House free of charge to fairgoers," I said. "The fact that Dr. Smoot is also running a town museum in the basement has nothing to do with the festival."

"But it's in the same building as the Haunted House," Mr. Griswald said.

"So are Dr. Smoot's living quarters," I said. "And they're none of the festival's business either."

"The museum is open to anyone who comes to the festival," Mr. Griswald began.

"But it's not a part of the festival," I said. "If you're concerned about the safety of your property, talk to Dr. Smoot. I have no idea what kind of arrangements you made when you agreed to lend him the brooch, but surely you included some provisions to cover insurance and proper security."

Mr. Griswald was sputtering in outrage. I wasn't sure if he was upset because he hadn't thought about insurance and security or merely because he wasn't used to people crossing him.

"Frankly," I went on, "if you're worried, I'd have Dr. Smoot bring the brooch back until the festival's over. And for that matter, I'm going to recommend to Mayor Shiffley that we require Dr. Smoot to do so. Even though the brooch is not the festival's responsibility, if there's a possibility that it's adding to our security problems at the Haunted House, we need to resolve that."

"This is outrageous!" Mr. Griswald bellowed. "I'm calling my attorney immediately!"

With that he stormed out.

"Oh, dear." Mrs. Griswald was shaking her head. "Would you like some tea? I never got the chance to offer you any before Harris pounced."

I couldn't help smiling at that.

"Thanks," I said. "But I should probably be going. Busy day. Unless you think Mr. Griswald expects me to wait while he talks to his attorney."

"Heavens, no." She grimaced. "He'll be shouting on the phone for hours. At upwards of five hundred dollars an hour. He always feels much better afterward. I suppose it's like therapy. Of course, real therapy might be rather cheaper and produce a more long-lasting effect, but Harris wouldn't hear of it. Are you really going to make us take the brooch back?"

"Sorry, but I think it would be a good idea," I said. "At least until the festival's over. It was very nice of you to lend it—"

"I didn't lend it," she said. "Harris did. I wasn't keen on the idea one bit, and after all, it's supposed to be my brooch, isn't it? He gave it to me for our twenty-fifth anniversary. Then a couple of months later, he goes and lends it to a museum. And the Caerphilly Museum, of all places. Of course, I happen to know the Virginia Museum of Fine Arts wouldn't take it. Why should they? They've got all those fabulous Fabergé eggs— what would they want with that ugly old thing?"

"Then you're not overly fond of your brooch?" I asked.

"I loathe it," she said. "I think it's supremely ugly, and the fact that it once belonged to the Duchess of Windsor doesn't mean much to me. I don't approve of her, if you must know. And when I think of what we could have done with all the money he spent on it, I'm almost sick."

"At least as long as it's in the museum, he can't expect you to wear it," I said.

"Thank goodness," she muttered. "But I don't want it down at the museum, either. People must be laughing at us, spending so much money for something that looks like cheap, ugly costume jewelry. No, I want it back here—or rather, back in our safe-deposit box down at the bank, where I don't have to look at it and no one else can either."

She looked anxious. Very anxious, considering that she hated the brooch. But then there was all that money. And maybe she wasn't so much anxious about the brooch or its cost but about having to disagree with her husband. I got the feeling she didn't do that very often.

"Call Dr. Smoot, then," I said. "And in case either he or your husband drags their feet, I'll ask Randall to issue a formal request."

"Thank you, Meg." She still looked a little anxious, but her smile was warm and genuine. "How's the Trinity food tent in the town square doing?"

"Business is booming," I said. "And the pie is as good as ever."

"Of course," she said. "It's your family's famous recipe, isn't it? I wish I could go down and help, but Harris won't hear of it."

"If you ever feel like sneaking away and pitching in informally, they'd love to see you," I said. "Or just drop by for lunch sometime."

"I just might," she said. "Are you sure you don't have time for that tea?"

"How about a rain check?" I said. "Assuming Mr. Griswald's continued absence means he's finished with me for now, I should get back to my job."

"I'll hold you to that rain check." She rose from the sofa and walked with me back to the front door. "And if you want to meet someplace other than this mausoleum, that would be fine." And then seeing the curiosity on my face, she added, "Harris picked the designer and gives her all her instructions. Not my idea of homey."

"How about lunch at Muriel's Diner after the festival's over and things calm down," I suggested.

"You're on!" she exclaimed. "I love the diner. Let me give

you my number—I'm not in the parish directory. Harris disapproves."

I added her number to my cell phone and said good-bye. As I walked down their front walk, I found myself wondering how Mrs. Griswald had put up with her husband all these years—how, and even more, why? When I reached my car, I made a note to call her for lunch, and another note to see what Mother knew about her.

I waited until I was out of Westlake before pulling over to call Randall.

"So I mouthed off and probably made an enemy of Mr. Griswald," I said, after I'd explained that the stolen cat was actually the brooch in the museum.

"He's hard to like and easy to offend," Randall said.

"But I think we should make good on something I suggested to him," I said. "I think it's a bad idea having such a valuable piece of jewelry down at the museum. Dr. Smoot has some security, but I'm not sure it's up to repelling serious jewel thieves. And even if it is, just having it in the museum exacerbates our already serious security problems down at the Haunted House."

"The chief said the body was moved," Randall said. "What if it was moved a couple of miles down the road from the museum? Even an ugly piece of jewelry worth half a million would be worth killing someone over. Though blessed if I know how the article about Arabella fits into it. She and Billy were highfliers in their day, but I doubt if they had anything to do with the Duchess or her jewels."

"The chief knows about Arabella's connection to the museum," I said. "I'm sure he'll check it out. And I'm not going to ask if he's showed Dr. Smoot pictures of Justin Klapcroft and the dead guy, to see if he recognizes either of them as people he had to shoo away from the museum. I'm sure he already has." I wasn't going to ask, because doing so would annoy the chief. But I was curious to know if Dr. Smoot had recognized them, and Randall, in his role as mayor, could probably ask without getting his head bit off.

"I'll look into it," Randall said. "How about if we just ask Smoot to send the brooch back for the time being? It's only common sense."

"Not something Dr. Smoot has a surplus of," I pointed out.

"True. But we can start by asking. And I'll also talk to the county attorney. Must be some kind of legal grounds she can think of for making him do it. Threat to public order or some such thing."

"Sounds good," I said. "Can you go talk to Dr. Smoot as soon as possible? Come down all official on him?"

"Yes'm," he said. "I'll head over right now."

"And we should start thinking about issuing a public statement," I said. "Warn the tourists."

Randall didn't say anything for a few long moments. Then he sighed.

"Better if it comes from us," I said. "Before the press gets hold of it."

"You're right," he said. "It'd be nice if we could say we have a suspect in custody."

"Not if Justin Klapcroft turns out to be innocent and sues us."

"Good point. I'll talk to the chief and the county attorney." He hung up.

As long as I was stopped anyway, I called Rob.

"Hold your horses," he said. "We're still just getting started."

"No problem," I said. "I just wanted to add one small search item to your list. Can you see if it's widely known over the Internet that Dr. Smoot's museum contains a piece of jewelry worth half a million dollars?"

"It does? Holy cow—what kind of idiot would trust Smoot with anything worth half a mil?"

"Good question," I said.

"Hey, maybe the owner's planning to have someone steal it and collect the insurance," he said.

"Possible," I said. "Or maybe the owner's an idiot who has no idea how little security Dr. Smoot has. Just let me know whether it's likely that any enterprising cat burglars could have found out online that the jewelry's there. I'll send you a picture of it."

"We're on it."

I hunted down my best picture of the cat brooch and sent it to Rob. Then, before starting off again, I finished tallying my list of Goblin Patrol members. Only two had failed to respond to my e-mail. I called and talked to one. My call to the other went to voice mail, so I left a detailed message.

I debated for a few moments. Did leaving a voice mail for the final goblin allow me to check off "confirm that all goblins are watching for pranksters" in my notebook? It didn't quite feel done. But it was so tantalizingly close.

I created a new, much smaller task: "confirm that Nelson Dandridge listened to my voice mail." And then I checked off the bigger task as done and went back to my patrolling. I could start by dropping by the New Life Baptist Church, where Mr. Dandridge was supposed to be patrolling.

My phone rang a minute or so after I began driving. I let it go to voice mail, with the idea that I'd call back when I got to the church. Of course it was Lydia. She left a cryptic voice mail: "Meg—have you called Mr. Brimfield yet? Can you call him ASAP?"

And of course her phone went to voice mail when I called back.

"Lydia," I said. "This is Meg Langslow. No, I haven't called Mr. Brimfield; I have no idea what you want me to call about, and I don't even have his phone number."

I hung up and sat in the church parking lot for a few minutes, fuming. Maybe I should have left a more polite message.

No. Hell, no. Lydia needed to learn how to do her job.

And maybe I was particularly annoyed at her because Mr. Brimfield was almost certainly part of the family from whom Dr. Smoot was trying to get funding for his museum and anything having to do with the museum or the zoo could have something to do with the murder. I'd be happy to call Mr. Brimfield if I could.

I mentally called Lydia a few unkind names. Then I shoved her out of my mind and climbed out of my car to look for Mr. Dandridge.

It turned out that Mr. Dandridge hadn't yet gotten my message because he'd been letting his grandson play *Minecraft* on his phone for the past several hours. But someone else had told him about the pranksters and the murder, and he'd been staking out the cemetery, watching for possible makers of tombstone rubbings.

"And what were you going to do if you caught one?" I asked. "It's not illegal to do tombstone rubbings."

"I planned to take their picture—well, actually that's why I brought along Colby—four years old and he already knows how to do more with this confounded phone than I do. And then I'd send the photos to the police. And then I'd engage them in polite conversation, to see if I could get any information."

"Good idea, on all counts," I said. "Which reminds me that I need to recruit watchers for the rest of the town cemeteries."

I made a few phone calls and steered reliable goblins to each of the town's cemeteries. It temporarily reduced the number on patrol, but Caroline had e-mailed me to report that she'd be arriving in town by two and would start deploying the Blake's Brigade volunteers around the zoo, so by the time we flipped over to the Night Side we'd be fully staffed again.

And after that flurry of activity, I felt momentarily blue. I started my car and headed back for the center of town, but my mind wasn't on the road. Was any of this going to do any good? And was there anything else I could do to help solve the murder, keep the townspeople and tourists safe, and keep the bad news from undermining the success of the festival?

An idea occurred to me—though I couldn't decide if it was a good idea or a terrible one. The brooch was the most valuable thing in the museum—but it wasn't the only valuable thing. I flipped through the photos on my phone. Arabella's dress? Dr. Smoot probably wouldn't want to contact the parents of the modern-day Arabella, but maybe he'd let me? Or at least move it to safety. I should go and ask him who owned the inaugural gown. And Mrs. Paltroon's painting was probably valuable. I couldn't imagine anyone bothering to haul away any of the museum's other contents.

I had a plan. Randall was taking care of the brooch, but I could investigate the other objects worth stealing. And first off, I needed to talk to Mrs. Paltroon.

Chapter 12

Of course, deciding to talk to Mrs. Paltroon and finding her were two different things. Odds were she also lived in Westlake, like the Griswalds, but I had no idea where. And even once I found her, there was the challenge of getting her to talk to me. I kept on my way toward the heart of town and as soon as I'd parked my car again in the Mutant Wizards parking lot, I called my expert on Caerphilly social matters.

"Mother," I said. "Do you have any idea where I could find Mrs. Paltroon?"

"Probably," she said. "Although I have no idea why you'd want to."

"I don't want to find her," I said. "But I need to. Goblin Patrol business."

"Is she in some kind of trouble?"

"You don't have to sound so eager," I said. "Not that I know of. I just want to talk to her about the painting she lent to Dr. Smoot's museum."

"That ghastly painting?" I didn't have to see Mother to know that she'd just shuddered. "If our ancestors looked that unprepossessing, I certainly wouldn't put them on display in the Caerphilly Museum."

"Especially since none of them actually lived here in Caerphilly," I said. "Then again, I gather Colonel Paltroon didn't either."

"Oh, is it Colonel Paltroon now?" Mother asked. "Last time I heard he was only a major. And some of the folks who've been attending the local DAR meetings for years tell me they can recall when he was only a captain. I've never seen a man so successful at obtaining posthumous promotions. At this rate, he'll probably make general in time for the Sestercentennial."

"The what?"

"Sestercentennial," she repeated. "The two hundred and fiftieth anniversary of independence, which will occur in 2026."

"Ah," I said. "Well, why stop at general? Mrs. Paltroon should aim for commander-in-chief. George Washington doesn't have any blood descendants around to put up a fight. Habakkuk Paltroon, father of his country. We could all visit the Paltroon Monument when we go up to the city of Paltroon to visit our congresspeople. I look forward to seeing his face on the dollar bill."

"I don't," Mother said. "Have you seen his face?"

"In the family portrait," I said. "Speaking of which— Mrs. Paltroon's whereabouts?"

"She's probably holding court down at the DAR's dried flower sale," Mother said.

"The Weed Patch?" I said. "Great! Thanks!"

I hung up before Mother could protest my using the sarcastic local nickname for the dried flower sale and turned my steps toward the town square.

I couldn't help thinking that while the town council might have decided to keep the official decorations in the tasteful fall/harvest range, the crowd in the town square was full-bore Halloween. Which made it all the more amusing that the Caerphilly DAR was holding its annual dried flower sale this weekend, in the front yard of the Methodist church, which faced the town square. Odds were that the genteel crowd who usually turned up every year to patronize the Weed Patch had been scared away by the Halloween hordes. And it was hard to imagine that many of the ghouls and witches roaming the square would even venture into the DAR

tent, much less emerge with expensive armloads of desic-
cated vegetation.

Then again, maybe I was wrong. I tended to avoid the tent
entirely because the dried stuff always made me sneeze.
Possibly a psychosomatic reaction, since Rose Noire's dried
herbs and potpourris never bothered me.

I followed the perimeter of the town square until I reached
the Methodist Church, and then hiked up the driveway and
entered the tent.

The curiously hushed and almost deserted tent. I gazed
around and saw nothing but dried plants. Plants lying in
sheaves on the tables and standing upright in buckets and
baskets. Baby's breath, larkspur, hydrangeas, Japanese lan-
terns, heather, statice, globeflowers, eucalyptus, flax, tansy,
wheat, and heaven knows what else.

I was already fighting the urge to sneeze.

"May I help you?"

A pleasant, if somewhat anxious-looking woman in a Colonial costume had approached me. I recognized her as one
of the Weed Ladies—Mrs. Paltroon's loyal troops who la-
bored year-round to collect and preserve local plants for the
sale. At least half of the plants in the tent were displayed
under huge banners that proclaimed them LOCALLY GROWN
AND PRESERVED! But still not very fragrant.

"I'm looking for Mrs. Paltroon," I said. "Is she here?"

The woman smiled and gestured toward the back of the
tent. A stately figure was slowly making her way down the
wide aisles between the flower displays. The woman who had
greeted me had been dressed neatly but not extravagantly,
in a plain blue gown and a lace-trimmed mob cap. Mrs. Paltroon would not have looked out of place at a court ball.
When she was about six feet away from me she stopped, as
if unwilling to risk closer contact, and fixed me with a gim-
let eye.

"May I help you?" From her, it sounded more like "How

dare you sully the purity of our tent with your modern Halloween nonsense?"

"Meg Langslow," I said. "I'm in charge of the festival's Visitor Relations and Police Liaison Patrol. I wanted to talk to you about your painting."

"My painting?"

"The portrait of Habakkuk Paltroon that you loaned to Dr. Smoot for display in his museum."

"Yes," she said. "That's mine. What of it?"

"Festival management is recommending to the owners of any valuable objects that they remove them from the museum until next week," I said.

"Are you saying you can't protect my painting?" she said.

"Protecting your painting is Dr. Smoot's responsibility, not ours. However, festival management is concerned that, given the increased crowds visiting the Haunted House and museum this weekend, the presence of valuable objects in the museum will make it harder to maintain crowd control in that part of the festival."

What was it about this woman that sent me into full formal bureaucratic mode? No doubt my suspicion that she had an expensive attorney on speed dial. With almost anyone else, I'd probably just have said, "Please take your precious family heirloom painting home before some clueless tourist Magic Markers a mustache on one of your ancestors."

"It's too much of a temptation," I said. "And were you aware that Dr. Smoot has already had several break-in attempts?" I decided against mentioning the murder, since I didn't know what information the chief had released already, and after all, it wasn't actually at the museum.

"No, I was not aware of any break-ins." She was frowning now.

I hoped I hadn't just unleashed the wrath of the Paltroons on poor clueless Dr. Smoot.

"They only began very recently," I said.

"That painting is a valuable artwork as well as a family heirloom," she began.

"Which is why I'm sure Dr. Smoot will cooperate fully if you decide to take it off exhibit until the museum traffic is down to its normal, manageable level," I said.

"Yes, but one can't simply wrap it in a blanket and throw it in the backseat of one's car!"

I didn't see why not, but I held my tongue.

"Fortunately, I had already arranged for Dr. Gwinnett Cavendish to pay the museum a visit. The noted art restoration and conservation expert," she added, when she noticed that Dr. Cavendish's name hadn't elicited glad cries of joy from me. "Dr. Smoot had expressed some concerns about the condition of the painting. After Dr. Cavendish inspects it, I will direct him to have it properly packed and restored to its normal position in my abode."

"I think that's a wise decision," I said.

She didn't look as if she much cared what I thought.

"Have you ever had any security concerns about the painting before?" I asked.

"No, of course not." From her expression, you'd think I'd asked if she were in the habit of breaking wind in public. "Of course, we've always had a state-of-the-art security system."

"Good," I said. "Well, I'll be off."

No one begged me to stay. I did linger at the tent's entrance for a few moments when I realized that a trio of twenty-somethings dressed as vampires were entering the tent and looking around in astonishment.

"Wow," one young man said. "It's like a mausoleum for dead flowers."

"Some of these would be very pretty if you sprayed them black," the young woman at his side said.

The third vampire sneezed vigorously all over a bucket of dried yarrow.

"Young man!" Mrs. Paltroon called out.

I ducked out and managed to get all the way back to the street before giving in to my laughter.

Chapter 13

Once I was safely out of the Weed Patch I strolled until I was in front of the Methodist minister's house next door, sat down on the low wall separating it from the street, and flipped through my photos from the museum. I still couldn't see anything else I'd have bothered stealing. I texted Randall, suggesting that when he talked to Dr. Smoot, he remove anything truly valuable, like the vintage dresses, from display. He texted back "Yes'm." I made a note to drop by later today or maybe tomorrow morning to make sure Dr. Smoot had done something. And with any luck we could persuade the Griswalds and the Paltroons to remove their possessions before tomorrow night, when the final influx of Halloween revelers arrived to make things really crazy for the weekend. Maybe when I dropped by I should talk Dr. Smoot into closing the museum for the weekend, in case one of tomorrow's tasks turned out to be "steal something from the museum."

I returned to making my rounds. Out at the Haunted House the line to get in was a quarter mile long. All the rides were whirling at the Fun Fair, and the games and concessions were booming.

At the zoo, I was delighted to see the Willner Wildlife Foundation's truck parked in the staff parking lot. The guards at the gate waved me in and I hurried up to Grandfather's office, where he tended to take refuge when the zoo was as crowded as it was now.

I found him at his desk, pecking away on his computer.

"Another scientific article?" I asked.

"Letter to the U.S. Fish and Wildlife Service," he said. "Damn fools want to take the gray wolf off the endangered species list. You need something?"

"Just came by to liaise with Caroline," I said.

He nodded, stood up from the computer, and strode off. I decided to assume he was taking me to Caroline. He led me down a corridor and out a side door. As he stepped outside he glanced up reflexively, then laughed and shook his head.

"Getting to be a habit," he said as we walked. "I seem to have shaken the blasted ravens off for now, but they'll show up sooner or later."

"What is it with all the ravens?" I caught up and matched his pace.

"Part of my costume," he said. "I liked the notion of a wizard with a raven on his shoulder. In some cultures they're considered good luck, and in others they're sinister omens. In Norse mythology, the god Odin had two ravens, Huginn and Muninn—thought and memory. He'd send them out every morning and every evening they'd come back and tell him what was happening in the world. In American folklore—"

"Ravens are cool; I get that part," I said. "But why so *many* ravens? I should think one would be enough, but you've got a whole flock."

"An unkindness," Grandfather said. "The proper collective noun for a group of ravens is an unkindness, not a flock. Although some sources also favor 'a conspiracy of ravens.' Now that I'm afflicted with them, I find both terms curiously apt."

"But why did you afflict yourself with so many in the first place?" I asked. "Why not just train one?"

"That was the original idea," he said. "At the beginning of the summer I set up a large habitat in a temporarily vacant office in the administration building and I picked out a likely looking specimen and established him there. I would go in for an hour or so a day and work on his vocabulary. Nothing fancy. A few dramatic words and phrases. 'Doom!' and 'Beware!' and such."

"And 'nevermore,'" I added.

"Of course," he said. "It's traditional. Unfortunately, it turned out that I hadn't chosen a particularly likely subject. In fact, I appeared to have chosen a total slacker. Least intelligent corvid I'd ever studied."

"Just because he wasn't much of a conversationalist doesn't make him unintelligent," I said.

"I assigned an intern to spend several hours a day trying to teach him." Grandfather was warming to his subject, and had begun waving his arms around as he walked. "I made recordings of my voice and had them played in the room for several hours every day. I tried to tempt him with treats. Nothing."

I wondered if he'd considered the possibility that the raven wasn't unintelligent, merely stubborn. Possibly as stubborn as Grandfather himself.

"So I returned him to the wild."

"You just let him go? Aren't you always telling me how cruel it is to expect zoo-raised animals to survive in the wild?"

"He was a wild raven to begin with," Grandfather said. "We have quite a few of them living in our woods. A little out of their normal range—here in Virginia you'd mostly find them near the mountains. But not unheard of. And they hang out at the zoo a lot, because between the animal feed and the junk food we sell the tourists, it's a food-rich environment. Anyway, I let him go where I'd found him—back near our composting facility. And before long I found out he wasn't nearly as stupid as I'd thought."

"And meanwhile you'd started teaching more ravens?" I guessed.

"No," he said. "It seems my slacker raven started vocalizing like crazy when he got home. Ravens started showing up here at the zoo croaking 'Beware!' and 'Doom!' and 'Nevermore!' So I thought, fine. I'll train a couple of them to sit on my shoulder for treats."

"And now you have the entire conspiracy on your hands," I said. "Or rather, on your head and shoulders."

Just then a raven appeared overhead and began circling. Grandfather looked up without enthusiasm.

"They're very intelligent birds," he said. "Especially when it comes to acquiring food. But once I stop feeding them, they should lose interest in me."

I nodded.

The raven landed on his shoulder, folded its wings, and looked at Grandfather expectantly.

"Stupid bird!" it croaked. "Go away!"

Grandfather sighed.

"Yes, eventually they should lose interest," he said. "Unfortunately they're pretty stubborn birds. Caroline's in here."

We had arrived at a small door in the side of the Creatures of the Night building. Grandfather shooed away his current raven passengers, waved his security badge at a small pad, then opened the door and led me inside into a small corridor.

"This would be the supersecret zookeepers-only part of the building?" I asked, as I followed him down the corridor.

Instead of answering he opened a door along the left side of the corridor and strode in. I followed, and found myself in a large, brightly lit room. Several young people in purple overalls were doing things with cables, hard drives, monitors, and other electronic devices.

"We were going to use this space for a special veterinary facility for the nocturnal animals," Grandfather said. "But for now it's electronics central."

"Meg!" A small figure clad in a gray hooded robe jumped up and ran toward me.

"Hello, Caroline," I said, returning her hug. "Just what are you organizing?"

"Damned technology," Grandfather said.

"We're setting up a state-of-the-art security center," Caroline said. "And when I say we, I mostly mean the technicians from the Security Wizards branch of your brother's company."

"Overdue," I said.

Grandfather growled. Caroline had probably been bossing him around. She was carrying a staff with a large crystal on top. Clearly she was also supposed to be a wizard, although I hoped she had not also saddled herself with ravens. Her plump, cheerful face made her a slightly incongruous wizard.

"Long overdue." Caroline walked over to a bank of screens mounted on the wall, three high and five wide. "Especially considering his own grandson owns one of the top security companies on the East Coast."

"Well, how was I supposed to know that?" Grandfather demanded. "I just thought his company made silly games?"

"He's set up all kinds of subsidiaries to do other stuff involving computers," I said. "You'd know that if you ever listened to the conversation around the family dinner table on Sundays."

"Oh, he does," Caroline said. "But only when he's the one doing the talking. Move a couple more feet to the right."

I was starting to follow orders when I realized she was talking into her cell phone. The picture on one of the screens wobbled, and then lurched a bit before settling down.

"We're ringing the perimeter with security cameras," Caroline said. "Of course, that will take some time, even with all these brilliant young people working on it, so we're also organizing patrols and posting sentries. That's perfect," she added into the phone. "Let me know when you're ready to work on the next one."

We conferred for a few moments, and I was reassured that she and the Brigade would be able to handle security at the zoo. I was relieved—this would let me pull the half-dozen goblins I had patrolling the zoo and reassign them to areas where our numbers were reduced when I'd assigned guards to all the cemeteries. I made a few phone calls to give the troops their new marching orders and headed back to town.

Assigning the cemetery guards turned out to be a good idea. Mr. Dandridge's vigil in the Baptist cemetery proved uneventful for the rest of the afternoon, but the watcher in the Catholic cemetery spotted one would-be tombstone rubber, dressed as a zombie. His counterpart in the Congregational cemetery, which was the oldest in town, spotted two—a vampire and a grim reaper, complete with scythe. Unfortunately, all three costumes were ones that made it hard to identify their wearers, and all three wearers were fleet of foot—fleeter than the pursuing goblins, at least—so all we could do was report the incidents and share with the police what photos they'd been able to take before the intruders fled.

"Do you know how many vampires we have in town at the moment?" the chief asked, when I showed him the latest tombstone rubbing photo capture.

"I know." I'd caught up with him on the steps of the town hall, and from our vantage point, halfway up, we could see at least fifty vampires scattered through the crowd. "It would be different if they all had wildly different notions of how a vampire should dress. But most of them—including our tombstone rubber—look as if they bought their costumes at Vampires R Us."

"Is there such a place?" The chief looked alarmed at the notion.

"Not that I know of," I said. "I thought I was making a joke. But seeing how many of them there are, who knows? Dr. Smoot would know—shall I ask him?"

"Let's not," the chief said. "He might think it sounds like a brilliant business proposition."

"If you want me to stop sending the photos of tombstone rubbers and other pranksters, just let me know," I said.

"No, keep sending them," he said. "You never know. The next shot could capture some detail that will let us identify the perpetrator. And if nothing else, it gives us an idea of the scope of the phenomenon."

"Yeah," I said. "At least a dozen, but thank goodness not hundreds."

"The day is young," he said. "And some of the participants may be planning to make their graveyard visits under cover of darkness."

So I continued arranging for an evening shift at each of the town cemeteries. And then I took a few hours off, so I'd have the stamina to stay out late on patrol myself. I picked the boys up from school and decided to take them to the library for a new book fix before going home to root through the pantry in search of something I could serve for dinner. Normally on days when both Michael and I were working long hours we could count on Rose Noire to take care of the cooking, but I knew she'd be putting in long hours of her own down at her organic herb tent in the town square.

"Mommy," Josh said, as I was buckling in. "We need to figure out costumes for Spike and Tinkerbell." His tone suggested that he was being deliberately and commendably calm in the face of a massive oversight on the part of his unfortunate parents.

"Well, dogs don't have to have costumes, you know," I began.

"Mom-my," Josh moaned.

"Noah's cat is going to be a unicorn," Jamie said. "And Mason's dog is going to be an Ewok."

Well, that answered the question of where the pet costume idea came from.

"We have to think of something even better for Tink and Spike," Josh said.

"I'll think of something," I said.

Maybe they'd forget about the dogs' costumes by the time we got home. I didn't much mind the idea of trying to put a costume on Tinkerbell, Rob's enormous Irish wolfhound, who was a mellow soul and would put up with almost any kind of human nonsense as long as there was hope of a treat afterward. But Spike, our eight-and-a-half-pound fur-ball, had not acquired the nickname "the Small Evil One" for nothing. I shuddered at the idea of putting a costume on him.

Then again, Spike was besotted with the twins and had never once bitten either of them in spite of what even I, their doting mother, recognized as extreme provocation. Maybe if the boys put it on him?

I'd worry about that later. It would make a nice change from worrying about murder and burglary. I followed the boys as they scampered toward the library door.

The walk leading up to the library was lined with what I thought of as middle-of-the-road pumpkins—not too scary looking to pass muster in the daytime, but not so cutesy that they'd be out of place when Caerphilly flipped into the Night Side. Inside, every room was festooned with black and orange crepe paper garlands, smiling pumpkins, happy ghosts, and fierce black cats. And displays of Halloween-themed books were everywhere. Collections of ghost stories, for children and adults. Nonfiction books on haunted houses. A major in-festation of vampires and zombies in the young adult section. Manuals on pumpkin carving and Halloween party decora-tions. Halloween-themed mysteries in the mystery fiction section—who knew so many authors had chosen to set mur-ders in the spooky season? An exhibit on Ray Bradbury in the science fiction and fantasy section, featuring *October Country*, *The Halloween Tree*, and *A Graveyard for Lunatics*.

We had arrived just in time for a special Halloween story hour, and the boys happily scampered to take their seats. I waved to the reader—one of Michael's grad students who was planning a career in children's theater—and left the boys in her charge while I roamed around the library, snapping pictures of some of the books on display with my cell phone, as a reminder to come back and check them out when I actually had some free time to read them.

Well, when the festival was over, and my free time was back to its normal, not-quite-nonexistent level.

I spotted Ms. Ellie Draper, the head librarian, carrying a stepladder down one of the aisles, and followed to see if she needed help. Or, rather, if I could offer to do something that a woman in her seventies might be better off not attempting to do atop a stepladder. She spotted me as she was setting it up.

"You're a bit taller than me," she said. "Can you reattach that?" She handed me a small two-sided adhesive patch and gestured up toward a poster that had come undone at one corner and was flapping down and in danger of falling.

I climbed up and performed the repair, revealing a poster printed in bright orange and black that proclaimed LIVE DANGEROUSLY! READ A BANNED BOOK! followed by the titles of fifteen famous books that had suffered banning.

"Banned book week was last month." Ms. Ellie nodded with approval of my handiwork, so I climbed down. "But I left it up because it fits the color scheme."

"Nice," I said.

And then it occurred to me that Ms. Ellie, both as a librarian and as a longtime resident, was something of an authority on town history. If the murder had anything to do with the contents of the museum . . .

"By the way," I asked aloud. "Have you been to see Dr. Smoot's new town museum?"

"Not yet." She frowned slightly. "Frankly, I've been a little afraid to. I'm not sure I want to see what kind of a picture he's painting of us. And since I'm not the world's most tactful person, I'm not sure I want him around when I take my first look. There could be swearing involved."

"Want a sneak preview?" I asked. "I have pictures."

I held up my phone, with one of the pictures on screen.

"I would love a sneak preview," she said, peering at the phone. "But not on that thing. Come with me."

She led me back through the "staff only" door and down the hall to her small but welcoming office.

"Sit," she said. "I'm pretty sure I have the cable to fit this. I can copy your museum pictures to my computer and we can look at them in comfort. There we go."

As we waited for the copying process to finish, Ms. Ellie began clicking through the first pictures. She seemed to find the non-wax waxworks as silly as I did. But she rather liked the wartime photos.

"Very nice," she said. "I must see if I can get copies of these for the library. As soon as Halloween's over we're going to put up a Veterans' Day display. I'll ask Dr. Smoot."

"Better yet, ask Fred down at the *Caerphilly Clarion*." I pointed to the small line at the bottom of one of the accompanying placards, which informed us that the photo in question was from our local weekly's files.

"You're right," she said. "And your photos of the photos will let me start planning our exhibit. Dr. Smoot doesn't really have very much information here, does he? I need to do some research!" She said this in the same tone the boys would use to announce that they'd found a stash of candy.

"I was hoping you'd feel inspired to research," I said. "You heard about the murder, right? It could have something to do with the contents of the museum." I clicked through until I found one of the pictures of Arabella's dress, and explained about the article the chief had found in the dead man's pocket.

"Oh, dear." She frowned and peered over her glasses at the bloodstained dress. "Let's hope not. But yes, I will definitely let you know if I find anything that would suggest a motive for murder."

"And the chief," I said.

"Of course."

"Ellie?" One of the other librarians stuck her head into the office. "Chief's on TV."

Ms. Ellie reached up and turned on a tiny TV sitting on a nearby shelf. The earnest face of a young newscaster from one of the Richmond TV stations filled the miniature screen.

"—from the mayor and the chief of police of Caerphilly," he said. Ms. Ellie and I both frowned—he'd mispronounced the name of our town. Then the screen cut to a shot of Randall and the chief standing in front of the police station, with a dozen reporters surrounding them.

"This morning at approximately nine thirty a.m., two local citizens found a body in the woods outside Caerphilly," the chief said.

"Nice that he didn't mention the zoo," I said.

"The deceased has been identified as a Mr. James Green, originally from Fresno, California," the chief went on. "Cause of death was a single gunshot to the head. We're treating this as a homicide. We ask anyone who has information related to the case to contact the Caerphilly PD." The number flashed on the screen, and the dozen reporters began shouting out questions.

"Do you have any suspects?"

"Could it have been a suicide?"

"Will you be canceling the rest of your Halloween Festival?"

Randall stepped forward when he heard that question and did a pretty decent job of conveying the notion that while they had no reason to believe the murder had anything to do with the festival, the town was taking every possible precaution to ensure the safety of the visitors and that visitors should feel free to enjoy themselves at the festival while taking reasonable precautions.

The channel cut to a photo of the victim, who didn't look any more prepossessing alive than he had when I'd seen him—although it was obviously a DMV photo, which meant we should probably make allowances. Then the face of the very earnest young newscaster reappeared.

"Anyone with any information about this case should contact the Caerphilly Police Department," he said—once again mispronouncing the town.

"Care-FILLY!" Ms. Ellie and I shouted back in unison. Then the newscaster began telling us about something the House of Delegates was up to and Ms. Ellie turned off the TV.

"Well, at least they've put a name to him now," she said. "That's progress. I'll see what I can make of these photos. Especially Arabella's."

I left her studying them and returned to the public area of the library, where Michael's student was finishing up the story hour. And a good thing, too, because I don't think I could have torn the boys away if she was still reading.

Just as I was getting into the car, my phone rang.

"Do you want to eat Baptist, Episcopalian, or Catholic for dinner?" Michael asked. "I have had it up to here with students and am in no mood to cook, and I assume if you've been dealing with the tourists all day you probably feel the same way. I'm dropping by the food tents on my way home."

"Ham, chicken, or fried fish?" I asked the boys.

"Yes," Josh said.

"All of them," Jamie agreed.

"I heard that," Michael said. "I'll surprise you."

He ended up bringing some of each, which met with the boys' approval. They consumed fried fish, hush puppies, fried chicken, mashed potatoes, ham, corn on the cob, Greek salad, and cupcakes with an enthusiasm that warmed my heart.

And in such quantities that I wondered, not for the first time, how we'd manage to keep them fed by the time they turned into teenagers.

"Don't eat all the vegetables," I warned. "We need to save some for Rose Noire."

Perhaps it was my imagination, but being warned off the vegetables did seem to increase their consumption, if only slightly. And Michael had brought such quantities that it wasn't as if Rose Noire was in any danger of going hungry.

Though I was a little worried when she came in. She had offered to watch the boys while Michael and I went out on patrol, but she looked so beat that I wasn't sure she'd be up to it.

"Are you going to be okay here tonight?" I asked.

"Yes, I'll be fine," she said. "In fact, it will do me good to spend some time with pure, innocent, loving children."

"I thought you were babysitting Josh and Jamie," I said. "Who are these paragons you're watching instead?"

"They're mischievous, but not evil," she said. "Sorry to be so down. I had some customers today who really disturbed me. They were asking for things like black candles and Jimson weed and—well, things I don't sell because there just aren't that many good uses for them. Good as in positive, life-affirming."

"Good as in the opposite of evil," I said. "I understand."

"They're probably not actually evil," she said. "They're probably just going through a phase. Acting out. Rebelling. But still—I don't want them to hurt themselves or anyone else. So after I closed up the booth, I stayed on for another hour just infusing all my herbs with as much positive energy as I could. I feel completely drained. But—the boys will help me recharge!"

She beamed over at them. I hoped she wasn't taking too

close a look at them, lest she change her mind about recharging with them. Josh had stuck a straw in each nostril and was snorting and pretending to be a monster. Jamie was biting into a cupcake, methodically adding a layer of chocolate frosting on top of the barbecue sauce that already covered most of the lower half of his face.

"That's great," I said aloud. "And remember, Michael's mother is coming sometime tomorrow to help over the weekend."

Actually, what she'd said was that she wanted to come up to see the boys in their Halloween costumes and spend some time with them. But I was pretty sure when she saw how chaotic our lives were at the moment she'd pitch in. And in fact, as long as she pitched in, I didn't even care if she decided to reorganize the contents of our kitchen cabinets again.

Armed with the knowledge that Rose Noire was actually eager to spend time with Josh and Jamie, Michael and I finished our dinner and even managed to get the boys reasonably clean and stuffed into pajamas. By the time we donned our costumes—the general and the swordswoman again— and took off, Rose Noire had them playing Parcheesi and eating popcorn.

I took one last look at this comforting domestic scene before we headed out into the Night Side.

Chapter 14

Night was falling by the time we took off for town. The ride was peaceful at first, but as we drew closer to town we began to see spillover from the festival. One farmer had turned his field into a parking lot and was having his son shuttle people to and from the town square in a small cattle truck. Another farmer had rented a dozen porta-potties and posted a sign offering his fields for "no-frills camping." There were probably other such entrepreneurs along the other roads leading into town.

We parked the car at the college parking lot and set out to patrol on foot for a while. Down at the town square the craftspeople had mostly shut up their booths. The food tents were closing up as well. Only the ice cream and soft drink vendors were still there. Here in town, the action was winding down.

Make that the official action. There were still quite a few people there, and they weren't all lining up for the refreshments or the porta-potties. Throughout the square masked musicians with guitars, drums, harps, flutes, portable keyboards, and who knows how many other instruments were playing, singly or in groups. More costumed revelers were listening, or dancing to the music—dancing in a variety of styles that were as varied as the music, which ranged from Bach minuets to rap.

And groups of people were talking, debating, flirting, and arguing. Was this merely a lively social scene or were some of the live action role players—LARPers—Rob had told me about, playing out dramatic scenarios of some kind on the streets of Caerphilly?

After we'd been patrolling for a while, I decided that the mixed groups were probably just socializing. The zombie Nixon flirting with the vampire French maid . . . the Frankenstein's monster arguing with the Freddy Krueger over whether to stay at the square or board one of the shuttles . . . the Pillsbury Doughboy taking a selfie with the two scantily clad lady vampires.

But the groups of people in Goth-themed clothing who all wore ribbon rosettes somewhere on their costumes—I'd bet anything they were part of a game. Especially since they tended to clump together in small groups of people with the same color rosette and prowl around together until they ran into a group with a different-colored rosette and acted out some kind of incomprehensible scenario.

"Is there a reason we're following the Goth vamps?" Michael asked at one point.

"They seem to be playing a game," I said.

"Yeah. But not necessarily the game we're worried about."

He was probably right. The Goth vamps, as he called them, seemed to be mainly a social group. We'd been drifting in the wake of one group of seven with purple ribbons for an hour or more, and so far none of them had done anything suspicious. They hadn't brandished fake body parts, nibbled insects, or menaced any of the many pumpkins they'd passed, and they were certainly far enough from the zoo and any of the graveyards. Of course, if one of their members were participating in the scavenger hunt they could have already finished their tasks for the day. Maybe they were just killing time, waiting for the next list.

Or maybe they were too caught up in their own game to be bothered with the scavenger hunt.

"You're right," I said. "I don't understand what they're doing, but it doesn't seem to have anything to do with our scavenger hunt. And we're not really following them, just drifting in the same direction."

"Let's drift in another direction, then," he said. "I think that purple crew is starting to notice us. We don't want to make the tourists too nervous."

We had been walking down the street along one side of the town square. The chief had closed it and the other three streets that enclosed the square to vehicular traffic at sundown, turning the area into a giant pedestrian mall. When we reached the far end of the street, the vampire posse turned right, obviously intending to continue circling the mall.

"Let's keep on straight," I said. "And catch a shuttle out to the Haunted House."

As we continued our course, I noticed that several of the purple-ribboned vampires were turning back to check on us. On impulse, I smiled and waved to them. They all looked offended and embarrassed and hurried out of sight.

"I meant that as a friendly gesture," I said with a sigh.

"Perhaps you destroyed their illusion that their cloaks of invisibility are working," Michael suggested.

Out at the Haunted House, things were hopping. Several members of my Goblin Patrol were keeping order in the long line of people waiting for their turn to go inside. The Ferris wheel, the merry-go-round, the tilt-a-whirl, and all the other midway rides were in dizzying motion, their orange lights twinkling. The barkers were calling customers to the games of skill and chance. We watched a ghost, a mummy, and a life-sized Barbie doll tossing Ping-Pong balls into fish bowls. Vampires firing toy guns at bats that fluttered by on sticks and strings. Batman tossing baseballs at targets, attempting to win a prize for a demure geisha. Cleopatra and Charlie Chaplin pitching darts at pumpkin-shaped targets.

I was relieved to see that zombies were able to enjoy cotton candy, and that vampires were not repelled by garlic-laden Italian sausages.

The hours wore on, and only once did we encounter anything that seemed related to the scavenger hunt, when a woman dressed as Pocahontas found a rubber finger in her buttered popcorn. I consoled her with a sheaf of the bright orange tickets visitors used to pay for rides and games, all the while glancing around to see if anyone was paying particular attention. But if anyone was, Michael and I couldn't tell.

The Fun Fair closed at midnight, and by 1:00 A.M. the area around the Haunted House was more or less empty. A few dozen costumed revelers were still there, standing in small groups or sitting in twos or threes against the fence. But then the last shuttle arrived—a horse-drawn shuttle, with two powerful Percherons pulling a hay wagon. The stragglers all boarded it, and we watched as it slowly rattled toward town.

Michael and I did a last check around the perimeter of the Haunted House, making sure the gates were closed and that no one was hiding in the shrubbery. Inside the house, the lights were all off, except for one on the top floor.

As we were getting into our car, another car slowed and stopped by ours. I watched it warily until the passenger-side front window rolled down to reveal Caroline Willner. A man I recognized as one of Grandfather's longtime volunteer helpers was driving, and Grandfather appeared to be dozing in the backseat.

"All's quiet at the zoo," she said. "And in addition to our Brigade members, we've got several of Rob's technicians staying on to mind the cameras."

"Was it a quiet day?" I asked.

She shook her head.

"We caught several people trying to cut through the mesh between the bats and the humans in the Bat Cave," she said. "Not sure what they thought they'd do once they got out into the guano piles. And we had to shoo a bunch of people away from the wolves and the tigers at closing time. But no more fake body parts. And if anyone managed to break in after we closed, they did a darn fine job of eluding us. Everything's going great so far, and everything seems secure. Time we hit the hay. I'm half dead, and I think your Grandfather's asleep in the backseat."

"Am not," Grandfather muttered.

"See you tomorrow," I said.

"Time for us to head home, I think," Michael said. "And leave the patrolling to . . . others."

"You were about to say 'younger people,' weren't you?" I asked.

"Less encumbered people," he said. "People who don't have to get up with the dawn to get two small boys ready for school. Some of them younger. Not all."

"Good idea," I said. "With any luck, the worst is over for tonight. Tomorrow night's going to be worse."

And I didn't have to mention that Saturday, Halloween itself, would be the worst of all. How had we ever let Randall talk us into this?

As Michael navigated his way through town, I called Charlie Gardner, my second-in-command, to let him know I was turning over the helm to him.

"Good idea," he said. "You need the rest. I'll see you tomorrow."

"Call me if anything dire happens," I said.

"If it's dire enough to be worth waking you for, sure," he said.

Michael and I were both quiet for most of the way home, but it was the comfortable silence of two people who don't have to talk to be in sync. We were almost in sight of the house when he finally spoke.

"I've got my graduate directing seminar all morning," he said. "And a blasted departmental meeting in the afternoon."

"That's okay," I said. "The Night Side's when I really want your company."

"That's what I figured."

We crept quietly into the house. Most of the lights were out, which meant that Rose Noire had probably fallen into bed as soon as the boys had settled.

Josh and Jamie were both sleeping peacefully. Jamie appeared to have been making yet another costume, this one involving quite a lot of orange and black construction paper that now lay in shreds all over his room. Josh had been drawing pumpkins again, and had posted the fiercest one on the outside of his door.

Michael fell asleep as soon as his head hit the pillow—an ability I envied. I lay awake for a while, thinking over my day.

I was just falling asleep when I heard the front door open and close again. Furtive steps ascended the stairs. Probably Rob, coming home late and trying not to wake anyone.

I got out of bed and made my way quietly to the bedroom door. Just then I heard a loud thud.

"Bother," muttered a voice.

I opened the door and stuck my head out. My brother was halfway up the stairs to the third floor, rubbing his shin.

"Rob?"

He turned and peered back down the stairway at me.

"You okay?" I stepped out into the hall and shut the door behind me.

"Just tired," he said. "Which makes me clumsy. Given how early I got up to start my Goblin Patrol duties, I should have gone to bed hours ago. But we've all been working on your scavenger hunt thing."

"No luck yet?"

He shook his head.

"Sorry," I said. "I know it's frustrating. But it was a long shot."

"No," he said. "It's not a long shot. At least it shouldn't be. Under normal circumstances, my guys should be able to find whoever's doing this game like that." He snapped his fingers. "There are places people go to plan things like this, or discuss them, and there's nothing about this on any of them. That's not right."

"So it was planned by someone who doesn't usually do stuff like this?" I asked.

"Bingo." He sat down on the steps and looked less tired somehow. "And you know what else is wrong? Nobody's talking about it online. And they should be. Maybe you can plan something like this all by yourself, or with a small group, but at some point you have to recruit people to play it, and that's pretty hard to do without leaving some traces online."

"So you're at a dead end?"

"Not quite. We have a theory." He grinned. "Okay, some of my guys who are a lot more tech savvy than me came up with a theory, but it sounds good to me."

"Let's have it." I sat down on the step below him.

"We think whoever started this game found players through social media," he said.

"You've lost me already," I said. "Like Facebook and Twitter and things like that?"

"Halloween in Caerphilly's all over the social media, thanks to Lydia."

"Lydia?" Probably not tactful to sound so surprised.

"Yeah." Rob grimaced. "She hasn't done anything else useful that I know of, but she has plastered the festival all over the Internet. It has its own Facebook page, and a Tumblr page, and a blog—you name it. People are tweeting that they're going to the Halloween Festival, and liking the Festival Page on Facebook and using it to arrange to meet up with friends. So our theory is that whoever organized this game watched social media for people who said they were coming to the festival, and then contacted them and recruited them for the game."

"And that wouldn't show up to your guys?"

"No, because they're not doing it publicly," he said. "I mean, it's not like they'd go to the Festival Facebook page and say 'hey, anyone interested in playing a kind of scavenger hunt that involves committing a bunch of misdemeanors, contact me at my real name and my very traceable real e-mail address.' They'd do it behind the scenes. Private messages. Or e-mails. In some cases, if people aren't careful with their privacy settings, you can find out their e-mails or even their phone numbers on these social media sites. I'd be surprised if the participants didn't get an e-mail from someone inviting them and warning them not to tell anyone else."

"Makes sense," I said. "If we can ever get Justin Klapcroft to talk, we'll find out."

"Although talking with him may not help track the organizer down," Rob said. "If I were running something like this that crossed the line over into illegal stuff, I'd set up a free e-mail someplace—you know, Hotmail, Yahoo, Gmail—and make sure I never accessed it from anyplace but a public computer. It could be difficult, if not impossible, to trace them. And by the way, that's another thing—this game incites people to break the law." Was that Rob's law school training bubbling up out of the past, or was he quoting one of the Mutant Wizards attorneys. "That's not typical. A LARP, for example—live action role-playing game—they're always careful to steer clear of anything illegal. But whoever's organizing this thing either doesn't know any better or doesn't care."

"So if it's not organized by someone who usually does this kind of thing, odds are your guys don't know him and can't find him."

"It's just going to take longer," Rob said. "We're combing through social media for anything that even hints that people are going off behind the scene to plan something like this. And if people are doing this, I bet some of them are posting selfies of themselves climbing over the zoo wall or sneaking away with a pumpkin."

"Who would be stupid enough to post a selfie of himself committing a crime?" I asked.

"Plenty of people." Rob looked as if he were shocked by my social media naïveté. "People are committing murder and hate crimes and tweeting about it. So why would they draw the line at stealing pumpkins?"

"So you're looking for self-incriminating tweets and posts," I said.

"And we're also setting out lures," he said. "I had a couple of guys online all day pretending to be tourists here for the festival and looking for something more exciting to do. I've got another one who's posting things that are sort of designed to make him look as if he is already in the game. Chief knows about it, by the way," he added. "If anything comes of it, I'll fill you in tomorrow morning."

With that he stood up and trudged the rest of the way up to the third floor.

I went back into the master bedroom. Michael was still sound asleep. I crept back into bed and wondered how long it would take me to find the off button in my brain so I could follow his example. And then I realized, with relief, that I was already dozing off.

I woke up again sometime in the wee small hours and my brain immediately kicked into overdrive, in a way that did not bode well for my getting back to sleep anytime soon. I deliberately avoided looking at the alarm clock, because I knew finding out the time would only make me feel more tired than I already was. I tossed and turned—but as gently as possible because Michael was sleeping quite soundly. Then a beeping noise began emanating from his side of the bed.

"Your pager's going off." I shook him gently, because I knew otherwise I'd have to listen to the pager for several minutes before he dragged himself to consciousness.

He pawed at the night table on his side of the bed until he found the beeper and pressed the right button.

"Box fourteen oh four for the structure fire. At Dr. Smoot's Haunted House. Engine companies fourteen and two, truck twelve, rescue squad two, ambulance fourteen respond. Oh four twenty-seven."

"On my way," he muttered, although obviously the pager couldn't hear him.

I felt a small twinge of satisfaction that Debbie Ann had taken my recommendation and started giving the call locations in terms the firemen could understand. At least when it came to landmarks like the Haunted House, the Caerphilly Zoo, or the New Life Baptist Church, no one in town actually knew the address, but they all knew exactly where to show up if you gave them the name.

And then it hit me. The Haunted House.

Chapter 15

"It's the Haunted House that's on fire," I said. "I'm coming, too. I'll take my own car so I won't slow you down, and I'll stay out of everyone's way, but this is going to affect the festival, and it could have something to do with the murder and the break-ins and—"

"No problem." He was heading out the bedroom door. "I might need you there to give me intravenous coffee. Is it really past four thirty in the morning?"

"Gee, thanks," I said. "So far I'd avoided looking at the clock. Aren't you going to need your shoes? And your pants?" To say nothing of his turnout gear, but first things first.

"Oops." He looked sheepish. "I guess I'm not as awake as I thought I was."

While Michael finished dressing, I dodged upstairs to make sure Rob, the other volunteer fireman in the house, was also awake. I met Rose Noire in the hall on the same errand.

"I'm awake, I'm awake," we heard Rob groan from behind his door.

"Keep an eye on the boys, okay?" I said to Rose Noire. "I'm going to tag along to see how much of a crisis this is for the festival."

"The festival that you're not in charge of organizing," she reminded me.

"This could be a security issue," I said.

"Of course," she said.

Just then Rob burst out of his room and clattered down the stairs. I followed him.

Michael and Rob took off in Rob's car—though I was relieved to see that Michael was driving, since Rob's eyes were still at half mast. I followed almost as soon as they left, but since I was observing the speed limit, I arrived at the Haunted House several minutes behind them.

There was definitely a fire. The firefighters had already set up a couple of portable spotlights, which illuminated a plume of smoke.

"What happened?" Dad had appeared at my side.

"Listening to the police and fire band again?" I asked. "I just got here myself, so your guess is as good as mine."

"Smoke's coming from this side of the house." We were standing in front, but slightly to the right of the Haunted House. Yes, smoke was definitely coming from the right. A lot of smoke. Was this the good kind of smoke that meant the firefighters almost had the blaze out already or the bad kind that meant we were in for a long, dangerous night? Michael would know but unfortunately I didn't.

I was reassured to see that Dad was holding his old-fashioned black medical bag. Although I hoped he wouldn't need it.

"What's in the right side?" he asked.

"On the ground floor, the living room," I said. "Not much in it apart from a nice black basalt fireplace and a ton of cheap Halloween decorations. I don't remember precisely what rooms are there on the second floor. Probably the vampire coffin and the witch's potion lab. In other words, more cheap Halloween stuff."

"Not good," Dad said. "The cheap decorations are mostly either paper or highly flammable plastic. Good fuel, and the plastic could cause some pretty nasty fumes."

"Let's hope the fire's not there, then," I said. "Though I don't think we want the fire on the third floor, either. That's the part that's not open to the public because Dr. Smoot's using it as his living quarters."

"The smoke appears to be coming from the basement," Dad said. "The far right end of the basement. What's down there?"

"The museum. Though I'm not sure which part of the museum. The spiral staircase leading down to it threw off my sense of direction. Can you see the outside stairwell? That would tell me whether it's the non-wax wax museum end or the historic artifact end that's burning."

"There." Dad pointed to where we could see, behind some shrubbery, the head of a fireman appearing to rise out of the ground. Apparently he was climbing up the outdoor stairway from the basement.

"Damn," I said. "If part of the museum has to burn, why not the wax museum end? The end that's on fire is where the artifacts are. Some of them valuable." Unless the Griswalds and Mrs. Paltroon had hurried to claim their valuables.

Dad nodded, and we watched for a few moments. The firefighters had broken through the front door, and I could see a couple of them doing something in the living room, but most of them were clustered at the right side of the house or had gone around back. Several of them were holding the hose, soaking something in the basement. Three police vehicles were also on the scene, though the officers were keeping their distance. I spotted Vern Shiffley standing in the open driver's door of his cruiser and leaning on the roof, talking on his police radio.

"Yeah," he was saying. "There's no big rush. The fire department's evidence eradication team is still at work."

I decided it probably wasn't the time to point out that saving lives and property was the fire department's mission, and evidence eradication merely an unfortunate but unavoidable by-product.

The chief's car pulled up and parked just behind Vern's

cruiser. The chief got out and the two of them began talking about something.

I noticed a small flurry of action at the side of the house. Then two of the firefighters appeared, carrying a stretcher, with the EMT walking at their side.

Dad dashed over to meet them. The firefighters stopped by the ambulance, and after Dad had examined their patient for ten or twenty seconds, he gestured. The firefighters hauled the stretcher into the ambulance. Then they hopped back out again and one of them raced around to the front of the truck and threw himself into the driver's seat. Dad and the EMT scrambled inside the ambulance with seconds to spare before the driver started the engine and raced off.

The remaining firefighter hurried over to where Vern and the Chief were standing. He pushed back his helmet and I could see that it was Michael. I drifted closer so I could hear what was going on.

"Who was that?" the chief asked.

"Dr. Smoot," Michael said. "Good thing Meg's dad showed up. Smoot's only slightly burned, but it looks as if someone hit him over the head before the fire started. At least he's alive."

Something about the way he emphasized "he" worried me.

"Do you mean someone else isn't?" I asked.

Michael nodded slightly.

"Who?" the chief asked.

"None of us could recognize him," Michael said. "And no, I don't mean that he was badly burned. He's hardly burned at all. Someone shot him."

The chief nodded and set his jaw.

"A tourist?" I asked.

"Young man in his twenties wearing a zombie costume," Michael said. "So yeah, probably a tourist." He turned to Chief Burke. "Chief Featherstone says he'll be releasing the scene to you any minute now."

"Good. Horace here?"

"Over there." Vern pointed to one of the cars, and I recognized the familiar figure of my cousin Horace standing beside it. He was holding a small suitcase—his forensic kit. Horace usually loved the occasional cases that called for him to use his crime scene training. But if it really was murder—the second in as many days . . . poor Horace.

I glanced over toward the house and saw a figure approaching us. He was only a silhouette against the floodlights, but I had no trouble recognizing Jim Featherstone, Caerphilly's fire chief. His barrel chest and pipe cleaner legs were unmistakable.

"It's a nasty one," he said when he reached us. "Pretty sure it's arson, so I'll be working closely with you. Though it's also possible that was only a stupid accident. Someone on the scene was carrying an ordinary candle. That seems to have been the ignition source."

"Let's take a look," Chief Burke said.

They set out toward a spotlighted area. Horace scurried over to follow them. Michael and I looked at each other briefly, and then fell into step behind them.

When we reached the house, I fell back. Michael went to help some of the other firefighters, who were packing up their gear. The two chiefs disappeared through a break in the hedge that ran all along the back of the house, about two or three feet from the foundation. I remembered seeing that hedge from the stairwell—was it only yesterday?

The chiefs' heads descended about a foot and then stopped, so I could still see them above the hedge. They stood in silence for at least a minute before Chief Burke spoke.

"Looks as if someone shot him in the back of the head while he was on his way out. Your people find a gun?"

"No." Chief Featherstone shook his head.

"Let's go take a look on the inside," Chief Burke said.

"Horace, you can get started here. We'll go in the other way, to avoid disturbing the body."

The chiefs emerged from the stairwell and Horace slipped through the gap in the hedge and disappeared.

"I should get Aida Butler down here," the chief said. "She inspected the basement yesterday. She might have some idea what's been disturbed."

"Chief," I said.

They both looked up.

"Chiefs," I amended. "I was also down there in the basement yesterday. Chief Burke, you may remember that Dr. Smoot complained of an intruder."

"That's what Aida was checking out," Chief Burke said to Chief Featherstone. "We don't doubt that someone was sneaking around, and maybe trying to get in, but she could find no evidence of anything amiss in the basement."

"Neither could I," I said. "But remember that I was going to go back and take a lot of pictures in the Haunted House? So we could tell if anyone left any new fake body parts there? I included the museum in my picture taking. In fact, I probably took more there—especially in the end where the fire was—than anywhere else." I held up my phone.

"Any particular reason?" Chief Featherstone sounded puzzled, but not displeased.

"That end of the room was where Dr. Smoot kept finding the intruders," I said, pointing to the smoke-wreathed right side of the house. "And I figured it was probably because they were getting in through the door to the outside, but then again it was always possible that they were going after something at that end of the museum. So I took pictures, intending to study them later and see if I spotted anything of interest."

"And did you?" Chief Featherstone asked. "Spot anything, that is."

"Haven't had time to study them yet," I said. "But those photos make up a pretty detailed picture of what that end of the basement looked like yesterday morning. I e-mailed them to Chief Burke yesterday."

"E-mail them to Chief Featherstone when you get a chance," Chief Burke said. "And since you're here—come with us."

"Chiefs," Michael said. "Unless either of you needs me, I'm going to head home so at least one of us is there when the boys wake up. And then take them to school."

"Good idea," said Chief Featherstone.

"And I'll try not to keep Meg any longer than I have to," Chief Burke said.

Michael headed off, while I followed the chiefs around to the front of the house, through the remnants of the entrance door, and down the steep, winding stairs to the basement.

"Notice anything different?" Chief Burke asked when we were all standing at the bottom of the stairs.

"It was a lot dryer yesterday," I said, stepping out of the puddle in which I'd landed.

"Sorry about that," Chief Featherstone said. "We did have a pretty serious fire to put out."

"Not a complaint, just an observation," I said. "The outside door was closed yesterday, and hidden behind those black curtains." I pointed to the waterlogged remnants of the curtains, which had been partially dragged down from their rods. "There were a lot of pictures hanging on the walls—probably knocked off by the fire hoses. And that case at the end wasn't smashed," I added. "It was full of jewelry."

"Valuable jewelry?" Chief Burke sounded slightly incredulous. Looking around at the rest of the museum I could see why.

"Only one piece that's actually valuable," I said.

I pulled out my phone and clicked through the pictures until I'd reached the one of the jewelry case. The chiefs inspected it, and then we made our way carefully to the other end of the room. Between the broken glass and the stuff that had been knocked off the walls and shelves by the force of the fire hose, there were a lot of obstacles underfoot.

"Try not to touch anything if you can help it," the chief reminded us. "Horace is still processing the outside. Normally I'd be keeping all of us out until he'd finished in here, but the crime scene's already pretty compromised by the firefighters' efforts. Unavoidably, of course," he added, with a nod to Chief Featherstone.

We reached the case, and I held out my phone again so we could all compare the photo with the real thing.

"Aha!" Chief Featherstone said. "That huge ruby ring is missing."

"Appears to be the only thing missing," the chief said, flicking his eyes back and forth between the picture and the case.

"Then whoever took it wasn't a very savvy jewel thief," I said. "The ruby ring's a fake."

"Then which is the valuable piece?" Chief Burke asked.

"Wait," Chief Featherstone said. "Let me guess. That black sparkly thing." He pointed to a black necklace. "Henry, what's your guess?"

"I wouldn't begin to know," the chief said. "Maybe that crown?"

"The black sparkling thing is a piece of Victorian mourning jewelry," I said. "The sparkly black stones are jet, which is not all that valuable. And the crown is the one they used to use to crown Miss Caerphilly County back in the fifties and sixties. Rhinestones."

"And you know this how?" Chief Burke asked. "I don't see any information tags."

"There were yesterday," I said. "And I read them. And also I can zoom in on the pictures on my phone, so I don't need to worry about the tags that probably got washed away by the fire hoses."

"The tags are here." Chief Featherstone was peering into the case. "They're just not waterproof. So which one is the valuable piece?"

"The cat," I said.

They both stared at it.

"That thing?" Chief Featherstone said. "Looks like a piece of yard-sale bargain-box crap."

"The gems are real," I said. "It was specially made for the Duchess of Windsor."

Chief Burke was peering over his glasses at it.

"No accounting for taste, is there?" he remarked. "I'd have taken it for a cheap dime-store trinket."

"And evidently so did our intruder," I said. "So the good news is that we don't have a brilliant, successful international jewel thief plying his trade in Caerphilly."

"And the bad news is that someone may have killed one person and seriously injured another to gain possession of something that actually is a dime-store trinket," Chief Featherstone said.

"I doubt that the ring was the actual motive for the break-in," Chief Burke said. "More likely the perpetrator snatched it in the hope of distracting us from his real motive."

"Which was?" Chief Featherstone asked.

"Well, if I knew that, I'd be making an arrest right now," the chief said. "Instead of scouring this blasted basement for any clue to what could possibly be worth burning down a building, killing one human being, and trying to kill another. To say nothing of the possibility that it's all related to yesterday morning's murder."

"Sorry," Chief Featherstone said.

"No, I'm sorry." Chief Burke sighed and massaged his fore-head for a moment. "Sorry to both of you. I woke up with a headache and it's not getting any better. But there's no use taking my mood out on the people who are trying to help. Jim, anything you can tell me about the origin of this fire could help solve the murder. And Meg—apart from the worthless ring, can you spot anything missing?"

Chief Featherstone handed me his large flashlight and I began to run it over the jumbled contents of the museum.

At first we had a couple of flurries of excitement as I spotted things in my photos that were missing from the museum. A Civil War–era spittoon that had been displayed on a side table. A pen once used by someone-or-other to sign some kind of important document. Nearly the entire collection of photos of Caerphilly soldiers from past wars. But as we continued to study the wreckage—study it, not sift through it, because we were still waiting for Horace to do his official forensic sifting—we managed to spot the spittoon, the pen, and several of the missing photos. They weren't missing at all, just blown out of place by the fire hoses. Odds were Horace would find the rest when he processed the scene.

"We've probably done as much as we can for now," the chief said. "Jim, you want to stay here and work with Vern and Horace?"

Chief Featherstone nodded.

"I've got to get back to the station," Chief Burke said. "See if news of this second murder makes Mr. Klapcroft rethink his decision to talk to me."

"I wouldn't bet on it," I said. "He'll probably be terrified that you'll suspect him of being involved and be more determined than ever to wait for an attorney."

The chief sighed.

"She's right, Henry," Chief Featherstone said. "At least if I were the wayward young rapscallion I was at his age, that's how I'd be thinking."

"Well, then maybe one of those forty-'leven local lawyers

I called yesterday will have returned my call by the time I get back to the station," Chief Burke said. "We should be getting out of Horace's way."

I assumed that by "we" he meant mostly me, so I began picking my way back to the stairs.

"Don't take off just yet," the chief said. "I want to ask you something, but I want a word with Horace first."

"I'll wait in the foyer," I said.

Chapter 16

Of course, I have always been constitutionally incapable of merely waiting, so I passed the time by strolling up and down the foyer, peeking into the adjoining rooms to see how much damage had been done. Not much, actually, which probably meant that we could open the Haunted House again shortly after the chief released it. Assuming he did release it before the rapidly approaching end of the festival. And also assuming that news of a second murder didn't send the tourists fleeing.

I was peering down the cellar stairs—okay, I was trying to eavesdrop on what the chief and Horace might be saying—when I was startled by a voice behind me.

"Oh, dear. Dr. Smoot didn't tell me there had been a fire."

I turned to see an odd figure standing in the doorway—a man who would probably have been close to seven feet tall if he stood up straight, but with such a pronounced stoop that he could probably have looked Michael straight in the eye—and Michael was six foot four.

Our visitor was elderly. He had taken off his hat upon entering the Haunted House, and I could see that he had a neat, closely cropped fringe of gray hair around the perimeter of his otherwise bald head. He was holding his hat in fingers so unusually long as to look positively freakish. Under his tent-sized dark gray raincoat I could see gray flannel trousers and galoshes.

"May I help you?" I asked.

"I'm Dr. Cavendish," he said. "I have a seven o'clock appointment with Dr. Smoot."

"I'm sorry," I began. "Dr. Smoot isn't available."

"He was expecting me." Dr. Cavendish hunched his shoulders defensively, which had the unfortunate effect of increasing his resemblance to an oversized vulture.

"I'm sure he was," I said. "Unfortunately, Dr. Smoot isn't here right now. He's in the hospital. Can you tell me what he was expecting you for?"

"Oh, dear." Dr. Cavendish pulled the left side of his raincoat open, revealing a well-worn Harris Tweed jacket beneath. He fished in the jacket pocket with two of those unusually long fingers—was it just my imagination, or did his fingers have more joints than usual? He pulled out a business card, then held it with both hands and presented it to me with a slight bow.

"Thank you." I glanced down at the card, which read G.Q. Cavendish. Fine Art Conservation and Restoration followed by the usual address, telephone, fax, and e-mail information. "Oh! I remember. Dr. Smoot and Mrs. Paltroon both mentioned that you were coming by today to take a look at the portrait."

"Yes." Dr. Cavendish sounded relieved that at least someone was aware of his mission. "May I see it?"

"Let me ask Chief Burke," I said.

"What is he chief of?" Dr. Cavendish looked anxious.

"Chief of Police," I said. "The painting's in the basement, which is technically still a crime scene."

"Crime scene?" Now Dr. Cavendish looked positively alarmed. "Dr. Smoot didn't tell me that there was a crime involved."

"I'm sorry," I said. "It's been a long night and I'm probably not explaining anything very well. There probably wasn't a crime when Dr. Smoot called you. I assume he called a day or two ago to examine the painting, right?"

"Yes," he said, nodding. "He and Mrs. Paltroon both. They informed me that it is a late eighteenth-century family portrait done by an unknown itinerant painter, on loan to the museum. As soon as it arrived, Dr. Smoot noticed that it showed some signs of deterioration. He notified Mrs. Paltroon and they agreed to have me come as soon as possible to determine the cause of the problem and assess whether it was safe to exhibit it here in his museum." He looked around at the waterlogged contents of the living room. "I gather this is not the museum's normal condition."

"We had a fire last night, remember?" I said. "Actually just a few hours ago. Dr. Smoot was injured and another person, apparently an intruder and possibly the cause of the fire, was killed."

"Oh, dear." Dr. Cavendish shook his head in dismay. "They were after the portrait, weren't they? They didn't take it, did they? Or—was it damaged in the fire?"

He looked so pale that I hastened to reassure him.

"If they were after the portrait, they didn't get it," I said. "And the portrait wasn't damaged. Not by the fire, anyway."

He breathed a sigh of such relief that you'd have thought I'd just told him his beloved mother was unharmed.

"Of course," I went on, "it did get a little wet."

"Oh, my goodness." He went pale again. "I must see it. Take me to it at once!"

"Just a second." I walked over to the basement door and called downstairs.

"Chief? May I see you for a moment?"

"Coming."

Chief Burke appeared at the top of the steps, looking distracted. I introduced the two and explained Dr. Cavendish's mission.

"I'd like to see the painting right away," Dr. Cavendish said.

I could tell the chief didn't like being ordered about at his own crime scene.

"And his expert opinion might help you figure out if the painting is valuable enough to have been a motive for what happened last night," I suggested.

The chief studied Dr. Cavendish for a few moments.

"I don't see why you can't take a look at the painting," he said finally. "But don't touch anything else."

He led the way down into the basement and then through the waterlogged room to the end where the painting hung. Dr. Cavendish kept looking around him with alarm, as if expecting something to pop out of the shadows, and his freakishly long fingers twitched convulsively.

"Oh, dear," he said. "Such a lot of damage. Those firemen with their jackboots! Couldn't they have been a bit more careful?"

"They put the fire out before it burned up the whole house and the painting with it," I said. "And if they had to do some damage in the process, it's the arsonist's fault." I decided not to mention that one of the jackbooted firefighters was my husband.

"Here's the picture," the chief said, gesturing toward the wall on which it hung.

"Oh, dear." Dr. Cavendish stood for a few moments and stared, his face disconsolate.

I could see why. Most of the Paltroons looked much the same, misshapen and awkward, with insipid smiles on their heavy-jowled faces. It was probably just my imagination that their painted smiles looked more forced this morning, as if they were resenting the indignities inflicted on them during the night but bravely putting on a good show. And I was definitely only imagining that the painted Mrs. Paltroon had made progress in her attempt to slip off the right side of the painting and escape from her overlarge brood.

But something had changed. All those areas where the paint had been merely a little puckered yesterday were now looking seriously the worse for wear. The wall behind the family was being transformed as little bits of the bland tan color flaked off, revealing that something else had originally been painted underneath. And Mr. Paltroon's fawn-colored coat was almost completely gone, revealing that he'd originally worn a green jacket.

"Fascinating," Dr. Cavendish breathed. "Pentimenti!"

"I beg your pardon?" the chief said.

"A pentimento is a place in a painting where the artist changed his mind," Dr. Cavendish said. "Or repented. Pentimento comes from the Italian for 'repentance.' The artist originally painted something in the background—a landscape would be most common, or possibly a fireplace or fountain. But then for some reason he painted it over with that rather atypical and compositionally unfortunate blank wall. And then changed the green coat to tan."

"Maybe the family didn't like whatever he'd done in the background," I suggested.

"Very possibly." Dr Cavendish was rummaging in his pockets. He fished out a small flashlight and a pair of tweezers. He turned the flashlight on and ran its beam slowly over the damaged areas of the painting.

"Of course," he added, "we usually discover a pentimento in less dramatic ways. Some paints become more transparent over time, so that what was completely obscured begins to be revealed. Other pentimenti are revealed by X-rays or infrared photography. Letting the top layer bubble up from damp conditions and then blowing it off with a fire hose is not a recommended method for investigating pentimenti. But now that it's happened . . .

Here he fell silent, stepped closer to the painting, and studied it with the light of his little flashlight for several minutes.

"I take it back," he said. "Not pentimenti after all. I think it's highly unlikely that the original artist made these changes. I can't be sure until I've done a full analysis, but I would not be surprised at all to find that these alterations were made years, if not decades, after the painting was completed, and by a different hand."

"But why?" The chief sounded puzzled. And I could tell by his expression that he wasn't at all sure any of this would be of the slightest use to him in solving his two murder cases.

"Well, it's possible . . ." Dr. Cavendish's voice trailed off as he reached up with his tweezers to Mr. Paltroon's shoulder and gently took hold of a large paint flake that was clearly on the verge of falling. Removing the flake revealed something else. Mr. Paltroon's coat wasn't just a coat. It had epaulets and gold frogging.

"That's a uniform, isn't it?" I asked.

"Why yes, it is." Dr. Cavendish seemed to find my question hilarious. Or maybe it was something about the uniform that had set him off. He went from a giggle to a guffaw and ended up leaning against the opposite wall with tears streaming down his eyes.

"What's so funny about the uniform?" the chief asked.

This seemed to set Dr. Cavendish off again. The chief and I waited with growing impatience until Dr. Cavendish recovered his composure. He pulled a handkerchief out of his pocket and wiped his eyes.

"I'm sorry," he said. "I forget sometimes that not everyone lives in the eighteenth century as much as I do. I should explain."

"Please do." The chief was clearly getting impatient.

"It's just that the uniform is so obviously the reason they defaced the portrait," he said.

"I don't understand," the chief said. "The Paltroons are quite proud of their ancestor's service in the Continental Army. Why should the uniform upset them?"

"Mrs. Paltroon is pretty much president-for-life of the local DAR," I added.

"Then the restored painting is going to come as rather a shock to her," Dr. Cavendish said. "Because that's the uniform of the British Legion. And an officer's uniform to boot— looks like a captain."

"The British Legion was not on our side, I presume," the chief said.

"No, indeedy," Dr. Cavendish said. "The British Legion was a loyalist regiment. They fought in the South Carolina campaign, under Lieutenant Colonel Banastre Tarleton. Known to the Americans as 'the Butcher,' because of his involvement in the so-called Waxhaw Massacre. He's supposed to have had his men slaughter several hundred American soldiers after they'd surrendered. The British side of it is quite different, of course, and we'll never know for sure what happened. But suffice it to say that if Mrs. Paltroon joined the DAR on the strength of this gentleman's service in the Continental Army, she was flying under very false colors."

We studied the portrait together for a few moments. I'm not sure what the chief and Dr. Cavendish were thinking. I was trying to figure out if there was a way I could manage to be present when Mrs. Paltroon learned the truth about her ancestor. And bring Mother along. She and the snooty Mrs. Paltroon had locked horns more than once.

"So I gather that the painting is fascinating to someone of your profession," I said. "But at the risk of sounding crass, is it worth a lot of money?"

"Well, I've seen some similar paintings bring nice prices at auction," Dr. Cavendish said. "But they would have been pictures by better artists. And in better condition," he added, as another large flake of paint detached itself from the tan background and drifted to the floor. "No, not worth a lot of money. I can't imagine anyone killing anyone over it—unless, of course, Mrs. Paltroon has a violent nature and is pathologically attached to her position in the DAR." He emitted a wheezy chuckle, so I deduced that he was joking. The chief and I, who both knew Mrs. Paltroon, exchanged a worried glance.

"Just how much is not a lot?" the chief asked.

"Oh, dear." Dr. Cavendish waved his long fingers dismissively. "I couldn't possibly give you a good estimate. It would so depend on market conditions at the time of sale. And the alterations significantly reduce the value, and who knows if the human interest story of how they happened would gain any of that back, and it's in such terrible condition—"

"If you had to buy insurance for it, how much would you buy?" I asked.

"I'd go for two hundred thousand," he said briskly. "You'd probably only get half that at auction, but you never know— you might get lucky."

Maybe in Dr. Cavendish's world a hundred thousand dollars wasn't worth killing for, but I had a feeling the chief didn't share that view. And if I were the chief, I'd be checking on how much insurance Mrs. Paltroon had on the damaged painting, and whether she was having any money issues.

I knew better than to tell him, though. He was probably already planning to do so. That was probably why he was scribbling so busily in his notebook. Definitely not a good idea to ask him.

But I could ask Mother if Mrs. Paltroon was strapped for cash.

"May I take this upstairs, where I can continue my examination under better conditions?" Dr. Cavendish asked.

"That's fine," the chief said.

He and I helped Dr. Cavendish take the painting down from the wall.

"I'm not sure we can get it up that circular staircase," I said. "Let's take it up the outside stairs and around front."

That worked fine, although I thought for a moment Dr. Cavendish was going to faint when we passed the place on the stairs where Horace's taped outline of the body was still in place. But then he appeared to remind himself that he was carrying an interesting if not particularly valuable painting and visibly pulled himself together.

We set him up in the dining room, which was on the other side of the house from the fire and thus not filled with puddles.

"Thank you," he said, once we'd set the painting flat on the dining table. "You know, this is quite exciting. I think that back wall's going to turn out to be a painting of George III. Definitely a Tory family!"

With that he appeared to dismiss us from his mind and focus on the painting. The chief and I withdrew to the hallway, then looked back to study Dr. Cavendish for a few moments.

"Seems harmless," I said in an undertone.

"Yes," the chief said. "But we should have someone keep an eye on him. Just on general principles."

"Roger," I said.

"I suppose it's always possible that this is somehow related to the murders," he said. "At least this latest one."

"Mrs. Paltroon, aware of her family secret, and fearing that the deterioration of the painting was about to strip away her claim to being descended from a Revolutionary War hero, attempted to sneak into the museum after hours to steal it back?"

"I said possible," the chief said. "I didn't say likely. And I don't really think even she'd kill someone over the painting, although I don't envy Dr. Cavendish the task of breaking his news to her."

"Yes," I said. "If she had any idea that the painting had the potential to reveal her family skeleton, she'd have locked it away in the attic rather than lend it to Dr. Smoot."

"Precisely," the chief said. "Still, let's keep this to ourselves for the time being. Dr. Cavendish?"

He stepped into the dining room. Dr. Cavendish had donned a headlamp and was using its light to inspect the painting through a magnifying glass. He was bent almost double and resembled some kind of ungainly insect. He didn't appear to have heard the chief or noticed our entrance.

"Dr. Cavendish," the chief repeated.

"This is fascinating!" Dr. Cavendish straightened up and beamed at us, not realizing that his powerful headlamp was shining straight into our eyes. "It will take extensive analysis to prove it, of course, but I can confidently predict that the paint used on these additions will turn out to be of a much later date—probably Victorian."

The chief was normally a very patient man, but I could tell that Dr. Cavendish was getting on his nerves to the point where he was doing his equivalent of my counting to ten before reacting.

"This is fantastic," I said. "And possibly a very important clue in the chief's murder case. Dr. Cavendish—I trust we can rely on your discretion?"

"Of course!" He drew himself up so straight that he knocked one of the hanging rubber bats askew with the top of his head.

"No one must know of this yet." I dropped my voice into a low, conspiratorial tone. "Lives could be at stake—to say nothing of the safety of the painting."

I could tell I'd won him over with that last bit.

"Of course!" he said. "I will keep my findings absolutely confidential until you tell me. And may I suggest that I could make arrangements to transport the painting to a safe location? A climate-controlled location?"

"Can you make it a location nobody but you and I know

about?" the chief said. "Not even Dr. Smoot and the Paltroons, even though they originally hired you? Because if
this painting is connected to the murder . . ."

The chief let his voice trail off. Dr. Cavendish's eyes grew
very big.

"Yes," he said. "I have good contacts at several museums
that would have the proper climate controls, the facilities
I'd need to continue my analysis, and more than adequate
security."

"Make an arrangement, then," the chief said. "Of course,
before we let you leave with the painting, we'll need to know
that you have an alibi for the time of the murder. Where were
you last night between midnight and three a.m.?"

"Somewhere over the Atlantic," Dr. Cavendish said. "I just
flew in from Venice, where I was consulting on the restoration of a Grigoletti."

"Good." The chief was scribbling in his notebook. "I'm
sending a deputy over to guard you and the painting. He'll
check out the details of your alibi. Just a formality, of course,
but we can't take any chances."

"Of course." Dr. Cavendish nodded solemnly. "The safety
of the painting is paramount."

"And your safety," the chief added. "I'll let you get back to
your work."

Was it just my imagination, or did Dr. Cavendish turn
back to the portrait with renewed enthusiasm, now that he
knew it was not only a professional puzzle but also a clue in
a murder?

I followed the chief back into the foyer. He was wearing
an expression that clearly showed that yes, he was capable of
suffering fools, but he wasn't going to be glad about it.

"We may or may not be able to give you the Haunted
House back by your normal opening time today," he said.
"I'll send Vern to interview the doctor and keep watch over

him. It would help if you could play watchdog till Vern gets here. And can you brief Randall?"

"Of course." I wondered if I should remind him that, technically, I wasn't in charge of the festival—just the volunteer security patrols.

"And that Ms. Van Meter, of course," he added.

I nodded. But I as followed him to the front door, I wondered if it would be sufficient if I filled in Randall and asked him to brief Lydia.

We saw Randall standing outside, across the street from the Haunted House. The firefighters had gone, so the immediate area around the house was deserted except for Randall, the deputy guarding the front gate to the house, and two disheveled tourists in vampire costumes who were blinking against the rising sun. I suspected they were on their way to bed rather than already out of it.

"Meg's going to fill you in," the chief said to Randall as he got into his car.

"Mind if we go back inside?" I said. "The chief asked me to keep an eye on Dr. Cavendish."

"On who?"

I explained Dr. Cavendish's presence as we climbed the steps. Randall was listening, but also frowning as he watched the chief drive off.

"Any particular reason why the chief's in such an all-fired hurry to get back to town?" he asked, pausing just outside the front door.

"He's probably eager to find out if this new murder has anything to do with the first one," I said.

"New murder!" Randall looked shaken. "I only heard about the fire. Not Dr. Smoot?"

"No," I said. "Not yet, anyway, and let's hope not at all. Tourist. Possible burglar. Also possible arsonist and attempted murderer of Dr. Smoot, for that matter. And shot in the head, just like the guy from yesterday—although this time in the back of the head. And he was dressed a lot like yesterday's guy, which might not mean much, because half the tourists in town are dressed the same way."

"Damn," Randall said. "This is going to take some dealing with."

We stood in silence for a few moments, gazing at the house.

"Okay, first of all, he wasn't just a tourist," I said. "As I said, he might be a burglar and an arsonist, and at the very least, he was playing a dangerous illegal game."

"Yeah." He nodded. "We need to get that message out."

"And encourage anyone else who's playing the game to talk to the chief."

"I should get back to the office and start writing a statement. Actually, maybe I should go down to the police station and work from there. In case any reporters show up. At least I can take the heat off the chief. Let him work."

He had pulled out his phone and was staring at it.

"Lydia again?" I asked.

"No," he said. "Just checking to see if she responded to the e-mail I sent her when I heard about the fire. Or the text I sent after I got here."

"Maybe she's a late sleeper," I suggested.

"Not usually." He punched some buttons on his phone and held it to his ear. After a few moments an expression of mixed concern and annoyance crossed his face.

"Her voice mail's full," he said. "Which means she probably hasn't even listened to the couple of messages I left her yesterday."

"Annoying as I find Lydia," I said. "I'm starting to worry."

"Me too."

Randall punched a few more buttons while I digested the fact that I'd finally admitted aloud to my dislike for Lydia and Randall hadn't even batted an eye.

"Hey, Branson," he said. "Sorry to bother you so early . . . you're right, but it is pretty early for me now that I'm a city dweller. Look, has my assistant, Lydia, been leaving messages with you by mistake again? . . . Okay, just checking. Haven't heard from her since sometime yesterday afternoon and that seems too good to be true. . . . Yeah, I'd appreciate it."

He hung up.

"She hasn't been calling the feed store by mistake?"

Randall shook his head.

"When was the last time you heard from her?"

He looked down at his phone.

"Two thirteen p.m. yesterday," he said.

We looked at each other for a few minutes.

"Let's go check on her," I said.

"Right," he said. "Mind if we take your car? I rode out with one of the deputies."

"What about Dr. Cavendish?"

"The deputy can watch him till Vern gets here."

We relocated the deputy into the front hall so he could watch both the gate and Dr. Cavendish and hurried out to my car.

"Where to?" I asked. "Town hall?"

"I already know she's not there," he said. "I just came from there. Head for 1510 Pruitt Avenue. You know where that is?"

I nodded and started the car.

I was slightly surprised when we reached 1510 Pruitt Avenue. The street, named after the family who had developed it, was mostly lined with cheaply built townhouses. But the townhouses ended at the 1400s, and the 1500 block was lined with tiny bungalows from the 1940s.

"Here we are," I said, pulling up in front of 1510. It was almost identical to the houses beside and across the street from it, except for being painted blue instead of beige or green.

"Her car's not there," Randall said.

"And unless it's well camouflaged, there's no garage."

"Let's go check on her."

Randall strode up the front walk to the front door and punched the doorbell a couple of times. We stood in silence listening, but we heard nothing and the door remained closed.

"If her car's not here . . ." I said.

"Maybe it's in the shop or something." He punched the doorbell again.

"We could go around and peek in the windows."

"The hell with that." He reached into his pocket and pulled out a massive key ring. He picked through the keys until the found the one he was looking for.

So Randall had a key to Lydia's house. Interesting.

My reaction must have shown on my face.

"Not what you think," he said, with a slightly embarrassed laugh. "Believe me, she is not my type. I'm her landlord."

He punched the doorbell button again, five or six times, then pounded on the door.

"Lydia!" he shouted. "We're coming in."

He unlocked the door and we stepped in.

The interior surprised me. We stepped into a tiny foyer area that was open to the rest of the living room. I wouldn't have thought Lydia had such nice, if old-fashioned, taste. The furniture was Victorian mahogany. The sofa and chairs were upholstered in faded but attractive green velvet. There was a tiny fireplace. Lace curtains at the window. Lamps that looked like antique oil lamps converted to electricity. The whole thing would have been charming if not for the layer of clutter and trash covering everything. Piles of newspapers. Pizza boxes. Coffee cups. Dirty dishes. Discarded pantyhose.

Randall and I surveyed it with frowns on our faces.

"I wonder what she did with the antimacassars," he said.

"Antimacassars?" I echoed.

"You know—those old-fashioned crocheted things people used to put on their furniture to keep men's hair oil from staining it."

"I know what they are," I said. "I just don't understand why you're worried about their absence."

"Aunt Bessie had antimacassars on all her upholstered furniture," he said. "That's who actually owns this place. And the furniture. Aunt Bessie's ninety-seven, and gone to live with her daughter out on their farm, so I offered to rent this place as a furnished house to Lydia. Aunt Bessie would have my hide if she saw the state it's in. I know I keep Lydia busy, but it wouldn't take five minutes to tidy this place up."

"If you like, I'll come back and help you tidy later," I said. "But for now, let's forget the mess and look for Lydia."

It didn't take long to search the rest of the bungalow. A tiny kitchen, full of dirty dishes and food debris. A tiny bathroom packed with at least ten times as many cosmetics as I'd ever owned. A tiny bedroom set up as a home office and strewn with paper. Another tiny bedroom almost completely filled with a queen-sized bed that was unmade and covered with clothes.

"It almost looks as if someone tossed the place." Randall was wrinkling his nose in distaste.

"Only here in the bedroom," I said. "Everywhere else, it's just bad housekeeping, but here, yeah. I can't be sure, but it's possible she was packing."

"Packing as in carrying a gun?" Randall sounded startled.

"No, packing as in dragging half her wardrobe out of the closet and throwing it on the bed," I said, pointing. "And trying to fit all of it into that small suitcase." I indicated a suitcase that had been thrown aside. "And then maybe getting out a bigger one and filling that with as much as it would hold, and not bothering to hang up anything she wasn't taking."

Randall nodded.

"We need to call the chief," he said. "Maybe there's some innocent explanation for all this, but it sure as heck looks suspicious to me."

I was already dialing 911.

Chapter 17

"I appreciate your calling so fast," the chief said when we had filled him in on what we'd found. "Any chance you two can stay there until I can get a deputy over there to secure the place?"

"No problem," I said.

"We'll hold down the fort," Randall added.

"Deputy Butler will be there in about ten minutes," the chief said. "When she gets there, both of you come down to the station so I can take your statements."

He hung up without waiting for an answer. Not that either of us wanted to refuse.

"Speaking of holding down the fort," Randall said. "Until and unless Lydia gets back on the job, I could use some help dealing with all of this."

He waved his hand as if indicating the clutter in the living room, where we had returned to await Aida Butler's arrival. But I suspected he meant "all this" in a larger sense.

"The festival," I said.

"And whatever we need to do to help the chief solve the murder before it torpedoes the festival," he said.

"I'll do whatever I can."

"And whatever the chief allows." He grinned at that, and I couldn't help grinning back. "I know he doesn't like having civilians interfering in his investigations, but . . . his department's already working to the limit and beyond, thanks to the festival. The festival I pushed the town and the county into. Maybe I should have listened better when he expressed some doubts over the wisdom of holding it. But that's water over the bridge now."

I opened my mouth to suggest that the usual metaphor was "water under the bridge," but thought better of it. Maybe the mangled metaphor, with its suggestion that we were in danger of being swept away by a flood, was deliberate.

"At the moment, the biggest thing that's not working right is the Halloween night duty schedule," Randall said. "I must have told Lydia half a dozen times that the whole point is to come up with a schedule that gives us the maximum number of people on duty while also leaving the maximum number of people free to take their kids trick-or-treating or answer the door for the trick-or-treaters."

"That's probably pretty hard for someone who doesn't yet know all the personalities." I was proud of how tactful I sounded.

"Also hard for someone who doesn't really give a damn about whether she's inconveniencing people," Randall said. "And maybe isn't even as good as she claims at organizing."

"Send me what she's got and I'll see what I can do."

The doorbell rang, and I jumped up to open it. Aida Butler was standing outside. Obviously she'd just come on duty—her deputy's uniform was still so fresh the creases showed.

"Morning, Meg, Randall," Aida said. "So what happened to Ms. Bossypants?"

"No idea," Randall said. "We have no idea whether she's another victim or a fugitive from justice. Or maybe she just got fed up with her job and decided to quit without notice."

"Um-hmm." Aida's face left no doubt which option she thought most likely.

"We're heading down to the station to talk to the chief," I said. "See you later."

It was only eight o'clock, but the town was already starting to wake up. Residents and shopkeepers were out, performing the tasks needed to flip the town décor over from the Night Side to the Day Side.

"Maybe we should have come down on one side or the other," Randall said. "Wholesome or spooky. Let's analyze it when the whole thing's over and see which one really generates more revenue."

I nodded. If I hadn't been driving, I'd have scribbled a task in my notebook. But I wasn't likely to forget. And I didn't need to remind him that I'd said the very same thing back when we first started to plan the festival. Odds were he already remembered that. And if he didn't—as Randall had said, water over the bridge right now.

The police station parking lot was bustling. I spotted half a dozen patrol cars from neighboring counties. Good—we needed those reinforcements more than ever.

Jabba the Hutt was behind the desk again and waved us back to the chief's office. We found him on the phone.

"Yes. . . . No, we can handle the computer forensics here. . . . Yes, I understand that. . . . No, we use an outside firm. Data Wizards."

I smiled. Data Wizards was a Mutant Wizards subdivision Rob had created to handle computer forensic work, once he realized what a booming business it was.

"Well, we couldn't afford them either if we had to pay their going rate," the chief was saying. "Their offices happen to be in Caerphilly, and they give us the local discount."

More likely Rob wouldn't charge the chief at all—just tell the Mutant Wizards accounting department to find a way to write it off as a donation.

"That's good, then. Yes, I'll be here."

He hung up and fell back into his chair.

"State police," he said. "They're going to send some resources."

"That's good," I said. "And I gather you've already talked to Rob."

"I caught him before he left the fire," the chief said. "Soon as we have the warrants, Rob will send over some experts to work on Mr. Klapcroft's phone and laptop. Randall, I assume I have your permission to let them work on Ms. Van Meter's office computer?"

"Absolutely," Randall said. "I hope you've put out an APB for her?"

"We call it a BOLO these days, but yes," the chief said. "Stands for 'be on the lookout.' For her and her car."

"You think she's definitely a suspect in this?" I asked.

"If she's not, it's a mighty big coincidence," he said. "Her taking off on the lam so close to a murder. At the moment, we're just describing her as a person of interest. Might help if we could figure out exactly when she took off."

"I haven't seen or talked to her since yesterday morning," I said.

"I talked to her about two yesterday afternoon." Randall pulled out his cell phone and looked at it. "Looks like she called from her office phone, instead of her cell. Two thirteen. That should narrow it down a bit."

The chief nodded and scribbled in his notebook.

His phone rang.

"What?" His scowl quickly smoothed itself when he heard who was calling. "Yes, Your Honor. Sammy should be at your house any minute and . . . The gist? Well, obviously the young man we talked about yesterday didn't commit the new murder, since we had him locked up in jail, but we suspect he may be involved, and at the very least he has information that could materially assist us in finding the killer. . . . Not yet, Your Honor. And Ms. Van Meter is missing—we don't yet know if she skipped town or if she's another victim, but her disappearance so close to the murder . . . Absolutely. Thank you, Your Honor."

He hung up with a look of satisfaction.

"Your aunt's getting me my warrants," he said to Randall.

"Now if I could just find a lawyer for Mr. Klapcroft, my joy would be complete."

"Have we figured out if he knows either victim?" Randall asked.

"No," the chief said. "If I knew the new victim's name, I'd toss it out and see if he reacted to it, but Horace didn't find anything on the body. No wallet, no ID, no cell phone. Just like Mr. Green, our first victim."

"Taken by the killer, you think?"

"Most likely. In both cases." The chief rubbed his forehead in a way I recognized as a sign that he was fighting a headache. "We've sent his fingerprints in. Maybe we'll luck out again. But I'm not optimistic. He's a lot younger than Mr. Green. And frankly, he doesn't look like a career criminal. He looks like a student."

"Was Green a career criminal?" I asked.

"He had a long criminal history—mostly petty fraud and confidence tricks." The chief shook his head as if more saddened than angered by this news.

"An old-fashioned con artist, then," Randall said.

"More of a new-fangled one," the chief replied. "He tended to troll social networking sites for his victims, and made use of e-mail and phony Web sites. Which makes me wonder if this scavenger hunt thing is somehow part of his latest scheme. Another thing I'd love to talk to Mr. Klapcroft about, when I finally find him an attorney. The county attorney's going to read the riot act to the public defenders when they get back, but that won't help me find an attorney now."

"Let me try," I said.

"With all due respect, I've already called just about every lawyer in town," he said. "At least anyone with any criminal defense experience, and since this is connected to a murder case, that's mission critical." He began rattling off a list of the attorneys he'd called.

I held up my hand. He stopped and frowned.

"Let me do what I'd do if I needed to get bailed out," I said.

He pursed his lips and watched as I took out my phone and punched one of the speed dial buttons.

"Good morning, dear," Mother said when she answered the phone. "Are you all right? Michael told me about what happened last night, and your father and I took the boys to school so he could nap a bit. Where are you now?"

"Down at the police station," I said. "I need a criminal defense attorney on the double. Can you round up one as soon as possible today? We must have at least a dozen in the family; surely one is available."

"Of course, dear," she said. "What is it you're being charged with this time?"

"You make it sound as if I'm a hardened repeat offender," I said. "It's not for me. The chief arrested the young man who scared the first-grade class with a fake foot during yesterday's trip to the zoo. He needs an attorney."

"I see," she said. "I must say, I can't imagine why you want to help him. Those poor children could be traumatized for life. Unless you want me to find him an incompetent attorney? Not, in that case, someone from the family."

"The chief thinks he has information that may be related to the murders," I said. "He won't talk till he gets a lawyer, and the chief needs him to talk before the killer strikes again."

"Right," she said. "I'll call you back." With that she hung up.

"She's on it," I said.

"I have every faith in your mother's ability to round up a lawyer," Randall said. "If it was a plumber you needed, or a carpenter, I'd have no problem, but so far Aunt Jane's the only lawyer we've had in the family, and she had to go and get herself promoted to judge."

"Even your mother might have trouble finding an attorney on such short notice," the chief said. "On a Friday afternoon, and not just any Friday but the Friday before a weekend of a very popular holiday. If—"

My phone rang. Mother.

"Hello," I said. "I'm putting you on speaker." Maybe I was overconfident, but I had utter faith in Mother's ability to manage her family.

"That's nice, dear," Mother said. "Your Cousin Festus will be down at the jail in about half an hour."

"Festus Hollingsworth?" The chief knew my cousin thanks to all the work Festus had done in helping the town combat the evil machinations of the Pruitt family, who had mortgaged the jail and nearly put the town into bankruptcy. "Does he do criminal defense?"

"He did quite a lot of it before he decided he was tired of his clients trying to pay him with counterfeit bills and grams of cocaine," Mother said. "That's why he moved into property law."

"Where the thefts happen on a grander scale," I put in.

"But he keeps his hand in doing pro bono work," Mother said, ignoring my remark. "And he happens to be staying with us at the moment."

"That's perfect," I said. "Thanks!"

"Well," the chief said. "That's moderately good news."

"Only moderately?" Randall said.

"Festus is a sharp cookie," the chief said. "He'll drive a hard bargain for his client."

"So Justin will have very little chance of coming back later with a charge of inadequate representation," I pointed out.

"True," the chief said. "And just between you and me, I'm perfectly willing to give Mr. Klapcroft immunity on any charges resulting from his breaking and entering at the zoo, provided he tells me everything he knows about this wretched game so I can determine if it has anything to do with the murder."

"And also provided that he isn't involved in either murder," I put in.

"That goes without saying." The chief was picking up his phone. "I'd better get the county attorney down here so we're ready to discuss terms if necessary."

Randall and I waited patiently while he briefed the county attorney. When he hung up, the chief looked at us.

"You'll be wanting your Haunted House back, I suppose," he said.

Randall looked at me.

"Only the Haunted House," I said. "I don't think the museum is a big draw for most festival-goers—only for trouble-makers."

"By which you mean the people playing this confounded game?" the chief asked.

"Maybe. So if Horace could do whatever processing he needs to do in the upper floors, we could lock up the basement and open the house."

"I can have a fence put up to keep people well away from the outside stairwell that leads down to the basement," Randall said. "And a secure padlock on the gate."

"That sounds reasonable," the chief said. "I'll check with Horace and let you know when I'm ready to release the scene."

"Why such gloomy faces?"

We all looked up to see my cousin Festus Hollingsworth standing in the doorway of the chief's office. He was wearing, as usual, a retro-looking three-piece suit that had probably cost more than my first car. He hugged me and shook hands warmly with Randall and the chief.

"So, where's my client, and what are you charging him with? I heard you found a body at this morning's fire. Was it a homicide?"

"Yes, but not of your client's doing," the chief said. "He's alibied for that one. We're holding him for trespassing and endangering the welfare of a minor, but he's not off the hook for yesterday's murder, and even if he's innocent, we think he has information that could help us solve both cases."

The chief sent a deputy to escort Justin to the interview room and then brought Festus up to speed on recent events before leading him off to meet his client.

"So now what?" Randall asked, as we watched the door close behind Festus and the chief. "Festival's starting up for the day. Assuming the news of a second murder doesn't scare all the tourists away."

Starting up? I pulled out my phone and checked the time. Not quite 10:00 A.M. I felt a sudden wave of exhaustion. Had I gotten two hours of sleep or three? I hoped Michael had slept a little before he had to tackle his graduate students.

"We need to find someone to run the Haunted House," I said. "And we need to brief the Goblin Patrol on everything that's been happening. As much as the chief will let us share. And then I need to turn everything over to my second-in-command and get some sleep, because tonight's when it's all going to get really crazy."

"Good idea."

"And we need to check on Dr. Smoot. Dad went down to the hospital with him." I pulled out my phone and dialed Dad. And then I punched the speaker button so Randall could hear.

"Meg!" Dad sounded cheerful. That was a good sign, wasn't it? "What's happening down there at the Haunted House?"

"No idea," I said. "It's a crime scene. Horace is there—ask him. How's Dr. Smoot?"

"His odds are good," Dad said. "He's got some serious burns, but ironically, the fire may have saved his life. The fire, and the fact that he had working smoke alarms. He was hit on the head and developed a subdural hematoma. Dr. Carper did an emergency craniotomy, and he's improving rapidly.

But if he'd gone untreated for another couple of hours, he'd have become the murderer's latest victim."

"Speaking of murder victims," I said. "Any idea what happened to the ones we do have?"

"Yesterday's was a gunshot wound to the head," Dad said. "The bullet wasn't recovered, but he was also shot in the shoulder, and we recovered that bullet for possible comparison with the bullet Horace found at the museum this morning. And I haven't done the autopsy on today's victim yet—been waiting till I was sure Dr. Smoot was stable—but most likely it will be the gunshot wound I observed at the scene. Went in at the base of the skull and out the top of the head. Which means either the shooter was a midget, or he was shot from below. Probably from the basement while he was trying to flee up the stairs."

"Was Dr. Smoot shot too?"

"No, just hit over the head, thank goodness. Oh, good—Horace has finished taking his photos of the new victim. I'm going to start the autopsy in a few minutes, if you're interested."

"Interested in the results," I said. "I'll skip the process."

"I'll keep you posted." He hung up.

"That's good news about Dr. Smoot, I guess," Randall said.

"Better news if he hadn't had to have a craniotomy," I said. "That means they opened up his skull, you know. To relieve the pressure caused by bleeding into his brain, which is the subdural hematoma part. But yeah. Under the circumstances, probably the best news we could hope for. Still, Dr. Smoot will be out of commission for weeks. We need to decide whether to close the Haunted House or find someone to run it."

"It's a pretty big draw," Randall said. "Heaven knows why. But I think we need a couple of someones. Dr. Smoot could have used the help, and he lived there. Got any ideas?"

"Let me think about it." I closed my eyes and began mentally scanning my lists of volunteers, trying to think of someone who would do a good job on the house. Why did visions of my pillow keep interfering?

"Ms. Ellie, maybe," I suggested, opening my eyes. "She's good at telling ghost stories, and so could probably manage to give a decently spooky tour of the house. She's probably better than Dr. Smoot at town history—at least she's more accurate. And most important, if anyone can keep the unruly tourists in line, it would be Ms. Ellie. Yes. I'll ask her."

"Good idea," Randall said. "And I think I can play the family loyalty card and recruit one good volunteer. I was thinking Aunt Jane."

"Judge Jane?"

"Like Ms. Ellie, she's pretty darn good at suppressing mischief," Randall said. "Even one of them could handle it, but together they'd be unbeatable. You tackle Ms. Ellie, and I'll call Aunt Jane. And you know, another thing—"

The door opened and the chief came in. He was frowning with annoyance.

"Dr. Smoot's in serious condition," I told him. "But Dad thinks he'll pull through. He'll be starting the autopsy on the victim as soon as he has done all he can for Dr. Smoot."

"Good." The chief smiled slightly, and then his face returned to its frown. "Our prisoner has suddenly become very chatty. Meg, you seem to understand this scavenger hunt thing—better than I do, at any rate. If you don't mind staying here for a few minutes, I'd like you to hear what he has to say."

"Rob and his employees are the experts," I said. "But if you think I can help."

Just then Justin stepped into the room, followed by Festus. The chief motioned Justin to a chair in the center of the room. Festus pulled up another chair and sat at his elbow.

"Now tell us again how you got involved in this game." The

chief sat behind his desk and fixed Justin with his sternest glance.

Justin glanced back at Festus, who nodded.

"This guy e-mailed me," he said. "Didn't give me a name—just called himself GameMaster41. And he said he'd seen my post that I was going to the Caerphilly Halloween Festival, and would I like a chance to win an advance copy of *Vampire Colonies II*. It's a computer role-playing game."

"Published by Mutant Wizards," I said, in case the chief hadn't heard of it.

"Yeah," Justin said. "And the festival's in Caerphilly, and Mutant Wizards is in Caerphilly, so I figured maybe it was a publicity stunt, and I said yes. And then GameMaster told me I had to sign a confidentiality agreement so if I told anyone about the game before the end or tried to get anyone to help me win, I'd forfeit the prize."

"Mr. Klapcroft has given us access to his e-mail." The chief held out a sheet of paper. I took it and held it so Randall could read it, too. It was a copy of GameMaster's original e-mail.

"Sent, you will note, from a Yahoo account," the chief said.

"Rob predicted that," I said, nodding. "Easy to set up, hard to trace."

"Precisely." The chief turned back to Justin. "GameMaster said nothing about the number of players you'd be competing with, did he?"

"Not exactly," Justin said. "He just said it was a select group of players. I hoped that meant a small group. And he said to watch my e-mail, and he'd send me the first day's tasks promptly at twelve oh one a.m. Wednesday morning, and if I finished them by midnight Thursday, and sent in photos to prove it, I'd get the next batch at twelve oh one Friday. I guess I'm out of the running now." Justin glanced at the chief with a slightly resentful look. "Being in jail overnight, I missed the midnight deadline."

"Look on the bright side," I said. "As far as we know, you're the only game player who has a solid alibi for one of the murders."

Justin grimaced. Maybe I wouldn't have been too thrilled either.

"Mr. Klapcroft also has an alibi for the first murder," Festus said.

"An alibi we're still checking," the chief said.

"I was still working at the college cafeteria at midnight," Justin said. "I didn't get here till nearly three a.m."

"By which point, according to Dr. Langslow, James Green had been dead for several hours," Festus added.

"Congratulations," I said. "And if that doesn't make you feel better, remember that all your fellow players are out there doing who knows what kind of stupid, dangerous, or unpleasant things to win a prize that doesn't exist."

"You mean there isn't a *Vampire Colonies II* game?" Justin looked alarmed.

"There is," I said. "But there's no way in the world that Rob's giving out an advance copy to anyone playing this scavenger hunt—it absolutely has nothing to do with Mutant Wizards."

"Oh. Bummer. For them, I mean. The other players."

"Glad you're not out there eating more insects?" I asked.

"The cricket wasn't bad," he said. "Tasted kind of . . . nutty."

An idea struck me.

"Are you sure you're out of the running?" I asked.

"Pretty sure, yeah." Justin glanced up at the large, industrial clock on the wall of the chief's office. " 'Cause it's more than nine hours past the deadline for sending in my proof."

"This says 'complete all five tasks before midnight and e-mail GameMaster the proof,' " I read. "I'd interpret that to mean that midnight's the deadline for the tasks, not the e-mail."

"Of course, GameMaster may not see it that way," the chief said. "But it's worth trying."

"I thought you said there wasn't a prize," Justin said.

"There is for you," I said. "A lot of goodwill with the chief—maybe even a get-out-of-jail-free card—if you can convince GameMaster to send you today's tasks."

Justin frowned for a moment as if puzzled, then his face cleared as he obviously figured it out.

"Oh, I get it," he said. "You want to get today's tasks to help you catch the other players."

"One of whom may be a murderer," the chief said. "Yes."

"But how am I going to explain not sending the picture in yesterday?" Justin asked.

"Easy," Festus said. "You were arrested while performing the last two tasks. You were in jail. Your lawyer didn't arrive to bail you out until today."

"That's almost completely true." Justin sounded surprised.

"When you tell a lie, it's always better to wrap it in as much truth as possible," Festus said.

"It's just the bail part that isn't true." Justin looked at the chief with a hopeful expression.

"Provided Mr. Klapcroft can talk GameMaster into sending him today's task list, and also provided that his alibi for the first murder checks out, we can discuss the possibility of bail," the chief said.

"Boy, will I be glad to get out of here," Justin said.

"If by get out of here you mean leave town, no way," I said. "He has to keep playing the game, right? Otherwise Game-Master might suspect."

"Yes," the chief said. "And since we have reason to suspect that GameMaster may already be responsible for at least one murder, we don't want him to suspect Mr. Klapcroft, do we?"

"So you want me to stay around here where someone might want to kill me?" Justin whined.

"GameMaster will have no reason to kill you if he thinks

you're still playing the game," the chief said. "And I'll assign a deputy to shadow you, to ensure your safety. In fact, I think we'll put you in protective custody, for your own safety, but I think we can find someplace a little more comfortable than the jail."

"And for heaven's sake," I added. "Don't tell anyone you're cooperating with the police. Not even your best friend."

"Meg's right," the chief said. "Indiscretion would jeopardize not only our operation but your life."

Justin looked a little scared, and glanced up at Festus.

"A moment," Festus said.

He and Justin went to the far side of the room and whispered together for a few moments. Then they came back.

"Okay," Justin said.

"My client agrees in principle to your proposal," Festus said, with a repressive glance at Justin. "Let's hammer out the specifics, shall we?"

"Meg, can you help Mr. Klapcroft draft his e-mail to Game-Master?" the chief asked. "Something that's in his own words as much as possible and doesn't accidentally give anything away."

"Roger," I said.

So while the chief, the county attorney, and Festus worked out the specific terms for his eventual release, Justin and I came up with a draft message.

"Hey, GameMaster," it read. "Sorry I'm late sending this. Finished the tasks way before the deadline, but then I got arrested right after I finished 2 and 4—can you believe it? My lawyer didn't get here to bail me out until today. Still got half the day left, so send me the Friday tasks, 'cause I'm determined to win!"

The chief, the county attorney, and Festus studied it carefully.

"Sounds good," the chief said. "Here—turn this on."

He handed Justin an iPhone. With all of us looking over

his shoulder, Justin entered his password, opened his e-mail, and typed in the message. He made half a dozen typos, but I figured that probably added to the authenticity. Then he held his phone up for inspection, waiting for approval.

"Send it," the chief said.

Justin obeyed.

"Now what?" Justin asked.

"Now we wait." The chief held out his hand for the phone and Justin handed it over. "The next move is up to Game-Master."

"Do I have to go back to the cell?" Justin asked.

Festus and the chief exchanged looks.

"We can put you in the interview room for now."

"Okay," Justin said.

The chief called in a deputy to escort Justin back to the interview room.

"So if he has an alibi for the first murder, why didn't he tell you sooner?" I asked, when Justin had left the room. "And is it really solid?"

"Your father wasn't able to do the autopsy until yesterday afternoon," the chief said. "That confirmed his earlier hunch that Mr. Green had been dead between ten and twelve hours by the time we found him. Mr. Klapcroft is a student at George Mason University, and has a part-time job with the campus dining services. At the time of the murder he was still at work in Northern Virginia."

"That must be a relief," I said. "For him at least. Frustrating for you."

"I want to get that phone forensics expert to start working on this thing," he said, looking down at Justin's phone. "But not until—"

The phone emitted a tiny ding.

Chapter 18

The chief looked down at Justin's phone in surprise for a few moments. Then he reached down and tapped on the phone as if more than half convinced it would explode if he made a typo. Evidently he'd been paying attention when Justin had typed in his password.

"It's from GameMaster." He was peering over his glasses at the phone. " 'Try to do better next time. Everyone else is getting ahead of you. Here are your Friday tasks. One: take a selfie with a bat. Two: do something amusing with fake blood. Three: put a spider on someone. Four: steal a gravestone—fake is okay. And five: toilet paper somebody's house.' Well, that gives us more clues to spotting the game players. Meg, I'm forwarding you a copy—can you get this out to your Goblin Patrol?"

"Will do," I said.

"And have them keep looking for yesterday's tasks," he said. "Maybe it's just coincidence, but I think we've seen some of these new pranks already. I'll check the incident reports, but I'm pretty sure we've had fake gravestones stolen along with pumpkins. And a couple of reports of houses getting toilet-papered. Which means that Meg could be right about there being three groups of players, working the same tasks, but not always on the same day."

"Remember we found that scarecrow on the steps of the town hall yesterday morning with stage blood dripping down a dozen or more steps," Randall said. "Damn stuff stained the marble—going to take a lot of work to get it off."

"And who knows," I said. "Maybe the third list includes 'steal something from the museum.' Which could have been what our murder victim was doing."

"Or 'set something on fire,'" Randall suggested.

"Not something they're going to be able to do today or tomorrow, stealing from the museum," the chief said. "I've sent over a couple of deputies with our patrol wagon and orders to confiscate pretty much everything. We'll be locking up the lot in our evidence room."

"Maybe we should publicize that," Randall suggested.

"And turn the station into another target?" the chief said. "I'd rather not. We have to keep an eye on the Haunted House anyway. Not just to keep people out of our crime scene, but if we catch anyone committing any of these pranks, we've got a fifty-fifty chance of getting that third list we think is out there. And now I'm going to turn over Mr. Klapcroft's phone to your brother's forensic computer specialist, and maybe he can start tracking down this GameMaster person. And if either of you hear from Ms. Van Meter, let me know. And don't tip her off that we're looking for her."

"Hey, one good thing," Randall said. "I guess this means our cyber-savvy con artist wasn't the GameMaster."

"Why is that good?" The chief was frowning. "If he was, maybe the confounded game would be over."

"Never thought of that," Randall said. "Well, I'm going to make my rounds."

"I'll send out new orders to the Goblin Patrol as soon as I get back to my computer," I said.

I was walking out the door when a thought struck me.

"Chief," I said. "Rob has had his people combing social media—Facebook, Twitter and all that—for anyone who's talking about coming here to the festival. It's possible they might have seen the dead guy. The latest dead guy."

"Good idea," he said. "I'll see if they can ID him. Thanks."

I headed down the corridor. When I reached the front

desk, I found Jabba the Hutt arguing with a tall fortyish man in a suit that looked at least as nice as Festus's. The man glanced at me as I approached the desk and then flicked his eyes back to Jabba—dismissing me, apparently, as uninteresting. I had the feeling I'd seen him before somewhere. He was almost handsome, in a gaunt, high-cheekboned way, but the most interesting thing about him was his eyes, which were so pale a gray that they seemed almost colorless.

"How much longer are you going to keep me waiting?" the man said.

I'd be the first to admit that I'm nosy, so I paused as if waiting my turn to talk to Jabba while I tried to figure out where I'd seen the man before.

"The chief is in the middle of a murder investigation," Jabba began. "I'm sure if you—"

"Do you know who I am?" the tall man demanded.

Jabba the Hutt had given up trying to reason with the tall man and was talking on the intercom.

"Chief," he said. "There's a Mr. Brimstone here to see you."

"Brim*field*," the tall man snapped.

"Brim*field*," Jabba repeated. "Something about the museum."

"Send him back," came the chief's voice, tinny over the intercom.

"First door on the right," Jabba said.

I watched as Mr. Brimfield strode down the corridor and disappeared into the chief's office. If he was Dr. Smoot's main hope for museum funding, odds were it would be a long while before those store mannequins would be replaced by real wax figures.

I couldn't see Jabba's face, and his costume didn't let me pick up much body language, but somehow I sensed that he wasn't entirely thrilled with Mr. Brimfield.

"Don't you hate people who say that?" I asked. " 'Do you know who I am?' "

Jabba made a noise that probably would have sounded more like a raspberry if his costume hadn't muffled it.

"Wish I could see the chief take care of him," he added.

"What does he want with the chief, anyway?" I asked.

"He seems to think poor Dr. Smoot has stolen something of his," Jabba said.

"Dr. Smoot?" I exclaimed. "Seems unlikely. Stolen what?"

"Something in the museum," Jabba said. " 'I do not care to have my family name connected with that travesty of a museum,' " he said, in what I deduced was an imitation of Mr. Brimfield's voice. " 'And I demand the return of my family's property.' "

"Well, a lot of us aren't that thrilled with the museum," I said. "But however peculiar the results, I'm sure Dr. Smoot is trying his best to put together a proper museum, and I can't imagine him stealing anything for it."

"Yeah," Jabba said. "It'd be pretty stupid to steal something and then put it on display for the whole world to see. Well, the chief will take him down a peg. Wish I dared listen in through the intercom."

I smiled at the thought.

"Especially since I know he's going to complain to the chief about my costume," Jabba added. "Even though I explained that I'm a civilian volunteer helping out so the police can put as many boots on the ground as possible for the festival. And that got him started ragging on the festival. He had no idea it was happening till he hit the traffic coming into town, and to hear him talk, you'd think we'd organized it for the sole purpose of making his life more difficult. I think he'd still be going on about that if I hadn't finally said that no matter how silly he thought it was, the festival made the town a whole lot of money. That seemed to shut him up. Guess he's one of those jerks who only respects the power of the almighty dollar and thinks he can get his way anytime he wants if he throws enough money around."

Just then the front door of the station opened and a uniformed state trooper entered.

"Sorry to vent at you," Jabba said quickly. "But some people just have a knack for getting under your skin, don't they?"

"They do indeed," I said. "You have a good afternoon."

I left Jabba to see what the state trooper wanted and left the station. If I hadn't been so exhausted I'd have been tempted to hang around to see how Mr. Brimfield looked when he'd finished his meeting with the chief. And then a sad thought struck me. Mr. Brimfield was not only unlikely to be the big donor the museum needed, he also seemed perfectly capable of harassing Dr. Smoot on his sickbed.

As I approached my car I pulled out my phone and called Dad.

"What's up?" he asked.

"Is there someone watching Dr. Smoot constantly?" I asked.

"Of course," Dad said. "Medically, he's still not out of the woods, so we have him in the ICU and heavily monitored. And I've asked the chief if there's any possibility that he can spare a deputy to guard him—after all, there's a murderer out there who could still be after Smoot."

"That's good," I said. "Tell the nurses to keep their eyes open for a guy named Brimfield, who thinks he owns something that's in the museum and came to town for the sole purpose of badgering Dr. Smoot about it." I described Brimfield in as much detail as possible as I opened my car and collapsed into the driver's seat.

"We'll keep an eye out for him," Dad said. "And if I catch him even trying to harass my patient . . . well, we'll see about that!"

I hung up. I felt a sudden wave of tiredness. I'd been fine when I was running on adrenaline, but now I was starting to crash, and getting a sleep-deprivation headache. I was glad that all I had to do was get home, send out my e-mail to the Goblin Patrol, and crash.

And then I had a brilliant idea. Why not stop by the library to send my e-mail from one of the computers there? I could get the word out faster. And while I was there, I could ask Ms. Ellie if she could fill in for Dr. Smoot at the Haunted House.

The library parking lot was crowded—had I missed an announcement of some special event? No, but even so, it wasn't business as usual here at the library. Most of the rooms were filled with costumed young people, occupying every seat at every table, every reading chair, and every computer.

I saw Ms. Ellie standing behind the circulation desk, surveying the crowd with a bemused expression.

"You're quite the popular favorite today," I said. "And here I was dropping in to see if I could use one of the computers."

"Come back to the office and use mine," she said. "And I'll show you what I've found so far."

She didn't say anything else until we'd passed through the door from the public area into the private. Then she stopped, closed her eyes, and took a deep breath.

"Are you all right?" I asked.

"Good Lord, give me strength," she said. "It all started yesterday afternoon. They figured out we had heat, bathrooms, comfy chairs, and free Wi-Fi. I've notified Randall and the library board that we're going to close early today and stay closed until Sunday afternoon."

"Sounds good to me," I said. "It's not as if any of them seem interested in the books. And that would free you up for a project I wanted to recruit you for."

"And that would be?"

"Filling in for Dr. Smoot at the Haunted House."

Her face fell.

"How is he?" she asked. "The rumors make it sound pretty dire."

"The rumors aren't all wrong, but Dad thinks he'll make it."

"Good," she said. "And if you need me, I'll be happy to fill in at the Haunted House—as long as someone can give me a ride there and back if it's after dark. I'm not fond of driving after dark these days. You know, by now I'm probably better equipped to give tours of the museum than Dr. Smoot. You should see what I've been finding."

"Let me use your computer to send an e-mail to the Goblin Patrol, and then I'll be all ears."

She waited impatiently as I composed and dispatched my e-mail. Then I stood up and gave her back her computer.

"Just let me call it up," she said. "By the way, thank you for bringing all that material to me. It's all very interesting, and one photo in particular is proving quite intriguing."

"You're welcome," I said. "Do you think this has something to do with the problems Dr. Smoot has been having at his museum? Or the murders?"

"I have no idea," she said. "Not sure how it possibly could. But you never know. And it is a fascinating historical puzzle."

I was tempted to suggest that if it was a historical puzzle— and presumably one that was decades old—then perhaps its solution could wait a few more days, until the Halloween Festival was over. But she seemed so enthusiastic that I bit back the words. And after all, it wasn't as if I had anything else to do at the moment. I was eager to get home and nap, but I could spend a few minutes to hear her out. And better now than later on, when the town had flipped over into the Night Side. I knew once that happened, I'd begrudge every minute I wasn't out in the festival as a minute in which something could be going wrong. So I smiled and tried to look more interested than I was.

"Okay," she said. "I blew up the photo so we could see it better. Gets a little fuzzy, but still pretty easy to make out the details."

She displayed the enlargement on her monitor and I studied it more closely than I had before. Two young men in uniform, standing in what I deduced was a World War I trench. They were up to their ankles in water, and the mud spattered on their trousers suggested they'd been through even deeper puddles. The trench's walls were slightly higher than their heads, and it was only just wide enough for the two of them to pass. They had pushed back their basin helmets to show their faces, thrown their arms over each other's shoulder, and were beaming at the unseen photographer. They were both handsome young men and there was a family resemblance between the two, including unusually pale eyes, though the one on the left looked older and thinner—perhaps only a sign that he'd been in the trenches longer. And they were clearly delighted to be together, and I had the sinking feeling that Ms. Ellie was about to tell me that one or both had never come home from those trenches.

They looked curiously familiar, and after a moment I realized why—Mr. Brimfield, the chief's indignant visitor, had the same uncanny pale eyes, and very similar handsome if gaunt features.

"The one on the left is William Henry Harrison Brimfield," Ms. Ellie said. "On the right is his younger brother, John Tyler Brimfield."

"Did the Brimfields also produce a James K. Polk Brimfield and a Zachary Taylor Brimfield?" I asked. I was rather proud of myself for being able to call to mind the next two presidents in order.

"Zachary Taylor Brimfield, yes, but not Polk," she said. "Good heavens, no. Harrison, Tyler, and Taylor—and presumably the Brimfields—were Whigs. Polk was a Democrat, so they skipped him altogether, and after Zachary Taylor Brimfield they produced Millard Fillmore Brimfield before quitting. Fillmore was another Whig."

Should I tell Ms. Ellie about the present-day Brimfield? Maybe later, when I was less exhausted.

"This is all very fascinating," I began.

"You'll notice that the brothers are wearing different uniforms," she went on.

"Actually, I hadn't," I admitted. I peered closer. "Military couture isn't exactly one of my specialties. Is there some significance to the differences?"

"America stayed out of World War One at first, you know. But a lot of young men wanted to get into the fight—especially those with close family connections in Great Britain. Apparently William Brimfield was one of those. He joined the Canadian Army."

"They let people do that?"

"They did then," she said. "Over thirty thousand Americans fought in the Canadian Armed Forces. You'll recall that we didn't enter the war until April 1917, and very few U.S. troops arrived in Europe before 1918. So for any American who wanted to enlist, the Canadians were the best option. John Tyler waited until America joined the war and enlisted in the U.S. Army. Zachary and Millard were too young to serve, thank goodness."

"Why thank goodness?" I asked. "Does that mean that at least one of those two in the photo didn't make it home?"

"Neither of them did," she said, with a sigh. "Such a waste."

"Definitely," I said. And I agreed with her, and at any other time I'd have been completely in tune with her melancholy fascination with the Brimfield brothers. But for now, I kept thinking that however sad it was, it was nearly a hundred years ago. Out there in present day Caerphilly, things could be happening. And back home, my pillow was calling. "At least before they perished, the two brothers were reunited in the trenches in France," I said aloud.

"So it seems," she said. "And that shouldn't have happened."

"What do you mean?" I asked. "The Canadians were our allies—what's wrong with William and John Tyler having a little family reunion."

"According to the records, William Brimfield perished in the Battle of the Somme," she said. "On October 11, 1916. Which is at least six months before any American troops landed in France, and a year or so before they had arrived in any kind of numbers."

"Maybe John Tyler got sent over early on some kind of special mission?"

"He was still in high school," she said. "The *Caerphilly Clarion* listed him in their article on young men who enlisted as soon as Congress passed the declaration of war. In April 1917."

"Maybe this isn't William Brimfield?"

She searched her desk and came up with a photocopy of a page from an issue of the *Clarion* from 1915. It contained an article announcing William Henry Harrison Brimfield's enlistment in the Canadian Army. She held it up beside the picture from the trenches. The young man in the trench photo was visibly thinner and dirtier than the one in the *Clarion,* but either it was the same young man or a dead ringer. Same strong high-cheekboned face, devil-may-care grin, and pale, pale eyes.

"They must have gotten the date wrong, then," I said.

"They must have," she said. "And also the name of the battle."

She showed me another photograph, a close-up of part of the engraving on the Caerphilly Cenotaph, a fifteen-foot obelisk honoring the county's war dead, which stood in a tiny park on the other side of the courthouse from the town square. It read "William Henry Harrison Brimfield. October 11, 1916."

"The Brimfields moved out of town a few years after the war ended," she said. "So maybe they weren't around to notice the error. Perhaps it was really October 11, 1918. That would be the end of the Battle of Cambrai. A lot of Canadian involvement in that."

She looked up and then cocked her head to one side, like a bird, and studied me with an eagle eye.

"And you're thinking all of this is fascinating, no doubt, but what does it have to do with anything that's going on right now?"

I had to laugh at that.

"Guilty," I said. "It does sound like a fascinating puzzle, and perhaps when the festival is over and I'm sane again, I will check back with you to see if you've solved it."

"It will probably turn out to be merely a typo on the part of the stonecutter," she said. "But it should be fun to try to solve it, and maybe in a year or two I can present a paper to the Caerphilly Historical Society, and begin the process of petitioning to have the inscription on the monument corrected."

"And I'll come and hear your paper and sign your petition and make a donation toward the cost of the correction," I said.

"I just thought you might like to know in case it does end up being related to the pranks," she said. "Or in case any of your graveyard watchers spot a ghostly figure in a doughboy helmet drifting through the tombstones."

"Are William and John Tyler buried in one of the graveyards?" I asked.

"No, they'd have been buried in France," she said. "They weren't much for shipping bodies home in those days."

"Then why would their ghosts haunt any of the graveyards?" I asked. "More likely they'd haunt the house where they lived."

"I should look up where that is," she said.

"Have you found out anything interesting about Arabella Shiffley Pratherton?" I asked.

"No." She tilted her head in a birdlike gesture. "Should I?"

"The dead guy had an article about her in his pocket," I said. "The first dead guy. The chief has no idea why. And he was a petty thief and con artist. The museum contains a portrait worth a hundred grand, a brooch worth half a million, and family photos that a wealthy curmudgeon wants to take away from Dr. Smoot, and the thief's carrying around an article about Arabella? There must be something interesting there."

"I'll see what I can dig up," she said. "Now you go get some rest. Any chance we could plan to open the Haunted House at dusk? If we're closing the library at five, and staying closed tomorrow; I'll be completely free to help starting at dusk tonight."

"Sounds fine to me," I said. "The Haunted House isn't much of a kids' attraction anyway."

"And maybe when things get slow, I can peek into the museum and see some of the artifacts firsthand," she added.

Should I tell her about all the artifacts being locked up in the evidence room? No need. The basement would be blocked off as a crime scene. And it wasn't as if things were ever going to be slow at the Haunted House tonight or tomorrow. So I just wished her a Happy Halloween and left.

As I let myself into my car, I realized that my short visit with Ms. Ellie had lifted my spirits. With her in charge, the Haunted House would be in good hands, and if Randall recruited Judge Jane, even better. And it was good to be reminded that, by Monday, we would return to the normal peaceful life of a small town, where a meeting of the local historical society was a highlight in our month, and the debate over whether or not a date carved in the war memorial cenotaph was correct could be the hottest topic in town.

Of course, by Monday, the chief might still have two

unsolved murders on his hands, with most of his suspects and witnesses scattering to the four winds, but at least, one way or another, the scavenger hunt would be over.

And just in case we were wrong and the motives for the murders lay in the contents of the museum, rather than the scavenger hunt, Ms. Ellie was on the case.

I managed not to fall asleep behind the wheel on my way home. It was almost eleven. I wondered if Michael had been able to get much of a nap before taking off for his first class.

As I pulled up, I saw Michael's mother carrying her luggage into the house. Rather a lot of luggage. I wondered how long a stay she was planning.

"Meg, are you all right?" she asked.

Did I look that bad? Or was it the fact that I'd stumbled twice on the cobblestones of our front walk.

"Only two or three hours of sleep last night," I said, giving her a quick hug and a peck on the cheek. "Would you mind horribly if I celebrated your arrival with a nap?"

"Of course not," she said. "And I can pick the boys up at school, so nap as long as you like."

Okay, with that kind of an attitude, she could stay as long as she liked. I mumbled my thanks, dragged myself upstairs, crawled out of my costume, and fell asleep almost as soon as my head hit the pillow.

Chapter 19

I may have fallen asleep quickly, but it wasn't a sound or un-troubled sleep. I kept waking up out of unpleasant dreams. Enormous alligators loomed up out of murky waters and threatened to devour me—or, worse, the boys. Menacing black-cloaked figures chased me down endless dark alleys. Worst of all, Dr. Smoot kept turning up, apparently un-harmed, until he smiled to reveal fangs that definitely owed nothing to the dentist's art.

"Why no," he kept saying. "I'm not dead. But I'm not alive, either."

Ridiculous. The boys had made it safely home from the zoo. There were hardly any alleys in Caerphilly. And even if I believed in vampires, I wouldn't be frightened of Dr. Smoot if he became one.

Of course, better to dream of things that looked silly in the light of day than of things that did scare me—like the fact that a murderer had struck at the zoo and the Haunted House and was probably still prowling the increasingly crowded streets of Caerphilly.

I woke up to peals of childish laughter—the sort of merry, innocent sounds that all too often signaled that the boys were up to something unusually dangerous or destructive. But before I could leap out of bed to check on them, I heard Michael's mother's voice and relaxed again.

On a normal day, I'd have been tempted to go back to sleep for another hour or two. But I realized that if the boys were home, it must be past three o'clock. I checked the clock. Three thirty. Even allowing for the sleep I'd lost to my nightmares, I should be rested enough to handle tonight's patrol. I dragged myself out of bed and donned my costume again. Time to get back to town. I suddenly felt intensely guilty for having spent so much time asleep. Guilty, and worried that something dire might have happened while I was fleeing from dream phantoms.

On my way downstairs, I ran into Michael coming upstairs.

"You look as bad as I felt a few hours ago," I said.

"Nap time," he said. "Or I won't be able to patrol tonight. By the way, I ran into Randall on my way to the parking lot just now. He tells me they caught another scavenger hunt participant."

"Where?" I asked. "And what was he doing?"

"Randall didn't say," he said with a yawn. "He was headed down to the police station to check it out."

"Anything else?"

"That's all I heard."

I was reassured. If anything really bad had happened, Michael would have heard. And Michael had also helped me decide what to do first—I'd check in at the police station to catch up on the news.

"I'll call you when I wake up," he said. "And you can tell me where to meet you."

I followed Michael back upstairs, helped him out of his general's uniform, and tucked him into bed. He fell asleep as fast as I had. I stayed long enough to brush off his costume and lay it out so he'd have an easy time getting into it when he woke up.

Then I checked on the boys. Michael's mother had them on the back porch drawing faces on pumpkins with black felt-tipped markers. Nice that she not only understood the wisdom of keeping them away from sharp knives but also remembered how dangerous it was to turn them loose indoors with markers.

"Mommy, look!" Josh cried. "Mine's the scariest."

"Mine's the nicest," Jamie countered.

"We're going to take the pumpkins to the library later," Michael's mother said. "Apparently some of Ms. Ellie's pumpkins were stolen."

Which meant the scavenger hunt was continuing. I shoved that thought to the back of my mind as I gave the boys hugs and admired all the pumpkins. They returned to their decorating with renewed zeal.

"I was going to take them into town to see the decorations this afternoon or maybe tonight," Michael's mother said. "But your father seemed to think it was a bad idea."

"I'd drive them around instead of walking," I said. "And this afternoon would be better, or just after dark. And avoid the town square—plenty of decorations to see in the residential areas. Though really, they'll get a chance to see the decorations when they're trick-or-treating, and that might be enough for this year."

"Then there is something going on," she said. "Your father said something about a murder, but knowing how much he loves his mystery books, I thought maybe he was just being . . . dramatic."

"No, there's a murder all right. Two of them." I pulled her a little farther away, to make sure the boys couldn't hear us, and gave her a quick update on everything that had happened.

"Goodness," she said. "No wonder you're not keen on having me take them to town. How are we going to handle the trick-or-treating tomorrow night?"

"Strength in numbers," I said. "Michael and I are both taking time off from patrolling to escort the boys, and you're welcome to come, too, and we're sticking to them like superglue."

"A good plan," she said. "And now I understand why your father came up with his plan to amuse the boys here this afternoon."

"What plan?" I hated to sound suspicious, but Dad's plans all too often were the sort of thing that delighted small boys and appalled their parents.

"Well, he suggested—oh, there he is now." She smiled and waved at something behind my back. "I'll let him explain."

I turned to see Dad bouncing into the backyard, followed by three young men and a young woman, all wearing purple Mutant Wizards t-shirts.

"Grandpa!" Both boys abandoned their pumpkins, leaving their grandmother to cap their markers, and ran to hug Dad.

"Meg!" Dad exclaimed. "Just the person I was looking for. Rob lent me a few of his staff for the project. Is it okay if we use your workshop?"

"What kind of project?" As the words came out of my mouth, I could hear Mother saying them, back in my childhood. And I could see my younger self awaiting her verdict with the same eager, anxious expression the boys now wore as they watched my face.

"We're going to help Josh and Jamie build truly awesome Halloween costumes for tomorrow night," Dad said.

"Mommy, please," Josh said.

"Pretty please with strawberries on top," Jamie added.

"I'll unlock the barn for you," I said. "And make sure there's nothing breakable in the way."

Dad, the boys, and the four Mutant Wizards cheered excitedly as I went back into the house to fetch the key. If I were a glassblower or a potter, I might have been less willing to turn over my workshop, but my wrought iron, my hammers, and my anvil were pretty impervious to damage, even from small boys.

I'd forgotten how much finished iron work I had out there, waiting until I had enough time to take it to a craft fair to sell. As I'd hoped, with the boys in school I had a lot more time to spend at my anvil. But my plan to resume my active blacksmithing career had hit another snag. Going to craft fairs to sell my work required spending weekends away from home—weekends that I now cherished as my main opportunity for spending time with Michael and the boys. Maybe the solution was to find a lot of craft shops willing to buy my work for resale or take it on consignment. Managing that could be just as time-consuming as attending craft fairs, but at least I could do it while they were in school. Not that I'd managed so far.

A problem I needed to solve, but not one I had the brainpower to tackle today. By the time I'd finished getting all the andirons and candlesticks out of the way, Josh was explaining his robot costume requirements to Dad and two of the Mutant Wizards, while Michael's mother and the rest of the team were brainstorming ideas with Jamie. Mostly ideas under discussion seemed to involve electronics, so I deduced that Rob had dispatched a hardware team.

"And we also need costumes for the dogs," Josh said, as he followed the costume crew into the barn.

"Excellent," Michael's mother murmured as she stood beside me in the barn door, watching the costume crew settling in. "With luck, we can keep them distracted until bedtime."

"Thank goodness you're here to provide adult supervision," I replied. And then, for the boys' benefit, I went on, more loudly. "Grammy, you're in charge. Call me if the boys need anything for their costumes."

As I headed for my car, I realized that the boys were gradually solving the problem of how to address Michael's mother. Michael and I had been married long enough that "Mrs. Waterston" seemed too formal, but I wasn't comfortable using "Dahlia," her given name, or calling her "Mom," as Michael did. I'd even toyed with "Mother Waterston" and dismissed it as too much of a mouthful, so mostly I just referred to her as "Michael's mother" and avoided any form of direct address. But "Grammy" was starting to feel comfortable—even in the boys' absence I could use it in a sort of half-ironic tribute to her status as a proud grand-mother. Maybe I'd work my way up to "Mom" after all, but in the meantime, "Grammy" worked just fine.

On my way into town, I could see that the expected Friday night crowds were definitely gathering. The farmer who'd set up his pasture as a no-frills campsite had a NO VACANCY sign up, and his neighbor across the way had opened up his pasture for the overflow. Starting a mile outside town, cars were parked up and down the road in every place where the shoulder was even close to wide enough, and you had to watch out for costumed revelers walking two and three abreast in the road, oblivious to the fact that cars and trucks might also want to use it. I was relieved when I got to the outskirts of town where the sidewalks began.

I picked my way through the residential streets until I reached the police station. On my way I tried to think of a good reason to drop by. I didn't think "I'm dying to find out what's been happening while I napped" would go over very well—especially if the chief was still running on very little sleep. Looking for Randall. That was the ticket. Looking for Randall, and someone said he was heading over to the station.

But when I walked into the police station, Jabba the Hutt merely nodded and waved me back toward the chief's office.

He and Randall were deep in conversation when I stuck my head in.

"There you are," Randall said. "Hope you got some sleep. We're expecting a bumpy night."

"We were always expecting a bumpy Friday night," I said. "Is there any reason to think it's going to be even worse than we expected?"

"The scavenger hunt, of course," Randall said.

"Devil's Night," the chief said. "That's what some people call the night before Halloween. Also Mischief Night. A time for pranks and minor vandalism and, in some benighted communities, waves of arson."

"That's never been part of our local tradition," Randall said, shaking his head.

"But who knows how many of the tourists come from places where it is?" the chief said. "Incidentally, Meg, there have been some developments while you were resting."

"Yes, Michael told me that you'd caught another scavenger hunt participant," I said.

"Alleged participant," the chief said. "We arrested him for trespassing at the zoo—he climbed over the fence and was attempting to gain entry to the Creatures of the Night exhibit. Several members of Blake's Brigade accosted him and managed to detain him until we could arrive to take custody."

"But the zoo's still open," I said. "I thought the task was to sneak in after hours."

"Our theory is that he was planning to hide there until the zoo closed," the chief said. "We confiscated another list from him."

The chief handed me a piece of paper. I glanced down to see that it was a printout of an e-mail from GameMaster, addressed to Tyler Rasmussen, giving him his Friday task list:

1. Find a scarecrow and put it someplace more amusing
2. Steal something from the museum
3. Do something with bones
4. Start a small fire
5. Take a selfie with a black cat

"He's definitely playing the game," I said. "That's probably the full text of the partial list we found at the first murder site. And numbers two and four could account for what happened at the museum."

"Yes," the chief said. "I've alerted Chief Featherstone to the possibility of arson—he'd already noticed an uptick, but had attributed it to Halloween mischief."

"Fulfilling item number two will be a lot harder now," Randall said. "The chief has confiscated nearly all of the contents of the museum and stored them in the police evidence room for safekeeping."

"Nearly all?" I said. "Then there still are some things people could steal?"

"And a few things that may already have been stolen." The chief picked up a piece of paper from his desk and looked over his glasses at it. "We're missing three framed photos—reproductions, not originals, according to the *Clarion*—the fake ruby ring you pointed out, and a pen once used by Virginia Governor Elbert Lee Trinkle to sign some piece of legislation back in 1925. We only confiscated the two department store dummies that were wearing authentic historical costumes, we didn't bother taking the furniture, and there's a brass spittoon that no one wanted to touch because it looked as if it hadn't ever been washed."

"Ick," I said. "I don't blame them."

"Getting back to Mr. Rasmussen—for all we know, he could be the person who broke into the museum this morning."

"Which would make him the killer?" I asked.

"Or a potential witness," the chief said. "Either way, he's refused to talk without an attorney."

"Festus not around?"

"We offered him Festus, but he seems to prefer waiting until his father can arrange representation," the chief said. "If his father can find an attorney willing to make the trip to Caerphilly on a Friday afternoon—soon to be Friday evening—more power to him. Here—" He handed me a sheet of paper. "Does he look familiar?"

I looked down to see a printout of what I deduced was an arrest form. Tyler Rasmussen was a nondescript young man of twenty or so, with disheveled medium-brown hair, beady red-rimmed eyes, and a black t-shirt.

"Not particularly," I said.

Just then the intercom crackled.

"Chief? Mr. Rasmussen again. Do you want to take it?"

The chief clenched his jaw.

"I suppose I'd better."

"Line one."

"Our prisoner's father," the chief said to me. He took a deep breath, picked up the receiver of his phone, and punched a button.

"Yes, Mr. Rasmussen?"

In the silence that followed—silence for Randall and me, but probably rather noisy for the chief—I stood up and pointed to the door, to suggest that I'd be happy to leave if needed. The chief shook his head and pointed back to the chair I'd just vacated, so I sat down again.

"I understand, Mr. Rasmussen," the chief said into the phone. "However, while at the moment we're only charging your son with trespassing and destruction of property, we have evidence to indicate that he is either a suspect in or in possession of material information related to this morning's arson as well as two homicides, so with all due respect, yes, we can continue to hold him . . . I look forward to meeting your attorney. Do you have any idea when he or she will be arriving?"

I suspected from the way the chief pulled the phone away from his head and frowned at it in disapproval that Mr. Rasmussen had resorted to a loud tone and unseemly language to express his feelings about having his son locked up in jail.

"Mr. Rasmussen?" the chief said into the phone. Then he put the receiver back on the cradle, ever so gently, as if slamming it down were a dangerous temptation.

"The senior Mr. Rasmussen is displeased with his son's

incarceration," he said. "He seems to think he can resolve the situation by flying here himself."

"Is he an attorney, then?" I asked.

"I think he would have mentioned it if he was," the chief said, with a grimace. "They usually do. But he clearly considers himself important—he's already asked me if I know who he is, and didn't seem pleased with my answer. But in the meantime, we have a young man in the jail who could help us if he so chose. Frustrating."

"That reminds me," I asked. "Speaking of people who seem to think their legends precede them, what did Mr. Brimfield want?"

"He wanted me to arrest Dr. Smoot," the chief said. "He claims that some of the photos Dr. Smoot has in the museum belong to him."

"I thought Dr. Smoot got them all from the *Caerphilly Clarion*," I said. "At least that's what it says on the labels he has beside the photos—or had, before the fire hoses knocked them off."

"Mr. Brimfield claims his family owns the copyright," the chief said. "Which, if true, could mean that regardless of who owns the physical print that was in the museum, Dr. Smoot couldn't display it without their permission. But that's a matter for the courts to decide if he chooses to take it that far. And in the meantime, the photo is evidence in my murder case, and no, I'm not giving it to him. Not to Dr. Smoot, either."

"You should have seen his face when the chief asked him where he was last night," Randall said, with a chuckle. "Don't think he gets asked for an alibi very often."

"And did he have an alibi?" I asked.

"Up in D.C.," the chief said. "Dining with his congressman and enjoying the luxuries of the historic Willard Hotel. I'm having it checked out, but I'm not listing him as a major suspect just yet."

"More likely a major nuisance," Randall said. "When he found out Smoot was in the hospital, he wanted to dash over there to confront him. To hear Brimfield talk, you'd think Smoot had put himself into a coma out of spite."

"I suggested that he go back to D.C.," the chief said. "And offered to advise him when Dr. Smoot was conscious again. He would prefer to stay here, and seemed to think he'd have no trouble checking into the Caerphilly Inn."

"Good luck with that," Randall said. "They've been booked solid since the week after we announced the festival. That's why Festus was staying with Meg's parents. If Festus couldn't get in—well, I've never known the Inn to be impressed by people who ask 'do you know who I am?'"

"Chief?" It was the intercom again. The chief rolled his eyes and punched the button.

"If it's Mr. Rasmussen again—" he began.

"No, it's Rob Langslow. Says he has important evidence for you. Shall I send him back?"

"Please do."

A few moments later, Rob popped into the chief's office, waving a sheaf of papers.

"I have your victim!" he said. He took the top piece of paper and placed it in front of the chief. I leaned over to see.

"Wayne Smith," the chief read. "Yes, that's him."

"He's a student at Christopher Newport University," Rob said. Then his face fell slightly. "Was, that is. The guys found out his parents' name and address. We figured you probably want to do a notification."

He slid another piece of paper across the desk to the chief.

"Yes," the chief said. "Thank you."

"And we've discovered something he had in common with Justin Klapcroft," Rob said, regaining some of his cheerfulness.

"Something in common?" The chief looked thunderous. "Mr. Klapcroft claimed not to know Mr. Smith."

"He probably didn't," Rob said. "They didn't have any friends in common on Facebook or anything. But both of them liked the Facebook page Lydia put up about the festival. And both of them posted on their own pages about planning to come to the festival. Both of them play a lot of computer games—including *Vampire Colonies*. And—this is important—both of them have their real e-mail addresses up on Facebook for the whole world to see."

"So this supports your staff's theory," I said. "That Game-Master, whoever he is, could have been watching Facebook for people who like computer games and are coming to the festival. And recruited them for his game."

"You got it!" Rob said. "Awesome, isn't it?"

I wasn't sure if he meant GameMaster's method of finding game players or the Mutant Wizards' skill in unraveling it. The chief merely frowned.

"Can you have your staff check to see if this young man meets the same criteria?" He held out a sheet of paper. Rob typed something into his phone, peering back and forth between the paper and the screen. Then he took a picture of something on the paper—probably the mug shot of Mr. Rasmussen the younger—and typed a little more.

"They're on it," he said, after a few moments.

"Aida is supervising Mr. Klapcroft as he completes the last of his day's tasks," the chief said, turning to me. "I've asked her to bring him in to see if he recognizes Mr. Rasmussen, after which we'll be returning him to protective custody. Meanwhile, I should fill you in on what we've learned about Ms. Van Meter."

Rob's phone dinged.

"They found him," Rob said. "The Rasmussen kid. He also meets all the criteria. Liked the festival page, bragged that he was going to come up for the whole weekend, has his e-mail viewable, and doesn't have any friends in common with either of the other two."

"Can your staff identify any other young people who seem likely candidates for GameMaster to contact?"

"We thought you'd ask that," Rob said. "So we've got a complete list of all the people who liked the Facebook page." He laid a thick wad of paper on the chief's desk. "A smaller list of those people who let you see their e-mails. We've highlighted the ones who have few or no friends in common with Justin and your victim. Rasmussen's in there." He placed a more slender wad on the chief's desk. "They're working on this list to see who we can definitely place here in Caerphilly—you know, people who do stuff like posting a selfie of themselves in front of the Haunted House. And also people who can be reliably verified as being elsewhere. Oh, and we're keeping an eye out for Lydia, but so far, nothing. Which is kind of strange, because usually she's tweeting every cup of latte she drinks."

"Excellent," the chief said. "And you're also looking for people who've posted anything that might indicate they're working any of the three task lists?"

Rob nodded.

"One more thing the guys tell me," he said. "There's a possibility someone else has taken over running the game in the last day or two."

"How can they tell?" the chief asked.

"GameMaster used to be very careful to make sure no one could trace where he was e-mailing from," Rob said. "If you want to hear the technical details—"

"I'd rather not," the chief said.

"That's good, because I don't understand it either," Rob said. "But the guys tell me that the e-mails he sent to Justin Klapcroft and Tyler Rasmussen were just sent from a cell phone. A burner cell phone we can't trace—but a cell phone. And from here in Caerphilly. It could just be that he's having to operate a little differently now that he's on-site."

"Or it could mean that someone else has taken over from

him," the chief said. "What if Mr. Green, who has a history of running online scams, was the original GameMaster, and whoever killed him took over running the game, using a cell phone he took from his victim. Would that fit the evidence?"

"Absolutely," Rob said. "Of course, we don't have anything to prove it yet. Just suspicions. But we'll keep working."

"Getting back to Lydia," I said to the chief. "You said you'd fill us in on what you'd learned about her."

"Her car was found in the long-term parking lot at Richmond International Airport earlier this afternoon," the chief said. "And she appears to have taken a one-way flight to New Orleans."

"That doesn't sound good," I said.

"We've asked law enforcement in New Orleans and adjacent parishes to keep an eye out for her," the chief said. "But it's Halloween weekend down there, too, and I expect what they're dealing with makes our problems look tame by comparison."

"Yeah, if they celebrate it even one tenth as wildly as Mardi Gras, watch out!" Rob said. "I remember one year—well, never mind." He seemed to remember where he was and composed himself, although he still had a silly grin on his face.

"Meg, you had more contact with Ms. Van Meter than most of us," the chief said.

"Not any more than I had to," I said.

"Join the club," Rob muttered.

"Did she ever mention New Orleans or say anything about having to leave today?" the chief asked. "Or say anything at all that would help us make sense of this?"

"Like anything that would contradict the theory that she killed James Green and Wayne Smith, set fire to the Haunted House in an attempt to cover up the second murder, and then decided New Orleans was as good a place as any to disappear in?" I shook my head. "Not offhand, but if I think of anything, I'll let you know."

"It's also possible that she's a witness and fled in fear for her life," the chief said.

Rob and I both nodded dutifully, but I could tell I wasn't the only one who found the notion of Lydia as a killer a lot more plausible.

"Well, I won't keep you from your patrolling," the chief said.

I can take a hint when I hear one. I stood up, wished Rob and the chief a good afternoon, and left.

Chapter 20

I decided to leave my car in the station parking lot and walk over to the town square to check on things there. A wise decision. Apparently the chief had decided to block off the town square well before dark, so I'd have had to turn around anyway.

There were long lines at every food tent and concession stand. But to the extent that I could see people's faces, the tourists all seemed pretty cheerful, many of them dancing along with the band's reggae-themed version of "Monster Mash." Rose Noire's booth, with its rapidly dwindling stock of organic herbs, lotions, and perfumes, was also crowded. She looked tired—I hoped merely from working so hard all day and not from having to beam positive vibes into herbs so her less savory customers couldn't use them for evil purposes. The dried flower tent was closing up—perhaps realizing that the crowds now pouring into the square were not likely to be customers.

I found myself feeling distinctly out of patience with the tourists, so I took one of those deep yoga breaths Rose Noire was always recommending and made a conscious effort to see them in a positive light. They were helping the town economy. And through the food tents, rebuilding the coffers of the churches just at the beginning of the winter when the need for funds for all their charitable activities increased significantly. And most of the tourists had come here not out of greed or ambition but to have fun. And they'd clearly spent so much time and money on the costumes that were, frankly, the main event as far as I could see.

Princess Leia marched between two Imperial Stormtroopers with such long legs that I suspected they were walking on stilts. Two people dressed as bunches of grapes walked by—one had dozens of light green balloons stuck to her clothes, while her companion's balloons were dark purple. A man wearing realistic-looking plate armor had decked out his mobility scooter with a horse's head and tail.

Watching the costumed revelers was getting me into a better mood, but now I had to fight the temptation just to find a good vantage point and watch the show.

Next year, maybe. For this year, I had work to do.

I spotted a familiar-looking costume—a well-worn gorilla suit that belonged to my cousin Horace. What was he doing out in costume instead of on duty? I fell into step beside him.

"What's up?" I asked. "Why aren't you on duty?"

"Shh!" he said. "I am on duty. Plainclothes surveillance."

Okay, in this crowd the gorilla suit probably qualified as plainclothes.

"Noticed anything interesting?" I asked.

"Take a look at that one."

He pointed to a man ahead of me whose costume made my jaw drop. He was wearing a black overcoat whose entire surface was festooned with thirty or forty extra sleeves. Not empty sleeves—each sleeve appeared to contain an arm, each arm ended with a black-gloved hand, and each hand was doing something different. One held a pencil. Another a cigarette. One was giving the V for victory sign. Another was making a rude gesture to the world. Two were shaking hands with each other.

"A coat of arms, obviously," I said. "And ingeniously done. Has he done anything suspicious, or are you tailing him merely because of the sheer number of fake body parts he's sporting?"

"He seems mostly harmless," Horace said. "I'm actually kind of keeping an eye to see if anyone tries to take any of his arms. I figure if I was a scavenger hunt participant and didn't know where to get a fake body part to scare people with, I'd spot him and say 'bingo!' "

I left him to follow his quarry and continued on my tour of inspection. And after one very slow trip around the square, I decided to head back to my car so I could check on what was happening out at the zoo and the Haunted House.

The road was completely lined with parked cars all the way out to the Haunted House—a few of them not completely off the road, creating spots where there was just barely enough room for two normal-sized cars to pass. In fact, I had to back up once to let one of the horse-drawn hay wagons by.

I drove all the way out to the zoo to check on things there. A large sign on the entrance gate read ZOO CLOSES AT 5:00 P.M. TODAY. I checked my watch—only half an hour to go. Though I suspected it would take an hour or two to make sure all the tourists were really gone. The area of the parking lot closest to the gate had been turned into a camping ground for the Blake's Brigade volunteers—it was filled with tents and campers and horse trailers. I saw Caroline briefing a trio of riders. Two were dressed as knights while the third was wearing a skeleton costume and had painted his black steed to look like a skeleton horse. As I watched, the three riders saluted and set off across the parking lot.

Caroline spotted me and came over.

"We've brought in the cavalry," she said, pointing to where the riders were following a dirt path into the woods. The paint on the skeleton horse was faintly luminescent. "Should make it easier to chase down any intruders who try to flee. And thanks for the offer of canine assistance."

"Canine assistance?"

"There they are now."

I recognized Michael's mother's car. She pulled up near us. Michael was sitting beside her in the front passenger seat, and I could see an enormous furry head bobbing between theirs. Tinkerbell. Yes, a full-grown Irish wolfhound would be a nice addition to the zoo's security.

Michael's mother stopped by the staff entrance and hopped out to open the back door so Tinkerbell could begin the complicated process of extracting herself from the backseat—a process made more difficult by the fact that she was wearing a pink tulle headdress, a pink tutu, and pink ruffles around all four ankles.

"That," I said, "is a truly scary costume. And what are you going to—oh, my God! What is that?"

I leaped back from a creature that suddenly appeared at Tinkerbell's side—the biggest spider I'd ever seen, with a hairy black body as big as a football and eight long, hairy, many-jointed legs. Had it escaped from the insect house at the zoo? Or—

Then the spider uttered a very familiar growl.

"Spike?"

The Small Evil One glanced up at me with a look that clearly said, "Don't you dare laugh or I'll bite your ankle."

Michael, already back in his Union general's costume, crept up behind Spike and carefully picked up the trailing end of his leash. Spike waited till the last minute and then lunged at him, snarling.

"He's in a bad mood," Michael said. "I don't think he really appreciates all the trouble the boys went through to make him the costume."

"Did they do this?" I asked. I risked life and limb by inching closer to inspect the costume. Spike had been dyed black—not, I hoped, with permanent dye—and the eight fake legs were attached to a wide fabric band fastened snugly around his belly. I might have managed to attach the belly band without getting bitten too badly, but there's no way I could have dyed him and survived with all my fingers attached. "And are they okay?"

"They're fine," Michael said. "He was good as gold with them, as usual. Now he's taking out his vexation on us."

Spike was gazing around with the sort of hopeful expression that suggested he felt like biting something or someone and liked the odds of finding a target in the crowd of tourists and Brigade members milling nearby. I deduced from the way Michael was holding the leash and frowning that the ride over had not been relaxing.

"That's excellent!" Caroline exclaimed. "Just looking at him scares the willies out of me. Do you think we should patrol with them, or just turn them loose to roam the Creatures of the Night?"

"What about the alligators?" I asked.

"I don't think Spike can possibly get at them," Caroline said. "The boardwalks in the swamp habitat are designed to keep toddlers from jumping into the habitats."

Did she really think I was worried about the alligators? Then again, maybe I should be.

"I'm sure Caroline will take good care of all the animals," Michael's mother said. "I'd better be getting back before the boys run Rob and his costume makers ragged."

She turned around carefully, to avoid hitting any of the dozens of tourists milling about, and headed away.

"I figured we could join forces," Michael said.

"Good idea," I said. "Let's head for the Haunted House."

I drove the couple of miles that separated the zoo from the Haunted House slowly, because at any given point somewhere between half of the road and the whole width was filled with costumed tourists.

And when we got to the Haunted House, we saw three Shiffley Construction vans parked in front.

"What's wrong now?" I muttered. "Surely they've finished

blocking off the back door by now. Or has there been some new problem?"

Randall spotted us as we parked and threaded his way through the crowds to meet us.

"Don't worry," he said, seeing my anxious face. "Nothing's wrong. I just had an idea to improve security, so I got some of the boys to come out and take care of it. We only need the front door open for the tourists, but Ms. Ellie and Aunt Jane said it was driving them crazy, keeping an eye on the back door, basement door, and a whole mess of windows. I thought it would enhance our security if we defended the perimeter a bit more—kept the tourists from wandering into the backyard or climbing the fence. So I sent a couple of my workmen out here to see to it."

He gestured toward the right-side yard, where a new stretch of eight-foot chain-link fence ran between the side of the house and the matching chain-link fence that defined the outer boundaries of the yard. A similar fence bisected the left side of the yard. And just to keep the new fences from being an eyesore, he'd had his workmen spray them black and decorate them with spooky silhouettes. A witch stirring a cauldron. Another riding a broom. Frankenstein's monster lurching with outstretched arms. A sinister creeping figure with a long cloak and clawlike talons. And an assortment of bats, cats, pumpkins, and skeletons. All were cut out of flat wood, painted black, and mounted on the fences.

"One of my cousins is an artist with a band saw," Randall bragged. "And you'll notice we added some barbed wire to the top of all the fences. That should slow them down a bit."

"And you seem to have created another tourist attraction," Michael said with a chuckle. Tourists were lining up to take selfies and pose in groups in front of the cutouts. In fact the new fences were almost as popular as the picturesque iron front fence—just about every time I visited the Haunted House, I spotted at least one person having his picture taken behind it—sometimes with both hands clutching the bars as if rattling them angrily, and sometimes with one hand stretched out through the bars in pitiful entreaty.

"You know," I said. "We should create some kind of site where the tourists could upload their photos."

"That's a great idea," Randall said. "It'd be great publicity for next year's festival. Assuming we have the festival next year, of course," he added hastily, no doubt realizing that one of the things getting many of us through this year's event was the notion that maybe we'd never have to do any of this again.

"Rob can probably get someone to set it up," I said.

We left Randall and his workmen to finish up the new fencing and continued on back to town. The road was filled with trolls, wizards, superheroes, hobbits, and other beings from worlds where automobiles had not yet been invented, so that their inhabitants didn't understand why stepping out in front of them was such a bad idea.

We parked in the college parking lot and began patrolling the town square. Night was falling, and the vegetable stands and craft booths were closing up. The food tents were probably hoping to close soon as well, but at the moment they still had long lines for the boxed dinners they had started selling for after-hours customers.

Including the Trinity Episcopal tent.

"Let's drop in and see how Mother is doing," I said. "I'm a little worried about her."

"Worried?" Michael echoed. "Why?"

"Look around," I said. "Does this look like something Mother would enjoy?"

A conga line of some thirty or forty particularly gross-looking zombies was winding its way through the square, shambling in time to Michael Jackson's "Thriller," which was booming out of speakers hidden in the ragged clothing of several participants. A dozen or so vampires wearing velvet

cloaks, pale makeup, and fairly fake-looking fangs were having some kind of discussion or altercation just outside the
tent door. Or maybe they were just acting out a scene from
some play or movie—overacting, more like it. A hairy-chested
man in a tutu was dancing the cancan with a man wearing a
grim reaper cloak and a Nixon face mask, and two people
playing the front and back halves of a unicorn.

"You're right," Michael said. "Let's check on her."

To my astonishment, Mother wasn't just supervising—she
was performing actual work. A short, round woman whose
face was hidden under a Darth Vader mask was cutting slices
of pie and putting them on paper plates. Mother, at her elbow,
was adding a small, artistic dollop of whipped topping to
each slice.

"You're making me wish I'd saved room for pie," I said, as
I came up behind them.

"If you like, dear, I can buy a whole pie for us to take home
and share later."

"Make it two," Michael said. "I'll help you pack them up
and Meg can take over for you for a few minutes."

Mother and Michael went off to deal with pie acquisition
and I stepped into her place and began wielding the whipped
topping spoon.

"Meg! Isn't this fun?"

Darth Vader pulled her mask up just long enough to see
that she was actually Becky Griswald. She seemed a lot happier, and even younger, away from her overbearing husband
and his obsession with the cat-shaped brooch.

"Actually, it looks like hard work if you do it for very long,"
I said. "Is the mask to make sure Harris doesn't see you?"

"To make sure no one mentions seeing me," she said. "He's
gone down to Charlottesville for the weekend for a meeting
of the Stuffed Shirts."

"The Stuffed Shirts?" I had to giggle, because it sounded
just like Mr. Griswald's kind of group.

"I call them that. Half a dozen old coots he went to business school with. They get together every quarter for an expensive dinner. Normally I have to go along to make polite conversation with their stuffy wives, but I pretended I had a migraine so I could stay home and enjoy the festival. Isn't it marvelous!"

She was beaming at the patrons who were picking up pie—a Spider-Man, a Wonder Woman, and a pair of pirates.

Just then Mother and Michael returned, each carrying a pie box. Mother handed hers to me and took up her station beside Mrs. Griswald. She was wearing what I thought of as her bravely suffering smile, and I suspected she was getting a headache.

"Mother, would you like us to run you home," I asked. "We need to go out to the Haunted House anyway—it would only be a small detour."

Michael opened his mouth—no doubt to point out that we'd just come from the Haunted House—and then he obviously realized what I was doing and held his peace.

"Thank you, dear, but Caroline is coming by to pick me up any minute now," she said. "It's been a long day."

A long day in uncongenial surroundings. In theory, Mother approved of Halloween—she approved of any holiday that involved decorating, and was enthusiastic beforehand about the idea of the festival. She loved the sort of tasteful handmade decorations Martha Stewart was always demonstrating, but the rest of the world so rarely met her expectations. Rubber bats, orange and black crepe-paper garlands, plastic skeletons—in practice, Halloween was one long assault on her decorating sensibilities.

"There's Caroline now." Mother's voice was filled with relief. "You know, if you're still patrolling, I can take the pies with me."

"Just as long as you don't eat both of them before we get home," I said, as I handed her my box.

"I think I can restrain myself, dear." She smiled wanly, gave us each a peck on the cheek, and sailed out of the tent toward where Caroline was standing. I suspected that she was probably going to go straight to bed with a cold cloth over her face, but if my teasing helped her keep her head high till then, all the better.

For the next few hours, Michael and I patrolled. Around the square. Back to the parking lot for the car. Out to the haunted house. Out to the zoo. Back to town. Either the news of the murder hadn't really spread to the tourists or it hadn't dampened their spirits. I was beginning to wish it had.

The town square seemed to be the favored rendezvous of what we'd come to call the vampire conventioneers—mostly young people in their teens or twenties, dressed almost entirely in black except for small ribbon rosettes pinned somewhere on their costumes. They tended to clump together by ribbon color—so far I'd noticed posses of red, blue, yellow, green, purple, orange, and gray. And they all seemed to spend their time acting out small dramatic scenes, so I'd pegged them as probable LARPers. And also as probably harmless.

"You know," I said, as we were halfway through another stroll around the town square, "I don't normally mind watching other people have fun while I'm working. Normally I can sort of share their enjoyment. Having a hard time with that tonight."

"It's not watching them have fun that's a downer," Michael said. "It's knowing that some of them might be plotting pranks. Or worse, more murders. Where do you suppose they're going?"

He was pointing to a trio of black-clad vampires sporting purple and black ribbon rosettes who had taken a sharp right turn at the corner, toward the less crowded parts of town.

"They're heading toward the campus," I said.

"Where there's absolutely no festival activity going on." He was frowning. Now that he was the heir apparent to the chairmanship of the Drama department rather than a despised rogue professor, he was taking a much more protective attitude toward the college. "The president and the board of trustees were absolutely dead set against hosting any festival events on campus. So where are those jokers going?"

"Maybe they're students, heading back to their rooms," I suggested. "Or even out-of-towners staying with friends in the dorms."

"Maybe." We had reached the corner where the LARPers had turned. He still looked uneasy.

"So let's just patrol that way for a little bit," I suggested.

Chapter 21

The three LARPers had already disappeared from view by the time we turned the corner, so we found ourselves walking through the tree-lined and increasingly quiet streets of the campus. The dorms were about the only place that showed any signs of life, but they didn't seem any different from a typical Friday night. And once we passed the dorms, the various academic buildings and the lawns surrounding them were absolutely deserted. When we finally reached the far end of the campus we stopped for a moment.

"Are you reassured that the vampires aren't taking over the campus?" I asked.

"Well, if they are, at least they're doing it quietly," he said. "I suppose we should head back."

"Let's turn that way," I suggested, pointing to a road that ran along the outer perimeter of the campus. "And go back by another route." Another route that would prolong, if only briefly, our time in the peaceful back streets of the campus.

Michael fell in with my suggestion and we walked in companionable silence for a few minutes. Then Michael stopped in the middle of the sidewalk.

"That's odd." He was peering into the darkness. "There shouldn't be anyone over there."

We were in a part of the campus I didn't know very well. I knew by the signs I'd read that we'd recently passed the Mechanical Engineering building and the Agricultural Sciences building, but I had no idea what was in the direction of Michael's gaze.

"What's over there?" I asked.

"The Ag Sci Department's demonstration barn," he said. "There shouldn't be anyone there right now."

"Not even someone tending the animals?"

"No." He shook his head slightly. "They were worried that the festival would upset the animals, so they trucked them all out to the main farm over a week ago. The building's supposed to be locked up tight for the duration."

"Maybe some cow with a homing instinct got out of her pasture at the main farm," I suggested.

"And walked ten miles to get back here? With a flashlight?" he added as we spotted a quick flash of light near the barn.

"Let's check it out."

We turned into a narrow asphalt lane that led to the barn. Fences ran on either side of the road. I got my bearings back and remembered coming down this lane before. There had been sheep and goats in the left-hand pasture, and at least a dozen different breeds of cow in the right. Now both fields were silent and presumably empty.

The lane opened up into a broad expanse of asphalt— also empty except for a single hulking piece of agricultural equipment. Possibly some kind of seed drill or tiller. Even a first-year Ag Sci student would probably know exactly what it was. All I could tell for sure is that it seemed to have a lot of sharp-looking points and edges so that we'd be better off giving it a wide berth.

We arrived at the broad double barn doors and stopped to listen.

"Rustling noises," Michael whispered. "There could be someone there."

"Or the rats could be having a field day while the legitimate occupants are away," I whispered back.

The door handles were chained together and padlocked. I pointed to a smaller ordinary door to the right of the main entrance.

Michael tried the handle gently.

"Locked," he whispered.

"Of course," I said softly. "If I were sneaking in there for some nefarious purpose, I'd probably lock the door behind me to prevent being surprised."

"And I'd run out the back if anyone rattled the door," he replied.

"You didn't exactly rattle it," I said.

"Yeah, but if they're listening . . ."

We looked at each other for a moment.

"Run around and check," I said. "I'll guard the front."

"Is it wise for us to split our forces?" he asked.

"We're also sending for reinforcements." I already had my phone out. "I'm calling 911."

"Good thinking." He took off running toward the back of the barn as I dialed.

"Hey, Meg, what's your emergency?" Debbie Ann asked.

"Not sure yet if it is an emergency," I began. "But—oof!"

Something hit me in the back. I stumbled, dropped the phone, and fell back against the side of the barn.

"What mere mortal dares to trespass on Clan Raven's territory?"

I looked up to see a tall, gangly young man dressed in black, from his ruffled shirt to his thigh-high boots. The only touch of color was a little rosette of black-and-purple ribbon near the collar of his cloak. He was grinning mirthlessly, probably so I could see his fangs. Even by moonlight they looked a little fake—not nearly as impressive as Dr. Smoot's. And he might have made a more plausible vampire if he'd worn a mask to cover his rather extensive acne. Though even without the acne, I'd never have mistaken him for a real vampire.

But the sword he was holding with its point almost touching the hollow of my throat—that was real. Real steel. Blacksmiths—especially ones like me who have done a bit of bladesmithing as well—can tell these things. The metal had an unmistakable satiny sheen to it. And while it made me cross-eyed to look at it, I could see that it had a nasty point. In fact, when his hand wavered a bit, I felt the point break my skin before he drew it back again.

"Mortal—I demand to know why you are trespassing on the ancestral lands of the Raven Clan!" he intoned.

"I heard you the first time." I decided my best bet was to ignore his game. "And if Clan Raven wants to claim this particular spot as part of their ancestral lands, they'll have to take it up with the Caerphilly College legal department. Now get out of my way."

"You dare assert your human laws against the immortal . . . um . . . wisdom of the Undying Ones!"

"Goblin Patrol," I barked. "And you're the one trespassing. Take that silly little toothpick away from my throat or you'll be sorry."

"Silence!" he roared. And then he narrowed his eyes and glowered at me. At my neck actually, where a few drops of blood were trickling down from the cut he'd given me. Was he really trying to make me think he was craving my blood? Or just killing time till he could come up with some more stilted dialogue? I reminded myself that both of our recent murders had been committed with guns, but somehow that didn't reassure me. It wouldn't prevent this lunatic from committing murder number three with his sword.

I needed to come up with a plan. Maybe I could back up in the direction of the agricultural machine at the edge of the asphalt and try to impale him on one of the pointy bits? No. Too complicated. And I was already talking as loudly as I could, in the hope that Michael would come along and tackle him.

Maybe a distraction.

"Look," I began. "If you—"

And then I deliberately broke off and glanced over his shoulder, as if I'd suddenly spotted something. He didn't completely fall for it and whirl around, but he did take his eyes off me for a few seconds, and that gave me my chance.

"Ay-yi!" I yelled, as my martial arts teacher had taught me so long ago. Fortunately I remembered a few other things he'd taught me. I ducked under the blade and kneed the Clan Raven dude in the groin while grabbing his sword hand with both of mine and twisting. He yelped and doubled over, dropping the sword. I rolled him over on his stomach—he was almost Michael's height, but weedy, and also, thanks to my knee, in no frame of mind to put up much of a fight. He squirmed a bit until I pulled one of his arms up behind and twisted it enough to be uncomfortable.

"Oww," he whined. "You're hurting me."

"Lie still, then," I said. "Or I'll hurt you worse. You're the one who drew first, remember. What are you doing here?"

He said nothing—just moaned feebly.

I tightened his arm a little.

"Oww!" he yelped. "All right. I'm just here to decorate for the ball."

"The ball?"

"The vampire ball," he whimpered. "Tomorrow night. All the clans are coming. And Clan Raven is in charge of decorating."

"In the barn?"

He nodded.

"You couldn't just hire a hall?"

Okay, that was a rhetorical question.

Then a voice came out of the darkness.

"You can let him go now, Meg." Aida Butler. "I've got my .38 aimed at him. Of course I didn't load the silver bullets this morning, but I'm betting Dracula here isn't immune to lead. Why don't you get up and find your phone and tell Debbie Ann I'm here."

"I need to look for Michael." It worried me that he hadn't showed up already. I spotted my phone and grabbed it.

"Wait till Vern gets here," Aida said. "Or let me cuff this creep—"

"I'm here," said Vern. "Where'd Michael go?"

"Around the back." I took off in the direction Michael had taken, over a fence into a paddock, and then down the side of the barn until I reached the fence at the other end. There were probably gates but I didn't want to waste time hunting for them in the dark. Okay, not so dark—Vern's flashlight came on, just in time to let me avoid stepping in a strategically located manure pile—but I still didn't want to waste time looking for the gate. "We heard rustling in there," I said over my shoulder. "In the Ag Sci department's demonstration barn," I added, since presumably Debbie Ann might also still be listening on my phone. "So I was guarding the front door while he went around to check on—Michael!"

I ran the last few steps to where Michael was lying on the ground just outside the barn, beside another people-sized door.

"I'm okay," he said. Then he winced. "Okay, I'm not okay. I think maybe my ankle's broken. But I'm not dead. The vampires went thataway."

He pointed away from the barn, where the Ag Sci pastures stretched away into the darkness.

"We'll round them up later," Vern said. "We need an ambulance here, pronto," he added into his police radio. Then he turned back to us. "What happened?"

"I found the door open," Michael said. "And I went in and surprised half a dozen people dressed like vampires. They were decorating the place—hanging lights and drapes and stuff. When they saw me, they all panicked and ran. One of them fell on her way out the door, and I tripped over her, and—voilà."

He pointed at his ankle. Vern shone his flashlight on it. The ankle was already grapefruit-sized.

"What's going on here?" I turned to see Chief Burke climbing over the fence.

"Trespassers in the Ag Sci barn," Michael said.

"The vampire clans were planning to have their Halloween masked ball here tomorrow night," I said. "Don't look at me that way—I didn't make it up. The vamp wannabe with the rapier told me. He's on the decorating committee."

"I don't doubt you," the chief said. "That would be the young reprobate Aida has in handcuffs at the other side of the barn? Debbie Ann seems to think he tried to attack you with a sword."

"What?" Michael exclaimed.

"He tried," I said, indicating the small wound on my throat. "But then I disarmed him and twisted his arm to tell me what he was doing here."

"I gather you mean that literally," the chief murmured. "Let me check this out. And it's starting to drizzle. Let's get Mr. Waterston inside where he can be more comfortable till the ambulance arrives."

Vern and I managed to get Michael up and helped him hobble through the barn door without putting any weight on his foot. We couldn't help staring at what we saw inside.

"Glory be," the chief muttered.

The vampire LARPers had transformed the place. They'd hung long lengths of black fabric from floor to ceiling along three of the walls, and I could see a ladder in place where we'd evidently interrupted someone decking the fourth wall. Someone else was starting to hang fairy lights along the already draped walls. At one end of the room was a large table covered with a black tablecloth, while at the other stood a black dais with two chairs sitting on it. The chairs were the only discordant note—although large, they were fairly ordinary armchairs upholstered in scruffy beige fabric. But I could see a heap of black fabric nearby, and I had no doubt that when they finished with the walls they'd have enough left over to camouflage the rather utilitarian chairs and transform them into vampire thrones.

"They're having a party here?" the chief asked. "Who authorized that?"

"If someone had authorized it, why would they have run away when we confronted them?" I asked.

"Barn's supposed to be locked tight till the festival's over," Michael said.

"Tell me what happened." The chief had taken out his trusty notebook.

Michael let me do the talking. As I was doing so, two EMTs arrived and began checking Michael out, which probably made the end of my tale just a bit less coherent than the beginning. Once I'd finished, Michael described the LARPers he'd seen.

"So we're looking for half a dozen young people dressed up as vampires," the chief said, with a sigh. "I'm afraid that's not much help."

"I can tell you what will help," I said. "All the people who are playing this game will be wearing those little ribbon rosettes. I'm pretty sure it tells the other players that they're part of the game, and also which clan they're in. The Clan Raven people will be wearing black-and-purple rosettes like my assailant."

"Yes," Michael said. "Black-and-purple ribbons, definitely."

"That's good," the chief said. "I'll put out a BOLO for vampires wearing purple ribbons. Meg, why don't you go down to the hospital with Michael? Once you're sure he's okay, come down to the station and we'll see what kind of charges we're pressing against these hooligans."

It sounded like a good idea to me. The EMTs were loading Michael onto a stretcher, over his complaints that all he really needed was a shoulder to lean on. I trotted behind them as they made their way to the other end of the barn, watched as they loaded him into the ambulance, and then, since our car was still over at the college parking lot, hitched a ride on the ambulance to Caerphilly Hospital.

Chapter 22

"He'll be fine," Dad said. "A simple fracture. We're just waiting for Dr. Sengupta to get here." Apparently only orthopedists were allowed to set bones and apply casts, and Dr. Sengupta, the local orthopedist, had fled to Richmond for the weekend, but had allowed himself to be persuaded by Dad to come back to take care of Michael.

"Why don't you leave me with your dad?" Michael suggested.

"I'm staying right here until you get your cast," I said. "And then I'm driving you home."

"But if you stay here, I'll have to wait until tomorrow to find out if they've caught the stupid LARPers who tripped me," Michael protested.

"And it could be a while before Dr. Sengupta gets here," Dad said. "You go handle your Goblin Patrol duties. I'll keep you posted on everything that happens here, and you can tell me what you learn at the station."

They both looked so determined that I gave in.

"Okay," I said. "But call me the minute Dr. Sengupta arrives. Or if anything else happens."

"Absolutely," Dad said.

"Of course," Michael said. "And now that your dad has given me some pain meds, I'll probably just go to sleep anyway."

So an hour or so after I'd arrived, I walked out of the hospital and turned left, toward the police station, which was only a few blocks away. The parking lot where we'd left the car was only a few blocks beyond that, and once I got to the police station, I could probably beg a ride from someone if I didn't feel like walking the rest of the way.

We were a few streets from the town square, but the noise still carried. Rancid Dread, an inexplicably popular local heavy metal band, was playing a concert in the town square tonight. The high-pitched squealing of the Dreads' guitars, and the incessant throbbing of their bass line carried easily, interspersed with the cheering of the crowds.

But wait—should they still be playing? If the concert ran past its agreed-upon midnight end time, we'd hear from everyone within earshot—which could mean half the county.

I pulled out my phone and glanced at the time. How could it possibly be just a little past eleven?

On impulse, I took a slight detour past the town square so I could see how the concert was going over. Either distance was kind to the Dreads' music or they had been practicing a lot more since the last time I'd been unable to avoid hearing them.

Amazing to see hundreds of costumed revelers either dancing in the town square or sitting on the courthouse steps, apparently enjoying themselves. The Dreads were all dressed in Goth-style Halloween costumes and flamboyant facial makeup, so if you were stone deaf you might think, just for a moment, that you were at an early KISS concert. They had improved a bit—musically at least. And with the costumes on, they didn't look nearly as weedy and disheveled as usual. Of course, their lead singer still enunciated so badly that it took me several bars to realize that they were doing a cover version of The Doors' "Riders on the Storm." Not a tune I could ever have imagined a heavy metal band playing until I heard the Dreads' hideous version of it. And unfortunately it seemed to be one of their signature numbers.

The song reached a crescendo, increasing in volume so much that I decided maybe I should continue assessing their progress from a few blocks away. I turned and collided with a human being almost the size of a Dumpster. Ragnar. Now that Blake's Brigade was guarding the zoo, I'd reassigned Osgood and Ragnar to patrol the town square. Though I thought their shift had ended hours ago.

"Sorry," I said. "Are you still on duty?"

"Is okay," Ragnar said. "I am technically off duty now, but I do not think the town square should be unguarded. And I like to listen."

He sounded rather wistful.

"By the way," I said. "If you happen to see the annoying Lydia anywhere, let the police know."

"Is she a suspect?" From his expression, I suspected he would be neither surprised nor unhappy if she was.

"No idea," I said. "All I know is she'd better have a good excuse for disappearing all this time, or she will not be around to organize next year's festival."

"Awesome," Ragnar said. "And if she leaves, perhaps next year we can have a small haunted house in Dr. Smoot's house and a big one in mine. And also perhaps by this time next year I will have another band to play with here in the square."

"I thought you were retired."

"Oh, not to make records with," he said. "Just to play for fun."

He was still looking longingly at the stage. An idea struck me. I peered at the stage until I spotted one of my Goblin Patrol members guarding the steps at one side of it. I texted the goblin and gave him a few instructions.

I watched as he darted over to Orvis Shiffley, the Dreads' drummer. They exchanged a few words. Orvis surged forward from behind his drums, grabbed the microphone from the lead singer, and began to address the crowd.

"I have some awesome news," he said. "Right here in the audience tonight we have a living legend . . . a musician who's been an inspiration to our whole band. And word is that maybe we could get him to play a few numbers with us. Ladies and gentlemen—Ragnar Ragnarsen!"

I could tell from the expressions on the faces on the audience members near me that most of them either hadn't ever heard of Ragnar or were under the understandable impression that he'd succumbed to drink, drugs, or fast cars, like the rest of his former bandmates. But they all applauded good-naturedly.

"Me?" Ragnar looked at me as if asking permission.

"The Dreads are asking for you," I said.

He lumbered off toward the stage, beaming like a grade schooler who has just been asked to hang out with the cool kids on the playground. By the time he reached the stage, the roadies—several of Orvis's uncles and older cousins—had pushed a spare drum set out of the wings. No doubt they kept one in reserve, in case Orvis demolished the primary one with the fury of his solos.

I waited long enough to verify that adding an unfamiliar and completely unrehearsed musician to their band didn't appreciably affect the quality of the Dreads' music. Only the decibel level. And Ragnar, who had been looking like a mistreated puppy, was in his element. I retreated from the town square and walked the few more blocks between me and the police station.

Only a few police vehicles occupied the parking lot, and those appeared to be only touching down in between patrols.

Inside the station, Jabba the Hutt had been replaced by a slender, balding, hollow-chested Superman whom I recognized as the relatively new civilian receptionist.

"Ms. Langslow," he said. "Shall I ask if the chief is available?"

"He's expecting me," I said as I breezed past.

If it ever came to leaping tall buildings in defense of the station, Superman wasn't going to be much help. I was already halfway down the hallway before he gathered his wits together to protest.

"Ms. Langslow." Chief Burke was in his office, talking to Randall, and neither seemed surprised to see me. "Good. Horace is still out at the barn, but he should be back soon. I want him to photograph your wound. How is Michael?"

"Simple fracture," I said. "Dad's staying with him."

"That's a relief. So, Meg, to bring you up to speed, your assailant is a Mr. Norton Brewer, a nineteen-year-old computer science major at the University of Richmond. His parents have been contacted. They were unaware that he was here in Caerphilly and have agreed to let Festus Hollingsworth represent him for the time being. Festus is on his way. So is the county attorney. In the meantime—"

"Chief?" It was Superman on the intercom. "I have some people here who want to see you."

"What people?" the chief barked.

"They say they're the elders of the Clan Raven," Superman said. "It's some kind of vampire thing."

The chief paused and looked at me and Randall. Randall shrugged. I nodded.

"Escort them back here," the chief said into the intercom.

"Yes, sir."

"I'm pretty sure that's the group your prisoner belongs to," I said when the intercom was off again. "He said Clan Raven were in charge of the decorations."

"Why don't you move your chairs over here beside my desk," the chief suggested to Randall and me. "Give them some room to get in."

And, probably not coincidentally, present a solid Caerphillian front to our visitors.

The door opened and three black-clad people walked in—two men and a woman. For elders, they were pretty young—mid-twenties perhaps. They all hesitated in the doorway—for dramatic effect, or just because they weren't entirely sure what to expect? They ended up standing in a clump in front of the chief's desk.

"Wes," the chief said—to Superman, I assumed—"bring in three folding chairs for our guests."

Superman popped out.

"Elders of Clan Raven," the chief repeated. "Mind telling me the names I'd find if I asked for your driver's licenses?"

"Bill Higgins," said the tallest. "I'm the leader of the clan."

"Celia Smith," the woman said.

"Tony Ruiz," the other man said.

Wes returned with three folding chairs, and conversation paused while the vampire elders set them up and sat down, being careful of their long black cloaks.

"So, if everyone's comfortable, would you mind telling me what you're doing here in Caerphilly?" the chief said. "Because we've already figured you're not just here to take in the festival."

"We're all participants in a live action role playing game loosely based on a computer game called *Vampire Colonies*," Bill said.

"Oh, God, *Vampire Colonies*," I muttered. "It would have to be *Vampire Colonies*."

The chief, Randall, and the vampire elders all looked at me in puzzlement.

"That's one of Rob's games," I explained. "The one that has a new version coming out shortly before Christmas."

"The one our other young friend was so eager to obtain?" the chief asked.

He meant Justin Klapcroft, obviously. And just as obviously didn't want to say his name in front of the elders, so I just nodded.

"I didn't know people were LARPing with it," I said.

"You know about *Vampire Colonies*?" Bill asked. He and his companions looked eager, as if they might have just discovered a kindred spirit.

"I was a play tester for the original game," I said. "The

computer game—as I said; I had no idea people were LARP-
ing with it."

"Ms. Langslow's brother, Rob, is the founder of Mutant
Wizards," the chief explained.

"Awesome," Tony muttered. All three elders seemed ever-
so-slightly awestruck at my proximity to greatness.

"Thus, she is somewhat familiar with the game you're playing," the chief went on. "I, on the other hand, am not. Fill
me in."

"Okay, so we've got people here from seven of the twelve
clans in our version of the game," Bill began. "Clans Raven,
Wolf, Owl, Bat, Tiger, Cat and . . . um . . ."

"Wombat," Celia put in.

"Yeah, Wombat," Bill said. "They're a little weird."

"The clans are semivoluntary associations of vampires
under a leader," I explained.

"Semivoluntary?" the chief echoed.

"If a vampire turns you into a vampire, you automatically
become a member of their clan, but under some circumstances you can change clans," Bill said.

"Or get kicked out for bad behavior," Celia muttered.
Evidently she already had some idea what young Norton
had been up to.

"We decided the Halloween Festival would be a cool place
to have our big annual Halloween LARP and masked ball,"
Bill said. "So we sent out the word for the clans to gather."

"In the computer game, the elders transmit their com-
mands telepathically," I said. "How do you replicate that in
your LARP?"

"We use e-mail," Bill said. "Tony runs our Listserv. And
we've been playing a scenario where all the clans are trying
to find a magical artifact that will give their clan great power."

"We're not talking about a ring, are we?" Randall asked.
Evidently he, like me, was thinking about the break-in at the
Haunted House.

"No." Bill looked puzzled. "It's a goblet."

"Which you've hidden someplace in Caerphilly?" the chief asked.

"God, no." Bill shook his head. "Do you realize what kind of a disaster that would be? We have three hundred and seventeen clan members here. Can you imagine if they all started tearing the town apart to look for the goblet? Give us credit for a little brains."

"Then where is this goblet?" I asked.

"In the trunk of my car," Celia said. "We're going to hide it at the ball. Well, we were going to hide it."

"The ball," the chief said. "Yes. Tell me about this ball." I could tell he was impatient with the vampires and what no doubt seemed like a distraction from the important business of solving two murders. But until we were sure they had nothing to do with the murders . . .

"We were going to hold our ball in that barn," Bill said. "Someone from the Owl Clan arranged it—a student here at Caerphilly."

"Arranged it how?" the chief said.

"I told you so," Celia said.

"We thought he'd gotten permission," Bill said.

"Maybe you thought so," Celia muttered.

"Unlikely." Randall shook his head. "Caerphilly College was very explicit. No festival activities on the campus."

"He had a key," Bill said.

"Which he probably stole," Celia said.

While they bickered back and forth, the chief pushed a paper across his desk so I could see it. On it, he had written "Find out if your brother knows about what they're doing."

"Okay to use your restroom, Chief?" I stood.

"Second door on the left," he said.

I went out into the hall, looked around until I found some privacy. The unused interview room. I closed the door behind me—checking first to make sure it had a doorknob on the inside—and pulled out my phone to call Rob.

"What's up?"

"Rob, did you know people were LARPing with your *Vampire Colonies* game?"

"Yeah, they do that with all the games, but especially the vamp games," he said. "We don't formally encourage it or even acknowledge its existence. Legal insists. They worry that someone LARPing with one of our games will do something illegal or insane and we'd get blamed. Which is unlikely, of course, but that's Legal for you."

Not for the first time I was glad Rob had such sensible people in his Legal Department.

"Is there a scenario in the game involving some kind of powerful goblet?" I asked.

"Yeah, the Goblet of Sorrow," he said. "Any vampire who drinks from it can walk in sunlight unharmed for the next twenty-four hours."

"Why is it called the Goblet of Sorrow, then?" I asked. "Why not something like the Goblet of Joyfully Biting People in Broad Daylight?"

"You know, I might share that suggestion with the developers," Rob said with a chuckle. "Goblet of Sorrow is more elegant, and also bad things happen to humans who are unlucky enough to be around when the vampires have drunk from it. But why are you asking about it? Does this have something to do with the murders or the scavenger hunt?"

"I don't know," I said. "I certainly hope not. But if anyone can find that out . . ."

"Roger," he said. "We'll expand our search."

"Look for a group of LARPers from the Owl, Wolf, Cat, Bat, Tiger, Raven, and Wombat clans gathering in Caerphilly."

"Wombat clan?" Rob said. "That's novel."

"They were planning to cap off their celebration with a Halloween Ball."

"And they didn't invite me?" he said. "Ingrates! Anything else?"

"All of this isn't messing up your schedule for releasing *Vampire Colonies II,* is it?"

"Nope," he said. "We're way ahead of schedule on that. In fact, doing all this research for you and the chief is kind of useful. We're so far ahead, I was worrying that some of the programmers might start trying to suggest that we add in new features, which we don't want to do this late in the process. So giving them something else to distract them from tinkering is priceless."

"Glad to oblige," I said. "Keep me posted."

I went back to the chief's office. Evidently in my absence he'd been trying to get the elders to explain LARPing to him. Not very successfully, I suspected, from the expression on his face.

"And the Bats and the Owls have been feuding ever since," Bill was saying. "So when you add that to all the sniping between the Cats and the Tigers, and the fact that the Wolves want to split into two clans, and the Wombats are . . . well, who knows what they're up to. Probably something pretty strange. Things have been unsettled. So since along with being one of the oldest and largest clans the Ravens have a reputation for being diplomats, we're hoping we can settle all this at the ball."

"And Halloween's the perfect time to do it," Tony added. "For vampires, Halloween's kind of like what Christmas is to mortals."

"Only it doesn't look as if we're going to have a ball," Celia said.

Bill and Tony had grown quite animated during their enthusiastic (if unsuccessful) explanation to the chief, but now their faces fell.

"Is that true?" Bill asked. "It's off?"

"Without permission from the college, I'm afraid you can't

use their barn," the chief said. "And most of the other possible venues in town are already booked with other events."

"Yeah, we figured that out weeks ago," Celia said. "That's why we were so excited when Karl came up with the barn."

An idea struck me.

"Chief," I said. "Could I have a word with you?" I glanced toward the door to suggest that I wanted that word out of the elders' hearing.

Chapter 23

The chief frowned for a moment, but then shrugged and stood up.

"If you folks will excuse me for a moment." He followed me out into the hall, closing his office door behind us.

"This may sound stupid," I said. "But maybe we should let them have their ball."

"Even if we had a place we could offer or suggest to them—why?"

"There are over three hundred of them who were supposed to be at that ball," I said. "So if they have to cancel, that's another three hundred tourists turned loose on what we know will be the most chaotic night of the whole festival."

The chief nodded at that.

"And even if the three elders in there understand why we're shutting down their party, what are the odds that all three hundred will understand? That none of them will get angry enough to try to get back at the town or the college in some way?"

"I hear you," he said. "If they'd found a legitimate venue for their party, it would have been just the sort of thing we've been trying to encourage. But the college isn't going to let them have the barn."

"What if we can get them Niflheim?" I suggested.

"Niflheim?" the chief echoed. "Isn't that part of the Norse underworld?"

"It's also what Ragnar Ragnarsen now calls his farm," I

said. "Mrs. Winkleson's old place," I added, in case the chief hadn't heard.

"Which I gather he has redecorated to look like something the Addams Family would feel right at home in," the chief said. "Yes, I can see that these vampire masqueraders would like his décor, but why on earth would he want to open his house to them?"

"He wanted to do something for the festival, and Lydia brushed him off," I said. "I have a feeling if we ask him to do it, as a favor to the town, he'd do it." Especially if we could catch him while he was still in a good mood from playing with the Rancid Dreads. "Think of it—we could get three hundred vampires off the streets tomorrow night. And having their ball so far out of town has other advantages. Out there, it would be a lot easier to keep an eye on them—especially since Ragnar is a duly sworn member of the Goblin Patrol. He'll need some help but out there it would be pretty easy to tell if any of the revelers are trying to sneak back into town to perform tomorrow's tasks."

"You had me at getting over three hundred vampires off the streets," the chief said. "Do you know where to find Ragnar?"

"As it happens, I do." I started dialing the number of the goblin who had helped me engineer Ragnar's appearance with the Rancid Dreads. "And since according to my phone it's a few minutes past midnight, now's the perfect time to call him."

"Midnight?" The chief looked at his watch to confirm the time. "I should call Aida."

The chief retreated to the other end of the corridor and pulled out his cell phone.

I was in luck. Midnight was not only the witching hour but also, more prosaically, the hour at which the Rancid Dreads were supposed to end their Friday night concert. I could hear the curiously enthusiastic cheers of the crowds in the background as I explained to my goblin what I wanted him to ask Ragnar. I was relieved to hear the cheers dissipating while I was waiting for him to return to the phone. Residents near the town square were not thrilled with how late the concert was supposed to go, and I feared even a single encore would flood the station with complaints.

"Ragnar thinks it's a great idea," the goblin reported. "Here—let me put him on."

"Meg, this is vonderful!" In his excitement, Ragnar's accent had grown more pronounced. "I vill begin preparations immediately!"

We discussed logistics for a few more minutes, and then I hung up. The chief had hung up and was striding down the corridor toward me.

"Ragnar's fine with it," I said. "In fact, he's over the moon at the idea of hosting an important vampire ball. He's going to transport all the vampires out to his place on a couple of his old tour buses, and he's calling a caterer to put on a feast."

"Excellent," the chief said. "Let's see if these elders have a way of getting out the word to all their people."

"What's up with Aida?" I asked.

"She's guarding Mr. Klapcroft," the chief said. "Waiting to hear from GameMaster."

"Has Justin completed today's tasks?" I asked.

"Hours ago," the chief said. "Under close supervision by my deputies. After which, their orders were to get him off the streets before dark and keep him safe until he gets the e-mail with the final day's tasks. Assuming GameMaster hasn't figured out he's cooperating with us."

"And assuming GameMaster still needs the game to continue to accomplish whatever it is he's trying to accomplish. So where is Justin?" I was hoping the chief hadn't had to lock him up again.

"We didn't want to risk having GameMaster spot him

going to and from the jail," the chief said. "So I deputized Aida's Aunt Niobe and she's helping us keep an eye on him."

"Doesn't that count as cruel and unusual punishment?" I asked.

"Oh, from what I hear, Niobe started off by giving him 'Hail, Columbia' for scaring the first graders, but now she's forgiven him and decided he needs fattening up."

Just for a moment, I felt acutely jealous of Justin, since Niobe Butler was accounted one of the best cooks in Caerphilly County. From the look on the chief's face, I suspected he felt the same way.

"Well, time's a-wasting," he said after a few moments. "Let's go in and give the Clan Raven elders the good news."

The elders were initially a little suspicious of the offer of a free party space.

"But why is this Ragnarsen person doing this?" Celia demanded. "Does he have some kind of ulterior motive?"

"Ms. Langslow can be very persuasive," the chief said.

"And why should any of you care?" Celia persisted.

"Because if you're out at Ragnar's house, you're his problem," I said finally. "Instead of our problem. And I'm not trying to imply that any of you LARPers are problems, but we're going to have even more tourists out there tomorrow night than there are tonight, so any large group we can get off the street makes the crowd control that much easier."

Learning precisely what our ulterior motive was seemed to reassure them a little. But they were still frowning in indecision when we heard a commotion out at the front desk.

"I want to meet my vampires!" Ragnar could be heard bellowing. "Where are they?"

He burst into the room a few moments later, with Superman trailing behind him. Upon viewing the vampires, who had drawn together in a clump and were gazing at him nervously, he beamed with delight.

"Yes!" he exclaimed, throwing his arms out with such force

that he knocked a framed picture of the Caerphilly Police Bowling Team off the wall. "This is going to be so awesome!"

Inexplicably, this seemed to reassure the elders.

"You're Ragnar?" Celia asked.

"Yes," he said. "But there cannot be just three of you. We need more. There are more of you, yes? Lots more?"

"Three hundred and seventeen of them," I said.

"Three hundred and sixteen," Celia said. "We're expelling Norton."

"Awesome," Ragnar said. "Come with me. You need to see Niflheim so you can tell me what you want me to do to get it ready."

The three elders left, with Ragnar shooing them along like a mother duck making sure all her ducklings made it to the water. Randall, the chief, and I followed them to the door and watched as they climbed into Ragnar's enormous black Lexus SUV. As Ragnar started his engine his stereo came alive and we both heard and felt the throbbing bass.

"Why does this remind me of the first time I put the boys on the school bus?" I muttered.

"They'll be fine," Randall said. "Ragnar's good people. Just a little eccentric."

Just then Horace arrived, and I went back into the police station so he could photograph my wound. While he was doing it, Aida arrived.

"Got the e-mail from GameMaster," she said, handing the chief Justin's phone. "Same list we got from Rasmussen earlier today."

"That's a relief." The chief nodded as he studied the phone's screen. "We've already had everyone watching for these pranks. Maybe the three lists we've got are all there is."

"So I gather the theory is still that the murders are somehow tied to the scavenger hunt?" I asked.

"That's *a* theory." The chief grimaced slightly. "The only coherent one we have so far. You may not have heard, but both victims were shot with the same .22-caliber gun, according to Horace's analysis of the bullets. We've sent them down to Richmond so the state crime lab can confirm this, but I have every confidence in Horace."

I nodded.

"Mr. Smith, our second victim, was definitely playing the scavenger hunt. So far we have no evidence that Mr. Green was, under any of his aliases—we've found nine of them so far. But he has a history of using the Internet to perpetrate a variety of scams, and whoever invented the scavenger hunt recruited players online."

"Yeah, that's suspicious," I said.

"Of course, it would make a little more sense if we could figure out how Mr. Green was planning to profit from the game," the chief said. "Mr. Green's previous criminal history suggests that he was nothing if not mercenary."

"I'm sure we—er, you will figure it out eventually."

The chief nodded, looking distracted, and I realized that he wasn't feeling quite as confident. I left him to his thoughts and went out into the waiting room to call Dad. He reported that Dr. Sengupta had arrived to do Michael's cast, and that he'd probably be ready to go home by the time I got there. So I collected my car and headed for the hospital.

As I passed by the town square, I peered down the block-aded streets to see what was happening. It wasn't exactly quiet, but the crowds had diminished considerably. Most of the people left were sitting or standing quietly in groups. I could see a lot of the *Vampire Colonies* LARPers milling about doing whatever LARPers do when they're gathered together. They weren't stealing pumpkins, eating insects, or menacing one another with fake body parts, so I told myself not to worry about them.

At the hospital, of course, I discovered that Dad had been overly optimistic about how soon Michael could leave. His cast was on, but we still had over an hour of paperwork and discharge procedures to get through. It was nearly 2:00 A.M. before we pulled out of the parking lot.

"Let's circle the town square and see how things are going there," Michael said.

"It's barricaded, remember?" I said. "And I took a look on my way over here. Pretty quiet. Only a few hundred tourists there."

"Only a few hundred," Michael said. "Normally we'd consider a few hundred tourists an invasion. But if there are still hundreds there at this hour, it makes me feel better about something I agreed for us to do tomorrow."

"Dare I hope it's something that would require leaving town for a while?" I asked. "Because right now that sounds pretty attractive."

"Tomorrow's the day the town is holding the usual big Halloween party for all the kids, to help them while away the hours before they can trick or treat," he said.

"The boys are looking forward to it," I said. "And Rob sent over some of his techies to help them create fabulous costumes, which would worry me a little if your mother weren't there to provide adult supervision."

"That's great," he said. "You do remember that we usually hold the kids' party on the town square."

"Oh, God, no!" I braked rather abruptly—good thing no one else was on the road. "We can't possibly have it there. The place will be full of LARPers and Rancid Dread fans and possibly players in this lethal scavenger hunt and—"

"Relax," he said. "The party has been relocated."

"That's a relief."

"To our yard. But don't worry," he hurried to add. "There are a couple of dozen parents on the party committee. They'll come over tomorrow to get everything ready. And your mother's going to supervise. They could have moved it to the school, of course, but even that's too close to all the festival craziness. And—are you okay with this? You seem to be taking it very calmly."

"I'm fine with it," I said. "I think it's very sensible to relocate the PG-rated activities away from the center of town this weekend, and as long as the party committee includes a cleanup subcommittee, I'm fine with the idea."

"Your mother will make sure there's a cleanup subcommittee," he said. "I gather she's pretty relieved to have an excuse to avoid working in the food tent tomorrow afternoon, and I hear the churches have decided to push box lunches all afternoon so they can close down the food tents before dark tomorrow night. Correction, tonight."

"Another sensible idea," I said. "And you know what else we should do? We should relocate tonight's Rancid Dread concert out to one of those fields near the Haunted House. Randall could have his workmen build a stage out there. They probably won't start playing until eight or nine o'clock, but the tourists who want to see them will start gathering out there earlier, which should clear out the town quite a bit and make it family friendlier for the trick-or-treating—to say nothing of keeping the decibel level down for everyone who lives in town."

"It'll mean a lot more tourists milling around near the Haunted House," Michael said. "Couldn't that be a problem?"

"Most of the problems at the Haunted House have happened after the crowds left," I pointed out. "And we can have someone stationed there. A deputy or two. Or maybe a few Goblin Patrol members."

"If I were a tourist, the Rancid Dreads would send me running back to town," Michael said. "But I'm probably only showing my age."

"I'd say your intelligence," I countered. "And I feel the same way."

The house was dark and quiet when we got in. Everyone had gone to bed except for Michael's mother, who had fallen asleep on the living room sofa while waiting for us. We woke her, and she and I helped Michael upstairs and got him settled.

"I'm off to bed," she said. "Got to get up early to deal with this party."

To my relief, she sounded eager rather than annoyed.

I pulled out my phone and tapped out a quick e-mail to Randall, outlining the bare bones of my idea about relocating the Dreads. I sent it, then put the phone back in my pocket and picked up my electric toothbrush. Thank goodness for small labor-saving devices that worked even when I was almost too tired to hold them.

Before I was halfway through with brushing, my pocket buzzed. I turned off the toothbrush and pulled out my phone.

"Good idea!" Randall had texted me. "Will get it going as soon as it's light."

"Good," I texted back. "Hope I didn't wake you."

"Wish you had," he replied. "Nite."

Michael was already asleep by the time I came out of the bathroom. I followed his example almost as soon as my head hit the pillow.

Though I did find a moment to feel grateful for the fact that we were already three hours into the very last day of the Halloween Festival.

Chapter 24

I could tell from the amount of light pouring across the bed that it wasn't early, but I didn't feel rested. I turned my head and opened one eye so I could see the alarm clock. Nine thirty. I decided not to calculate how much sleep I'd had. I'd survived on almost none for weeks on end the first year or two after the boys were born. I could do this.

I crawled out of bed and went over to peer out the window into the backyard. It was full of people. Michael's mother was standing in the middle of the yard, apparently giving orders, while around her the school decorating committee members were hanging decorations, setting up tables for the refreshments, and arranging hay bales for seating.

And if Grammy was out there giving orders, what was Mother up to?

I threw on my costume and hurried downstairs.

To my relief, Mother and Michael's mother appeared to have divided up the available territory in an equitable fashion. Grammy was in charge of the outdoors, while the house was Mother's domain.

"A little farther that way, dear." I started, but she wasn't talking to me. Apparently Mother was in the living room, supervising the rearrangement of the furniture. Mother never overlooked an excuse to rearrange furniture.

I slipped into the kitchen. Several volunteers were slicing fruit into giant bowls. Someone was rinsing punch bowls in the sink. I could smell chocolate chip cookies being baked.

My stomach wasn't ready to contemplate cookies. I grabbed

a yogurt and a spoon and fled before any of the kitchen workers could draft me to help with their tasks.

Mother was still giving orders in the living room, and I could see that the dining room was filled with people assembling party favors, so I slipped down the corridor to the library and let myself into Michael's office. I'd been hoping to find him there, holed up from the madness, but no such luck. Where could he be? He couldn't have gone far on crutches, and I doubted the two mothers would have let anyone draft him into a work party.

I pulled out my phone and texted him.

"Where are you, and are you taking care of your ankle?"

I started on my yogurt. If he hadn't answered by the time I finished—

"Barn," he texted back. "Sitting. Supervising."

I'd have texted back and asked "Supervising what?" but his terseness suggested he was busy with something. I could wander out to the barn in a few minutes.

I finished my yogurt while checking my e-mails. Nothing urgent. According to Randall, the chief now had four scavenger hunt participants in custody, but none of them had been able to provide any information we hadn't already heard from Justin Klapcroft. Charlie Gardner, my deputy chief goblin, reported that things had been quiet all morning, as if the majority of the tourists were resting up for new feats of partying this evening. I spent some time adjusting Goblin Patrol schedules and making sure everyone knew about the change of plans—that the food tents would be selling boxed dinners all afternoon and closing at four, and that the Rancid Dreads would be playing out near the Haunted House. And suggesting to Randall that maybe, if we offered half-price tickets at the Fun Fair between 5:00 and 8:00 P.M., it would lure a lot more of the teenaged and twenty-something revelers out of town during the trick-or-treating phase of the evening.

"Good idea," he texted back. "I'm on it."

At some point I looked out the window and spotted Jamie, who was standing in the middle of the front yard, looking as if he'd lost something. And as if he were on the verge of bursting into tears about whatever it was. I put my phone away and hurried outside to see what was wrong.

"Mommy!" He greeted me as if I'd abandoned him for weeks, and ran over to cling to me. He wasn't just on the verge of tears—they were starting to leak out and trickle down his cheeks. Not the sort of face you expect from a six-year-old on Halloween. And I noticed Josh standing nearby watching us. He wasn't as upset as Jamie, but he definitely didn't seem as excited as he had yesterday.

"What's wrong?" I asked Jamie.

"Daddy breaked his leg," he said.

"Broke," I said, automatically. "It's okay. He'll be fine."

"But if he can't walk, how can he trick-or-treat with us?"

Good question.

"Don't worry," I said. "Daddy has a plan. He'll be there."

"You're sure?"

"Absolutely!" He'd be there, even if I had to load him into the boys' Radio Flyer wagon myself and haul him all over town. "Let's go talk to Daddy."

The boys scampered ahead of me to the barn. We found Michael sitting on a hay bale, holding a rubber bat in one hand, and studying something that was out of our field of vision.

"What are you doing?" I asked.

"Ghouling up the llama cart," he said, pointing to the vehicle in question.

Until Michael had come home one day with the llama cart—which looked rather like the sort of vehicle you'd hitch to a Standardbred horse for harness racing—I hadn't known that llamas could be used as draft animals. Pack animals, yes—we'd already taken the guys on several camping trips. But apparently as long as you had the proper harness, a llama could easily pull a cart. Michael had been trying to train the llamas to pull ours, though last time I'd heard, with only limited success.

Upon its arrival, the llama cart had been bright red. Now it had been repainted a matte black, and Rob and Dad were fussing over it, adding decorative bats, rats, and skeletons.

"It's shaping up pretty well," Dad said.

"Needs more bats," Rob countered, shaking his head.

"We'll have to make them, then," Dad said. "The craft store has been out of bats for weeks now."

"How about adding some of that orange glitter stuff?" Rob asked.

Orange glitter stuff? Making bats?

Hosting the Halloween festival had certainly revolutionized Halloween decorating in Caerphilly. There had been a time when most people just popped a jack-o'-lantern on their doorstop and called it quits. The few people who went further, with things like orange lights on their shrubbery, fake gravestones in the front yard, and skeletons dangling from the rafters, had been somewhat admired but little emulated. But this year, Caerphillians had applied to their Halloween decorating the frenzy they usually saved for Christmas. The local craft store had made valiant efforts to keep up, pumping tons of black and orange decorations into the local economy. The more energetic householders had made pilgrimages to larger craft stores and Halloween emporiums in Richmond and Washington, D.C., and not long ago, at one of Trinity Episcopal's potluck suppers, I'd spotted two matrons off to one side, in furtive conversation. I sidled close enough to eavesdrop and found that one was lending the other her collection of mail order catalogs with a good selection of Halloween merchandise.

I found myself wondering how hard it would be for some people to manage the transition from bats and skeletons to pilgrims, turkeys, and in due course, reindeer.

But in the meantime, it was both useful and amusing that even Rob and Dad could manage a reasonably competent Halloween decorating job.

"Are any of the llamas actually ready to pull the cart?" I asked.

"Groucho has been showing the most promise," he said. I assumed this meant that unlike Harpo, Chico, Gummo, and Zeppo, Groucho didn't pitch a fit the minute he saw the cart. "If we bribe him with enough cantaloupe he'll be fine."

"I'll drop by the grocery store and stock up," I said, pulling out my notebook. Groucho would do anything for cantaloupe. Harpo was similarly fond of cucumbers. Perhaps we could change his mind about pulling the cart if he saw us offering cucumbers to Groucho when we harnessed him?

Time enough to worry about that later.

"What's this, then?" Grandfather and Michael's mother had appeared at the barn door.

"Grouchy is going to take Daddy trick-or-treating," Jamie said.

"And if the boys' bags get too heavy, they can put them in the cart with me," Michael was saying. "In fact, if they get tired out when we're half a mile from the car, like last year, we can put the boys in the cart."

Learning that Grouchy would be taking Daddy trick or treating had restored Jamie and Josh to good moods, and they began discussing which of his costumes the llama should wear.

"Even the llamas have costumes here in Caerphilly," Grammy said.

"Llama shows almost always have costume competitions," I said. "Michael doesn't enter those, but Rob seems to enjoy them. Boys, how about the vampire llama costume for Groucho?"

The boys dragged Grammy off to the other end of the barn to inspect the contents of the llama costume closet—yes, we now actually had such a thing. I called Randall to ask if he could send a truck to haul the llama cart to town—not that Groucho couldn't cover the distance from here to there, but it would take rather a long time and tire him and Michael both.

"I'll have cousin Shep pick it up this afternoon and drop it off in the college parking lot," Randall said. "And wait till you see what's going on in town."

"I don't like surprises right now," I said. "Give me a hint. What is going on in town?"

"Nothing at all," he said. "The town square's almost empty—even the protesters didn't show up today. About ninety percent of the tourists are out at the Haunted House, or the Fun Fair, or just hanging around in the meadow, watching my workmen put the final touches on the new stage."

"I assume we got permission from whoever owns that meadow to turn it into a concert venue."

"My cousin Peewee owns it, and he's fine with our using it for now. The stage is portable—built on the back of an old flatbed truck—so if Peewee tries to hold us up for outrageous rent next time we want to have an outdoor concert, we can haul it someplace else. That was a stroke of genius on your part, moving the Dreads out here where the only creatures they can annoy are Peewee's cows."

"As long as the Dreads don't curdle their milk," I said.

"They're beef cows," Randall said. "They're pretty stolid. And if the Dreads' music makes them suicidal, I'll save you and Michael a few steaks."

Another problem solved.

For the next couple of hours, I pitched in to get ready for the party and followed the action in town from afar. More accurately, the lack of action. I'd have been delighted to hear that things were so quiet in town if not for the nagging fear that a quiet day meant an all-too-lively night.

I also helped encase Josh and Jamie in their costumes. Josh was an evil robot, complete with glowing red eyes in his mask and lights shooting out of the ends of his fingers when he pushed a hidden button. Jamie was a space alien. His headgear featured a Plexiglas panel that appeared to give a view of a glowing green brain, and when he flexed his fingers, little clusters of slimy green glow-in-the-dark tentacles shot out of the ends of his fingers. Rob's techies had outdone themselves—maybe in addition to Mutant Wizards, Data Wizards, and Security Wizards he should start another division: Costume Wizards. The boys roamed around, happily showing off their lights and tentacles to the assembled parents.

Around 11:30, Luigi, owner of Caerphilly's beloved town pizza restaurant, showed up with boxes of pizza.

"But the pizzas aren't supposed to be here till four!" the mother in charge of refreshments moaned. "The kids won't even get here till one!"

"My guy will be back at four with the kids' pizzas," Luigi said. "These are for your volunteers. On the house. *Mangia!*"

While we were still eating pizza, Frank Ledbetter, the owner of the *Caerphilly Clarion,* showed up with his digital camera to document the festivities. Mother and Grammy wanted to drag him all over the house and yard to take pictures of their work, but he managed to convince them that the decorations would show better with costumed trick-or-treaters included, so even he managed a slice of pizza. By the time the kids began arriving, we were all tired from our decorating efforts, but well fed, and the children's excitement buoyed everyone's mood.

Mother shooed the children inside for party games—

bobbing for apples, throwing darts at orange and black balloons, and that old Halloween favorite, Pin the Tail on the Headless Horseman. This was intended to keep them busy while, outside, Grammy and her team spent the next hour or two hiding candy all over our yard for the candy hunt.

I stationed myself in the front hall with Frank so I could steer the arriving partygoers to the games.

"Nice of you to come and cover the party," I said, during a lull between arrivals. "Especially with so much going on back in town."

"I like to do it every year," he said. "It's a popular feature. And frankly, I'm happy to have an excuse to get out of my office right now."

"Too close to the festival action?" I asked.

"Festival's okay," he said. "I'm getting a lot of great material—not just for the paper and the Web site, but for my freelance business. I sell a lot of my shots through stock photo agencies, and this Halloween stuff is going to be a gold mine. No, it's not the festival that's bugging me."

"Is it the murders making things crazy at the office?"

"No—we're a weekly. We don't have the frantic scramble the dailies do. I bet the chief will have solved it before we put out our next issue. No, what's really bugging me is that some creep thinks he owns some of the photos in the *Clarion* archives. He must have called eight or ten times, and then yesterday he dropped into the office and I thought I'd have to call the police to throw him out."

"Let me guess," I said. "Josiah Brimfield."

"You've run into him, too?"

Just then another pair of guests arrived—an eight-year-old little girl in a princess dress, and her younger brother, who made an adorable baby koala bear. Frank took their pictures, separately and together, while I admired the costumes. The children and their mother scampered inside to join the party and Frank and I resumed our conversation.

"I've met Brimfield," I said. "I was there at the police station when Brimfield stormed in demanding that the chief take his pictures back from Dr. Smoot."

"Yeah, he threatened to sue me for giving prints to Dr. Smoot for the museum," Frank said. "He doesn't have a leg to stand on, but he can make my life a misery while he finds that out."

"So maybe I shouldn't tell him that I took photos of all the photos?" I said. "And shared them with Ms. Ellie at the library? Heck, maybe I shouldn't tell you. Is that a copyright violation?"

Frank chuckled.

"I'd keep it to myself when someone as litigious as Brimfield is around, but you're not in any trouble as far as I'm concerned. Look—first of all, the person who owns a photo isn't the person in it or his heirs—it's the photographer. So the fact that his great-great-uncles are in the photo doesn't prove ownership. We have no information on who took that photo. About the only thing we do know is that it was first published in the *Clarion* in 1919, which is important because, according to copyright law, anything published before 1923 is now in the public domain."

"So if he tries to sue you, he'll lose."

"And if he's consulted a lawyer, he already knows that," Frank said. "I'm guessing he hasn't, or even if he has he just figures he can browbeat me into giving him the photos."

"But why does he care so much?" I wondered aloud.

"Beats me," Frank said.

"Not sure if it's relevant," I said. "But Ms. Ellie says the photo's proof that William Henry Harrison Brimfield didn't die in 1916, as recorded in local history." I gave him the capsule version of her explanation.

Frank grew thoughtful, and almost failed to notice the entrance of a set of twins dressed as Dr. Seuss's Thing One and Thing Two. Then he jerked to attention and took their photos. When they and their father had moved on to the party proper, he spoke again.

"It could be relevant if there was some hanky-panky with their wills," he said. "What if, for example, William Brimfield made a will leaving everything to some French barmaid he met on leave in Paris? They might want to hush up the fact that he outlived his brother, who left all his worldly goods to his grieving family."

"That would make sense if William had actually inherited the family fortune before he was killed," I said. "Did he?"

"No," he said. "When I was checking the files to find material for Dr. Smoot's museum, I found a photo of his aged parents looking solemn at the ceremony where they unveiled the war memorial. And besides, the Brimfields lost all their money in the depression anyway, so there wouldn't be much for my hypothetical French barmaid's descendants to lay claim to by now."

"The Brimfields struck it rich in California," I pointed out.

"But they seem to have started out fresh with nothing," Frank said. "I looked it up on the Brimfield Corporation's Web site after he started badgering me. John Adams Brimfield, the old man, went out to California with his two surviving sons and carved an empire out of the wilderness, to hear them tell it. So I don't think it's a money issue. More likely they're hiding something disreputable. What if William, the one with the inconsistent death date, didn't actually die in the war? What if he deserted or got court-martialed or something and they drummed him out of the family?"

"And he just went quietly?"

"If the rest of his family was anything like Josiah, he might have gone off singing 'glory, hallelujah!'" Frank said. "We may never know."

"Ms. Ellie's going to do some research on it," I said. "After the festival is over."

"Good," he said. "If she finds any dirt on the Brimfields,

I'll do a front page article on it, and send a stack of copies to the Brimfield Corporation. Probably cost me an arm and a leg in legal costs, but it'd be worth it."

"Talk to Festus," I said. "He takes a dim view of big corporations beating up small businesses. You never know; he might take it on cheap for the chance to take a whack at this Brimfield Corporation."

"I'll do that," Frank said. "Well, one good thing about Brimfield showing up this week—the festival seems to be driving him bonkers. You should have seen him freak out when he found someone had tucked a fake finger into one of his overcoat pockets."

We both chuckled at that. And then, since a flock of small Ewoks, Stormtroopers, and other *Star Wars* characters had arrived, I left Frank to the task of capturing their cuteness for posterity.

In due course, Grammy's crew announced that they were ready for the great Halloween candy hunt, and we herded the children outside and turned them loose. Astonishing that it only took them fifteen minutes to find the candy that had taken the adults nearly two hours to hide.

Meanwhile, Luigi's son had arrived with the kids' pizzas and the party ended with a delightfully noisy and enthusiastic meal. Pizza was a good choice, I realized, because most of the kids liked it enough that they would actually put down their candy and eat a slice or two. And then all the parents began the chore of dragging their kids away from their friends so they could get home and refresh their costumes before nightfall.

Michael watched while his mother and the boys decked out Groucho in the black cape and fake fangs that made up his vampire costume while I attached the horse (and llama) trailer to the back of the Twinmobile and fetched the boys' empty goody bags.

"Not quite sunset yet," he pointed out.

"It probably will be by the time we get to town and hitch Groucho up," I said. "And besides, we're going to stop at Mom and Dad's.

So the five of us set off. Michael's mother drove the Twin-mobile, and I followed in my own car, in case anything really dire happened and I had to split the party.

Mother and Dad and Grandfather made a big fuss over the boys' costumes, even though they'd already seen them at the party. Dad had been waiting until our arrival to head out to his medical tent, relocated from the town square to across the street from the Haunted House. Mother and Grandfather were going to stay in and hand out candy to any trick-or-treaters who made it this far out of town.

"Actually, I expect I'll handle the brats for the rest of the night," Grandfather said when he was sure Mother wasn't near enough to hear. "Your mother's had a rough day."

"Don't scare them too badly," I warned him. "Dad, how's Dr. Smoot?"

"He hasn't regained consciousness yet," Dad said. "But all his vital signs are good. I think it's only a matter of time."

We finally left Mother and Dad's and drove to the college parking lot, where Randall's cousin had left the llama cart. I led Groucho out of the trailer and hitched him up. Then I handed each of the boys their enormous black-and-orange canvas treat bags and turned them loose. They made a bee-line for the nearest houses, with Michael's cart trotting on behind them. Grammy and I brought up the rear.

"What's that," she said, pointing to the paper I'd pulled out of my tote.

"A map of Caerphilly," I said.

"I should have thought you'd know your way around town fairly well by now." Was there a note of disapproval in her voice?

"I do," I said. "I'm going to use it to keep track of where we've already been. Last time we figured out about halfway down one street that we'd already been to all the houses on it. Hard to tell whether the boys circled around deliberately, because it was a particularly generous street, or whether it was accidental, but we're not having that again. If they say 'but we haven't been this way yet!' I can tell if they're lying."

"Good thinking," she said.

The boys were scampering up the walkway of the first house, and Grammy and I scrambled to catch up.

This part of the day was delightful—like having our town back again. Almost the only people we met were other parties of trick-or-treaters. The boys recognized some of them, or thought they did, and called greetings to their friends, while Michael, Grammy, and I trailed after them. And the boys had the whole routine down pat. They knew not to go up to the occasional darkened house. They smiled proudly when their costumes were praised, gave Uncle Rob's employees due credit, and so ostentatiously took only one piece of candy that at least half of the householders urged them to take more. And they paused at the end of every block to plot their next course.

"We should go that way." Josh pointed to the right at one such intersection.

"But there are lots of houses down that way." Michael's mother indicated the street ahead of us, which was dense with townhouses.

"Yeah, but they're all those stuck-together houses that never answer the doorbell on Halloween," Josh said.

"Or they close the door and make you wait while they find something and then all they give you is raisins," Jamie said. "That way's better."

They scurried off in the direction they preferred, and Michael steered his cart after them.

"Mostly groups of students or young working people in the townhouses," I explained to Grammy. "They tend to be more interested in partying on Halloween than giving out candy."

She nodded and hurried on after the boys. I paused long enough to make a note of our route on my map.

And then just as I was turning the corner, I realized—we were just leaving Pruitt Street. The darkened house the boys had just passed by was Lydia's house.

Why was there a car in her driveway?

Chapter 25

I put a thick stand of bushes between me and Lydia's house. Then I pulled out my cell phone and called Randall.

"What kind of car does Lydia drive?"

"Little silver compact," he said. "Honda, I think, or maybe a Toyota. Why?"

The car in Lydia's driveway was a silver Honda Civic.

"We've been trick-or-treating in her neighborhood," I said. "And I noticed that there's a car in her driveway."

"Wasn't her car supposed to be down at the Richmond airport?" he asked.

"No idea," I said. "Would they have impounded it or just left it there and kept an eye on it?"

"Not sure they'd have any grounds to impound, would they?"

We both fell silent for a few moments. I didn't know the answer. Neither did Randall, apparently.

"Did you check to see if she's there?" he asked.

I glanced at the house.

"The lights are out, so if she's there she may not want anyone to know it," I said. "And I'm not all that keen to knock on the door of a murder suspect. I'm hanging up and calling 911."

"I'll be over with the key," he said, just before I cut the connection.

"Nine-one-one, what's your emergency." Debbie Ann was more businesslike than usual. Probably due to the number of out-of-towners who might be calling these days.

"There's a car in Lydia Van Meter's driveway," I said. "At 1510 Pruitt Avenue. A silver Honda Civic. Matches what Randall can remember about her car. Which I know was found out at the Richmond airport, but I didn't know whether it was impounded or whether maybe she could have come back and claimed it."

"Dispatching a deputy. Can you see the license plate?"

"Not from where I'm standing," I said. "Too dark. Do you want me to stroll closer so I can see it?"

A pause.

"Let me ask the chief."

As I waited, peering through the shrubbery at the car, I began to hear voices coming from down the block, where Michael and Grammy and the kids had gone.

"Meg! Where are you?" Michael was calling.

"Mommy?"

"Blast," I muttered. I didn't really want to draw attention to where I was crouching in the shrubbery. But neither did I want Michael and the boys circling back to a house where the police might be about to confront a murderer.

I ran a few yards down the street.

"Coming! Just a minute!" I shouted, waving my arms.

Then I ran back to my position in the bushes. As I did, I heard the noise of a car engine starting.

"It's moving," I said into the phone.

The car had been nose out, as if its driver had anticipated the need for a fast getaway. It darted out into the street, turned left and disappeared into the night.

"It pulled out before I could get the license," I said. "Heading north on Pruitt Avenue."

I could hear Debbie Ann relaying this over the police radio.

"Randall's on his way with the key to the house," I said. "I'm trick-or-treating with the boys—I should get back before they start to worry."

"That's fine," Debbie Ann said. "You call us if you see anything else suspicious."

I didn't for the rest of the trick-or-treating, but my fleeting encounter with a car that might or might not belong to a murderer cast a slight pall over my enjoyment. The boys probably wondered why I was following them up to every doorstep and studying the people who opened the doors, instead of waiting at the foot of the driveway as I had earlier in the evening.

I was relieved when the boys finally agreed that yes, they had hit all of the really good houses, and it was time to go home. Of course, no six-year-old would ever admit that he has more than enough candy, but I could tell by their tired yet satisfied expressions that they were not unhappy with their haul.

And thanks to my useful little map, I'd managed to steer our party in a giant circle, so we ended up only a few blocks from where we'd parked the llama trailer. Grammy and I helped Michael into the car while the boys scrambled to sit in the far back of the Twinmobile. Then I unhitched Groucho, led him into the llama trailer, and pulled the llama cart into the parking space where Randall would be picking it up later.

"I wish you weren't patrolling alone," Michael said, sticking his head out of the window.

"I'll be careful," I said. "And I'll call or text you as often as I can. Don't let them make themselves sick."

"Boys!" Grammy called back from her post in the driver's seat. "Remember, we have to take the candy home for the count to see who got the most. Anything you eat on the way doesn't count!"

Michael and I grinned. Grammy had figured out how to slow the boys' candy consumption—appeal to their overly developed competitive spirits. As they drove off, I could see that Josh and Jamie were both clutching their candy bags and eyeing each other with suspicion.

I walked to my own car and set out for my evening of patrolling.

Evening and morning, more like it, I thought with a sigh.

I started with a long, slow crawl through the residential
streets of Caerphilly. Trick-or-treating was trailing off—only
a few of the older kids were still out, twelve-year-olds pretending cynicism about the whole thing but not passing up the
chance—their last chance, since Caerphilly had an ordi-
nance against trick-or-treating after the age of twelve. And
maybe a few thirteen-year-olds hoping no one remembered
their birthdays, or dragging along weary siblings to justify
their presence on the streets—"I'm not really trick-or-treating,
I'm just taking my kid brother around."

I spotted and reported a few pranks. A small bungalow not
far from Lydia's had been toilet papered. Three more toilet
paperings in Westlake, where the great distances between
the houses and between the houses and the street probably
made it easier to prank unseen. On an otherwise quiet side
street a scarecrow appeared to be trying to crawl out of a
manhole. Another scarecrow was sitting sedately on a bench
at the base of the War Memorial Cenotaph. I took pictures
of them all and called them in to Debbie Ann.

Then I headed out to the Haunted House area—which,
between the house itself, the Fun Fair, and the impending
concert, was now Halloween Central. There was a line of
people waiting to get into the house. More lines at all the
rides and booths in the Fun Fair. And an enormous crowd
of people had taken over the field across the road from the
Haunted House, where a couple of the Rancid Dreads and
their entourage could be seen making desultory preparations for the concert.

The night wore on. I thought longingly of home, where
Michael and his mother had probably allowed the boys to eat
a small amount of their candy before tucking them into

bed. Where Rose Noire was probably off in the nearby woods, performing her annual Samhain blessing ritual to dispel dark forces and call down peace and positive energy on the town. Mother had probably gone to bed and was happily dreaming of tomorrow's grand All Saints' Day service at Trinity Episcopal. Last time I checked on him, Dad was snoozing in his tent, though that would probably end when the Dreads began playing—or sooner, if anyone needed his medical services. Michael was home and fretting. I tried to text him every fifteen or twenty minutes to help ease his anxiety. "All fine," I texted more than once.

Because it really was. Not a quiet evening, of course, particularly not after ten, when the Dreads began their concert. And it wasn't free from incident. A few more pranks happened, and the chief rounded up yet another suspected scavenger hunt player. But things really were running smoothly. Out at Ragnar's mansion, the Vampire Ball was going splendidly, and the deputies watching had spotted no departures— only a continuing trickle of arrivals. Almost no one was left in the town itself. The crowds milled happily between the Fun Fair and the concert field. Some of them were surreptitiously sipping from bottles and cans concealed under their costumes, but after much discussion, Randall and the chief had agreed that the deputies would turn a blind eye on this as long as those involved were discreet and didn't become rowdy. As if by osmosis, the revelers had figured this out, and were policing themselves far more effectively than the chief could have ever managed with his limited number of officers—even with help from the Goblin Patrol.

I amused myself with thinking of things we could have done better. Things we could do better if we decided to hold the festival again. Some of them new ideas, others things I had suggested, in vain, to Lydia. Not that I'd have much luck getting Lydia to consider any of them, but then I suspected Lydia wouldn't be in charge if we had another festival.

I checked in from time to time at the zoo, where Caroline was standing vigil.

"We've seen a few prowlers," she reported. "But so far, our patrols have kept them away. I expect they'll get more desperate as their midnight deadline approaches, and maybe we'll catch a few."

Things weren't as quiet at the Haunted House. I was on my way back from a trip to the zoo when Ms. Ellie called me.

"Meg? You anywhere nearby? Something weird's going on here."

I pulled to a stop in front of the Haunted House and shoved my way through the crowds to the door.

"Out back," Judge Jane murmured to me. "Someone's trying to get over the fence. Debbie Ann's sending a deputy."

She unlocked a door that led to the kitchen—which was not on display yet, being at the moment a highly utilitarian vintage 1950s kitchen full of stark white metal cabinets. We peered out the back door.

Something was flapping at the top of one section of chain-link fence in the back left corner—the section that, thanks to the overhanging branches of two enormous oaks and an impressively large weeping willow, was least visible either from the house or anywhere else. I opened the door and stepped out onto the concrete back stoop.

At first I thought it was merely someone's cloak that had blown away and snagged on the fence. Then I realized that there was a human figure beneath the cloak.

"Call the deputy," I said. "We have a trespasser."

"We already did," Judge Jane said. "I thought I told you that."

"I wanted to make sure our intruder knew," I said in an undertone.

I decided to get closer to keep an eye on the trespasser. I made my way carefully down the back steps and strolled across the yard. Which was empty, thanks to Randall's extra fences. As I drew closer, the trespasser struggled more and more wildly.

"Give up," I called out. "You're well and truly stuck, and the deputy's already on his way here. If you promise to go quietly, we can probably find a ladder to get you down before you lacerate yourself too badly."

The figure grew limp.

"Oh, bother," it said. She said, actually, and her voice sounded familiar.

"Hello?" I said. "Is that—"

"Hi, Meg. It's me, Becky Griswald. Yes, you've caught me. It was a pretty stupid idea to begin with."

Just then Deputy Sammy Wendell arrived, and for the next few minutes we had to focus all our attention on the difficult task of extricating Mrs. Griswald from the barbed wire and helping her climb down the chain-link. Irritatingly, although no one appeared to have noticed her climbing up, a large crowd eventually gathered around outside the fence to watch the rescue operation.

"Thank goodness," she said when her feet were finally on solid ground again. "I'm getting too old for acrobatics."

We led her into the kitchen and let her sit down on the least rickety of Dr. Smoot's vintage aluminum kitchen chairs. Judge Jane handed her a glass of water and then went back to the public part of the house to help Ms. Ellie deal with the tourists.

"You want to give me a reason not to take you down to the station and charge you with trespassing?" Deputy Sammy asked.

Mrs. Griswald shook her head.

"Just why were you trespassing?" I asked.

She set her jaw as if prepared to resist thumbscrews or Chinese water torture. Then her face fell.

"If you must know, I was going to try to steal the brooch back."

"The cat brooch?" I asked.

"But that isn't even—" Sammy began.

"But it's your brooch," I broke in, shooting Sammy a look to stop him from mentioning that the brooch, along with most of the rest of the smaller museum exhibits, was locked in the police department's evidence room. "Why not just ask for it back?"

"Because if the museum gives it back, Harris will just take it and lock it up in the bank again," she said. "It's my brooch, and I want it."

"I thought you hated it," I said.

"I do," she said. "But it's worth a lot of money. I want it so I can sell it. I've decided to dump Harris and make a new start in life, and that brooch is how I'm going to do it."

"Was that why you broke in Thursday night?" Sammy asked.

"That wasn't me," she said. "I wouldn't have hurt Dr. Smoot, much less killed that poor tourist. But it did give me the idea, you know. I figured if someone was going to steal my brooch, it might as well be me."

Sammy and I looked at each other. I suspected he was thinking much the same thing I was. Mrs. Griswald seemed harmless enough. But if she was that desperate to dump her husband, and thought the only way she could do it was to get her hands on that ugly half-million-dollar brooch . . .

"I'm afraid I'll have to take you down to the station," Sammy said.

He pulled out his radio and exchanged a few words with the chief. Then he helped Mrs. Griswald up. I was a little worried about her—she was limping rather badly.

Sammy saw my face and looked faintly guilty.

"We can call your Dad to check her out once we get her down to the station," he said.

I followed him out the door and watched from just inside the front gate as he led her down to the police cruiser. Just as he was about to guide her into the backseat, his shoulder radio crackled again.

"Wendell here," he answered. "What's—ow!"

Mrs. Griswald kicked him in the shin and ran away with no trace of a limp, disappearing into the crowd almost immediately.

Sammy tried to give chase, but she was wearing a black cape, and at least three-fourths of the crowd swirling around his cruiser wore all or mostly black. And the few who weren't oblivious to his predicament—or pretending to be so— seemed to be taking Mrs. Griswald's side, smirking at his discomfiture and clumsily stumbling into his path.

I pushed my way over to his car.

"The chief will kill me," he said.

"Have him put out a BOLO on her," I said. "Five foot four, wearing a black cape and possibly a Darth Vader helmet. And I'll notify the Goblins."

And just as I was composing my alert to the Goblins, the chief called me.

"I gather you're going to have your volunteers look for Mrs. Griswald," he said. "Please make it absolutely clear that if they locate her they are to report her whereabouts—not attempt to detain or apprehend her."

"Understood," I said.

"And could you also ask them to be on the lookout for Ms. Van Meter?"

"So that was her car in the driveway?"

"No, her car is still in the long-term parking lot at the Richmond airport," he said. "Under observation. But if she's up to something, maybe she wouldn't use her own car. And although Mrs. Griswald just shot to the top of my suspect list, Ms. Van Meter is still very much on it. So, same instructions as for Mrs. Griswald: If you or any of your volunteers spot either of them, call it in immediately and give them a very wide berth."

"Roger."

I finished my message and sent it out, then pushed my way back to the front door. Ms. Ellie was shepherding out the last tourists.

"No, I'm sorry," Ms. Ellie was telling several who were trying to push in. "We're closed." She was having to shout to be heard over the Rancid Dreads.

Judge Jane stormed out of the door holding a hand-lettered sign that said CLOSED. GO AWAY. She held it up and turned slowly so everyone could see it. Then she slapped it against the front door and attached it with a small strip of duct tape.

The two of them stood on the doorstep looking fierce while I chivvied the last of the tourists out of the yard. They didn't all cooperate very well, and it took longer than it should have, but at least once they were out of the yard they all seemed to shrug their shoulders and wander off, either toward the Fun Fair, which was going on for another hour, or toward the field where the Dreads were blasting out a vaguely familiar song.

"What are those wretched boys playing now?" Judge Jane asked when, after locking the gate behind me, I returned to the front steps.

"I think it's 'Welcome to the Jungle,' " I said. "By Guns N' Roses."

"Never heard of it," Judge Jane muttered.

"Are you sure it's not 'Ding Dong! the Witch Is Dead'?" Ms. Ellie asked.

We all cocked our heads and listened.

"To me, it sounds more like they're attempting 'A Mighty Fortress Is My God' and failing utterly," Judge Jane pronounced. "Well, as long as the tourists like it."

We trooped inside, locked the door behind us, and all collapsed on three of the spindly black chairs.

"Where's that deputy who's supposed to be taking over from us?" Judge Jane asked.

"Probably chasing Mrs. Griswald," Ms. Ellie said. "Do you really think she did it?"

"She definitely tried to break in here," Judge Jane said. "As to the murder—well, who knows? I'll probably have to recuse myself anyway, now that I've had this run-in with her. Seems like a nice woman, but I've passed sentence on plenty of seemingly nice people."

"You know how neighbors always describe serial killers as perfectly ordinary quiet people who they thought wouldn't hurt a fly?" Ms. Ellie said. "Well, she fits that."

"My money's on Lydia Van Meter," I said. "Of course, I could be biased."

"Or perhaps you've just had more opportunity than we have to assess her character," Ms. Ellie said.

"Blasted music is giving me a headache," Judge Jane said. "Well, that and the fact that it's way past my usual bedtime."

"Why don't you go home," I suggested. "Ms. Ellie and I are both night owls—we can wait here for the deputy."

"I'm taking Ms. Ellie home," she protested.

"I can take her," I said. "It's out of your way."

"Don't you have patrolling to do?"

"Yes, and this is a valid part of it," I said. "Go on."

She grumbled a bit more, but gave in fairly easily, which suggested how very bad she really felt. I saw her safely to her pickup and then scurried back in to lock the gate and the front door before any of the tourists got their hopes up that the house was reopening.

"You're sure you don't mind?" Ms. Ellie said.

"Mind a chance to sit down for a bit, in peace and quiet? Well, more peace and quiet than I'd have if I was out there," I added, wincing as the Dreads emitted a particularly power-ful guitar riff. Or was it only a blast of feedback? Sometimes it was hard to tell with them. "And Michael will be happy. In fact, I should text him."

I pulled out my phone and texted: "Safely locked up in

Haunted House with Ms. Ellie, waiting for a deputy to arrive to take over. Love."

I figured he'd probably be asleep by now, but the speed with which he texted back showed he must have been awake.

"Hope the deputy's a long time coming so you can stay safely locked up there for a while. XXX."

Ms. Ellie opened her mouth, but whatever she said was drowned out by the enormous wave of sound that signaled the end of one of the Dreads' songs, and then a huge roar of applause and cheering from the audience. She shook her head and leaned back in her chair.

Outside, the cheering died down and the Dreads launched into another number. This one started slow and, for the Dreads, relatively quietly. Ms. Ellie sighed.

"I suppose I should be pleased that those young men are becoming so successful," she said. "But being pleased for them is one thing, and listening to them quite another. How much longer are they going to play?"

"We were going to hold them to a two a.m. curfew in town," I said. "Which was going to be even less popular than last night's midnight ending time. Out here? We told them they could play as long as they liked."

She shuddered slightly.

"It's not as if either of us has to stay to the end," I said.

"I was just wondering how much longer before Sammy gets back," she said. "Of course, if they catch Mrs. Griswald—or Lydia, for that matter—the wait will be worth it."

"Should I feel guilty for recruiting you to do this?" I asked.

"No." She put her hands on her hips and gently stretched backward, as if easing her back and shoulders. "It's been fun, in a peculiar sort of way. And Jane's good company. But tell your Mother not to expect me at the early service tomorrow morning."

"You mean later this morning," I said. "And she won't give you a hard time—she'll be too busy reproaching me. Look,

I'm going to check all the windows and doors from the top floor on down. In theory, since it's after midnight, everyone who needed to break in here to play that stupid game has either already done so or missed his chance. But just in case."

"Want help?"

"No, you keep an eye out front for Sammy. And make sure everyone's still paying attention to the concert and not trying to sneak over here."

"All right." She sat back down on one of the spindly black chairs and I could tell she was weary.

"If he's not here by the time I get back from checking all the windows, I'll recruit a few Goblins to stay here till he arrives," I suggested. "Or borrow a few of the Brigade."

"Good idea." Ms. Ellie brightened at the thought.

"And don't let anyone in," I said, as I climbed up the stairs to begin my search.

Chapter 26

I started with the third floor. I unlocked Dr. Smoot's private quarters. Nice to know that he wasn't putting up a false front—his taste in décor for his living quarters didn't differ much from the public areas of the house. All of the furniture was either painted or upholstered in black—a black velvet sofa and matching chair, a black lacquer coffee table—didn't the man ever yearn for a bit of bright color? I locked the door behind me as I entered and searched every spot that could possibly hold an intruder. Not many spots in the living room other than the coat closet, with its dozen assorted black capes, and all the windows were shut tight and locked. In the bedroom, I checked under the bed and in the closet, which proved that nearly any garment a middle-aged man might possibly want to wear either was made in or could be dyed black.

I also noticed a small pile of mail on the dresser and found my fingers itching to tidy it and take it back to the desk I'd seen in the living room. And why not? Assuming he eventually came out of his coma—and Dad seemed reasonably optimistic—he'd still need a lot of help before he got back on his feet. And some of those envelopes looked like bills—not a good idea to let those get scattered. I should make it easier for whoever stepped in to help him. Especially considering that it could very well be me.

I gathered up the envelopes and returned to the living room. The desk was black, of course, like nearly everything else, but really rather nice—a small black lacquered Oriental writing desk. I set the stack of mail on top.

"What the heck," I muttered. I picked up the stack again and sorted it. Four bills, three of them not yet opened. I set them in one pile. Six pieces of what I would define as junk mail, but Dr. Smoot's definition might be different, so I set them in another pile. And a nine-by-twelve brown envelope.

I was about to set it in a pile of its own when I noticed the return address: Mr. and Mrs. W. P. Walmsley. A familiar-sounding name. Arabella Pratherton Walmsley's parents?

The envelope had already been unsealed so I pulled out the contents. A sheet of cardboard. A letter. And a vintage black-and-white studio portrait of a pretty, dark-haired young woman in an elegant bias-cut satin evening gown sitting in a chair with a tall, handsome man in a tuxedo standing at her shoulder. A Brimfield, I decided; his features bore a striking resemblance to those of William Henry Harrison, John Tyler, and Josiah, and he had those same odd pale eyes. But the young woman's gown looked like something from the thirties, so I deduced that this was probably Zachary Taylor or Millard Fillmore.

Then I turned the photo over and saw the inscription on the back, in an elegant, almost calligraphic handwriting: Mr. and Mrs. William Pratherton.

I flipped the photo over in surprise. So this was Billy Pratherton, the bootlegger? Still, with those eyes, he had to be related somehow to the Brimfields. It was a small county. I'd tell Ms. Ellie about it and let her chase down their family trees.

Looking at the picture didn't really feel like snooping—after all, odds were the Walmsleys had sent it to Dr. Smoot so he could display it in the museum—but reading the letter certainly would. I turned it facedown and picked up the envelope to stuff it back inside.

What the heck. In for a penny. I turned the letter over again and read it.

Dear Dr. Smoot,

I'm enclosing the picture we discussed. You're welcome to keep it if you want it for your museum. To me it would only be a sad reminder of Arabella's accident. And don't ask me for anything else. I know it's not your fault, but I can't help but think that if Arabella had never visited your museum, never gotten interested in trying to trace the family genealogy, and never gone to San Francisco, maybe we'd still have her with us.

Respectfully yours, Mary P. Walmsley

"Wow," I murmured. Dr. Smoot was right—Arabella's parents did blame him for her death.

And what was the connection between Billy Pratherton and the Brimfields? This was definitely a case for Ms. Ellie's research skills.

Speaking of Ms. Ellie, she was probably getting impatient. And with any luck, Sammy would have arrived so we could leave. I'd fill her in on the ride home.

I locked Dr. Smoot's apartment door and went down to the second floor. No one hiding behind any of the black velvet curtains. No one crouching beneath the tablecloth of what I'd finally decided was probably a re-creation of Miss Havisham's wedding feast. No one crammed in beside the animatronic vampire in the coffin.

When I came down to the ground floor again, I noticed that the basement door was open. I couldn't help smiling— Ms. Ellie had probably been unable to contain her curiosity and had decided to take a peek at what was left of the museum. I probably should have warned her that most of the historical exhibits weren't there. Perhaps she'd find the ruins of the non-wax wax museum amusing.

I checked the rest of the ground floor. She didn't emerge while I was doing so. At any other time, I'd have let her have her fun, but it was late. Maybe the thrill of the hunt for historical clues had reenergized her, but I was already afraid I'd fall asleep on the way home. And I was getting a headache, too. It was probably the stress and lack of sleep causing it, but proximity to the Rancid Dreads wasn't helping.

"Ms. Ellie," I called—not all that loudly, because shouting would bother my head.

No answer. She probably hadn't heard me over the music. But what could be keeping her?

I sighed, and then began trudging down the circular stairway to the basement, walking carefully because fast movements really hurt my head. Time to get home and get some sleep—if possible before my headache reached killer proportions. And as I descended, the music faded to a tolerable background roar, and I realized why Ms. Ellie might have preferred to stay in the basement even after she realized the artifacts were gone. You could hear the music just fine, but it wasn't quite as eardrum-shreddingly loud down there.

I stepped out into the basement and saw Ms. Ellie on her hands and knees on the floor, searching through the ashes and rubble there, while above her stood a figure in a black hooded cloak wearing a Darth Vader mask. Not Mrs. Griswald, though—this Darth Vader was much taller.

And carrying a gun. Not a very large gun, but both James Green and Wayne Smith had been killed with a .22.

I froze. No way he could have heard me over the Dreads, so if I could just duck back up the stairwell—

"I see you, you know," he said. "And if you run away, I'll shoot her." He stretched out the arm with the gun to make it obvious that he was pointing it at Ms. Ellie. "If you find what I'm looking for, I might let you go." His voice was familiar—not so familiar that I recognized it, but familiar enough that I knew I'd heard it before.

"I already told you, they're not here anymore," Ms. Ellie said.

"Shut up," he told her. And then, to me: "Step into the

room. Away from the staircase. Come over here. Down on your hands and knees and look."

"Look for what?" I asked. I was following his orders, but as slowly as I thought I could get away with. I was trying to figure out where I'd heard that voice before.

"Photos," she said. "He wants the framed photos that were here. I told him I had no idea where they went."

"I do," I said. "They've all been taken down to the police station and locked up as evidence."

"Then what's this doing here?" He held up a charred frame. The photo inside it was visibly waterlogged.

"They must have missed one," Ms. Ellie said. "I can't find what isn't here."

"You'd better hope the rest of them are here." There was a slight note of panic in his voice as if he was starting to suspect that we might be telling the truth. "Get busy," he snapped at me.

I picked a promising patch of charred rubble and started sifting through it.

I glanced up and noticed something. The Darth Vader mask hid his face, but not his eyes—spooky pale eyes. Our masked intruder was either Josiah Brimfield or someone who shared his DNA.

"Why do you want the photos anyway?" Ms. Ellie said. She was sifting through her own patch of ash and rubble with her hands—pretty much the same rubble she'd been searching since I came in.

"He's not searching for all the photos," I said. "Just that World War One photo of the two Brimfield brothers. I have no idea why."

"I have," she said. "Probably something to do with my theory that there was something fishy about the dates of William Henry Harrison Brimfield's death."

I couldn't be sure, but I thought Brimfield stiffened slightly.

"Oh, I remember," I said. "The one you told us all about in the paper you presented to the historical society last month."

"Paper?" Ms. Ellie only looked puzzled for a second, then she caught on to what I was doing. "That's right, you were there. You know, I really think the World War One Historical Association may run it in that magazine of theirs."

"I know what you're trying to do," Brimfield said. "You're trying to convince me that everyone already knows everything so there's no use trying to get the photos back and I should just give up and go home. But I know better. You haven't published any papers."

Okay, that didn't work. But I had another idea.

"Yes, you've been keeping your eye on Caerphilly recently, haven't you?" I said. "It all started when poor Dr. Smoot contacted you, thinking your family connection to Caerphilly would make you willing to provide financial support for his museum. Instead, he inadvertently alerted you to the fact that an old family secret was in danger of being exposed. You tried to bully him into giving you that World War One photo, or at least taking it off display, but he wouldn't budge. I expect he'll confirm all this when he wakes up."

"If he wakes up," Brimfield said.

"So that's when you created the GameMaster e-mail and started up this stupid scavenger hunt game," I said. It was a guess, but as far as I could tell from his eyes, a good one. "I'm not sure whether you were expecting one of the players to steal the photo for you or whether you planned all along to use the game as cover for making your own trip to the museum, but anyway it backfired. The murders caused the police to close down the museum and move most of its contents to the evidence locker, so now it's only a matter of time till your secret goes public."

"What secret?" Ms. Ellie asked. "We suspect that William Henry Harrison Brimfield didn't die on the date that's on the War Memorial, but even if he deserted or was court-martialed, who really cares after all these years?"

"He didn't desert or get court-martialed." I wasn't exactly guessing—the pieces were falling into place. "Or even if he did, that's not what you were trying to cover up. He came home and became Billy Pratherton, Caerphilly's most disreputable bootlegger, didn't he? The bootlegger even the Shiffleys looked down on because he'd poisoned so many people with wood alcohol."

Brimfield didn't say anything, but I could see through the holes in his mask that his eyes had narrowed and figured I was on target.

"How do you know William Brimfield turned into Billy Pratherton?" Ms. Ellie asked.

"He's not denying it, is he?" I said.

"No," she said, glancing at Brimfield. "But how do *you* know."

I decided it was not a good idea to let Brimfield know that a critical piece of evidence was still lying around on the third floor.

"I saw a picture Arabella Walmsley sent Dr. Smoot," I said. "A picture of her grandparents, Arabella Shiffley and Billy Pratherton. Billy is William Brimfield—you can't miss it. That means the modern-day Arabella is—was—a Brimfield, too. A great-granddaughter of John Adams Brimfield, who founded the Brimfield Corporation. I don't know anything about California inheritance laws, but I bet if they got a good attorney, the Walmsleys would have a fighting chance of getting a piece of the Brimfield fortune."

"They could certainly cause the Brimfields a lot of expense and embarrassment trying," Ms. Ellie said. "And the good attorney would be pretty easy—haven't you heard of the big Richmond law firm, Venable, Walmsley, Lightfoot, and Wythe? But do you really think he killed Arabella?"

"I bet she showed up on his doorstep waving a copy of

that picture," I said. "She was delighted to have found another branch on her family tree. But all he saw was someone who might take money out of his pocket. Yeah. I'm sure he killed her."

"I'd love to see that picture the Walmsleys sent," Ms. Ellie said.

"I bet Mr. Brimfield would, too," I said. "But the chief has it. He plans to work with Arabella's parents to get her death reinvestigated as a possible homicide."

"So the police have it all figured out." Brimfield reached up, pulled off the Darth Vader mask, and scowled at us. "If that's the case, I'm in a bit of trouble, aren't I? But maybe it's only you who has it figured out. So maybe if I get rid of you, I'm home free."

"And if you're wrong?" Ms. Ellie asked.

"They can only fry me once." Brimfield shrugged and smiled a cold, thin-lipped smile. I decided he didn't look that much like the World War I–era Brimfields after all. There had been light and warmth and laughter in their eyes, in spite of their grim surroundings, and his just looked like slabs of pale gray stone.

"Was the scavenger hunt your idea?" I asked.

"Hell, no," he said. "It was Jimmy Green's idea from the start. I just told him to get the damned photos. I should have known. He never could do anything straightforward. God, but he was annoying."

"Is that why you killed him?" I asked. "Because he was annoying?"

I didn't really expect an answer.

"No," he said, with a chillingly humorless smile. "I killed him because he tried to extort more money from me. He called and insisted that I come down here to meet him because he had something important to tell me. And when I showed up, his important news was that the publicity about the museum was making his job harder and he wanted double his original fee."

"And you didn't like that," I said.

"I didn't like his threat to go to the police if I didn't comply with his demands," Brimfield said. "I decided he'd outlived his usefulness."

"And I bet you decided it before you even came down here," I suggested. "Why else would you have brought a gun with you?"

"I came prepared to deal with any eventuality," Brimfield said. I took that for a yes.

"And what if they trace the gun?" Ms. Ellie asked.

Brimfield glanced down at the weapon in his hand.

"I shall dispose of it after tonight," he said. "And in the highly unlikely event that it falls into police hands—well, I doubt that they would be able to trace it, but if they did, it would only lead back to poor Jimmy."

"Did he kill Arabella for you?" I asked.

"The greedy little bitch." Brimfield suddenly looked angry for the first time. "Pretending she wanted to be reunited with the family she'd never known. I knew what she was really after."

From what Dr. Smoot had said about Arabella's wealthy family, I didn't think she had much need for money. Brimfield could be projecting his greed on a young woman who only wanted to learn more about her own family. What a jerk.

I was not going to let this jerk kill us. And I sure as hell wasn't going to die listening to the Rancid Dreads mangle "Riders on the Storm."

He could have fired off a machine gun under cover of the Dreads' performance without anyone noticing. But maybe if I could just keep him talking. The longer he talked, the more chances we would have.

"I still don't understand why Jimmy thought up the whole

elaborate rigmarole of the scavenger hunt?" I asked. "What was wrong with just breaking in and stealing the picture?"

"Because Dr. Smoot would have remembered my interest in the picture," he said. "I told Jimmy to make sure it wasn't obvious that the picture was the target. Of course, what I thought he would do was make a clean sweep. Empty the miserable little museum, so the photo would be only one of dozens of things lost. Still, the scavenger hunt wasn't totally useless. Bet your chief of police is pretty busy trying to track all the players down, much less check their alibis. Pretty easy for me to slip under his radar. And without you two around, the odds of anyone spotting the family resemblance and figuring it out are pretty low."

Unfortunately, he was probably right. And even if the chief put the pieces together tomorrow, it wouldn't be much of a victory if we weren't around to share it.

"I need to finish this off." Brimfield glanced at his watch. "I've got an eight a.m. breakfast meeting at the Old Ebbitt Grill. On Capitol Hill," he added.

As if we cared where he was planning to celebrate our demise.

"So can we stop searching this filthy rubble?" Ms. Ellie asked.

What was she doing? Searching the filthy rubble was keeping us alive. Or did she have a plan?

"You've convinced me that it's useless," he said. "Get up and go over there."

Ms. Ellie began following his orders, but as slowly as possible. She glanced at me as if expecting me to do something. I moved as if I was about to get up, then faked a loud sneeze. Brimfield started.

"Bless you," Ms. Ellie said.

"Sorry," I said. "It's the ashes. They—*achoo!*"

Brimfield looked annoyed, but didn't seem to notice that along with jerking my head forward violently with each sneeze I was also inching forward a bit. I'd spotted a potentially useful item in the rubble.

"Bless you again," Ms. Ellie said.

"Get on with it," Brimfield snarled.

"They usually come in threes," I said. "The sneezes, I mean. *Ah-ah-ah-choo!*"

With the third sneeze I jerked forward, grabbed the object I'd spotted—the detached head of one of Dr. Smoot's department store mannequins—and flung it at him. Then I rolled, so the shot he fired in my general direction went wide. And Ms. Ellie seemed to have gotten the hint that I'd be sneezing a third time—while Brimfield was focused on me, she lurched forward and slashed at him with the first weapon that came to hand—a wicked six-inch shard of glass from the broken display case.

"You old witch!" Brimfield exclaimed. He shoved her backward with his foot and raised his right hand to point the gun at her.

But while his attention was on Ms. Ellie, I'd grabbed up another weapon—the enormous brass spittoon—and hit him over the head with it. He keeled over into the remains of the glass display case.

"Get his gun," Ms. Ellie said. "I'll get the roll of duct tape from upstairs."

She strode out. I carefully plucked the gun from Brimfield's limp hand and moved back to a safe distance before calling 911.

Chapter 27

"So we thought Brimfield had an alibi," I said. "What happened?"

After several lively hours out at the Haunted House, Randall and I were sitting back in the chief's office, sipping coffee and hot chocolate. Daylight was now peeping through the venetian blinds at the chief's windows. We were waiting for the county attorney to review the official statement to the press we'd crafted. The chief had my signed statement. Brimfield was safely locked up in the Caerphilly jail, awaiting the arrival of the high-powered Washington lawyer he'd summoned. Part of me wanted to go home and crawl into bed, but I knew I'd never get to sleep as long as there were still unanswered questions about last night's events, and as long as he'd put up with me, the chief's office was where I could get those answers.

"One learns to be skeptical of alibis," the chief said.

"But his sounded like such a good one," I said. "Hobnobbing with his congressman till the wee small hours of the morning, so he couldn't possibly be down here committing a murder—wasn't that it?"

"You haven't been following this morning's news, then," Randall said, with a chuckle. "The representative from Brimfield's district just had a press conference. He's checking himself into rehab. Seems he has a drinking problem and is prone to blackouts. Can't remember anything that happened after eight or nine in the evening for the last several months."

"Convenient," I said. "Do you think he was lying for Brim-field or does he really not remember?"

"We may never know," the chief said. "Whether or not he's actually an alcoholic, I suspect his handlers have decided it's a shortcoming his district will find more acceptable than be-ing an accessory after the fact to murder. Suffice it to say that since last night's events, the congressman has demoted our suspect from 'my old buddy Josiah' to 'a constituent who has been persistently attempting to sway my position on agricultural tariffs.'"

"The county attorney is considering whether it's worth the trouble of filing charges of making false statements to the police," Randall said.

"Meanwhile, now that we have probable cause," the chief went on, "I'm subpoenaing the records from Brimfield's rental car. These days, many of the rental agencies equip their vehicles with GPS tracking devices."

"So we'll be able to verify that he was in Caerphilly the night of the murder?" Randall asked.

"The odds are good," the chief said. "And the fact that we caught him in possession of the murder weapon doesn't hurt either. Oh, and I've already heard from the San Francisco police."

"Let me guess," I said. "They're reopening the case on Arabella Walmsley's death."

"And also the deaths of two Brimfield cousins who would have considerably reduced the amount of Josiah's fortune if they'd still been alive when his granddaddy died a couple of years ago," the chief said.

"And the second victim, Wayne Smith—he was playing the game?"

"He was." The chief shook his head sadly. "He broke Game-Master's rules by texting a friend about what he was doing. The last text the friend received said that Mr. Smith saw someone going into the museum, and he was going to see if he could sneak in behind him."

"Brimfield?" I asked.

"Almost certainly," the chief said. "In Mr. Brimfield's pockets, we found a brand new key wrapped in a piece of paper with a four-digit number written on it. Any minute now I expect Vern will be calling me to confirm that they are a duplicate of Dr. Smoot's key and a copy of the code to his security system—obtained, no doubt, by Mr. Green as part of his plan to steal the photos."

"Well, that explains how everybody was getting into the basement without our knowing it," I said. "And did he really think stealing that one copy of the photo was going to keep his secret from getting out?"

"Maybe that's one reason he killed his henchman," Randall said. "Because he'd found out the guy had gone to all this trouble to steal something that was only a copy. I bet arson at the *Clarion*'s offices was next on his list."

"Chief?" Jabba the Hutt, still in costume, appeared in the doorway. "I just heard from Deputy Paulsen."

"Since when do we have a Deputy Paulsen?" Randall asked with a frown.

"On loan from Goochland County," the chief said. "Since he was unfamiliar with the local topography, I decided he would be of greater use guarding Dr. Smoot than patrolling the town. What does Deputy Paulsen want?" he added, turning back to Jabba.

"Dr. Smoot's awake," he said. "And hopping mad at Brimfield for whacking him over the head and making him miss Halloween. Dr. Langslow and Dr. Carper are checking him out, and they'll call you in a little bit to let you know when Smoot's ready to make a formal statement."

"Excellent," the chief said.

Jabba disappeared.

"The pieces are coming together." I could hear the satisfaction in the chief's voice. "All of the game players we've captured are talking now, and with your brother's offer, we expect even more to come forward to give information."

"What offer?" Randall asked.

"Rob's offering a free copy of *Vampire Colonies II* to anyone who comes forward to talk to the police about the scavenger hunt," I explained. "Not an advance copy—they get it on release day. But still—free is good."

"Wish we'd thought of that a day or so ago," the chief said. "Ah, well."

"What about Mrs. Griswald?" I asked.

"Now that we're sure she had nothing to do with the murder, I've released her on her own recognizance," the chief said. "She wasn't happy when I told her we'd be hanging on to the brooch as evidence for the time being, until I pointed out that as long as it was in our custody, her husband can't get his hands on it, either. I gather she's going to be staying with Reverend Smith for the time being, and Festus has promised to find her an excellent divorce lawyer."

"Good," I said. "She seems like a nice woman—at least when she's away from her husband."

"Chief?" Jabba again, this time on the intercom. "Dr. Blake is here to see you."

"Send him in."

Grandfather appeared in the doorway, still clad in his wizard's cape, which looked as bedraggled as if he really had made a journey from the Shire to the gates of Mordor in it. He was wearing the fiercely triumphant expression that usually meant he'd succeeded in foiling some large corporation's efforts to despoil the environment.

"I've got your evidence back." He threw his cloak open, patted the pockets of his safari vest, and eventually reached into one to pull out the object he was seeking. "Voilà!" he exclaimed. He tossed a ring onto the table—a familiar-looking ring.

"That's the ring that was stolen from the museum the night of the murder," I said. I'd recognize that grape-sized cubic zirconia anywhere.

"One of the ravens picked it up somewhere and came back to the zoo with it," Grandfather explained. "They're as bad as magpies with shiny objects. Silly bird flew up to his nest with it. Had to send one of the keepers up in a cherry picker to retrieve it. Nearly fell out of the tree and killed himself. Damned nuisance, but I figured apart from the monetary value, the thing could be an important clue in your case."

I could tell from the look on the chief's face that he remembered the ring. But I could also tell that he wasn't going to deflate Grandfather's pride at having retrieved what he thought was a valuable artifact.

"I'm deeply grateful," the chief said. "We probably won't need to introduce it at the trial, since it wasn't the killer's primary target, but if you hadn't found it, that could be just the sort of small unsolved mystery that a clever defense attorney could exploit. Thank you."

"Happy to oblige," Grandfather said. "Well, I've got to get back to the zoo. I'm taking the Brigade on a tour of the Creatures of the Night this morning."

With that he strode out.

"Thank you," I said.

"And what happens when he visits the museum and finds out that the ring's a fake?" the chief asked, with a sigh.

"I can't imagine him visiting the museum," I said. "And we can ask Dr. Smoot to pull the ring from the exhibit. I'll figure out some excuse."

"Perhaps that we have advised everyone not to entrust any valuable objects to the museum until Dr. Smoot has made substantial improvements in his security," the chief suggested. "It will be the truth. Speaking of valuable objects in the museum, now that we know the Paltroon painting's not connected to the murders, I'm setting up a short meeting tomorrow to enable Dr. Cavendish to return it to its rightful owner. Would you be interested in attending? In your role as head of the Goblin Patrol."

"This would be the meeting at which Dr. Cavendish breaks the news to Mrs. Paltroon that she's on thin ice as the local DAR president? I wouldn't miss it for the world. May I bring Mother along? Someone should be there to help console Mrs. Paltroon if she takes it badly."

"We should sell tickets," Randall said with a chuckle.

"Chief?" It was Vern, sticking his head in the door. "Got someone you might like to talk to."

"Who?" From the chief's slight frown I deduced that he couldn't think of anyone else he particularly wanted to talk to just now.

"Lydia Van Meter." Vern smirked. "I suppose we're no longer considering her as a murder suspect, but the BOLO was still out. Her car disappeared from the airport this morning, and we picked her up when she crossed the county line. If you ask me she has some explaining to do."

"Bring her in," the chief said.

"Mind if I give her a piece of my mind?" Randall muttered.

"Let me talk to her first," the chief said. "There's still the possibility she's somehow mixed up in this."

Vern returned, escorting Lydia. Was it mean of me to be amused by the fact that he had her in handcuffs? She was at least a head shorter than Vern, and probably half his weight. Then again, the other deputies were still giving Sammy a hard time about letting Mrs. Griswald escape, so I'm sure Vern didn't want to follow in his footsteps.

"What's going on?" Lydia demanded. "Why am I being treated like a common criminal?"

"Because up until a few hours ago, that's precisely what we thought you were," the chief said. "I think we can dispense with the restraints for the time being," he added to Vern.

Vern nodded, took out a key, and unlocked the cuffs. The

chief leaned back in his chair and studied Lydia for a few moments before speaking. She sat down in his guest chair, and from the look on her face, I was pretty sure she was preparing herself to accept an apology.

"At approximately five a.m. Friday morning," the chief began, "you left Caerphilly, drove to the Richmond International Airport, left your car in Economy Lot B, and took a United Airlines flight to New Orleans by way of Atlanta. Mind telling me why?"

"You've been spying on me!" she exclaimed. "What business is it of yours what I do?"

"Immediately prior to your departure, a man was murdered at the zoo, another at the Haunted House, and Dr. Smoot was very severely injured," the chief said.

"Oh, my God! But I had nothing to do with any of that!" Either she was genuinely surprised or she was a much better actress than I'd thought. "Randall, why didn't you tell them why I was going?"

"I might have if you'd had the common courtesy to tell me," Randall said.

"I left a voice mail." She sounded highly indignant.

"Not on my phone," Randall said.

Lydia uttered the kind of sigh that suggested that she was tired of dealing with idiots. Then she looked at our stern faces and decided maybe she'd better explain.

"My best friend from college needed me," she said. "She was trying to throw this killer Halloween party, and her caterer folded—two days before the party. I figured since the festival was already pretty much planned, I'd fly down and help her out."

She sat back in her folding chair, and from the expression on her face, she clearly thought she'd explained everything quite satisfactorily.

"You ran out on your responsibilities here to help a friend throw a party?" Randall said.

"All the planning here was done," Lydia said.

"The planning may have been done," Randall said. "But plans fall apart, and you need someone on hand to make new ones. If you'd asked me if you could go, I'd have said no. You didn't even notify me."

"But I left you a voice mail," Lydia said. "It's not my fault you didn't get it."

Randall, Vern, the chief, and I all exchanged looks.

"Yes, it is your fault," Randall said. "You ran out in the middle of an event for which you had major responsibilities."

"When you disappeared," the chief said, "we didn't know if you were the killer, an accomplice, or maybe another victim, so we used up a lot of valuable time and resources that could have been better spent trying to catch the real killer."

"You never liked me," Lydia said, turning to me. The chief and Randall had been doing most of the talking. Why was Lydia lashing out at me? "You resent me because I took what used to be your job."

"Resent you?" I said. "I was thrilled to be off the hook. No, I resent you for doing such a lousy job on my old volunteer position and then expecting to be paid for it."

"Randall, I won't stand for this," she said. "I won't be treated like . . . like . . . a kindergartener."

Randall had closed his eyes and was taking deep breaths. Then he opened them again.

"Sorry, Meg," he said. "This counting-to-ten thing may work for you, but it just gives me time to get madder. Lydia, you're fired. I'm going to ask the chief to send a deputy to escort you while you clean out your desk, and when you get back to my Aunt Bessie's house, you can start packing. I'll have a moving truck waiting in the driveway, and I'll be there to make sure none of Bessie's antiques leave with you."

Lydia's mouth fell open in astonishment, and she stared at Randall for a good thirty seconds. Then she shut her mouth firmly, stood up, and put her hands on her hips.

"Well," she said. "I'm not going to stay around where I'm not appreciated."

She flounced out, head high, as if she'd just resigned over some issue of principle instead of being fired.

"Good riddance," Randall muttered.

"Amen," the chief said. "Vern, you go do the desk cleaning detail."

Vern saluted and hurried after Lydia.

"Randall," the chief went on. "You can tell me to mind my own business if you like, but when you start hiring Lydia's replacement, why don't you let Meg help you interview the candidates? I think she probably has a pretty good idea what the job requires."

"I have an even better idea," Randall said. "Why don't I just hire Meg?"

"Sounds good to me," the chief said.

"Me?" I squeaked.

"You're better at this job than anyone," Randall said. "Nobody was badgering me to hire someone to do it because they weren't satisfied with your work. They just thought I was exploiting you because I was dumping so much on a volunteer. So how about if I pay you for it?"

"I'm trying to get back into my blacksmithing, now that the boys are in school," I protested.

"But having the boys in school doesn't solve the whole problem, does it?" he said. "I heard you say so yourself the other day—you're finding more time to do the iron work now, but to sell it properly you'd have to spend your weekends at craft fairs when you'd rather be spending them with your family. If you take Lydia's job, you can make your own hours."

"Except when events like the festival are happening," I pointed out.

"Yeah, but what are the odds that anything big like this is going to happen without you volunteering for some kind of job anyway?" he said. "Heck, you put in more hours as Chief Goblin than Lydia ever did as my assistant. Isn't it better to be the boss? And any old time you find someone you think can take your place, you just tell me and I'll hire her."

I was tempted. Getting paid for doing things that I would probably end up doing anyway sounded sweet.

"If you like, I can install a forge and an anvil in your office," Randall said. "You can blacksmith whenever things get slow."

"I'm not making any decisions until I've talked to Michael," I said. "And had a full night's sleep."

"Let's talk tomorrow," Randall said. "We've got to start planning the Christmas festivities right away."

I was about to answer when I heard shouting outside. The chief got up and walked over to the window to look out.

"I'll let you know," I said. "Meanwhile—"

"Where is she?" bellowed a powerful voice.

We turned to see Ragnar Ragnarsen bursting through the door. He raced over to stand in front of me.

"I have found you!" Ragnar shouted. "You are my blacksmith!"

"I am?" I wasn't quite sure why Ragnar needed a blacksmith—though my imagination conjured up the vision of a horse large enough to carry him with ease, an enormous draft horse with shaggy fetlocks and hooves the size of hubcaps. Time to give my explanation of the difference between an ornamental blacksmith and a farrier. But then I noticed that Ragnar was holding a copy of the *Vampire Colonies II* poster.

"You made this?" He was pointing to the intricate dagger with the bat-shaped hilt. "And this?" The candelabra that appeared to be made from blackened fingerbones. "And this?" The iron balcony, with its bats, gargoyles, claws, teeth, and eyes. "Rob tells me that these are not made with Photoshop but with real iron?"

"I made all of it," I said. "I'd be the first to admit that some of the ideas came from Rob and his art staff, but Rob wanted real ironwork for the cover, so he could hold contests to give away reproductions as part of the publicity campaign."

"Fantastic!" Ragnar exclaimed. "My house needs you! It needs candelabra! Chandeliers! Railings! Andirons! Sconces! I travel everywhere looking for the perfect ironwork for my house, and I find it here in Caerphilly! This is wonderful! You are my blacksmith!"

He seized me in an embrace that would probably have broken bones if he'd tried it on a smaller, frailer person. Fortunately, being a blacksmith has toughened me up more than most people.

"You must come to the house so we can make plans!" he said when he'd finally released me.

"After we recover from the festival," I said.

"Of course, of course," he said. "You are tired. And I still have many vampires infesting the house, recovering from the revelries of last night. But when the house is quiet again, we will begin! Please, I beg of you—do not take on any other commissions until you see my house. I think perhaps I will keep you busy for years."

With that he beamed at me and strode off.

I'd heard worse offers.

"There you are," Randall said. "No reason why you can't run the special events for me and still do commissions for Ragnar."

"I'll talk to Michael," I said. "Because—"

"Meg, dear."

I looked up to see Mother in the doorway.

"I came to pick you up for the All Saints' and All Souls' Day service at Trinity," she said.

"I was just going to go home and nap," I said.

"We'll run you home after the service," she said. "I think it would be nice if you were the one to read the name of that poor young man who was killed in Dr. Smoot's museum. In addition to honoring all the saints," she added, turning to Randall and the chief, "we also read the names of everyone who has died during the year at the service—if possible by someone who was close to them. I'd do it myself, but I think it would be so much more suitable if Meg did, since she was instrumental in solving his murder. And besides," she added, turning back to me, "you have to come and see the boys in their saint costumes."

"Saint costumes?" the chief echoed.

"It's a new idea that dear Robyn has introduced," Mother said. "All the children come dressed as their favorite saints."

"Oh, no," I said. "I forgot all about the saint costumes for the boys." Robyn probably wouldn't mind if they came as a robot and a space alien, but some of the other parents would probably look down their noses at our parenting skills.

"Don't worry," Mother said. "Dahlia and I took care of that while Rob's costume experts were here. Would you like to see them?" She turned again to Randall and the chief with that question.

"If you have time, sure," Randall said.

"I'd be very pleased," the chief said.

Mother bustled out and I held my breath. I couldn't, off-hand, think of any saint that would appeal to the boys nearly as much as space aliens and robots. I hoped they were wearing whatever their two grandmothers had devised with reasonably good grace.

And then, to my delight, the boys raced in, looking very excited.

"Mommy!" Josh exclaimed. "Look at my costume today!"

"This is almost as good as the space alien," Jamie added.

The costumeless reality of November second was going to come as a great shock to both of them.

"Aren't they adorable?" Mother asked from the doorway.

Josh was dressed as St. Sebastian, in a toga festooned with

so many arrows that he'd probably have to stand during the entire service. Jamie was St. George, wearing silver lamé armor and a helmet borrowed from his role as a Roman soldier in this year's Easter pageant. Around his shoulders curled a three-foot-long stuffed dragon made of red and gold metallic fabric.

"Mommy, I got a hundred and ninety-one pieces of candy," Josh said.

"I got two hundred and thirty-three," Jamie countered.

"And it's all locked up in the candy boxes ready to be doled out for good behavior," Michael said from the doorway, where he was balanced on his crutches.

"Mommy, this was the best Halloween ever!" Jamie exclaimed.

"Can we do it again just like this next year?" Josh asked.

I tried not to wince at the "just like this" part. There were many things about this Halloween that I hoped we never repeated.

"I took a pulse check this morning," Randall said. "So far the merchants are happy. And I don't know about the other churches, but First Presbyterian's going into the holiday season with our fund for relief of the poor and unfortunate fatter than it's been for years."

"We Baptists are also well supplied for this winter's good works," the chief said.

"Robyn is delighted with how well the food tent did," Mother said. "The women's shelter's future is secure."

"And Ragnar's excited about taking a bigger role in the festival next year," Randall said. "Prepared to throw a lot of money at it. And he had a pretty good suggestion—we could have all the family friendly stuff here in town, and push the vamp and ghoul stuff out to his place. He's got plenty of space out there."

"All we really need is for someone to agree to organize it all," Mother said.

"We'll see," I said. But I couldn't help smiling as I said it.

"Hurray!" Everyone joined in the cheers, even the boys, who probably didn't really understand what they were cheering for.

"But we'll talk about that later," I said. "After the services. And my nap, which I will be working hard to postpone until after the services are over. Let's go."

I strolled over to the door and linked my arm in Michael's— not easy to do with him on crutches, but I managed.

"Come on boys," Mother said. "Let's go show off your latest costumes."

"See you later," I called over my shoulder as we headed out. "And Happy Halloween."